Loose Ends

By Anastasia Goodman

A Sasha Perlov Novel

© Copyright 2012

ISBN-13: 978-1479160815
ISBN-10: 1479160814

Published by Ocean Breeze Press

Cover Design and Layout by Parry Design Studio, Inc.
www.parrydesign.com

LOOSE
Ends

by **Anastasia Goodman**

A Sasha Perlov Novel

CHAPTER 1

I know that I should feel morally conflicted, torn by my actions or what could be more accurately described as my lack of action. Am I feeling guilty and remorseful? After all, I am a law enforcement officer—a police detective sworn to obey the laws of the land and an aspiring law student. But I don't because I have learned to live with ambiguity. Sometimes justice doesn't follow some narrowly prescribed set of rules. Can there exist an unassailable and immutable set of laws? People are more complex than the law assumes. Life should be simple, but it's not. I should have been satisfied with what was presented as facts. But I can't let things so. I must know exactly what happened. As a police officer it drives my partner and my superiors nuts. I just hate loose ends.

My story started routinely. There was nothing to suggest how an ordinary call would give me permission to cross the line.

I'm known across Brooklyn South, beyond my precinct as the Russian Jew boy—I have no real name just this moniker. Whenever a call involves a Russian in South Brooklyn I'm called—supposedly I can deal best with my people. I identify with those first black cops all assigned to the Harlem and

Bedford-Stuyvesant precincts and never to the Upper East Side of Manhattan or Forest Hills in Queens.

I came from Russia as an adolescent following my parents to be free from the shackles of Soviet discrimination—this was before the fall of the great Evil Empire known as the Soviet Union. A signed photo of former President Ronald Reagan hangs on the wall in my parents' dining room along with an autographed photo of Scoop Jackson, the late Senator from Washington State and renowned anti-Communist crusader. There's a federal law bearing his name that Russian dissidents used to cite to denounce Soviet human rights abuses.

My mother never stops reminding me how she was a prisoner of conscience in the Soviet Union and resettled in America with hopes and dreams. And how did I reward my parents—I became a police officer, a very odious profession back in Soviet Russia.

"A police officer," my mother tells me, "You wear a uniform. We should have stayed in the Soviet Union. We brought you here so you could become an artist, a doctor, or a lawyer. A policeman," she mutters to herself. Now I'm a detective so I don't wear that dreaded uniform. My goal once I joined the force was to quickly achieve a promotion to shield me from my mother's reproaching frown. I'm not ashamed to admit it—I'm a mama's boy as are all self-respecting Russian Jewish boys. What my mother thinks or says matters. Nonetheless I love to 'yank her chain'. What a keen expression, you can picture the person wearing a dog collar being dragged against their will. I adore the English language; it possesses so many wonderful slang phrasings—who needs elegant prose in America. Forget Faulkner, which I struggled with when I arrived in America from what was then called Leningrad and has now reverted back to its older name—St. Petersburg.

I take the call to respond to an emergency at a house off Coney Island Avenue that hot, sunny afternoon in July. The uniform officer has some suspicions and an unidentified but nagging gut feeling that this case is not as it appears. It's Brighton Beach, the NYC Russian Jewish ghetto, and my home turf, Brooklyn South, 60th Precinct.

The sergeant tells me what he knows. There's a frantic 911 call from a woman. "My husband not breathing, come quickly," in a heavy immigrant accent.

So the ambulance arrives and the guy's stopped breathing; but the EMT knows he hasn't been breathing for several hours. He's a fat, ugly middle-aged guy and she's a young beauty. It's assumed that she's Russian because it's Brighton Beach and she is having difficulty with the English language. She tells the responding officers that she's his wife. So I get the call.

"One of your people needs you," says my Lieutenant and off I go with my partner Jimmy, a guy of Polish descent whose family has a long memory of hating Russians, not to mention Jews. I try explaining this to my Captain but to no avail; he's Irish, his family left the Old World during the Potato Famine 150 years ago. What does he know about Eastern European differences? According to the brass, "Polish—Russian, it's all the same."

The officers try to question her but her English language skills are lacking. They're not certain if her story is inconsistent or she doesn't understand the questions. So we arrive, Jimmy and I, to start the investigation.

Jimmy Sutton a.k.a. Solewski, whose Polish-born father changed the family name because of discrimination—employers thought the family were Jews. The old man chose the name Sutton because he happened to be the lead carpenter on a construction site on Sutton Place, the natty neighborhood on Manhattan's East Side around 58th Street. My first reaction to working with Jimmy was Poles and Jews have an anguished but shared history. Jimmy's grandfather probably helped the Nazis load the Jews into the cattle cars on their way to the death camps in Auschwitz. We were dealing with a story that was a thousand years old and each party thought they were the victims. Just because a Pope or two said otherwise—according to Jimmy's family the Jews were still Christ-killers. Of course, they never said anything to my face. But I understood the slurs because I spoke a little Polish and I overheard the old people talking.

The only people Jimmy's family hated more than Russians once they came to the New World were blacks—the devil incarnate. Jimmy held his prejudices in check when it came to Russians and Jews, but when it came to the blacks—well this was a relatively newly acquired hatred not ready to be given up for Lent. His family never met a black person until they moved to Brooklyn and then they never met one they liked.

Despite my religion and Russian nationality, Jimmy's father liked me. I spoke better Polish than his son, having learned the language from my mother. Jimmy's father and I go man-to-man; I got his respect. I go against the stereotype of the Jew as meek and mild—I was one tough son-of-bitch. He also thought because I knew so much about Brighton Beach and its inhabitants that I must have ties to the Russian Mafia. Now I don't do anything to encourage this line of thinking, but I certainly don't deny it.

We pull up in our unmarked car behind the patrol car and the ambulance with its strobe lights pulsating; luckily for our ears the sirens are off. We never really know what to expect. A cop's mind revolves around suspicion. We look for the worst in people and claim the high ground as the seekers of truth, but the truth is relative. Say I have four witnesses to a crime. Each one has a story, which is labeled the truth. And, each truth is slightly inconsistent if not entirely contradictory with the other truths. Yes, and then there's the suspect's and the victim's stories which are also called the truth. My job is to ferret out the facts and determine whether we have a crime. Crime and punishment; oh, and yes, what about justice; they are all part of the same equation. In the end, I often don't learn what exactly happened. I am forced to make assumptions and usually the brass is so happy to get a case off the books that "I think this is what happened" is good enough. Confessions help but are not necessary to close a case. Most criminals don't confess. Killers go to the electric chair professing their innocence. I know from the bottom of my dark Russian heart that all people have secrets to hide. Search out the secrets because they often lead to the facts of the crime.

Observation is the first tool of a good cop. The clothes, the car, the patterns of speech, are just starting points for an investigation. These simple beginnings could all be deceptions, conceived by a perpetrator to hide what happened. On this muggy day I am sent as an interpreter and cultural attaché. So I begin my questioning in English for the benefit of my Polish partner and the officer on call, but switch to Russian when her answers become too choppy and fragmentary.

She's a beauty; I can smell her fresh-scented perfume, almost fruity. It reminds me of the wild blueberries that I would pick at my grandfather's dacha many years ago. There's an innocence about her that mixes with an irresistible sensuality; she's a woman who can't decide which of her many alluring features are her most marketable. She stands next to me, close but not too close, swaying her body as she rocks back and forth on her heels. I quietly breathe in her scent through my nostrils; I feel like a bloodhound that must lock in her smell so I don't lose it or confuse it with somebody else. She doesn't flirt with me, but she looks me straight in the eyes and I know she knows that I find her attractive, as do many men.

The new widow is tense, she rhythmically rolls back and forth on her heels; most immigrants are afraid of the police so that's not revealing. She's not a Jewess with those blue eyes. I can tell that and the fat guy lying on the floor is wearing a Star of David around his neck. I can feel my mother's instant dislike of the dead guy with a blond shiksa. This woman is treife—not kosher—the forbidden.

I take a long look at the corpse spread out on the carpeting—I know this person. I review the name and address again. I'm from the neighborhood—my family doesn't live too far away. Do I know him from shul, synagogue? It's been awhile, maybe during Pesach in the spring. A cop's work hours and regular religious attendance don't accommodate each other. I am always given time off for Yom Kippur—the holiest of holy days, the day of fasting—a true sacrifice for a Jew—but the other important days and keeping the Sabbath holy don't jibe with a detective's hours.

I look at the name—doesn't sound Russian, certainly not a new immigrant or first generation. I'll ask my mother about this guy. I continue staring at him. I'm waiting for the coroner's guy to finish so I don't want to touch the body. Her, I don't know. I would remember a face and a body like hers. She's watching me looking at her deceased husband and then a light goes on in my head. He's one of the regulars at the Seaside summer concerts at the Brighton Beach Bandshell. Of course, I recognize him—Jack—I think—no last name.

I loved those summer concerts every Thursday night near the Boardwalk. They were a seaside institution. My mother dragged my father and me, further proof of our assimilation. In America, people congregated like penned chickens to hear washed-out, has-been singers. For a small price you got the privilege to sit on a cheap, metal, folding chair. If five dollars was too expensive, you brought your own chair or blanket.

The acts were usually performers popular with older baby boomers, people who grew up during those heady, early days of rock n' roll in the 1950's and 1960's. The sounds were familiar to a large segment of the Brooklyn population but they were never favorites among Russian immigrants. For my father and me, these were amusing events; opportunities for watching people; we went to please my mother. Always seeing the political, she viewed these simple activities on a grander, symbolic scale. To my mother growing up in the Soviet Union, American rock n' roll had a subversive message. It was forbidden, and therefore there must be something to be gained by listening to what the authorities condemned. When my mother actually heard the Beatles in the mid-1960's she immediately recognized the seditious potential. The sounds pulsated in a clearly sexual way and the lyrics exalted the listener to make their own choices—liberation was at hand. The individual didn't need the state to dictate who to love and what to believe. It was a powerful new message.

One feature of these Bandshell concerts was the parading of local politicians before an indifferent audience—an act of pure political theater. Our master of ceremonies, the Borough President, entertained us with bad jokes and silly puns. Hours were wasted as he gave every local politician running for any office the opportunity to speak to the concertgoers. That was every politician who was running as a member of the Democratic Party.

We left before the Soviet Union totally collapsed and something Russian officials termed multiple party elections emerged. Multi-parties run candidates for the same position but one person, Vladimir Putin, controlled the process. So at first glance, Brooklyn politics felt very familiar and not so reassuring. Here was a place where a person's name appeared on a ballot running unopposed. It was a curious feature of living in New York City. As a result, my mother, the passionate activist back in the Soviet Union, purposely stayed away from political parties in America.

I am more than an observer of the Bandshell scene; now as a cop I get some overtime money working security at the shows. Since 9/11 and the election of the new Borough President, the man behind those shows, there's a lot more security. It's one of the few times when I put on my uniform my mother actually smiles. She points me out to concert acquaintances. "There's my son Sasha, the police officer. Doesn't he look handsome in his uniform?"

Then, beyond the advertised entertainment and the political chatter, there was always the side show where spectators entertained each other. Jack was the guy with a reputation as the man who was literally first-on-line. I got to know the regulars. I never learned last names but I recognized familiar faces. Week after week, summer after summer, they took their same places on line. For the deceased and the other regulars, the Bandshell concerts represented their fifteen seconds of notoriety. Standing on line was their badge of courage. Occasionally, the police were called to break up a fight among those on line. These people were a territorial bunch and the deceased's reputation included his big mouth.

So on a steamy July afternoon, I am standing over the body of the late Mr. Jack whoever—Brighton Beach Bandshell concert regular—a legend in his own time. I am the detective called to investigate his death. My mother will be interested in this case since she will know about Jack, one of the regulars, even if she hasn't been personally introduced to him.

Jimmy is standing around talking to one of the uniforms that he knows from playing on the precinct softball team. He is wearing a tapered shirt under his suit jacket. He likes people to admire his muscular build. My partner is the athlete. When he's not playing on all the precinct sports team, he's lifting weights. His passion is boxing and before he gets too old he dreams to represent the precinct at an interdepartmental boxing match.

It's hot under that expensive suit, but Jimmy doesn't break into a sweat. We are known in the precinct as the Cool Team, reliable and fearless if you need back-up. We should be breezing through the questioning. The guy lying on the worn, stained, reddish-pink carpeting is quite dead; there's no visible blood, no shooting or knifing. Mr. Jack is wearing a light colored sweat suit, size 2X, and nothing but food stains can be seen. The guy from the coroner's office is kneeling on the carpet examining the deceased. He looks up at us and announces, "It looks like a heart attack." It's not an official verdict but it's all we will get today.

I say to my beautiful hostess, who already has offered me tea, "Heart attack?"

"Minute," she tells me, and walks away across the living room and out of sight. My eyes follow her until she disappears behind a wall.

We have no reason to believe that she will flee the scene so Jimmy and I wait for her return, which she does in a few minutes.

She hands me some pill bottles. I reach over the dead man and collect the bottles. Our fingers touch in the process and I can feel her soft skin. She is certainly not working at anything physically demanding. I notice her nails are done in a deep purple tone, complementing her big blue eyes.

I show the bottles to the coroner's man still resting his copious body on one knee next to the body. He reads the labels and says to all of us as we wait patiently for his medical expertise. "Pills for heart disease, high blood pressure, high cholesterol, angina. Some potentially life threatening problems."

He hands me back the small bottles. I examine the pill containers again staring at the labels and making a mental note to check with the pharmacy nearby where they are filled.

I start my inquiry in Russian, which is why I am here and not any other detective. "When did you discover the body?" I ask her, watching for signs of distress or guilt. Suspicion, I never entirely trust what I can see. She's tense and doesn't answer at first.

Finally, she speaks. "When I returned from shopping," she turns her head so our eyes meet.

"And you left the house when?" I could stand here on this spot, nailed to the carpeting looking at her eyes for hours.

"Just before noon. I like to eat at Juniors," she smiles sheepishly; a widow in mourning should not look too happy. Juniors is a renowned downtown Brooklyn eating establishment and bakes a cheesecake you could die for.

"Did you go alone?"

"No, no—my sisters were with me. We all went together."

"Sisters, how many people were with you?"

"The three of us," she nods her head.

"Where are your sisters?" I didn't notice anyone else.

"They're here," she says, looking around the room, but there are no women present.

I check the room with my eyes and see no one but police and emergency personnel. The room is filling with uniforms of all types.

"So you got home when?"

"Just a little while ago, this afternoon." Her eyes return to my face. She is nervous but I see neither guilt nor do I see anguish over the death of a husband.

"I know 911; we have a card from the police department we keep near the phone." Then she points towards another room, probably the kitchen.

She smiles shyly, "Jack," the dead husband, "He doesn't like me to go shopping too much but I go with my sisters," she points to the two other blonde young women who just make an appearance. I look at the uniforms and point with my eyes to the other young beauties now entering the room. The uniforms look surprised; here they are spending too much time yakking to each other instead of checking the surrounding area.

"We saw the body on the floor and his chest wasn't moving. I didn't know what happened so I called 911." The two other women walk towards the widow.

I would take bets that these women aren't her sisters. Unless they are from the countryside, Russians don't have such large families. She is well-educated; her Russian pronunciation is perfect, and therefore, I deduce that she must be city-bred. But I continue to listen.

"We all live here." Now that's interesting. This fat piece of lard has three beauties living in his house. Now where's the justice. Of course, I'm alive and he's dead so I'll reconsider this line of thinking.

The two women walk across the room, close to the widow, providing her emotional support. The taller one places her hand on the widow's shoulder. I don't recognize either one. They are nice looking but don't match the widow's pure, silky beauty. The women are both blonde and thin; their eyebrows are light so they dye their hair and eyebrows or they are natural blondes.

I tell my attentive audience that, "I know your husband."

The widow looks surprised; her pupils grow larger. I am looking into the deep blue sea.

"From the concerts. The Bandshell on Thursday nights," I add.

All three study my face as if I had just announced a major scientific discovery.

"Jack, first-in-line," I say. "I work security for those concerts."

I hear a faint sigh of relief.

"Concerts. Yes, few blocks away. I don't like them. I don't go." That confirms my observational talents. I didn't remember ever seeing her.

We return to the moment and all stare at the dead body on the floor. Does her story make sense? I can't decide but I have only a limited amount of time to determine whether we should have the coroner do an autopsy. An unobserved death can require an autopsy to medically determine the cause of death. The bureaucrats demand a reasonable explanation that life insurance companies and Social Security will accept.

"He had heart condition," she says in Russian, which none of the officials understand except me but nonetheless the other men watch as she places her hands gently on her heart. She looks across at Jimmy and points her head down so the coroner can see where she's pointing. Naturally, Jimmy and I stare at her chest; even the coroner's man looks up at her chest.

"He's not as old as you might think. It's the disease."

Requiring an autopsy is a touchy subject. The Medical Examiner's Office has an attorney dedicated to legally securing the right of the city to perform autopsies when relatives are unwilling to agree. The city doesn't like to pay the expense if it's unnecessary and a large segment of the public finds the process objectionable on religious grounds. I know Jews don't approve of having their loved ones' body parts cut out, weighed, measured, and examined. It's a sin, my mother often reminds me so I tread carefully about this decision. I can hear her voice in my head warning me. My mother is my conscience as I do my job as a police officer.

It was difficult to explain to my parents about joining the force, so I didn't. One day, five years ago, it became clear because I appeared in the kitchen of our Brighton Beach home in a rookie police uniform.

"Sasha, a policeman," my mother's exasperated arms flung into the air, "Sasha how could you take that test?"

I often pictured that moment especially when bored sitting in a cold police car during a stakeout. I imagined her thin arms as they clung to the damp air of that summer day. Her arms had that way of appearing as if they were being pulled towards heaven; a place she was certain doesn't exist. Nonetheless at those moments, I pictured her as a giant marionette, like the ones I remembered as a child on the stage in Leningrad. Not real marionettes, but ballet dancers acting like giant puppets being pulled by imaginary strings. But my mother was not a marionette; this feisty woman from an ancient land had seen too much to be unwillingly pulled in any direction.

"Sasha, a Jewish policeman, a Jewish policeman," the words an oxymoron. "A Russian Jewish policeman," her sense of betrayal deeply felt, a thousand years of persecution hung on each word. The dark history of Russia was heavy on her heart and it didn't matter whether it was either the Czar's or Soviet police. It was always the police who waged war against the Jews in somebody's name. The police had the guns and the dogs while the Jews at best had quick tongues—usually they didn't fare too well against the powerful. That was the allure of joining the police, not to spite my mother whom I loved dearly, but to challenge her ideas of what was true in Russia was not true in America. Every day in this new land I discovered fresh new truths. I compared my immigrant life to what I knew in Russia. I have now spent half my life in the Motherland and half in the New Jerusalem.

History defined my mother's life since she survived the Battle of Stalingrad. She doesn't really remember the winter of 1942-3 since she was only a child during the siege, but it was the defining modern moment of our long family saga. Being labeled a survivor enabled my mother to endure bleak times in the 1970's and early 1980's in Soviet Russia, proclaiming to the world her Jewish identity while the Soviet authorities wanted its citizens to deny all things Jewish. My mother was only saved from what could have been a very harsh and brutal punishment by the Soviet authorities by her birthright. She was the daughter of one of the Heroes of the Battle of Stalingrad. My grandfather was fiercely nationalistic and a brilliant Soviet soldier and administrator in charge of the city during the Nazi invasion. It was because the Soviet authorities even forty years later recalled his role and his continued support for the Soviet Union that she was not permanently imprisoned and sent off to Siberia.

In that dreaded winter during the Great Patriotic War few names meant more than Field Marshal Zhukov, General Romanenko and Dmetri Aronovich, my grandfather. It was his job to literally count the grains of salt—he had to keep enough people alive from starvation or freezing to death to ensure the triumph of Mother Russia.

Our family should have had a life of great accomplishment and prestige in the Soviet Union. My father was a brilliant mathematician in Russia and my mother a recognized inventor. So they sacrificed the good Soviet life because they refused to accept the fact that there were no Jews in Russia, only good Soviet citizens.

They carried their education, their enormous technical skills and all the honors bestowed by a grateful Mother Russia to capitalist America. There was no place of distinction for my father in America. While he should have had a tenured professorship in mathematics at MIT, instead he toiled as a good corporate citizen in the actuarial department of a New York insurance company. My mother, first in her class in engineering school, took a job as a computer programmer at a bank.

My mother was a blazing fire, sometimes roaring out of control while my father was the shimmering, cool, smooth steel of a new skyscraper. When my mother got exasperated with me she always said, "Like Uncle Vanya, the Cossack." I have his blood, this Uncle Vanya that family folklore said abandoned his wife and children and ran off to join the Russian Army. He was not conscripted, not one of the young cantonists forcibly recruited by the Army of Czar Nicolas I and forced into military service. No, he ran off—the adventurer—the scoundrel. He returned a decade later with his own horse, money, and a deed to land—in a country where the serfs were slaves to the land of their feudal lord. So he came to be called Uncle Vanya, the Cossack and although there was the element of irresponsibility in the label it also suggested something of the Russian soul-- a darkness but also a yearning to be something more than you are. I enjoyed being labeled with the distinction of being the most recent incarnation of Uncle Vanya.

The dead man belonged to an earlier generation of immigrants running from the Czars. Most New York Jews are descended from Eastern European immigrants and Russia was the largest source of this emigration. The widow was a recent escapee from the former Soviet Union but not necessarily Russian because the educated in the former Soviet republics all spoke perfect Russian.

The EMTs want to stuff the corpse into a body bag. They wait for Jimmy or me to give the sign, which we do. Because he's so big the EMTs would love to just drag the body out of the house but since the widow is in the room, how would that look? So the two EMTs roll the body onto the stretcher and out he goes, through the wide doorway, down the worn steps and out the fenced-in yard.

The widow watches as the EMTs remove the body.

"What happens now?" she asks completely perplexed. Her two sisters are listening.

"The coroner will just check a few things and then if he's satisfied they will issue a death certificate and release the body to a funeral home you select."

"How long does it take? He should be buried quickly."

She's not a Jew but she knows Jewish ritual about quickly burying the dead.

"A day we need, to confirm the cause of death."

"You won't cut him up?" she asks in exaggerated horror, her mouth stretching open so far you could examine her tonsils if that is your object of interest. That part of her anatomy is of little importance to Jimmy or me. I stare at her eyes and I begin to see small droplets of tears moving down her cheek.

"You understand," she tells me. "He's Jewish, his family would object."

Jimmy collects the information about his family and I put the pill bottles in a baggy and drop them in my jacket pocket. I'll chat with the doctor whose name is on the bottle; Jimmy can speak to the local pharmacist

The three sisters cast glances to each other.

Am I dealing with conspirators?

As I take my leave, I kiss the mezuzah on the doorpost. Mezuzah, which means doorpost in Hebrew, contains a parchment written in Hebrew with specific citations from the Bible. A Jew on leaving a house kisses the mezuzah for good fortune. I am searching for good luck in every corner.

I look back and see the sisters watching me. I see the large crack on the wall above their heads. I don't see anything in the house that looks like it has gotten any recent attention. Cracks are common when you live near the sea and Brighton Beach is nestled right against the ocean. The paint is peeling from the constant dampness and all the exposed metalwork is rusting from the bite of the salty sea air.

Here I am back in Brighton Beach in the middle of a summer day. Am I investigating a crime scene or just overseeing a natural death? I pull out the bottles and look intensely at them. Not that I know what the drugs are or what they do, but I study the labels because I have to maintain my all-knowing policeman demeanor. Its part of the role I play.

There's nothing here. Yet, I feel something's not right—a

cop's intuition, still there's no indication of foul play. I just need excuses to see her again.

I confer with Jimmy—my expert on how never to approach or treat women. However, he does know police procedure. Jimmy likes to intimidate all the men he meets on the job and flirt shamelessly with all the women even the old and unattractive ones. He didn't join the police force so he could help people. Jimmy has an expression; "If I wanted to help people I would be a social worker. If you want to kick ass, you become a cop."

"Should we order an autopsy or do we go with a heart attack?" I ask my partner.

Jimmy turns his body and looks at the three women in the doorway. His eyes are looking at the widow's legs moving slowly up her body. The presence of the two sisters distracts him. There's so much to feast on he can't decide which one is most worthy of his attention.

At first, Jimmy is not speaking. "Let the coroner do a preliminary examination—we can wait before ordering an autopsy," he finally says something and it's sensible. I can count on Jimmy to come up with sensible actions when I'm indecisive.

"Is there something here?" I ask for reassurance.

He straightens up and brushes off a piece of lint from his ivory-colored linen suit jacket. "No, but she has nice tits."

"She's not too upset," I tell him.

"Would you be? Big piece of shit like him. She probably married him for a green card, so what do you expect. Love?"

We both stand together while the uniforms move around us. Jimmy calls out, "Bye," to his softball buddy.

"There may be something here. Not overt, like they shot him. Maybe, just maybe, he has a heart attack around eleven this morning and they don't do anything. They flee the house. They run from the scene and wait till they're sure he's dead. Then they return and call 911." I look at him, "It's possible, right?"

He breathes in deeply. Jimmy likes the smell of the salty ocean air and that's why he's a constant visitor to my parents' house.

He's a second son.

"Anything is possible. And in your black Russian heart you sense that this immigrant is hiding something."

Jimmy shakes his head and continues."Okay, I think you got nothing, but sometimes… Actually, you're more often right than wrong when it comes to these immigrants. Could be that there is something. So we'll wait for the coroner's preliminary report. Okay."

I smile with satisfaction.

On my way out of the house I spot Vasily standing among the other curiosity seekers. A small gathering of neighborhood nosy-bodies surrounds the outer edges of the property. My pal Vasily, the reported neighborhood gangster, is a familiar figure in the neighborhood. He's my age and we're actually from the same neighborhood in Petersburg. We went to school together there. It's a very small world for us Russian Jews—America, the Motherland, we're all together.

When I see Vasily I stare, not in a harsh way but to show my recognition. A policeman can't appear too friendly with a gangster, but I remember my father's words, "He's one of us and you never go against one of us."

When I first joined the police force my father warned me about delving too deeply into the affairs of Vasily or his brother Mikhail, the reputed head of the Russian Brighton Beach Mafia. I was certain he wanted to protect me or even our family. But I was wrong. Neither my father nor my mother was afraid of Vasily and his pals. "We have nothing to fear because they aren't going to bother us."

"You know Papa, Vasily and his pals are involved in drugs, arms dealing and maybe even a little extortion. Not nice things," I told my father, shaking my head with a confidence that was necessary for the job.

The wisdom of a thousand years is in my father's eyes. He knows the black heart of the Russian soul. When he answers he is speaking for Mother Russia whether ruled by Soviets or

Czars—"If not Vasily then someone else? If not Russians then some other group? Who takes that poison? Is it many Russian Jews? Do many seek out prostitutes? Everyone has to make a living." 'Enough said' is written in my father's eyes.

Vasily watches me and smiles. We both have that certain thin, angular Russian face. There are two Slavic looks—first, the sharp edged one that belongs to many city-bred Russians. It's the telling sign of most Russian intellectuals, who always have some Jewish blood. Then there's the peasant look, which belongs to the country folk, the result of too little protein and too much potatoes and vodka. Most recent Russian Jews don't fit into that peasant category but many immigrants soon become nicely rounded once they stay awhile in America. Instead of boiled potatoes we have McDonald's and Burger King.

I don't wave to Vasily, that would be imprudent, but I smile shyly and he knows that I am acknowledging him. Vasily, the gangster, and I, meet again on shared turf. He lets me find and prosecute the murderers who in a rage of passion kill their wives. He lets me bring to court the men who beat their wives or girlfriends. The common thieves belong to me. The money laundering and the sins of consenting adults belong to him. We both watch them load the corpse into the ambulance and turn our attention to the three blonde sisters standing on the stoop. If Vasily knows the deceased he appears unemotional as the dead body is being hoisted into the ambulance. I watch to observe if he acknowledges the three sisters. I see nothing. A few old ladies stare. One says to the others, "My God, it's Jack."

I pause to take in the pungent salt air. Right beyond this block is the Boardwalk and the ocean. To the casual eye it may not look like a fierce ocean but it can be deceptively dangerous. People drown—I know I have examined bodies on the beach. In the summertime, the beaches all along this stretch of sand are packed with humanity. They arrive by car, bus, and subway in all sizes, colors, and shapes, placing their blankets and chairs in rows, looking like sardines in a giant tin can. If I walk to the Boardwalk now, I will see hundreds of half-naked bodies lying on their stomachs and backs sun bathing, small children along the surf's edge playing with the sand, and people of all ages sitting on mesh chairs receiving the sun's rays.

I am a frequent visitor to the beach. I can tolerate the crush of humanity on a hot sweaty summer day, but for me the perfect moment is the dawn when the sun appears out of nowhere and lights up the surface of the sea. A cop's life is one filled with constant stress. You don't dwell on the possibility but there's the occupational hazard of being faced with an assailant's gun or knife. Even good neighborhoods possess bad people and just as the most docile dog can turn on its owner, all people can be brought to the brink of uncontrollable rage.

I refresh my soul by regularly returning to my parents' home in Brighton Beach. I now live in another country as far as my parents are concerned, Kew Gardens, Queens. It's home to many Russian Jews but whose ancestors left the Motherland in the 1880s. I return to this ocean to be reborn at that exact moment when the ocean meets the land and a glimmering orange ball called the sun crosses over the horizon. I am a witness to this miracle many times but still I stand on the Boardwalk gaping as if I am a child amazed and dumbfounded by this magnificent sight of a sunrise.

A cop works all hours so it's not unusual to be coming home at dawn. When I am most on edge, I find myself driving on the Belt Parkway along that section that stretches from north of the Rockaways to Coney Island. I can travel east, turn around and travel back. On a particularly intense evening, when I have seen too much of human misery or too much brutality, I can repeat this ritual over and over again. It's the combination of the smells of the sea and the sounds of the gulls piercing the dawn air that consoles me. The great Talmudic scholars perceive the dawn as a metaphor for redemption. I completely understand that intense feeling. If it's still dark while I travel my route, I can see the lights flickering on the bridges separating Brooklyn from the Rockaways. This scene is ceaselessly soothing to this savage beast.

Welcome to Brighton Beach—the New Jerusalem—and my home turf. Every new Russian immigrant has a story to tell—maybe all recent immigrants have stories—but this is mine.

CHAPTER 2

A new day begins, redemption lies before me. Spending the night at my parents, I wake early, walk three blocks and watch the rising sun. Standing alone on the deserted Boardwalk, my arms resting at my sides and as the glorious sun makes its appearance, I raise my arms, like a phoenix, readying myself for the chaos of the day. The great rabbinic sages are right; dawn brings on the light and rebirth. My inner code of justice stands ready to right the world's wrongs.

Two hours later, after my cycling and breakfast activities are complete, I walk to the station house to begin my shift. As of yesterday, the case is dangling. Nothing definitive can be decided without lab results or a confession of contrition. Since neither is available we're rolling again on the streets of Brooklyn with time to assess our case. Our Lieutenant likes cases that produce quick results. It's not necessary to have all the answers, but I'm uneasy when the threads are left hanging. Just as I can't help myself from pulling at dangling threads on people's clothing, I can't rest unless I know exactly what happened.

"So Jimmy, what do we have?" I ask my partner when we meet in the station house.

Jimmy unwraps the gum and puts a stick in his mouth. He's a

quiet chewer unlike my first partner. Nothing puts me more on edge than someone sitting close to me making smacking noises as they attack a stick of chewing gum.

"Nice legs and a pretty face. Promising, but I need to see her in a bathing suit. We need to continue to investigate," he says and I'm glad we agree.

"Right," I answer. "But what do you think about the case itself? What happened?"

"Heart attack," his quick response.

We walk to an unmarked police car waiting for us in the parking lot. The traffic is normal for this time of day—crawling. I'm driving so I can't actually see his body movements; but after riding with him for two years, I can feel his shoulders shrugging. Jimmy is reviewing in his procedural head the scene from yesterday. I know how his gray cells work, slowly but deliberately synthesizing the evidence.

Jimmy doesn't possess too many expressions and they all emanate from his well-developed shoulder blades, a result of his efforts attacking a punching bag and lifting weights. There's the 'don't know and don't care' shrug that lacks vitality and energy. If we move based on this type of shrug it's because we're going by the book. Jimmy thinks it's a waste of our time, but it's required that we look like we can solve these problems—our NYC public demands we try. This shrugging is reserved for cases that are hard to solve like street muggings, where we rarely catch the punks unless they stab or shoot someone. Most car thefts remain unsolved because if the auto is worth stealing by the time we find it the tires are gone, the air bags have been ripped out and the sound system is nothing more than a gaping hole in the dashboard. We conserve our labors for finding the big fish, working to nail the stolen car rings.

Then there's the enthusiastic heavy shrugging accompanied by head wagging. This means real business. These are the cases that will win us brownie points with the brass. We rarely find many of these cases in Brighton Beach. We're not homicide cops so we usually don't get involved with the messy, gory, gang-related murders playing out in the Coney Island housing projects. The Case of the Russian Lady doesn't fit into any regular category— it's a case to pursue because the lady is interesting to pursue.

We drive around the neighborhood for several hours doing nothing but observing from our patrol car. It's why cops get fat and lazy—too much time sitting. We spend the idle moments talking about shared passions—boxing and cars.

"Okay, so what do you think happened?" he asks, as he looks my way. I see the curve of his round face in my peripheral vision.

"Let's stop to eat," I suggest as I give a fast glance to my watch. "We can talk inside." I try to explain myself. "I don't really want to waste the taxpayers' money or disappoint the Lieutenant dwelling on the obvious." I have a part of my mother's Soviet sensibilities about misusing public resources. "I don't think what we have been told is actually what happened."

"So genius, what happened? Stop here." Jimmy points to the diner where he wants us to stop. Although we are not supposed to get free food from restaurant owners, we can't help it if they find it necessary to reward us with extremely generous discounts.

We both love this small, box-shaped Brooklyn diner with the huge, dirty windows and cheap drapes. It's located on a busy interchange, where all types of humanity come to ease their thirst and hunger. The Greek owner waves at us as we emerge from our climate-controlled car into the hot muggy air. What a pleasure then to enter his nicely air-conditioned diner. The linoleum squeaks as we walk across the recently polished floor. A few heads turn in our direction. We're not in uniform but everyone knows we're cops. I have that cop look with my Sears' suit and sensible shoes. Our eyes glance across the room, always observing and categorizing each face into good citizen or bad guy groups.

The waitress doesn't ask us what we want. She brings two tall, frosted glasses filled with home-made ice tea and sandwiches piled so high with fresh, quality ingredients that we take the extra half with us in the car for an afternoon snack. She knows our routine. For me it's tuna fish; Jimmy has the corned beef.

We eat at our favorite booth that allows eye contact with the front door as well as the bathrooms. We are never off guard, always waiting for a bad guy to make a move. Everyone has something to hide; but most indiscretions do not require action by the NYPD.

"I think what we have is a case of omission not commission," I answer as Jimmy digs into his corned beef sandwich. He's learned from me to ask for rye bread and mustard. No self-respecting Jew can even tolerate watching anyone eat meat with mayonnaise on white bread.

"Here's what I think went down." I'm the expert on human motivation because I'm Russian—we eat dark bread so we have dark hearts; so goes the logic in police headquarters. Besides psychology is what I studied in college. I enjoy playing into their notions of Russian immigrants and there's a deep vein of truth in the stereotype. It becomes shorthand for explaining my actions.

Jimmy is paying attention between bites and sips of iced tea. His eyes rest on my mouth so I continue."She hears a big bang; the sound is coming from downstairs. She's upstairs doing something, I don't know. And he's watching TV alone downstairs. Maybe she calls down to him to see if he's OK."

Jimmy is looking intently at me and following my words. He respects my detective instincts, assuming that as a Russian I have x-ray vision, capable of seeing into the mind of a suspect. I understand the inner workings of the psyche and conscience; and the proof is my taste in reading. I'm the only person Jimmy has ever met that actually read Dostoevsky's *Crime and Punishment*. I admit to him that I read the book both in Russian and English several times. His reading of great literature is limited to high school English class and then only the Cliff notes. He tells me that once he watched on the late show a movie version of *War and Peace*, but he didn't remember any of the storyline.

I go on. "He doesn't respond so she goes downstairs and she finds him on the floor. Maybe he's clutching his heart," I illustrate crossing my hands across my heart. My lips are pleading.

Jimmy can see that I am trying to speak the words, 'Help me,' but no sounds are uttered; I can only gesture. "Maybe he finally manages to whisper help or call 911." Jimmy is nodding his head as he follows my outline of the case. This is a good sign. Jimmy is actively engaged in my line of reasoning.

"She turns away and goes out the door and leaves the poor bastard to die," I add.

"What about the sisters?" he asks.

"I don't know maybe they weren't even in the house at the time. We really don't know anything at all about them."

"And?" Jimmy asks, waiting for the rest of the story to unfold.

"She, and maybe the sisters, return in a few hours from shopping and eating at Juniors. Maybe they take the subway," I reply, between bites of tuna fish; not too much mayonnaise is how they know to make my sandwich.

"Do we have a crime?" I ask.

Jimmy stares at me. "Of course we have a crime, if she intentionally left him while he was dying. She should have called for help. But it will be a bitch to prove unless we can get the sisters to turn on each other. What kind of evidence will we find?"

It doesn't matter whether the women are sisters, Russians do not turn on each other especially to rat on someone to the police. They're probably all glad he's dead.

"It could of happened that way." Jimmy likes my version—it's logical and in its own way obvious. Proving the case and bringing it to the DA is a different problem. So in Jimmy's view, the case remains viable. No one is skipping town so the possible felons are available and so far we haven't heard from any friends or relatives screaming about foul play. We can conduct an investigation without an autopsy.

We need to learn much more about our couple. What kind of a relationship did they have? The first suspect in any questionable case is always the spouse or significant other—who else has the necessary hate or fear or resentment to trigger an unholy act?

Then I tell my partner my other news.

"I'm going to the Lieutenant's Bar-B-Q." I hate to go to these functions. I don't like to drive out to Suffolk County and play politics. Jimmy loves to go and he's been nagging me since I joined the 60th Precinct to follow tradition. It's an honor to get an invitation because not every cop in the station house gets invited.

And lately my father is suggesting that I do the political thing and go, even if I just stay for an hour. "Sasha," he tells me yesterday, "you must go and present yourself. A man must do everything necessary to promote himself before his superiors." A very Soviet bureaucratic response and usually my mother, the anti-Soviet, the proponent of American free-will, disagrees with him and denounces conformity. Yesterday, her response is different. And this morning, in unison, they begin their helpful chats about my future.

As she pours me a glass of freshly-made orange juice, my absolute favorite beverage, she adds her observations of life in America. "Sasha, listen to your father, he knows about these things. Look how far he's gotten in the insurance company. We force ourselves to go to these stupid affairs. Go, it will be good for your career."

I don't understand what's going on in my mother's head since as far as she's concerned, I can't possibly make a career out of being a police officer. In her mind, I'm a law student on loan to the police department. My mother suggesting office parties as a means to obtain new stature at the station house? I don't understand and that's one of my mother's most endearing characteristics. She always keeps my father and me on our toes, expecting the unexpected.

"Jimmy, I'm going to the Lieutenant's shindig with Roberta."

Jimmy is just swallowing his ice tea when I make my announcement. Whatever is left in his mouth at that microsecond he spits out on the table and the rest is circulating in his throat causing him to choke. I am not certain what I should do, smack him on the back or get him water so I just watch for a couple more seconds.

Finally after the choking stops and with tears running down

his pleasant face he tells me in a very harsh tone. "Roberta, are you nuts. She's a dyke." This diner is not gay-friendly so I don't expect any reaction from our fellow customers.

"You don't know that." I'm shaking my head.

"Yes I do. You asked her?" Jimmy can't believe his ears. He sticks his index finger into his ear pretending he has water in it and shakes his head like a dog does after getting soaking wet from running in the surf.

"No, she asked me and I couldn't refuse."

"Yes, yes you can say no, no. What do you mean she asked you?" Jimmy's face is getting very red, which isn't a good sign.

I describe for Jimmy, in full detail, my conversation with Roberta earlier today on my way into work. "Roberta asked me if I was going to the Lieutenant's party. I told her that, with reluctance, I planned to go to keep my father happy." I pause after each word for emphasis while Jimmy continues to poke at his ear pretending he's still checking for the imaginary water that is blocking his hearing. "She said that we could go together, and I was more than willing to have some company."

Jimmy is going with his girlfriend Lori, and he will spend hours making small talk and complimenting the Lieutenant on his gun collection and the house's landscaping. Jimmy's the best partner a fellow officer could ask for but he's a 'tuchis lecker,' ass kisser. We all know how much time the Lieutenant spends on his lawn and shrubs. He brings in roses from his prized collection and places them on his credenza behind his desk next to the photo of his wife. A member of the community Grange, he's always talking about non-toxic fertilizers and organic gardening. I know Roberta is only going to make an appearance so we will spend perhaps an hour or two doing the politically smart thing. How long can I stand listening to gardening tips?

I planned my escape as part of my decision to attend. Fleeing the party with Roberta after an hour or two made sense although when she asked, I just blurted out, "Yes." I knew the rumors about Roberta. When I first heard others gossiping about Roberta it reminded me of the Biblical story of Miriam, who was punished by God with leprous skin for speaking ill of her brother Moses. Even if the stories about Roberta were true, if the result caused harm it was forbidden.

Jimmy is now holding his stomach as if he is in great pain. At first, I'm thinking that the ice tea is too cold. He places his strong, Polish hands over his face, completely covering his big blue eyes with those sexy, puffy eyelids that the girls just love. He's got his mouth completely masked by his hands. "It isn't bad enough that you're a Russian—and a Jew—now they're going to think you're a queer."

He continues in his pained condition. "How am I going to save you," he asks himself out loud.

It's at that exact moment that I realize how much Jimmy likes having me as his partner. We are truly mates. I am bursting with happiness as I watch him figure out the possible angles to save me.

All cops depend upon their partners. It's necessary for survival. But a really great police partnership is special like the intricate mechanism of an expensive Swiss watch, all the delicate pieces move precisely together—the tick closely follows the tock.

When I was first introduced to Jimmy, it felt right. We would make a great pair although at first glance it looked like a mismatch. A well functioning partnership was important to me because I knew I was perceived by most of my fellow officers as an outsider, an oddball. They wanted me as back-up because of my sharpshooter's eye and steady hand, but not as a companion to chat with for endless hours while waiting at a stakeout in a police car.

I drink coffee but give me a hot glass of tea with lemon and lots of sugar even in the summer heat. I don't eat cheeseburgers, ever. I don't hunt although I could easily kill anything moving from a hundred yards away.

Russians search their hearts and make decisions based on their instincts, seeking a perfect balance between fate, the cards that they get dealt, and control over one's destiny. Jimmy, being of Eastern European descent, understands this fatalism.

People who are too similar don't make great partners. You need a complementary personality, someone looking over your shoulder that understands your weaknesses and can compensate for them. You don't merely want to survive you want to flourish. Jimmy and I are just that kind of different mix and it works.

Despite this unpleasant news that I am dumping in his lap, our relationship endures because Jimmy is going to make good on my impulsive behavior. He's going to find a way to take this problem and re-invent it as a splendid decision. Always the political animal, he sniffs out the news, and determines who to follow and whom we can ignore.

The truth is whatever her sexual orientation, Roberta and I enjoy more in common with each other than most of the officers in the station house. Unlike most of our station house peers, we didn't study law enforcement in college, although I did get an "A" in a criminology class.

Roberta is typical of the middle class that remains living in the Big Apple; she's a product of a Catholic education from kindergarten to high school. Me, I am a graduate of Stuyvesant High School, one of New York City's elite public high schools.

I was a good student in high school but, according to my teachers, I never worked to my potential. Still with my solid school achievements, I was accepted to an Ivy League college and my parents were so proud; they told all their Russian Jewish friends. It wasn't Harvard or Yale, and cost a small fortune. I refused to go and instead went as a Merit Scholar to a state school and saved my parents a tidy sum, which my father later acknowledged was a smart use of scarce resources.

When I graduated from college, with no particular vocational goal, my father said he could get me an entry position at his insurance company. My mother found a place for me as a computer programmer trainee at her bank.

I didn't want my parents' help. I was an independent spirit—

living in America. Naturally, I did something to 'yank their chains.' And my inner Uncle Vanya, the Cossack, had other plans. I dropped them suddenly on my parents because I knew they would disapprove.

At age 22 and feeling very much at home in the New Jerusalem, I told them.

"Sasha you joined the Army," my parents looked at me as if I had just sold the dacha in the countryside to gypsies for a broken violin.

"A Jewish boy in the military, are you mad," my mother never stopped repeating that phrase as she and my father drove me to the bus that would take me to my military training.

My mother questioned my sanity. "There's not even a war going on," this being between Iraqi wars. "Do you know how many Jews fled Russia rather than serve in the army of the Czar?" She poked with her thin index finger on my arm like a woodpecker, a true sign of her displeasure.

My father did not want to be too critical yet he remained convinced that I had not carefully analyzed all my options. In his mind this was not a logical decision, more likely an impulsive gesture. "The military, any military, is run by mental midgets."

Words, words, mental midgets; I taught my father the tricks of turning a phrase so he sounded more like an American. Alliteration, what a concept, the sounds linked together as they rolled off the tongue. Mental midget, almost Shakespearean, how those two words captured the essence of his thinking about the military, mendacity, and bureaucratic sloth; realistic descriptions of the military at peace.

I kissed them good-bye as the bus was leading me to Officers Candidate School. I was not a total fool; if I was going to join a world of mediocrity then at least I'd have status as a junior officer.

My mother yelled at me as I stepped onto the bus." At least learn a trade."

My father was right, of course. So I was stuck with my impulsive decision—this was going to be my sacrifice. In my family we needed to have stories of sacrifice to share. Those years in the military represented my first contribution to the family history of sacrifice. On the grand scale of degrees of sacrifice, through which generations of my family had managed to live and survive, my military experiences were pretty tepid, more boring than life threatening or life changing. Whenever I'm completely bored as a police officer, I remember those truly worthless days spent as a soldier protecting the land of the free and the brave. Becoming a soldier had one positive advantage; it helped to speed up my citizenship process.

The Army asked me about my career plans. I studied the glossy brochure. There was the part about computers, my mother was correct—I could find a marketable career path.

Why join the Army to learn something I could have studied at the bank? So I told them about a special skill of mine that I learned from my Uncle Alexei, my mother's brother who served in the Soviet Army. I asked to join the marksman corps. I wanted to be a sharpshooter just like Vasily Alexandrovich Zaitsev, who reportedly killed 242 Nazis during the Great Patriotic War, what the rest of the world called World War II. This Vasily assassinated a score of Nazi invaders during the deadly but illustrious Battle of Stalingrad.

They did not believe I had this hidden talent. A Russian immigrant from Brighton Beach, Brooklyn, familiar with guns, not likely, they immediately replied. Then I showed them my stuff on the rifle range. I demonstrated my steel nerves, steady hand and dexterous fingers. I was a surprise to my superiors— the NYC Jew with an eagle eye. They were soon discussing my training as a member of the US Olympic team. They could not believe their luck.

"What an honor," my mother said when I called. But there was a drawback. I had to re-enlist for four years in order for them to commit to my training. "It makes perfect sense," said my father, the only logical decision the Army was making, according to his mathematician's mind.

"So Jew boy, are you going to re-enlist," asked my Army bunkmate, Richard from Prairieville, Indiana who couldn't find Russia on a map. I listened to my Army associates, consulted my parents and peered into my dark Russian soul to find my inner Uncle Vanya.

"Well, Perlov, are you ready to represent your country in the Olympics?" asked my colonel.

No, I was not ready. I was not going to re-enlist so before I realized it, I was back in Brooklyn. I brought home my Army trophies for marksmanship. I still possessed these impressive sharpshooter skills but I needed a different vocation than US Army soldier. It was time for a new career choice.

My mother was relieved. "What's the point of marksmanship—to kill people? There is no war, Thank God." My mother often thanked God although I know she never believed that there was one watching over any of us. Where was this mysterious, merciful God at the Battle of Stalingrad? Yes, we won the battle and later the war, but at an enormous cost.

"Uncle Vanya, the Cossack," mother was pecking at my arm after I told my parents my next career move, "from the Army to the police," she was shaking her head.

New York's finest was mightily impressed with my Army trophies. I was assigned to the SWAT team. My job was to perch on rooftops, lie on grassy knolls and wait for my prey. Problem was I didn't really want to kill anyone. As an Army sharpshooter, since we were at peace, I never shot a real person. I entered contests and won trophies against other Army divisions and later the Marines—but my targets never once breathed or bled.

"Sasha," my mother cried tears of anguish to my father when she saw me wearing my SWAT team uniform on the TV during a nasty hostage situation. "Leonid, he is killing his fellow citizens." My father told me later how he had to comfort and soothe my mother's rattled nerves.

I couldn't stand to break my mother's heart as a member of the SWAT team. I'm basically a good Jewish boy—a mama's boy and her reproach was too daunting. I didn't have the emotional detachment to remain cool and seemingly unaffected by her disapproval. My Uncle Vanya impulses had to find a different outlet.

With little enthusiasm, my police superiors permitted me a transfer. Being Russian, their next suggestion was to work undercover against the Russian Mafia in Brooklyn.

"The secret police Sasha, you want to join the secret police, even Uncle Vanya, the Cossack would never stoop so low." My mother thought that the Army had permanently damaged my brain. My father couldn't believe a son of his would spy on neighbors. I declined that opportunity. My standing in the police department continued to fall.

Then there was my sorta Russian Jewish girlfriend named Natasha. She was the only white girl not from Brighton Beach or Staten Island named Natasha. My mother found this very confusing to read about girls named Natasha in the newspaper and only see black faces. No Russians she knew were marrying black people.

Now my Natasha had a Jewish father of Russian descent— among the ones whose family left Czarist Russia a hundred years ago. The name was right out of the greatest Russian literature. Problem was her mother was a Christian and not Russian. She was brought up in her mother's faith.

"I survived Stalingrad, Soviet jails so you could live free in America to marry a goy," my mother's heart hardened when she thought of my betrayal.

So I slept with Natasha but I never married her. She eventually moved on to someone offering her a more promising future. It was not that my parents actually believed in religion like most people. God and religious observance were two separate notions. We kept a kosher home and we always attended services at the Russian Jewish synagogue on Brighton Beach Avenue in the heart of the new Russian Jewish ghetto, but believing in God was something for the Hasids—the ultra orthodox Jews from the other part of Brooklyn.

"Why not stay in Israel?" I asked in the late 1980's when we left the Soviet Russia for Israel. But the sojourn lasted only six months. My mother found endless faults with the Land of Milk and Honey.

"Who wants to live in a theocracy," my mother said. "America is better than Jerusalem, we can have anything and everything," spoken like a true immigrant with their boundless faith in the American dream.

So here I sit in a Brooklyn diner deciding the course of events involving a fat, dead Jew and his Russian lady. Meanwhile, Jimmy is preoccupied not with the case, but how to explain my impulsive decision to go the Lieutenant's party with Roberta. I see him concentrating, devising several explanations and testing the theories quietly out-loud to himself. He doesn't need my input.

"So," I need to bring him back to the case. There are decisions to be made.

He's still shaking his head at me, my stupidity. How much more Jimmy needs to do to mold me into a proper police officer. Tolerance is not only unnecessary, it's an impediment to working well with the other guys.

"I have to use the European angle. You being Russian— you can't refuse a woman's invitation—chivalry." His head and shoulders remain in motion like a kewpie doll at a circus midway.

"That's the best angle. European guys are always polite with women." He likes this path he's following.

"The way you're always opening the doors for all the women in the station house even that black bitch sergeant." He's comfortable—he's found the explanation.

"You dumb bastard," he tells me smiling. "Next time stay away from her."

He's ready to move back to the case having solved our personal dilemma, which is to him of vastly more significance than this case.

"Our Russian lady," I chuckle, a wide grin on my face. Then I wink and I can see him picturing her beautiful body; we can only imagine.

Jimmy is focusing on the widow. "You should not be wasting your extravagantly elegant manners on Roberta, save it for the widow—after we close the case, of course." Anything else gets me in big trouble with the police brass, the kind Jimmy cannot make right. Rule one of police procedure—no fraternizing with possible suspects in a case.

"I'll go see the doctor whose name is on the pill bottles," I tell Jimmy. We need to know more about his heart condition if we intend to label the case death by natural causes. The lab boys are performing some toxicology screening. I am hoping there's no arsenic because I don't really want to lock her up in prison.

Jimmy doesn't like doctors or hospitals, and he hates going to the morgue. "I'll check his assets and see what our Russian Lady will inherit." We both know money can be a very tempting golden calf. Then there's the immigrant holy grail—the green card. The Immigration authorities should have useful information. Is she really married to the dead guy? Are the three women really sisters?

Jimmy and I are on the case dedicated to finding the truth or at least to try to piece together the events of that fateful afternoon. The clock is ticking so we have to speed up our investigation since it is not a high priority case unless we find immediate evidence of foul play.

As I start daydreaming again about the widow, Jimmy's cell phone punctures my fantasy world.

"Yeah," he answers. "No," I hear him say.

"No, we don't want to go there." He closes the phone. "Sarge is requesting our return to the station," and he buries his head into his folded arms. "It's the worst possible assignment, talking to mugging victims, senior citizens from Coney Island. They don't see well; they can hardly hear; and a smart lawyer makes mincemeat of their testimony in a court room."

We both hate these calls, but the Lieutenant demands our presence and we must obey.

We stare across the desk of our Lieutenant. He is genuinely pleased I have decided to attend his party.

"Great, Perlov, my wife has something special for you to eat." Everyone knows about my unusual eating habits. Some attribute it to healthy living habits since I am known to be an avid cycler and surfer. Jimmy has some vague ideas about my observing religious rules—keeping kosher. He understands religious rituals; he gives up meat for Lent.

"I want you to go to Harbor House," the Lieutenant directs us. This is a senior housing complex run by the New York City Housing Authority, home to hundreds of poor immigrants, mostly from the former Soviet Union. The complex consists of three 14-story buildings, sitting right in the midst of Coney Island surrounded by mean, crime-ridden, low-income housing projects where gang activity is commonplace.

Unimaginative thinking is responsible for this mess. Thieves and low class criminals, preying on the old and fragile in the senior housing, are making a magnificent beachfront into an urban battleground. These old, defenseless people, many who barely speak the language are easy marks for the local thugs. But the resentment in Coney Island is thick and tinged with racial hatred. The politicians want to deny the truth. Ask the immigrants if the rough hooligans don't shove them and shout, "Go back to Russia" while they're walking on the Boardwalk. The resentment exists because the unemployed and truant adolescents and young men living in the public housing hear complaints about these older residents from their families. It is the adults who curse these old Jews because the politicians favor white immigrants over the native born black and Hispanic residents.

Jimmy rolls his eyes. The Lieutenant ignores him and looks at me.

"These old people deserve our attention, and besides the brass is breathing down my neck," he tells me. He has a hard stare for Jimmy. Several levels of the political bureaucracy are screaming to find the culprits and protect the old people. Justice is required. Or at least we have to make the streets appear safer. The reality is the streets are really safe in the 60th Precinct, unless you happen to become a crime victim.

"I know you sympathize with their problems. Old Jews from Russia," he returns his gaze on me.

"Go back and interview a few of them. The sergeant has the names and addresses. How does it look for so many cases and only one arrest? Bring me an arrest." He pounds the desk. Jimmy has lost interest and is daydreaming but the sound jolts him from his seat. It is exactly the reaction the Lieutenant is seeking. "Get the bastards," he orders us.

Jimmy and I are not afraid of the Coney Island projects; we patrol without hesitation, rarely are our guns out of their holsters. We know these mean streets and are completely comfortable demonstrating the power represented by our badges without the overt use of force. The karma we give off tells the residents we are tough but we're honest and fair. Unless you're breaking the law, there's nothing to fear from us. We don't patrol the streets harassing the youth, we never shake down the storeowners, and we're not interested in sampling the commerce on the streets. We live in Brooklyn, a mosaic of humanity, not in a pure white suburban community in Suffolk County or northern New Jersey.

"Let's drive around the Garden," Jimmy tells me. We enjoy cruising around this place, a local reference to the basketball courts surrounding the Coney Island projects, named for the illustrious Madison Square Garden courts of the New York Knicks. The hopes and dreams of black Coney Island youth are here in this square of asphalt. You can hear the applauding by-standers blocks away. Ten thick are the crowds, watching for fresh new talent to emerge. The college and professional basketball scouts are here watching for a future Stephon Marbury, the Knicks megastar and product of these projects. The scouts promise everything and these young kids put all their hopes into landing that lucrative contract that will get them and their families out of this urban jungle. And how many will succeed? They might as well be betting on the lottery.

Down the street about a mile, the immigrants of Brighton Beach put their faith and hope in education. Study hard; learn as much as you can. These are words we hear repeatedly from our parents. You practice your spelling and the vocabulary of this new language, learn to conjugate verbs, study algebra, and practice that violin. Practice. We practice not ball handling and three point shots, not the hockey we love to watch on TV, but SAT practice exams. And for those not destined for Harvard, there's Kingsborough Community College down the street in Manhattan Beach. Even if you're not college material, you learn a trade that pays, car mechanic, carpenter, something honest. Russian immigrants performed those trades back in the Motherland and fathers teach their sons in America. Or borrowing the example of the Koreans, you combine all your earthly possessions and open a store on Brighton Beach Avenue where all the members of your extended family work. It's not that these young black kids don't work very hard but the goals are different. Immigrants have dreams but they want better odds than the basketball scouts are offering.

"Should we stop?" I ask Jimmy as we find an illegal space by a fire hydrant.

I know he loves to watch the raw talent out on the courts, but the athlete says, "Later; they'll be out here all day and half the night."

Harbor House awaits our attention. There's an official parking space for the police so no need to double-park on the street. We take the elevator to the fifth floor to visit Mrs. Svetlana Chervony, crime victim.

"Police," I announce as we ring the doorbell. A plain wooden mezuzah hangs above my head on the doorpost, a sure sign of a

Jewish household.

We know she is watching us through the security keyhole. I take my badge close to the hole so she can see it.

She slowly opens the door; the latch remains hooked. I show her the badge again.

I speak in Russian. "Mrs. Chervony we are from NYPD. We're here to talk to you about a mugging. Can we come in?"

"A Russian?" she asks in a hushed tone, and a small, hunched-over woman beckons with a thin finger. She releases the latch. It's always difficult to tell the age of the old. They're winkled, their skin is translucent, and folds appear where once there was elasticity.

She leads us to the living room that also serves as a dining area. Every available inch of space is put to good use, but it doesn't have a cluttered feel. The windows are open wide and the sea breezes cause the drapes to flap in the air. The sofa is spotlessly clean although worn, probably a present from the Jewish Aid Society. Cotton doilies cover the spots where the cloth is most tattered. A Russian language newspaper is on the kitchen table; the books on the shelves are all in Russian. I notice a threadbare Siddur, Jewish prayer book, on the sofa, which she kisses and moves away so I can sit.

"Mrs. Chervony, we want to ask you about what happened last week." I continue to speak in Russian.

She sits next to me while Jimmy pulls up a chair from the kitchen set. He rests with his elbows on his thighs watching me question the old lady. Her eyes are small but she stares intently.

"You don't know what it feels like," she sighs.

"Tell us, what happened." I sympathetically ask.

"I was just about to press button for elevator," her speech becomes more animated.

"My finger was," she picks up her crooked index finger and is about to rest it on the imaginary button.

"When," she screams. Both Jimmy and I jump. "He grabs me around neck. I can feel his big arm across my neck." She begins to breathe faster.

"I think to myself, I can't die." Her words are tumbling out of her mouth. "I can't die. All I have been through. I can't die in America. I can't die in the hallway. I don't want to die," and she begins to sob quietly at first and then in a tidal wave. Her small chest is heaving. I watch her face as she struggles for breath. I hope we don't have to perform CPR.

Jimmy rises quickly and goes into the kitchen space, which is directly in front of us. He flings opens cabinet doors and finds a glass. He watches the cold water flow into the glass then glances at us on the sofa. Her tears wash her thin face and so he searches for a tissue box, which he finds on the counter. Hurriedly, he returns and hands her a glass. She also takes the tissue he offers.

She is trembling and so I place my arm gently around her shoulders, "It's OK, Mrs. Chervony," I whisper in her ear. I rock her softly. She could be my Bubbe, my grandmother. I want to place a kiss on her sweaty forehead but that would be too intimate.

She begins to hiccup from the crying. Her tiny body shakes with each motion.

"Sugar," I tell Jimmy, "find a sugar cube."

He obeys and finds a glass container and brings it to me.

I select one square cube. I urge her to eat it. "Sugar best medicine for hiccups."

She takes the cube from my hand and sucks on the sugar; it slowly dissolves and in a few moments the granules coat her throat, relaxing her spastic body motions.

Jimmy looks worried. His palms are damp; and his eyes stare at the old woman's face looking for more signs of physical distress. Then he turns back to my face for reassurance. I smile. The old woman is already calmer.

I want to make small talk. "Mrs. Chervony, where are you from?" I will give her time to calm down before I begin my questioning.

"Volgograd," she says and a faint smile appears.

"Yes, my mother is from there," I answer with surprise because you don't find too many immigrants from the former Stalingrad. The Jews come from the bigger cities, Moscow and Petersburg.

She gives me an intense stare as if she is memorizing all of my facial features. "What is her name?"

"Anna Aronovich."

The old woman's mouth opens wide. "Any relation to Dmetri Aronovich?"

"I am his grandson," I answer proudly and my back straightens up.

She clutches her loose fitting blouse near her heart. Her fingers are gripping the white cloth. She asks, "The grandson of the Hero of the Battle of Stalingrad? There is a God in heaven. Hashem in his mercy has brought us a protector."

She takes my hand and turns it around so that the palm shows. Then she gently kisses it. I don't dare move my hand away although I am uncomfortable. She gingerly places her hand against my cheek.

"Yes, God in his infinite majesty has brought you to us. I know you will protect us like your grandfather did in the Battle of Stalingrad."

She pauses and her eyes drift to another world.

"Did your grandfather tell you about those brutal months? No one knows unless you were there, how Russians suffered in those years."

"He told me few things," I say while she continues to hold my hand.

"It was so horrible, words fail any of us in trying to describe those times. Your grandfather he was there, everywhere. The Nazi Army marched into the city. Those cocky, arrogant dreck." The last word is said with such venom you could feel the poison flowing from her taut mouth.

"The bombs fell and the tanks exploded their shells throughout the city. And there was your grandfather directing us to safety or at least out of the greatest danger. In the morning, Hitler's tanks plowed over everything standing. And in the evening, the Red Army moved, house-to-house, block-to-block killing every Nazi. Colonel Aronovich traveled throughout the city, day and night, in his open car, regardless of the weather, getting us to move to another sector of the city. We walked in line. Sometimes he would reach out and grab a child or an infant, sometimes an elderly person and put them in his car. He had to keep moving us along away from the fires and the Nazis. There was no one to fight those fires." She sighs heavily. Jimmy is glued to his seat and although he doesn't understand a word, he sees the gravity of the conversation on her face.

"Your grandfather distributed all the rations to the civilians. We all got the same." She nods her head and sighs again.

Her mind returns to sixty years ago. "He came to our neighborhood where there were Jews. He stood on the hood of his car. He told us what we already knew. 'You must fight not for the Soviet Union, not even for Mother Russia.' He pointed to each one of us and told us. 'You fight with the Red Army because they are the only thing separating you from certain execution by the Nazis.'"

She takes in a deep breath. "We knew. We heard the stories from the Russian western front that the Nazis were shooting all the Jews they found, men, women, children, even babies pulled out of their mother's arms. People shot and buried alive. They were going to exterminate all the Jews. We knew what fate was before us. Your grandfather reminded us this was a fight till the death. Because death surely awaited us if the Red Army failed."

My mother, the anti-Soviet dissident, always spoke affectionately about the heroic Red Army during those brutal times. At the Battle of Stalingrad, Stalin himself ordered the Red Army not to retreat under any circumstances. It was victory or death.

She continues her remembrances, her face deep in thought.

"We had nothing to eat."

She touches my hand. "We put old belts and shoes in boiling water and drank it like soup. Can you imagine drinking leathery water, how desperate we were?" She sighs again as she relives those days.

The tears come but not gushing out; slowly they lead a trail from the corner of her left eye to the edge of her dry lips. "We had water because it was winter and there was snow and ice everywhere."

She shakes her head and dabs her eyes with the tissue.

"We got rations from your grandfather, sugar, a thimble full, that's all. Crumbs, we ate crumbs. We stood on line for these meager rations to keep us alive."

I gently pull her close to me.

"We were hungry, always hungry. I'd wake up in the morning, ravenous and all day I thought of nothing but food. I went to bed at night, dreaming of food. It was good to sleep because then you weren't consciously thinking about eating. We all grew weaker but because of your grandfather we never gave up. He provided us rations, as little as they were."

She holds my hand. "Your grandmother was killed in the first bombing?" she asks in a whisper.

"No, she was severely injured at the first attack by the Nazis and there was not enough medicine so she grew weaker. After a few months she died during the winter."

"We knew the Colonel took only what he gave to the rest of us. Nothing more."

She stops and then looks into my eyes. "His baby son also died."

I know the story. "As my grandmother grew weaker she had no strength to nurse. He starved to death."

She sighs again and holds my hand tighter. "It was so bad. You do what you must to survive. I killed man. Yes," her face tightens.

"We were hiding in cellar in building without roof. We burned books to keep warm. It was bitterly cold and snowing. Russian winters."

I lived through fifteen Russian winters.

"Two Nazi soldiers with their guns raised entered our hiding place. We had no guns, but we weren't defenseless. Your grandfather's soldiers taught us self-defense."

She grows more excited in the telling.

"We were afraid. I was standing up and at first I thought he would surely shoot me. But we had some food and he was hungry so he approached, and I offered him some bread."

She looks at us both. Jimmy doesn't understand a word but he sees her mood is changed from victim to someone with confidence in her voice.

"I speak German so I tell him that I have bread to share. I ask him to come closer. He puts down the barrel of his gun. My friend is sitting behind me and silently she puts a kitchen knife in my hand. When he was right in front of me I plunge the knife into his gut. The second soldier is frightened and was about to fire his gun when an old woman hits him over the head with a frying pan. When he was down on the ground this old woman hit him over and over again with the heavy pan. The blood was everywhere."

She smiles a devilish grin.

"I had the knife in his stomach and turned it around and around just like your grandfather's soldiers showed us. Never lift your arm over your head, don't strike from high is what we were told," and she demonstrates the wrong approach.

It is a dramatic swoop. The humid air is stirred by the force of her hand movement. Jimmy is startled by her sizeable gesture.

"We took their guns. Then we stripped them. The boots were worn but better than what we had. Their coats were warm. We even took their socks." She sighs again.

"They may not have died from our blows but we left them for the Russian winter air to finish off what we started."

This time when she sighs, it is a sign of accomplishment. "I never want to see death so close. I thought when I was attacked last week that after all I have lived through, I would die in the hallway."

She kisses my hand. "You were sent by Hashem. You will protect us."

"God helps those who help themselves. Tell me what you remember about your assailant," I answer.

She sits as straight as her frail body permits. "Yes."

I look calmly into her eyes with my warm dark, Russian eyes. "What did he look like?"

"Shvartzer," she replies; he is black.

"How black, the color of coal? Or maybe," I point to a page in a magazine resting on the coffee table. "This color?"

"No, very black like coal."

"How tall was he?" remembering that she is a very small woman and everyone must look tall.

I tap Jimmy on his kneecap. "Stand," I say in English and he obeys.

"As tall as my partner?" I take her by the arm and help her to stand next to Jimmy, who is over six foot tall.

"When you look at Detective Sutton's chest can you remember where you were in relation to the assailant's body? Did you have to look up?" She nods.

I continue, "And how far did you stretch your neck?"

She moves her neck as gracefully as a swan. It appears that the assailant is a few inches taller than Jimmy.

"His build?"

I motion to Jimmy to take off his suit jacket.

"Sturdy and strong like my partner?" She looks, "or thinner like me?" Her eyes dart from Jimmy's muscular chest to my thinner frame.

"Or was he fat?" She is getting a little wobbly on her feet so I help her sit. She just looks at me.

She looks uncertain so I change direction. "What was he wearing?"

"Crazy in this heat, he was wearing a wool cap and a sweatshirt. You see the boys in 95-degree weather dressed for winter wearing long sleeve sweatshirts. Or they wear nothing. They can't have much of a wardrobe."

"Think about his physical shape. Was his flesh pressing against the cloth? Did you get that close to his body?"

"He was fat. He was busting out of his sweatshirt."

"Good, very good." And I softly tap her hands, taking them in mine. "Think, was there anything else that you remember?"

She stares at my hands.

"What about his shoes? Was he wearing sneakers?"

She quickly lifts her head and the words pour out. "Yes. First, he grabbed my arm and he was able to pull me around so that he held me tightly, his big arm across my neck but I was able to forcibly step on his feet." The words a torrential wave; I could see her pounding heart through her blouse, clinging to the perspiration on her chest. "His grip on my neck loosened but he held onto my purse." She frees her hands from mine. Her fingers open the top buttons on her blouse. "I keep my money and key here." She unpins a small cloth purse that she hides inside her bra. "Here's where I keep my money. The purse that the crook took has nothing in it but tissues and one dollar."

"And you noticed, what?"

"Yes, as I tried to free myself I saw his red shoelaces."

"Red shoelaces," I say in English.

Jimmy says, "Bloods, hitting on old ladies in Harbor House?"

"Maybe Bloods wannabees," I answer in English.

"Bloods make their money selling crack in the streets and whoring their women on Surf Avenue not hitting old ladies for dollars." Jimmy finds this incredulous.

"Maybe he was bored," I suggest.

Jimmy was the knowledgeable one when it came to the gangs of Coney Island. His first assignment at the 60th was to work on controlling the gangs, but it was a truly thankless job. Jimmy had neither sympathy nor empathy for most of the victims of gang violence since they were usually other gang members. But he knew the cops in charge at the precinct.

"We'll get Lewis and Murphy on this," Jimmy says referring to the two detectives who handle gang-related activities in Coney Island. They are the latest "salt and pepper" team trying to keep the peace between the housing project gangs.

Mrs. Chervony doesn't understand what Jimmy and I are saying, but she knows we are making plans of some kind. "Those shvartzers think we old Jews have money hidden in our mattresses." She shakes her head with disgust.

"Anything else?" We need the best description if we hope to find the guy.

I wait for her to concentrate. "Any other markings, a tattoo?" I take her hands in mine.

"On his wrist. When he grabbed my purse, I fought back. I know there was nothing in the purse. But it is mine not his. He pushed me hard and I was able to grab his sweatshirt and then his wrist. I saw what I thought at first was a bracelet but pulling on his wrist I realized it wasn't real maybe a drawing."

"What did it look like?"

I take off my jacket and pull a pen from my pocket. Jimmy is hanging on to every word like a trusty bloodhound. I draw a few different designs on my wrist for her to consider as imitations of the tattoo.

"That one," and she points to a simple design of thick woven threads like a friendship bracelet you might see being sold by those pushcarts in the shopping mall.

"Wonderful. You have given us a good description of the assailant. We will find him."

She wraps her thin arms around me. "You will protect us, I know now."

"Listen Mrs. Chervony. You know that they added security guards during the daytime. Only go out when they are on duty and never alone. You have friends in the building. Yes?" Under pressure from the local politicians, the Housing Authority added security guards for an additional four hours during the daytime. Originally, the guards were on duty from 9 PM to 6 AM, times when these old people rarely left their apartments.

She nods her head.

"So make sure you go with your friends when the guards are downstairs. Soon there will be security cameras added." The political pressure was intense and even though this was one of the safest complexes in the city despite the recent muggings, funds were secured to install security cameras. The other complexes were scenes of murders, drug dealing and prostitution. These old people couldn't vote but their children were good citizens and campaign contributors.

"But they didn't get us the best security cameras but cheaper version," she adds. Typical of Russian immigrants, they are always complaining even when the authorities do something good.

"They will work, remember what I said. I will call when I have something."

"You will visit again?"

"Of course, Detective Sutton and I will return. Don't worry."

We left her apartment and on the way downstairs, Jimmy was full of questions.

"So what was that all about, the hugging and hand kissing?"

Jimmy has already heard family stories, but I gave him her abbreviated version of my grandfather, the Hero of the Battle of Stalingrad's exploits. "She got a little carried away, calling me her protector, as my grandfather protected her and others from the Nazis 60 years ago."

"We have to find the bastard. She has such faith in you. And if we do she'll make an unreliable witness on the stand," Jimmy knows how poorly old people make witnesses. I don't think we need to worry that she would refuse to testify out of fear of retaliation by the gang bangers. Something tells me despite the tears she's made of strong stuff, a survivor of the Battle of Stalingrad.

"No, we'll never use her as a witness, but if we can identify the bastard then we'll watch him because you know he'll make some stupid move and break the law. We'll get him but not likely for this assault."

Jimmy takes his arm and wraps it around my shoulders. This is a new move.

"Hero of Harbor House, Perlov the Protector," he says with a hearty laugh. He slaps me on the shoulder, smiling and laughing.

It's true. I have my mission. My grandfather will be proud of me. Maybe my protective shield will offer expansive powers and reach my Russian Lady.

CHAPTER 3

After my shift is finished, I can't get back to my parents' house quick enough to tell my mother about Mrs. Chervony.

"The name means nothing but maybe a face," she says.

"Please, you were a child how would you remember and she was a young woman, now very aged," I reply, while my father nods his head in agreement.

"Still, I must meet this woman," my determined mother replies.

Perhaps that can be arranged. For the moment the issue is food, good Bar-B-Q and ocean breezes, so I will spend another night here. I try to be helpful but my gestures are dismissed because they are not genuine. A Russian man likes to be served although my father enjoys being the chef working by his stone Bar-B-Q in the backyard. The juices spill on my shirt and I don't care who will see me except the neighbors. The temperature is perfect and the sea air pushes away the oppressive heat so that ten miles inland people can't sleep without air-conditioning but not us in Brighton Beach.

It's so pleasant after dinner that we walk on the Boardwalk after eating too much. We are not alone; the wooden planks are filled with happy faces of mostly Russian immigrants. We allow strangers among us but immigrant heads turn at the sight of black or brown bodies.

I sleep like the dead, satisfied, although in the early hours my dreams become more vivid—I see her, the blue eyed beauty, a flash of the dead man slips into view and a glimpse of old Mrs. Chervony appears. Dreams, messengers of God, or the unconscious, wow, is all I can think upon rising.

Missing the dawn, still I manage to see the second hour of the new day returning to the Boardwalk. The sky is lit by a brilliant ball of orange matter that is zapping me from a million miles away. I can feel the power entering my body and energizing each cell. From afar, the sun appears completely smooth and circular, but I know this star is a mass of fluid gases flickering and dancing into space. The whole universe requires my attention today.

I skip breakfast and practically dance into the station house.

"Morning, Perlov." The desk sergeant actually lifts his head from his newspaper. Now that is strange. My inner magnetism must have a stronger pull than I imagine. Members of the public line up to complain about wild dogs, vandalism, stolen cars, and abusive husbands while the desk sergeant is known to make no effort to lift his head. He barely registers their existence. I am flattered by his attention. I don't want to know why he has taken this sudden interest in me.

I dash up the stairs. I am never one to take the creaky elevator. I might be stalled on it between floors and have to wait hours for the fire department to come and rescue me. Some poor fools are lured into its gated cage only to fall victim to the elevator's malfunctioning, a most unforgettable experience.

I enter the usually noisy second floor where the detectives sit and suddenly silence comes over the room as if Moses has just proclaimed a new plague on the house of Pharaoh. I look around the room for a sign.

Clapping. First it starts slowly with a few isolated gestures and then into a thunderous roar. My fellow officers are applauding. I hear whistles. A few guys are standing on their chairs.

I hear my name. "Perlov, Perlov, Perlov."

I see Jimmy approaching. He screams above the din. "Welcome, the Hero of Harbor House, Perlov the Protector."

More screams, "Perlov, Perlov." But the sounds seem to have stretched into the phrase 'Perlov the Protector, Perlov the Protector.'

The Lieutenant emerges from the standing bodies; silently and expertly, he maneuvers through the crowd and stands in the center of the room. "The Hero of Harbor House, Perlov the Protector," and he points towards me.

The hooting quiets. The Lieutenant commands center stage. He bellows. "Perlov the Protector, go get those bastards knocking down old people for dollar bills. Bring me arrests."

Then in a moment, the Lieutenant is gone having made his appearance and his pleasures known. I, his loyal vassal, have my charge.

Jimmy comes over and slaps me on the shoulder blade. The cheap fabric of my suit catches the edge of his fancy pinky ring. He doesn't notice because he is laughing and so are all my other colleagues.

"Good show, the Hero of Harbor House, Perlov the Protector. How's that for a title?" he asks.

It beats my former moniker, Russian Jew boy.

One of the guys moves forward. He hands me a platter. I take off the paper napkin and see what are clearly homemade cookies.

"My wife baked them for you," says Geary. Always a nice guy although his days of rising into the ranks of the big boys are a decade gone. The cookies are made into the shape of stars of David, with generous blue sprinkles.

"My wife said you can eat them. All the ingredients had that little 'O' on the label with the 'U' in it, and then it had a little 'D'." His daughter is married to a Jewish guy. He's always asking me what to bring to his daughter's-in-laws for dinner.

"Yes, so nice of you, please thank your wife." I am genuinely and pleasantly surprised. I can't think of any act of equal kindness by any of my fellow officers.

"You can bring back some to your mother."

"Yes, I will." She can sample them since she's always looking to improve her limited culinary skills. She will analyze the ingredients, checking the proportions. She often thinks she fails to bake a perfect cake or muffins because she doesn't exactly follow the directions. Really she has no taste buds; she is incapable of creating a great cake because she can't smell the ingredients.

Jimmy is still laughing.

"Nice," I break into a wide grin. I am pleased.

"What the hell is this all about?" I know, I probably shouldn't question anyone's generosity, but there has to be a motive.

"Last night, I mentioned to a few guys from the softball team about your grandfather, the Hero of the Battle of Stalingrad, and how I started to call you the Hero of Harbor House, Perlov the Protector."

The family history from the Motherland is blending into my present career. My grandfather devoted his life to service to the state, at a huge sacrifice.

"Well, Geary just keeps repeating—Hero of Harbor House, Perlov the Protector. Like it became our team mantra and we came from behind in that game. In the last inning, old Geary," he is the oldest guy on the softball team and the station house's most senior uniformed officer. "He hits a home run. Can you believe it, a home run with the bases loaded? I mean, get real. This is Geary we're talking about. We're thinking strike out so now it's like he's adopted you and your new tag line."

Jimmy and I are both amazed at Geary's success.

"He got his wife to bake the cookies? Who told the Lieutenant?"

My partner lightly drums the pencil point on my nose. "Me, who else." He continues to annoy me with the pencil. He often does that to get my absolute attention. "You know that means we got to find the bastards. That place has got to be safe. We're responsible."

This is all very flattering but, "anything about our Russian lady?" I ask.

"Nothing from the lab. Summertime is slow at the Medical Examiner's office, too many dead bodies and people on vacation. We don't get any priority status, but," and he motions me to follow him back to our desks. "Immigration comes through."

From a manila envelope he pulls a photo. "Our widow, Olga, Mo-. I can't pronounce these names... M-O-I-S-S-E-Y-E-V." He slowly spells out the name, one letter at a time.

We stare at the grainy photo. "A mug shot. Looks like she hadn't slept for days," I add.

I take the photo in my hand. "Can't tell she has blue eyes."

I put it down on my desk. We are like two little boys panting and staring at an object of devotion. Should we erect a shrine to her with flowers, a candle and burning incense?

"What else do we have?" I ask.

"Yes?" Says Jimmy. And slowly he pulls out the remaining photos. "Sister Irina." We look at her face but without the same enthusiasm. She actually looks good, certainly more refreshed and alert than her sister.

"Is this her sister?" I ask.

"According to Immigration she is listed with the same last name and they entered the country together."

"And for the finale, "and Jimmy pulls out the last photo. "Sister Masha, the taller one."

I look at the photos. "You said, Olga, Irina and Masha?"

"Yeah."

"Three sisters?" I say.

Jimmy begins to get impatient. "So?"

"Chekhov's *Three Sisters.*"

"Who's this Chekhov?"

"The Russian playwright. The three sisters in his play are named Olga, Irina and Masha."

"We're being played," Jimmy shakes his head and the half grin on his face is threatening-looking.

"Do you think Immigration knows?" I should not be too surprised by bureaucratic idiocy.

"Those jerks can't find their own dicks. Homeland Security,

my ass." He throws the empty envelope to the floor.

He looks down at the floor but leaves it alone. "We have a contact and I'll call. Maybe someone at Federal Plaza knows something."

We both look again at the photos, examining them closely for hidden messages. Can they talk to us, tell us their secrets? We all have secrets to hide.

The phone's jarring rings bring us back to the moment.

"Sutton, yeah, yeah, I understand." I observe Jimmy's talking in his official abrupt tone, must be some bureaucrat.

He turns to face me. "You better find something because the widow has requested release of the body and it's leaving the morgue."

"We still have the lab results arriving at some time." There is hope of finding some clandestine hieroglyphs among the scant evidence.

"What's your plan, Perlov the Protector?" He loves his creative invention and its popularity is spreading throughout the station house.

"I have an appointment with Feinstein's doctor. His office isn't far from here."

He shakes his head. "I'll be spending my time with Lewis and Murphy. Maybe we'll find a fat, tall black kid with red shoelaces who likes knocking down old ladies."

"Good luck," I brush against his shoulder as I leave. I have a doctor to see.

"I'll nail the nigger," Jimmy says quietly but forcefully.

I never quite know what to say to Jimmy after he says the "n" word. What's the point of reminding him of his insensitivity, that's why he uses the word, to make a statement, to shock me.

My mother often remarks that she finds it incomprehensive that black people call themselves niggers.

"Can you imagine if I would speak to your father or any Jew and say, 'kike, come here,' what insulting nonsense."

Well, I'm on my way to visit with a kike who I hope has a story to tell.

I call on Dr. Gelman, the late Mr. Feinstein's cardiologist. The receptionist is surprised to see a cop visiting the good doctor. She looks suspiciously at me when I show her my badge. There are secrets here; I can sense it in my black Russian soul. Probably it's a little Medicare fraud.

My mother is constantly complaining that the number of doctors accepting Medicare is shrinking. The older women in the neighborhood come to my mother to complain. A few remember her as a refusenik back in Soviet Russia. Here in America, she naturally is willing to take on this new government. She writes letters of protest and complaints to our local Congressman, our Senators, and the regulators for these old bubbes.

She's always the voice of the oppressed and the underdog that will be the epitaph on my mother's gravestone. She doesn't quite get the gay rights movement or the feminist revolution, but the old women wearing babushkas on their heads, these people she knows, and opens our door to help.

The doctor slides me in between the 85-year-old with congestive heart disease and the 88-year-old with painful angina.

I am ushered into the doctor's office. It's perfect looking. The walls are dark oak paneling and the carpeting a deep pile; my shoes sink into its richness. Russians appreciate the fact that a man who serves people is entitled to make money. Therefore, it is his right to demonstrate this wealth—not ostentatiously, but certainly his office should be bigger and more luxurious than an accountant's office.

"Detective Perlov, what can I tell you about Jack Feinstein," the doctor begins. "He had a heart condition. I'm not surprised that he died; with his ticker it was only a matter of time." He shakes his head, a slight frown on his face. Maybe he's thinking how he can continue to bill the insurance company after Feinstein's death.

"Do you know Mrs. Feinstein?" I'm watching for a physical reaction because this is a man with a personality for a face.

"The first or the second?" He smiles mischievously; he knows where I'm going.

"The young blonde is the second?" With my easy smile and a wink, I encourage him to tell me all the little rumors and dirt. A good doctor and a few nosy neighbors are the best sources of information.

"Yes," and he begins. "I've known Feinstein for years. He was a fatal heart attack waiting to happen." The doctor explains that with his pear-shaped body, smoking, obesity and generally poor living habits, he was a poster boy for all that's wrong with the American life style.

"The first Mrs. Feinstein was a lovely woman, an ordinary woman, a school teacher like Jack. I think they met while they were teaching at the same school in one of those black hell holes in central Brooklyn." He's happy to fill in the details.

"Poor thing, she died of ovarian cancer at 45, maybe five years ago." The doctor was deep in thought either about ovarian cancer—a diagnosis meant a sure death sentence—or something beguiling about the late, ordinary Mrs. Feinstein.

"And the second Mrs. Feinstein?" Now I'm waiting for the more intriguing part of Feinstein's family history.

The doctor's face is fleshy and soft with a double chin that moves when his head nods up and down. "Mrs. Feinstein usually accompanied her husband to my office." The good doctor must have looked forward to those visits.

"When was the last time you saw either one of them?" I doubted that the doctor was anything other than a voyeur when it came to the second Mrs. Feinstein.

"Not too long ago, I was still trying to manage his heart medicine better." He calls the medical records clerk to find the deceased's file. He is not one of those holier than holy doctor types who won't give up any information without a subpoena and a court order. Psychiatrists are the worst to work with on obtaining evidence. They all must have studied the evils of the Soviet psychiatric hospital system. When I approach they see danger—red flags fly—and their lips and tongue turn to stone.

"Was his condition worsening?" I ask—already on death's

doorstep so the widow was counting on how she would spend her inheritance.

"No," then he edges a little close to me. He has a secret to share.

"I don't want to speak ill of the dead," he says and I get ready to hear some real dirt.

"You've met Mrs. Feinstein?" he asks me.

I nod, "she was the one who called in the 911." The good doctor moves his large torso across the desk beckoning me to move closer.

"Well he felt that he had to perform," his head shakes and his double chin jiggles. I'm guessing he isn't going to talk about the late Mr. Feinstein performing stand-up comedy at the Comic Strip on Second Avenue.

"Sexual performance," he gestures with his hand, pointing to his crotch.

He continues. "Most of these heart medicines decrease sexual performance. It's far worse than not ejaculating. I mean just getting hard." Then he stops and waits to make certain that I'm really interested in this story.

I nod and encourage him to continue.

"So I try to balance the drugs," then he stops and points his finger at my chest.

Raising his voice he tells me in a severe, preachy tone. "And I warned him, again and again not to take Viagra—that stuff would be poison for him."

His voice returns to a quieter intensity. "He asked me for a prescription for that drug and I refused. I said if you want to kill yourself then I won't be responsible."

I could understand the willingness to take on the risk—I mean why be married to such a piece of ass if you couldn't do anything. Now that had to be the equivalent of living in hell.

"But I couldn't stop him. You go on-line today and everyone is selling you Viagra—who needs a bona fide prescription? You answer a questionnaire on-line and you lie. No, I don't have a heart condition. No, I'm not a candidate for a stroke. No, I'm not taking any drugs that would have a counteracting effect. No, I'm a perfect physical specimen." Clearly, the doctor must have practiced this diatribe on more than the late Mr. Feinstein.

"Do you know if he was taking Viagra," I asked, although I don't need his opinion because the blood screening should tell us that.

"Sure, he told me. But what more could I do. I'm not responsible," he answers in genuine anguish. His reaction is sincere, not the mouthing of someone afraid of a future lawsuit.

Then he moves his large frame against the desk with his hands outstretched towards me. He has another secret to tell me.

"I probably shouldn't say this because it may be idle talk," he's almost whispering.

"He used to boast that she was his sex slave," he tells me. I expected a hint of envy on his part as those words tumbled out but there was none; it was closer to revulsion.

"He was a fool—a sick fool," the doctor vigorously states. "What was he doing with a beautiful young woman seemingly in good health and with a great body? Just a fool," he adds with disgust.

The doctor is a good family man, no impure notions floating in his brain.

"Do you think the second Mrs. Feinstein encouraged him to take the Viagra?" Maybe she really wanted a good tumble in bed or to kill him off as quickly as possible.

"He once told me in a moment of despair how much she loathed him." The doctor was saddened by the memory, "as I was taking his blood pressure and reminding him how much weight he still had to lose that's when he said that to me." He sat motionless, thinking.

He continued to divulge more information. "I don't think she wanted him to touch her. I think Viagra was all his idea," the doctor wanting to exonerate the widow of all responsibility.

So I bend over the desk getting closer to the doctor, but not too close to invade his personal space. This is something an immigrant needs to learn about in America. In Russia, we don't know about personal space—imagined or real. When you live four, five, six to a small apartment, there is no personal space. In America, the land of endless spaces, big houses and every child has their own bedroom and a private bathroom, there's such a thing called personal space.

"Well how did this relationship begin?"

The doctor is looking weary from thinking about the deceased. But he knows his former patient.

"It sounds so stupid but he was lonely," the doctor says respectfully. "I don't exactly know how it all got going, but she was a waitress in one of those Russian restaurants on Brighton Beach Avenue." He points at me, rightfully assuming I know these places. I have not lost my accent so he assumes I am a foreigner and with a name like Perlov, Eastern European, what else but Russian.

"She was living with lots of other girls in one of the old, decrepit walk-ups near the Boardwalk." I know those places because that's where my adventures in America began, in one of those ratty, cockroach-infested buildings owned by one of our mishpocheh—slimy dogs among the kinfolk.

"One thing leads to another and she moves in with him. He had a nice little house; his mother left it to him. His wife is gone—poor Irene. She couldn't have children. She never discussed all the facts with me and I didn't probe—she wasn't my patient. After she's gone with no one to keep watch over what he eats, he stops dieting and exercising, and naturally his condition deteriorates. His heart is so bad that the city lets him retire early from teaching. So now he has a lot of time on his hands." There's the story, at least the part the doctor knows.

"What about the sisters," I ask, and at first I get a blank expression from the doctor.

Then a light bulb goes on, "Yeah, yeah, sisters?" He nods his head and he puckers up his big lips to form a small pout.

"I don't know whether they're actually her sisters, but who knows. Jack said she had two sisters and they all lived together in Jack's house."

"Did you ever meet them?" I see that the doctor is looking at this watch. I don't have much more of his time today.

"No," he answers impatiently, in a tone of voice reserved for his difficult patients. He doesn't have any more secrets to share.

As I take my leave from the doctor, he reiterates his diagnosis. "He had a very bad ticker. If he had taken better care of himself twenty years ago he would be alive. Too young to die." Disappointment, perhaps recognition of professional failure at not getting Feinstein to change his ways, is apparent on the doctor's face.

I left the doctor's office confident that we had all the puzzle pieces in place if Viagra showed up in the deceased's blood. Exactly what happened that afternoon remained for me to unravel and determine if a crime had been committed. A servant of justice was my police motto. It will take a little more delving into other secrets to learn the facts. There was no need for an autopsy; his heart was badly broken before she met him.

I call Jimmy after I leave the doctor's office. "Any word from the lab?"

"No, but if you're finished with the doctor why don't you head there and shake them up a bit. Remind them that we have important cases too. Pompous asses, but behave or we'll never get the report." I love it when Jimmy gives me pointers on working with the bureaucracy. I do have a tendency to want to tell them to kiss my Russian ass.

Jimmy can apply the charm, but not at the Medical Examiner's office. He leaves this task to me. He knows that I know his tricks, some things he will do anything to avoid. I ask him about this aversion to the dead. He never analyzes his actions. My conclusion; attending too many wakes as a child. The psychology major finds the explanation.

"Hey, Perlov the Protector, I'm here holding down the fort. Lewis and Murphy and I are reviewing all the photos of big, fat, black kids with wrist tattoos. You would be surprised how many possible suspects fit that description. Remember Mrs. Chervony is tiny so she probably doesn't know big and fat, but the tattoo is the key."

"Okay, I'm on my way to the morgue."

Before I stop at the Medical Examiner's office, I have a little personal business to take care of at Downstate Medical Center. There's a certain Russian-born doctor whom my mother wants me to meet. She's a medical resident in the Emergency Department.

When my mother isn't writing letters of protest she's a shadchen (matchmaker)—always on the lookout for a beloved for me. All of the other matches didn't work out—my father says it's about the chemistry, not quite right. My mother always tells the parents—usually she makes her matches through the young woman's mother—that I'm a law student. Among the families of Russian Jews being a cop is not an acceptable occupation for a future son-in-law. Their lovely daughters need a more dignified provider. Uniforms are not considered desirable accoutrements. I work strange hours and meet some of life's most miserable specimens of human beings. My dating in the Russian community often hits a major obstacle when the girl's mother learns what I do for a living. Fathers and mothers from the old country all have stories to tell about the secret police.

To a young lady, I appear unreliable and distracted but actually this job takes a toll on you. I can promise to meet someone and then at the last minute a call comes through that puts the date in jeopardy. I am never "not" on call.

Once when I was out with a new lady friend through one of my mother's introductions, we stopped at a small grocery to buy a soda after a movie. My luck, who walked into the store but a bad guy I recognized with several outstanding warrants. I called for him to stop, that I was a police officer. So what did this fool do? From his waistband he grabbed a handgun and pointed it at the Korean store clerk.

Now I was in a big mess. The young lady horrified. I was afraid that she was going to faint and fall down on the hard, dirty linoleum floor. The clerk was so frightened that he peed in his pants. However, I remained calm; that's part of my job and training. I quietly approached the young thug with my hand stretched out in front of my body and asked him to put the gun down. My left hand was visible and in the thug's line of vision, which distracted him from my other hand. Discreetly, my right hand went for my gun. I am known as the best marksman in Brooklyn South. I could have killed this man in less than a moment, but I asked him again, slowly, and in a hushed voice to put down his gun.

Then I got lucky. He turned coward, dropped the gun and ran out of the store into the arms of two uniforms that just happened to stop for cigarettes. So I never fired a shot. And I wasn't running into the street chasing the stupid loser. After that the young lady refused my phone calls. I even sent her a dozen roses with an apology although what was I apologizing for—this was my work. Finally, her father got on the phone and told me to stop calling.

At first, my mother was angry with the girl's family. No matter what, I am her bright-eyed baby boy. Then she said, "I can't blame them." She gave me a big hug. "I don't know what I'm going to do with you."

In my favor are my two best traits—my quick wit and my dark Russian sense of humor. I'm also an OK guy to look at, nothing particularly special but good-looking for a Russian Jew. Maybe I reach 5' 10" when I'm wearing thick, wool socks—the kind I love to wear when we're on a stakeout in the wintertime. Forget the stereotypes of Russians grinning and bearing Siberian winters when the temperature barely reaches 40 degrees below zero. I hate the bitter cold. I hate snow and ice; give me the sun and hot tropical ocean breezes.

This time I have a better chance with the young doctor and getting the mother's approval. The lady in question is actually the daughter of someone my father knows from the insurance company so I have the mother's initial approval. She already knows I'm a cop going to law school at night. It also plays in my favor that my father is simply a mensch, a good guy, so the son must also be worthy.

Her name is Dr. Marina Lublin. We speak on the phone several times but now is the perfect opportunity to meet. My mother is vague about a physical description, usually that's not a good sign, but my father assures me that there is a photo on his colleague's desk and she is an attractive woman. My father does not recommend ugly women. He thinks of himself as dashing, in an intellectual sort of way. My parents make a striking couple; strangers remark how wonderful they look together. He wants something equally impressive for his only child.

My father knows the doctor's mother through the informal Russian Jewish network at the insurance company. They don't work in the same division or on the same floor of the 30-story building in Lower Manhattan, but there's a small and growing group of a half dozen who eat lunch together. Marina's mother is a recent hire.

All these immigrants shared stories of their lives and careers before they emigrated and what they now must do to prosper in America. My father arrived in the actuarial department as a clerk, an assistant's assistant. Fifteen years ago, he was the first new immigrant Russian hired in his department. He never asked questions. He learned from observing who in the office received the most praise and was promoted—these were the actuaries. And how one became an actuary was a straightforward method not too dissimilar from how the bureaucracy in Russia worked. You sat for scheduled exams and weeks later the grades were posted, and months later if you were successful you were rewarded. It seemed a sure way to gain money and maybe a little prestige.

Most actuarial students were recent college graduates and were selected to be part of the insurance company's structured program, which actually allowed for paid periods of study during the workday. Despite these elaborate plans for sitting for these exams that were held semi-annually, the dropout rate was high. Many students failed to pass their exams and most did not successfully pass all ten exams. At best one took an exam each year, studying diligently at work and at home. The students spent hours reading their books and taking practice exams.

My father read the books, which he borrowed, from an actuarial student in his insurance department. Then he sat for his first exam, not too difficult, and he passed with the highest mark in the whole actuarial division. His superiors wanted to know who was this man? They still did not include him in the special actuarial program, but he continued on his own and sat for the next exam. Again he passed with the highest mark. He decided to sit for an exam each time they were offered. Once he sat for two exams on the same day. By the time he was sitting for his fourth exam he had been noticed—he was marked as special and officially enrolled in the program, becoming one of the oldest actuarial students in the insurance company. Each passing grade led to more money and a slight promotion.

He was enjoying himself. While the best students usually took a full ten years to become the master Actuary, my father accomplished the task in five years. His superiors were most impressed and a genuine promotion followed his ascension to the title of Actuary. The assistant he started working for was now his assistant. But my father was never a man to use power or his intelligence against a fellow human being. My father, the humanist, was beyond such trifling.

I arrange to meet Dr. Marina in the hospital cafeteria. She doesn't have much time and I have to meet the forensic guys in the basement. Then Jimmy is waiting for me back at the station house. This is going to be a brief, casual chat, a harmless way of feeling out each other. Do I merit an evening of her valuable time, and is she pleasant looking enough and possessing of some charm?

I entered the cafeteria. Although we have never met and the photo was of poor quality, I knew it was her. She was sitting alone at a long institutional-looking table in the middle of the room.

Of course, she was wearing the appropriate clothing—white doctor jacket with a stethoscope wrapped around her neck. And she had that Russian intellectual look—dark, deeply set eyes, angular face, prominent cheekbones and a silky, glowing skin. She was from Moscow—normally a sign that someone in the family worked for the Soviet bureaucracy.

I unconsciously touch my hand to my best feature—my very dark almost Asian black, thick, wavy hair. The girls always tell me they wish they had my hair, such a waste on a guy.

I straighten up aware of my poor posture—I can hear in my head one of my old teachers from school in Petersburg scolding me—"Perlov straighten up." I button my jacket and move forward to introduce myself.

"Marina?" I ask. Just because I'm a detective, doesn't mean I don't make mistakes of identity.

"Sasha," she extends her hand.

I sit down and we go through the usual pleasantries.

"Can I get you something to eat or drink?" I speak in English although I'm perfectly happy to speak the Mother tongue. I must bring her an offering and act generously to demonstrate that I am capable of being a provider.

"No," she politely refused. "It's too late for lunch and too early for dinner. I'm fine with my coffee and my apple," she says, showing me the items.

"Another cup," I offer because it would be too impolite to get her nothing.

She probably doesn't need the extra caffeine but she nods. "Sure, lots of milk and sugar."

"Would you prefer a cup of tea?" I know my fellow citizens.

"It's just ordinary tea bags; the coffee is the best thing they have." I don't know how fresh the coffee can be in the late afternoon.

I dash to the food area. There is an array of different snacks and a willing cook who offers to make a sandwich, put a hotdog or hamburger on the grill. I shake my head and grab a few objects sitting on the metal shelves.

I bring her coffee and an orange, a cellophane package of pound cake and a cookie.

She takes the cookie and coffee. "Thanks."

I open the package of the pound cake; it's too yellow in color to be freshly made, it's probably mostly chemicals. I offer her a piece, but she refuses with a nod of her head.

I ask her. "How's life in the ER at Downstate? We bring in our most serious emergencies here." It's a distance from Brighton Beach and Coney Island but we bypass the closest hospital when the cases require the best trauma care.

"Busy, always busy, but that's why I love the place. I went to Medical School here so I know the whole place," she adds, slowly sipping the last of her first cup of coffee.

"I know the Medical Examiner's office downstairs at Downstate," I try to make a silly pun.

She smiles at my flat joke. It's a beautiful wide smile; a smile of compassion. All young doctors should be as dedicated.

"When I was in medical school we spent time in the Medical Examiner's office. I couldn't think of a branch of medicine I would less like to study—being a forensic pathologist, examining and taking apart dead bodies. Ugh," she crinkles her nose and face. It's exactly my sentiments.

"Exciting in the ER?" I can remember bringing in one good cop who got shot and was very well treated in the hospital ER and a few bad guys who should have died here; but, unfortunately, the doctors managed to put them back together again.

"It's great—never a dull moment. We have shootings and stabbings, children who've been neglected to the point of starvation—and then the usual heart attacks, cuts and bruises. I went into this kind of medicine because I didn't want to be bored and it's hectic. It's just as I expected." She smiled again and I wanted to reach across the table and kiss her.

She turns serious and the smile fades. "Things here are not the same as the Motherland. Such a rich country and yet so many poor." It was more than pure propaganda in what the Soviet authorities used to say about America. In the middle of affluence, an underbelly of poor second-class citizens lived. It was the reason why my Uncle Boris said he never wanted to live in the New Jerusalem but preferred Berlin, Germany. Not everyone wanted to be a rich capitalist.

"It's the nature of capitalism," I say with a laugh. "The rich get richer and the poor get poorer."

She isn't smiling any more. "It pains me to see so many people without any health coverage. I had a woman come in this morning who had a disfiguring skin condition that could have been taken care of years ago if she had a place to turn to for medical care." I sense a humanist—still looking for justice, just the type of crusader my mother will like.

She's somber but still friendly to me. "You know my mother was a physician in Russia." Actually, if my father knew that fact, he never mentioned it to me.

"When we arrived from Moscow eight years ago she expected to become a physician here in America. But the requirements were onerous, especially for someone not completely fluent in English. She could sit for the medical boards now and certainly pass, but then she would have to start all over and begin an internship and a residency. So I'll be the doctor in the family." She smiled with pride edged with a little regret, knowing her mother's professional disappointment.

She shifts her body and leans forward. "Let's talk about you." She smiles again, and it's my turn to be examined and studied. When first meeting people, Russians like to quickly size the person up and determine their character, imagine a continuous chess game. First, you attack your opponent, and then you wait for their move—will it be defensive or will they make an offensive move to create an element of surprise. How much will your opponent reveal? Where are the weaknesses? My father the master player always says, 'life is a chess game.'

"You know I'm a cop," I reply.

She shakes her head and her eyes fully explore my whole face. Do I possess her and her mother's dedication? "I know my mother tells me you are a police officer studying the law at night." It was the line my father learned to parrot from my mother—can't afford to scare off too many more potential brides.

"My father is impressed with you being a policeman," she says. Now this is a first.

"Yes?" I wait for more information.

"My father always says that the Jews are too civilized. It's the reason we were brought almost to the edge of extinction in Europe; just too much the people of the Book. We have styled rituals to kill animals for the dinner table. We have 613 mitzvoth to follow so we live an orderly life. We have completely reduced any violent leanings."

"I'd like to meet someone who thinks I'm in an honorable profession. When can I meet your father?"

She turns her face flirtatiously. "What about me?"

"Of course you. How about dinner when you aren't saving all of humankind?"

"Thursday I have some time." She has great dimples when she smiles.

Then she asks me rather sheepishly. "Have you ever killed anyone?" This is a most unusual first meeting. Perhaps it will be a good omen since my dates are ordinarily so afraid of asking questions about what I do. It must be because she is a doctor and sees life and death on a daily basis.

I never quite knew how to approach the question of killing. I have heard the rabbis speak of the difference between murder and killing—one a sin and the other a responsible act.

So I respond, cautiously. "Yes I have; more than once. I was a marksman in the SWAT division." Everyone knows the term SWAT even if they don't exactly know what the initials stand for. Her lips are about to form a new word, but she stops herself, too much for a cafeteria coffee break. I see in her inquisitive eyes a thirst for the answers to many more questions.

I add. "I was a marksman in the Army where I never shot anyone."

"Where did you learn to shoot?" she asks incredulously.

"My Uncle Alexei, my mother's oldest brother, taught me when I was about 12 years old."

"Is he here in America?"

Is she thinking that her father will want me to bring along Uncle Alexei on our first date? "He was killed in Afghanistan." Our family history is filled with stories of sacrifice.

"Was he a government official?" she asks and you can feel the curiosity in her tone. She already must know something about us, my mother's refusenik days or about my grandfather, the Hero of the Battle of Stalingrad. Occasionally, someone stops my mother in the street in Brighton Beach to ask about the family.

"No, he was a Colonel in the Soviet Army and his convoy was ambushed. Uncle Alexei was assassinated in the name of Mother Russia." My mother adored her older brother. Totally disagreeing about Soviet politics and the future of the Soviet Union, they were committed idealists in their own very different ways.

Marina isn't certain what to say. Does she offer sympathy or ask more questions? She says the expected. "I'm sorry." Then she adds, "Does it make you uneasy what America is doing in Afghanistan?" The doctor is a political animal. In America, most people are apolitical, even the educated ones, while in Russia, especially the Jews were intellectuals and always political; it's one of the chief reasons for the Soviet authorities fear of the Jews— too many independent opinions.

"It's kind of eerie if we are witnessing a parallel here in America—still chasing the Afghans and now the Iraqis—maybe the war on terror will bankrupt the country. Then where will we go?" I ask jokingly.

"To Canada," she says assuredly, but politics are left aside as Dr. Goldberg from the medical examiner's forensics lab walks to our table and introduces himself.

They appear to know each other by sight. "I've seen you around," she says. He is looking far too interested in her. I don't want Dr. Goldberg poaching so I stand to make my departure.

"Let's plan on Thursday," I bend my head and whisper.

"You know where I live." And I do.

"Let's plan on 6 PM." I tell her and it's an official date.

She also stands to leave. She extends her hand and I feel the strength in her fingers as she squeezes my hand. I notice Goldberg watching her walk towards the elevators. We both stand in silence while she waits for the elevator doors to open and swallow her up.

Now the powers of destiny must cooperate and nothing should interfere with our Thursday schedule.

Goldberg and I head towards the basement and the forensics labs.

"Nice customer service. You find all your clients in the cafeteria?"

He ignores my sarcasm. "I came for a cup of coffee," he explains.

"So what do we have?" I ask as we head towards the elevators leading to the labs.

"There's Viagra in the blood but no heart drugs."

"What does that mean?" I stop walking and turn to stare into his face.

"It means he had mega doses of Viagra in his blood stream but nothing else. No aspirin, no meds for high blood pressure, or cholesterol; pretty clean."

We are heading down into the bowels of the building. The elevators doors open and we are in the offices of the Medical Examiner. I find myself following him through the corridors, wide enough to hold two lines of dead bodies. The rooms are cold and stark in their nakedness. I feel my tongue and brain freezing. We descend further into the rooms of the dead. I stand in a corner of the room with my arms wrapped around my body trying to keep warm. Upstairs there's heat and humidity in the real world. I never venture alone into these places; someone always leads me to get the news I seek. An assistant of Goldberg walks by dressed in his huge rubber apron; splashes of blood and perhaps other human remains decorate the garment. I cannot bring myself to smile or even acknowledge the doctor, who is too preoccupied to care about me.

Goldberg brings me to the heart of the labs where all the analysis is conducted.

"So what's this mean?" I ask Goldberg, the expert.

"It's obvious," he remarks in a condescending tone. "The guy had ingested maximum strength Viagra but I found no heart drugs. I noted the drugs you said he was taking, but nothing."

"Does that mean he never took those drugs or he stopped taking them for 24 hours or what?"

"It could be he never took the drugs or maybe it means he didn't take the drugs for the last few days. We would have found traces if it was only 24 hours ago but it could have been a week ago. These drugs would leave some traces within a week, but he could have taken them eight days ago."

"What killed him?"

"The chief medical examiner has to pronounce cause of death."

"Okay," he's being a pain. "So what will he say will be cause of death?"

"Heart failure, possibly brought on by the Viagra, but we would have to do an autopsy to determine that and I think the body has been released. Because unless you have a compelling criminal reason to know more exact details, we don't want to do anything more."

I stand there and wonder what I should do.

The doctor's stare is confrontational. "Are the heirs thinking of suing the doctor or the drug company? What more do you need."

"Why didn't he take his pills?"

"How should I know?" says my helpful doctor.

"Aren't there more tests you can do?"

"You watch too much TV. We don't do anything exotic; we use test kits that we buy off the shelf. This is all standard."

"Do lots of other men stop taking their heart medicine?"

"People stop taking medicines of all kinds—diabetics refuse to take insulin, the mentally ill are always neglecting to take their drugs, heart patients don't like the sexual side effects and don't take their medicine. The morgue is full of men who don't take their prescribed medicine."

I don't move.

"Case closed," and Goldberg walks away without looking back.

I call Jimmy back at the station with the news. "So what's this mean?" he asks.

"I really don't know but let me call the guy's cardiologist and ask."

Jimmy doesn't hang up. "Check back in with me. I think we're closing in on a suspect at Surfside Gardens. Perlov the Protector, your subjects need you."

When I get outside and into the fresh air of the living, I call the doctor's office and to my surprise he takes the call.

"The coroner did not find any traces of the heart drugs; just Viagra in his blood. What do you think that suggests?"

The decibel level of the doctor's voice raises several notches and I have to pull my ear away from the speaker of the cell phone. "That fool—I warned him. He stopped taking his medicine. It's no wonder he's dead."

CHAPTER 4

I'm heading back to Brighton Beach. I know I'm going in the right direction because the gulls are leading the way. Stopping at the traffic light, I look up to see a group of them sitting on the weather-beaten electric lines, which are hanging dangerously, sagging loosely above the street. One gull makes an indiscriminate deposit on the windshield of my unmarked police car. Pesky little scavengers those birds, but they have a purpose in God's scheme. One appears to be staring at me, squawking, demanding payment for keeping the beaches and streets free of nasty vermin. He's hungry and so am I.

If I arrive at my parents' house now I can expect dinner grilling outside on the little stone Bar-B-Q my father and I constructed one summer, years ago. I can smell the pungent, spicy flavors of a kosher hotdog. Nearby, sitting on the grill, is a small pot of sauerkraut growing browner and browner, as the heat gets hotter. The mustard is strong with a touch of horseradish. I can feel the salty food penetrating the cracks of my dry lips. Jewish heaven must be a room lined with tables filled to the ceiling with food; all of it preserved in salt and spices designed to raise the blood pressure, but when you're dead it can't matter. The juices of my stomach cry out for sustenance, only the gulls are hungrier; and if they follow me to my parents, my father will surely reward them for their efforts.

I am rounding the curve. I see the house and I notice a gull right overhead.

The phone rings. I shouldn't answer it; first I should eat. I deserve to eat. Taxpayers should appreciate how devoted I am to this job.

I pick up my cell phone. "Yeah," knowing by the number it's Jimmy.

"Get your ass in here, we got the guy."

"Can I stop and get a quick bite at my parents and meet you somewhere."

"No, I know your mother. You'll be eating course after course, talking politics. Forget it. Get in now. I want to pick up this guy before it gets dark. We don't want to be in the projects waiting for this guy too late. I got a date tonight."

It could be hours of waiting and I get crabby when I'm hungry. This lean body needs nourishment on a regular basis, but I obey my partner's order.

The three of them are waiting for me, standing outside, as I drive up to the station house.

"So, what's the hurry," I am already getting annoyed.

"Hero of Harbor House, Perlov the Protector, you have responsibilities," Jimmy tells me while Murphy and Lewis are laughing. Murphy is a light-skinned black man whose family comes from one of the Caribbean Islands. He speaks softly, but he has a sharp right punch. Jimmy knows personally the power of that mean right hand since they sometimes spar as boxing partners.

Lewis shows me a photo.

The kid is dark black just as Mrs. Chervony described and his face is large. How large he is exactly I don't know from a mug shot.

"Well, who is he?" I want all the details before we attempt to apprehend him. Preparation is the key to minimizing risk on this job.

"He's a runner for the Bloods. JJ Reynolds is the boss-man," Lewis tells me.

He looks at a printout. The kid has a rap sheet at nineteen, typical for a kid from the projects. "No parents, living with his grandmother. Spent time in the juvenile system but for nothing too serious, mostly petty, drug-related crimes," Lewis explains.

I look over Lewis' shoulder and read. He doesn't seem like a killer but he's not a choirboy. Already he has the markings of a career criminal.

Lewis closes the folder. "What do you want to know?" He resents the over-the-shoulder routine, which is how Jimmy and I study a case together. We don't worry about personal space; we're from a Europe that doesn't understand the concept.

"OK, OK, don't get too hot." I make an exaggerated step backwards. "What's his name?"

"Does it matter?"

"Yes, so I know what to call out before I shoot him."

"Albert Speer spelled S-P-E-E-R." Lewis enunciates each letter very slowly.

"Albert Speer," I speak the name quickly. "Really?"

I look at the three of them. "Do you know who Albert Speer was?"

"No," Lewis says. "But you'll tell us." His voice is filled with spite and vinegar.

"Albert Speer," and I wait a second so I have their undivided attention, "Was the Armaments Minister and Master Architect for Adolph Hitler."

I move closer to Lewis while Murphy is laughing and grinning. I can't imagine being Lewis' partner.

"So this is the irony. Mrs. Chervony, WW II survivor, is attacked by someone with the same name as an old nemesis." I wait again for emphasis and look directly at Lewis. "You do know what irony is?"

"Smart fuck, let's go." Lewis is finished with talking.

They proceed in their unmarked car. I'm not leaving before I feel prepared.

"I'm going to get some real protection." And Jimmy knows I'm going to my police locker. Tonight requires at least an automatic pistol and one rifle. I have a small army of weaponry in my locker, which is the result of my service on the SWAT team as well as my Army time. I shouldn't have possession of these guns, but my commanding officer was a cool guy and let me leave with US Army materiel. The Lieutenant turns a blind eye because he knows we need more protection on the street than the NYPD provides. The rules require some bending.

"Are you ready?" Jimmy asks with a smirk. But he's no fool; he put two bulletproof Kevlar vests in the back of the car. Gang members are unpredictable sons-of-bitches. This kid is just a runner, but who knows if he doesn't have a cousin, brother, or uncle higher on the food chain who hates cops.

We drive to the projects of Surfside Gardens and wait. Cops spend hours waiting. Talking to their partners while waiting for suspects to make an appearance; that's the nature of stakeouts and it gets boring, with a big yawn. It's early evening not yet dusk and we sit in our unmarked car, which the whole neighborhood knows is a cop car.

"So are you going to buy a new outfit for the Lieutenant's party?" I ask my always fashionably dressed partner.

"You making me out to be a girl?" There's a trace of hurt in the voice.

"I know you want to make a great impression with the Lieutenant's wife."

"Forget my clothes. You don't know what bullshit I had flowing from my mouth to explain away your party date."

While his tone is mocking, he's no longer angry; absent is the harshness he earlier expressed.

"So what happened with that doctor your father knows? Did you see her at the Medical Examiners?"

"Yes, I met her in the cafeteria. Nice, very nice; smart."

"Yeh, you like the smart ones. What does she look like?"

"Striking in a dark, exotic way. Some Russians have Asian blood from the passing Mongols of hundreds of years ago. She has that mysterious, foreign look."

"Sounds good. Better than your usual blind date from your mother who has no taste in women. Any Russian Jewish girl is OK with her. Now your father is a man of class. This sounds like something he would choose." Jimmy has long admired my father's tastes in clothes and cigars. "What's the plan?"

"We're going out Thursday."

"Well, if this one ever moves into the girlfriend phase then we can double date. My mother's on my ass to marry Lori. I think she's tired of cooking and cleaning for me. Now the old man, he thinks I got the best of all worlds. But these women gang up on you." Resignation, the absolute acceptance of his fate; there is no escaping from his probable marriage.

Jimmy still lives at home in Bay Ridge. It's too expensive to get a nice apartment in New York City. This way he can save his money for the nice clothes he loves to wear to impress. Despite the bravado, Lori is special to him. He speaks affectionately of her, "You know how difficult it is to find anyone who half-way understands the kind of shit we go through being cops. Look at us, sitting here waiting for a fat piece of lard to arrive. We could wait here all night and he won't show." Jimmy has no illusions about this job.

Jimmy rearranges his body in the seat of the car, playing with the curly wires of the police radio. "I don't care about Lewis and Murphy. I got a date with Lori and we are leaving by nine."

I'm hungry so nine is fine with me.

"By the way, I got news about our Russian lady case. Between reviewing mug shots with the salt and pepper team, I got to call around."

Now I'm listening. "So?"

"The deceased was not the life of the party. I called his old school for the names of friends. Someone we could talk to about him and the Russian lady. I made a dozen calls and I got one lead in Manhattan Beach."

I press my head against the seat rest and close my eyes. Her face appears, those crystal blue eyes staring out into a luminous sky. She turns and looks at me without flinching, steady, sure of her actions. Is she complicit in a crime?

Jimmy taps a pencil point on my nose. "Stop daydreaming. What did you say about her, frayt?"

"No treife, forbidden," and I unconsciously lick my dry lips with my tongue.

I answer Jimmy. "So we got friends to talk to, good. The case is open. The question is why wasn't he taking his medicine?"

"Because the pills interfered with fucking his lady love. It's simple," Jimmy has the logical answer.

Jimmy shifts his attention to our favorite conversation, boxing. I listen, but it's the Russian lady occupying my thoughts. The minutes drift into hours. Jimmy has his own conversation going while I half listen about the Golden Gloves championship just thinking about her, blue eyes, lovely skin, nice tits. The ocean breezes roll through the open car windows and although it's hot and humid, we are comfortable, bathed by the swaying air currents. At exactly 8:55 PM Jimmy calls Lewis on the car radio.

"We're going. If something breaks call me or Perlov the Protector. We'll be back early tomorrow morning to continue the stakeout."

I get to go home and eat that hotdog, which I refuse to share with a seagull perched on the garage roof.

Morning arrives and the stakeout begins. I pull up to the curb in my unmarked car. The projects are quiet at seven in the morning. No school and not enough adults are going off to work. There's no paperboy delivering his wares as you might see a mile down the road in Brighton Beach. It's a different world.

Jimmy jumps into the car. He has a cup of coffee with him, but when he sees my thermos, he throws his coffee out the window.

"I walked here from the station house. Thought I'd do a little reconnaissance work, but there's not much stirring." He pours some of my mother's coffee into his used cup.

"Your mother makes the best coffee. She put in that vanilla. Um. She can't cook but she has her strengths in the kitchen."

We chat about his date with Lori. We don't see Lewis or Murphy. I start to call but Jimmy hands me a bulletproof vest. "Put this on and we'll wait."

Jimmy is carefully examining his nails with their perfect half moons when I think I see our man.

"Jimmy." His eyes quickly look out the windshield.

"Fat fucker, I'll call for backup. He must have eaten his way up two sizes since that mug shot." Jimmy's hand goes for the radio while I go for my second pistol lying on the floor of the car.

We don't wait for the backup. I leap out of the car towards our suspect. Jimmy is by my right hip ready for the unexpected.

I call out, "Albert Speer. Police. Stop, we want to talk to you."

Albert Speer starts to run in the opposite direction, but his mammoth body does not move quickly.

Jimmy follows him while I run around the back towards his apartment building entrance. I spot my partner as I run in another direction. Jimmy isn't even trotting, but walking quickly just a few steps behind Speer's lumbering body.

We are waiting for him to tire. He's too much trouble with all that bulk to bring down. I don't want to jump on his back, and try and wrestle him to the ground. With minutes to spare, I run to the children's playground so that he is approaching me with Jimmy following behind.

"Albert Speer. Police, just stop there." And I stand in a marksman's stance. My legs are spread apart and my arms are stretched forward with my handgun pointing directly at Albert Speer's chest.

Albert is clutching his sides. We can see him panting.

"Albert stop," I repeat.

Albert obeys; he continues to hold his left side. Sweat is dripping from his forehead onto his hooded sweatshirt.

"Put your hands behind your head." We hear the sirens of our backup.

I stand ten feet away; you can't be too careful until his hands are visible and incapable of mischief.

"Albert get on your knees." He is still breathing heavily. My gun is pointing at his head. Jimmy is right behind him to cuff him, but he knows not to stand between his legs even if he is on his knees. Big guys like this are dangerous.

Jimmy cuffs him. For our suspect this is going to be very uncomfortable because the department hasn't bought any super extra large handcuffs so this will pinch.

I place my gun back in its holster. "Albert, why are you running from the police?"

Jimmy kicks the suspect's legs to spread them further apart. The uniforms arrive.

Checking in the pocket of his sweatshirt I find little packets. "Albert, what are these? Crack cocaine?"

Jimmy puts them in baggies for the evidence room.

I lift up his hooded sweatshirt. His chest is a slimy mess of dirt and sweat. His baggy pants have managed to get tangled and now rest inches above his knees.

"Nice boxers, Albert." I stretch the waistband of his boxers with my pencil, and there resting under his boxers in the waistband of his briefs is a handgun.

"Albert, look what I found in your tidy whiteys, a gun." With the pencil as a prop, Jimmy pulls the gun up and out, and places it in a baggie. I continue, "You could have shot off your balls with that gun. Is the safety off? Albert got a permit for this?" Albert takes a deep breath, sucking in the moist air.

Roberta and her partner are watching us and snickering.

"Albert, we are arresting you for fleeing an officer, possession of crack cocaine with intent to sell and assaulting Mrs. Svetlana Chervony. Do you understand these charges Albert? Anything you say will be used against you in a court of law. You have the right to a lawyer and if you can't afford one, the city will provide one for you."

It takes the four of us to get Albert to his feet with his pants dragging. Roberta's partner pulls them up.

"Albert do you understand your rights?"

"I got to eat breakfast. It's time for breakfast. My Grammies has breakfast for me. Will I get breakfast?" He stares ahead not looking at anyone.

"Albert do you understand your rights?" I ask again.

"Breakfast, where's my breakfast? My Grammies expects me for breakfast." He rattles on.

"Albert," I place my hand under his chin and sharply jerk his head so he is looking directly into my eyes.

"Albert, do you understand your rights?"

"Yes, yes, yes, yes. My breakfast." He lives on a different planet where all of life centers on regular disbursements of food.

"Take him to the station," I tell the uniforms. Roberta turns him towards the squad car.

"What are you arresting him for?" I turn around and see a light skinned black man wearing a white Muslim cap.

"Who are you, his lawyer?" and I walk past him.

"You got my cousin, where are you taking him?" A young, thin woman approaches me. "My grandmother will be upset."

I look her in the eyes. "Tell his grandmother; Albert has been a bad boy. He keeps bad company. He's carrying a gun, narcotics and he's been assaulting old people at Harbor House. If you want to see him, he'll be at the 60th Precinct."

By the time we get back to the station house, Albert is being processed.

"Don't forget and check all his cavities for drugs," Jimmy tells the uniforms.

"I'd have Roberta stick her hand up Speer's ass but she's a woman. I'll find another loser." I watch Jimmy checking the faces of those who are milling around.

"Hey, Lenny. You go check out the fat fucker. Make sure you put your hand up his anus for drugs. We don't want him ingesting anything. Take away the shoelaces and the belt. We don't want a suicide. Then bring him to the downstairs interrogation room." Lenny casts Jimmy a nasty look.

"Don't look at me. Do it. That's why I'm wearing a suit and you're in uniform."

That's what I love about Jimmy; he knows who's in charge. The station house has a methodical pecking order.

We find Lewis and Murphy and they follow us to the interrogation room. Albert can't see us from the doorway. Roberta brings him in and cuffs both hands to the table. Despite his heft and menacing gang attire, he sits like an obedient child.

Jimmy and I enter the room while Lewis and Murphy stand outside watching us through the one-way mirror.

"Okay Albert, before we lock you away for the gun and drugs, I'll give you a chance to come clean," I tell our suspect, who is tugging at the tight cuffs.

"Albert are you listening?" I ask.

"I got to have my breakfast. My Grammies always says I got to have my breakfast." He hasn't stopped asking for food.

Jimmy shoots me a look and rolls his eyes.

I begin again. "Albert have you been attacking little old ladies at Harbor House?"

"Where's my Grammies? She always has breakfast for me. I got to eat my breakfast." The words leave his lips in a constant beat. It's a steady rhythm without being at all musical.

Albert is now pulling at the handcuffs as a chained dog might do.

Jimmy turns away. Albert looks at him and then returns to the handcuffs.

Jimmy slams his hand against the table.

Albert jumps out of his chair. I can see his heart thumping through the sweatshirt. I know this routine so I'm prepared.

"I peed. I peed in my pants," Albert cries. His big, bulging eyes swell with tears.

Jimmy sighs.

"Albert," I plead. "Albert look at me," and he does.

"Albert I'll get you some breakfast, coffee and donuts, just tell us. Were you at Harbor House?"

"My Grammies doesn't let me have coffee. No donuts for breakfast. I got to have milk. Milk. I like chocolate milk. Sometimes my Grammies lets me have chocolate milk. Can I have chocolate milk?"

Jimmy is losing patience but I feel we have something here. Time; it takes time to get a confession.

"Yes, Albert I'll get you some chocolate milk. What do you want for breakfast?" My tone of voice is soft and sweet enough that the honey rolls from my tongue.

"I eat three eggs. Corn bread. Pancakes and if I'm good, I get waffles with syrup."

Jimmy in a needling voice says, "He'll eat you broke."

"Albert choose your favorite."

He studies his hands. We wait.

"Albert, now." I raise my voice.

"Pancakes with blueberries."

"Alright. We'll see about the blueberries." I take out a five-dollar bill from my wallet. Jimmy stands, takes the money and hands it to a dangling arm in the doorway. At this point, I don't know who is watching us.

"Don't forget the chocolate milk." I shout to the mirror.

I tap Albert on the head with my open palm. I try again, more forcibly. "Albert, so tell us. The old ladies at Harbor House."

Albert looks directly at me. "Those old bitches. I take their money, but they don't have much." His face is filled with satisfaction for a job well done.

"Do you remember one tiny lady? You only got one dollar."

"That bitch," the words come out with his spit. "She hurt me."

Jimmy looks at him eying his width, and says. "This I can't imagine."

Albert is nodding his head back and forth. "Yes, she hurt me.

She stepped hard into my foot. She hurt me. Those kikes have money in the mattresses."

I'm calm. "You think so. Who told you that?"

"My Grammies tells me. Those kikes have money hidden in the mattresses. They don't need nice apartments. They foreigners."

"What else does your Grammies tell you?" I look at his clumsy body and enormous baby face. He's not intimidating looking, but still capable of committing great destruction.

"Those Jews, they have money. They don't speak English. They don't belong here," he says with assurance.

I ignore his remarks because my goal is a confession. I ask him, "What did you do with her purse?"

"She had a big, big pocketbook for that dollar. She had only one dollar. One dollar. One dollar." His repetitive speech has a certain unconscious beat. He focuses on one word at a time. He drills down to the one thought.

"Albert," I tuck my finger under his fleshy chin giving him a little pinch.

He jerks his body. For a big, fat guy he seems super-sensitive to touch.

"Albert did you throw away that purse?"

Albert is twisting in his chair, probably from the sticky urine settling around his thick thighs.

"No, I keep those purses. They mine. I have them in my room. I got a money clip that has a dollar bill sign. I got that from an old Jew kike man. I took that. I tried to get a little purse from a fat old Jew lady but she fought with me. I tore her blouse. I got a little cloth but no money."

Jimmy yells to those watching behind the mirror. "Get a warrant for his apartment. Get the evidence before the grandmother gets smart and throws away the stuff. We want his souvenirs. Hurry. We want his souvenirs."

"Albert, you hold on to those keepsakes from your crimes?" I ask the smiling suspect.

"Yes, they mine," he answers. Albert feels the excitement around him; loud voices are making demands but he doesn't appear alarmed. He pumps his fists as if he was a spectator in a sporting event.

We get ready to leave the room. We have what we need, the fat man delivered.

"My breakfast. I need my breakfast. You promise. You promise. You promise breakfast." He clings to these words as others might to ideas.

"You'll get it," I answer.

We leave the dirty, hungry Albert to sit in his own bodily juices. He begins to rock and it looks like he's singing the word, "breakfast."

Murphy slaps me lightly across the shoulders. "Nice job."

"What do you think his IQ is?" I look at the three of them.

Murphy answers, "50."

"Well, I'd guess closer to 75, but he's retarded. Maybe he's autistic."

Lewis answers. "So we shouldn't do anything. He takes money from defenseless old Jews, calls them kikes."

"Oh no, he's very dangerous with that bulk and no brains. If his crew boss tells him to shoot these old people, he'll kill them. He doesn't understand the consequences of his acts. We got to put him away." My sympathies are with the victims. He is only a victim in some abstract vision of a socially dysfunctional country divided by race and class. I remember the diatribes we heard in our Soviet classrooms about what's wrong with America.

The breakfast arrives. Jimmy takes it from one of the uniforms. "I like blueberry pancakes."

I take it from him.

Albert continues rocking and then suddenly he bursts into tears. We all watch through the mirror as the tears and snot roll down his face. Repulsive is how he looks and Murphy shakes his head in disgust. Jimmy is eyeing the pancakes with intense interest.

"I know things," Albert wails between the sobs and the mucus. He continues crying. "I see the shootings at Surfside."

Lewis gives Murphy a light tap. Lewis begins to walk into the room, but I stop him by pulling on his forearm. He doesn't have a chance to react.

I take the breakfast with me back into the room.

"Albert here is your breakfast." I put it down on the table. Albert tries to reach for it; he tugs at the tight handcuffs.

I slowly open the paper bag. He can smell the pancakes. He sniffs the air like a dog; his nostrils actually flutter. I can't stand looking at his face with trails of dried, caked tears mixing with runny mucus and crusty snot.

I take one of the napkins from the bag. "Wipe your nose," and he manages by bending his head sufficiently close enough to one of his hands cuffed to the table.

I pull out of the bag a paper cup with the milk. I can see from the closed lid that it is dark.

"Albert I have the chocolate milk."

He wets his lips.

"So tell me Albert, what about the killings?"

"I got to have my breakfast. I got to have my pancakes. My pancakes."

"What did you see?"

He is concentrating on the white bag. I loudly snap my fingers. Then he looks at me and says, "I see Red Roy kill Ernie and those two others. Yes. I see it."

I yell to my observers. "Get the tapes working. Get the video going. He can't write what he saw. Get this going." I can't see what they are doing, but I know they are readying the newly installed video cameras designed specifically for a case just like this.

"Is it working? Test it."

Jimmy enters the room. "Go."

"First test it." I don't want a screw up, this is too important. "Let it roll. This is a test. I have Albert Speer with me." I stop. "Now go backwards and make certain it's working."

Albert is watching all the frenzied activity, distracted from the food, but not for long. His eyes return to the bag.

Jimmy is back in a few minutes and taps me on the shoulder. "Go."

"So Albert," I push the milk towards him. "Take a sip and then we'll talk."

I let him take a sip. I hear him take this giant gulp; he doesn't stop to take in air. He will finish the entire large cup of milk in one swallow.

He smacks his lips. How I hate that sound.

I take away the cup and he grabs for it but the handcuffs prevent him from getting it. "Okay Albert. Tell me what did you see?"

"I see it all."

I wait for more details. I pick up the cup and wiggle it in front of Albert. "I was hiding in the janitor's closet. I like to collect bottles. I bring them to Key Food for money. The closet has big barrels filled with bottles. I go look for all the bottles, one by one. People throw them out, not me, never me."

I cut him off sharply. "Albert, I don't care about bottles. Tell me what happened with the killings."

"Yes, I was looking in the barrels and I hear loud noises. Yelling. I don't want to stop but I hear Red Roy's voice and I know he don't live in my building so I look out."

"Was the door open a little? Did you see him through a crack in the door?"

"No, a hole in the door, like you look at strangers."

"Like a peephole."

"Yes, but bigger. The janitor's closet got a big hole."

I nod my head for encouragement

"I got to eat my breakfast. I got to eat my breakfast," Albert starts again. He rocks.

I open the plastic top and show Albert the pancakes. He reaches for them but the handcuffs prevent him from going too far.

"My pancakes," I know that I am teasing him, but I'm enjoying it.

"Ok Albert. I'll give you a bite, but tell me what did you see?"

"My pancakes, my pancakes," he is struggling to get at the pancakes.

I cut a piece, dip it in the artificial syrup and drop it into his open mouth, like a mother bird giving her youngling his feeding.

He swallows without breathing. His mouth stays open.

"Albert, now tell me what did you see. I'll give you the rest."

He licks his lips; his tongue searches for any vestige of syrup.

I knock the table with my fist. He speaks. "I see Red Roy and Ernie from my building pushing each other. Ernie's cousin goes to help Ernie and I see Red Roy takes his gun and shoots Cousin Tom. Ernie goes for Red Roy but too slow. Red Roy shoots him. The other guy I don't know, he tries to run away but Red Roy fires and shoots him. I don't see him fall but I hear him fall; I hear a big bang on the ground."

"Then what?" I ask.

I cut another piece of pancake for Albert. I drop another big piece into his waiting mouth. He swallows it at once.

Albert smiles. "Red Roy run away. And I stay in the closet. I peed in the closet, a little puddle. I afraid of Red Roy. He's a bad motherfucker. O-o-o. I afraid of Red Roy."

"How are you so sure it was Red Roy?"

"His red hair. Everyone know Red Roy. He got red kinky hair and real light skin. He kind of scary-looking. Everyone know Red Roy."

"You never came forward?"

"I afraid. I got to have my pancakes. I got to have my breakfast."

"So you will, so you will." I take away the plastic silverware and push the dish towards Albert. He doesn't wait for me to leave. His hands dive into the food.

I leave him to his vision of heaven, blueberry pancakes. I tell Lewis, "We'll get a warrant and arrest Red Roy." A minor case has turned unexpectedly into a homicide investigation. Successful police work often depends on simple luck, not computers or fancy expensive forensics, just blind, dumb luck.

Weeks have gone by without any good leads on solving this triple murder. No one is willing to talk to the police; people in the projects are afraid. The police pride themselves on solving murders; lowering murder rate statistics is the drum roll heard repeatedly by precinct inspectors. Solve murders. Pancakes and chocolate milk are the secret ingredients for finding our murderer.

"No warrant," says Lewis, with Murphy by his side, assuming control of the case.

Jimmy and I look perplexed. Losing lead status on the case is one thing, but making irresponsible decisions, well we wait for an explanation.

"You think Fat Albert is a good witness or even that he would testify." Murphy is agreeing with Lewis' plan.

"We're the police, we'll protect him." I look to Murphy for assurances; he was always the more reasonable of the two.

"No," Lewis adamantly answers without being overly harsh or arrogant-sounding.

He continues. "We let him go and we spread the news through snitches that he ratted out Red Roy is the plan."

"And, for what purpose do we do this except as a sure way to get Albert killed," I say in complete bafflement.

Murphy answers. "We smoke out Red Roy. He's the one we want."

Lewis looks at me and snaps. "You care what happens to Fat Albert."

I am infuriated, "Yes, yes. I do care."

"He's a moron who hates Jews. What's the loss?" Lewis shrugs his shoulders.

Jimmy is uncomfortable playing judge and jury. "Yeah, but do we want our witness killed? You got a real plan? This doesn't make any sense."

"We let him go. Red Roy will seek revenge, either by taking direct action himself because he's a hothead, or if he's thinking he'll send someone else after our fat fuck. Then we wait to nail Red Roy for attempted murder or the murder of Albert. That's how we solve the triple murders." He dramatically wipes his hands in mid-air. End of case.

I am totally opposed to this plan and pace the small hallway before I answer. "You can't do that."

"What's your idea?" Murphy asks as he braces his body against the wall preventing me from pacing.

"At least we got to try and protect Albert when we release him and get Red Roy for attempted murder," I see Jimmy nodding his head, affirming my decision.

"Okay SWAT man, we post you on the project roof tonight. You take one of the guns from your arsenal and take care of any lurking dangers," says Lewis in complete seriousness.

"No, no, not at night. If we're going to try and protect him we release him in the daylight. And we station sharp eyes around the building and get them positioned hours before we dump Albert home." I reply with Lewis and Murphy listening.

"We get uniforms to escort him home?" Murphy asks.

I am picturing in my brain the layout of my plan. "No, unless we want to endanger them." I've walked every inch of Surfside Gardens during my years at the 60th. I know the physical set-up of Albert's building. "No, we get them to take him to the central path of the project's east side. Then they leave him to walk to his building entrance. We are laying in wait in the grass, behind the shrubs, as invisible as possible, positioned all around the pathways. That's where someone is most likely to go after Albert. These guys are experienced killers but not trained assassins. They will not be using sights and high power rifles, just handguns, up close and personal."

I see my companions sizing up my plan. One by one they nod in agreement.

I tell my attentive audience, "Tomorrow morning around 6 AM, we position cops in the right places before anyone is stirring. We get cops on the roofs; everywhere we can find a line of sight. You get the word out today that he's being very cooperative and then you have one of your informants spread the word he is being temporarily released around 8 AM. Get someone from the Housing Authority to give us complete blueprints. I want to know all the landscaping details."

90

We are in team mode. It doesn't take me long to get the Lieutenant's blessing for a large-scale operation. We have the Housing Authority's cooperation and permission to stage this action on their property. Albert is cleaned up and put in a holding cell until morning. We call in for pounds of food to keep him quiet.

There are still a few hours left in our shift. I am pumped and eager to continue our investigation of the Russian Lady using Jimmy's leads. Detective work is endlessly talking to strangers about what they remember, their opinions about people they like and hate, and just simple observations. Can we determine my Russian Lady's character through conversations with people who know her? The sisters are unlikely to provide illuminating answers. They have too much at stake in protecting the image of the dutiful wife. Justice demands my dogged search for the truth.

I still need to know did Feinstein keel over and collapse? Did he cry out for help? Were the widow and the sisters in the house at the moment of his heart attack? Did they ignore his cries or did he quietly stop breathing and they left the house unaware he was in physical distress? The uniforms at the scene reported that the nosy neighbors didn't see the widow or her two sisters in the house during that afternoon.

Jimmy has already checked on the man's finances. The new widow isn't going to collect a fortune, only a teacher's pension, though she will get the house. There doesn't appear to be anyone contesting the widow's rights. The deceased has a sister in California who will be coming to the funeral. Jimmy has chatted with her on the phone and she doesn't request any details about her brother's death, which is interesting.

The brother and sister don't seem too close and that's common in America. People seem to drift here both physically and then emotionally or maybe it's the other way around. This is unthinkable behavior for a Russian Jew. Out of obligation and simple guilt, a sister should be crying on the phone when we call about her brother's death. She should be inquisitive, want to know the facts. She informs Jimmy that she will be in New York should we want to question her.

Jimmy has located the address of Feinstein's only good friend who lives in Manhattan Beach on the other edge of this little peninsula that includes Coney Island and Brighton Beach. We arrive at the friend's house, which is typical for the neighborhood. From the street it looks small with almost no property, but it's deceiving because it probably has three maybe four bedrooms, a full dining room, and a couple of bathrooms. This is dense living space. The houses were built in the 1940's right after the war, and were not the product of a developer's cookie cutter method of building houses. A sense of individuality lives here. Who wants to live like the Lieutenant in Suffolk County or like my Uncle Viktor in Staten Island in a neighborhood where all the houses look similar and were built during the same five-month period? Not me—give me an old neighborhood with charm and character.

The name of the friend Jimmy has located is Bernstein. He's probably Jewish like the deceased although in the age of interfaith marriages, a name can be deceiving. They aren't expecting us, which is better because we don't want people to have created a story line. It's fresher and usually more honest if we just make an appearance.

The voices are coming from the back of the house.

Jimmy calls out as we open the gate of the fenced in yard, "Police." We always pray when we make a sudden appearance that the owners don't have an unleashed Pit Bull or German Shepherd waiting to sample a piece of a stranger's leg or arm.

A man—we assume Mr. Bernstein—appears from the back of the house followed by a woman. They are both in their 50's, white and middle class gauging from the type of siding and general appearance of the house. At least on the outside not too much has been done to upgrade and modernize the house to twenty-first century tastes. There's a newer model Jeep in the driveway, and as we approach with our badges showing, we see a Harley Davidson motorcycle. Somebody enjoys thrills.

"Hi," I smile so all my front teeth are visible, trying to look non-threatening while Jimmy follows me through a narrow path separating the driveway from the house and a side door. He can barely squeeze by but he manages. I notice my vain partner looking down at his stomach to check whether it's time for him to put away those chips and six packs of beer.

"I'm looking for Mr. Robert Bernstein," I say.

The man eyes me suspiciously. It's not about secrets here but mistrust. If he's not an immigrant, he's still uneasy around police. Forget about the love and admiration the public has towards the police since 9/11. This guy doesn't like police. He probably has a story to tell but I don't want to hear his complaints. I have a case to investigate.

"We're here about Jack Feinstein," I wait for the name to register. I watch the man and woman glance at each other.

"You know he passed away?" Jimmy looks at them while he's speaking to make certain they're listening. Meanwhile, I visually study the house. I'm instinctively looking for newly dug holes in the backyard, fresh cement on the patio, anything indicating recent changes. Crime and changes, especially a house's physical appearance, often are related.

"Can we ask you a few questions," Jimmy continues. I'm taking in all the body language. The man squints from the sun in his eyes and the woman pushes her eyeglasses closer to her face studying us. They're trying to figure out why we are visiting with them about Jack Feinstein. The suspicion turns to confusion. We can handle confusion easier than suspicion.

They both are wearing swimsuits so I guess there's a pool in the back. Neither one of them is in top physical shape although the man looks more athletic than the woman. The man motions for us to follow him to the back of the house. I don't see a dog or any sign of a dog—no doghouse, no bones lying around under chairs or in unlikely places where a stranger would innocently step and fall. No balls soaked in dog saliva nor is a leash on the ground. We're safe from a canine attack.

"I thought he died from a heart attack, what's with the questions?" Mr. Bernstein asks inquisitively.

"We're just finishing the investigation. We like to make inquiries anytime someone dies relatively young in their home," Jimmy responds, waiting for a reaction from the two of them.

"That's the job of the medical examiner's office; checking for cause of death." Mr. Bernstein is still a little hostile. We know from the information Jimmy checked that Mr. Bernstein is a scientist with a Ph.D. working for one of the big teaching hospitals in Manhattan. He is probably very familiar with the work of the medical examiner's office.

"Nice pool," I turn my back towards the couple and gaze into the water. Although he's flabby around the middle, I guess that our host is a swimmer and probably was a lifeguard at one time. He has the right type of body. His shoulders are wide and muscular and his chest has that certain fullness that belongs to a swimmer. He didn't get those muscles from bodybuilding.

"Do you swim every day?" I ask, just to try to get the conversation moving in a more friendly direction.

He dips his fingers into the pool and stands near me. "Yes."

I laugh a bit, my attempt at removing the lingering hostility. We need to make these people into willing informers. "You were a lifeguard at one point, right?" I ask.

He smiles; it's a little smile but his nice white, straight teeth show. "Yes." His shoulders relax and I think we have a connection.

Jimmy immediately notices and we eye each other for less than a second. He turns to Mrs. Bernstein and asks, "Do you think I could have a cold drink—water—it's hot out here."

She is at heart a good hostess and she replies, "Certainly, I'll get something from the kitchen." Jimmy follows her into the house.

"Where were you a lifeguard?" I place my hand into the pool and then touch my wet fingers to my forehead to cool down.

"Near here in Coney Island," he answers.

"I was a lifeguard too," I reply and then Mr. Bernstein is interested. His whole face loosens up and I actually see a real smile emerge.

"No kidding, where?" now I have his full attention.

"In the Rockaways—Beach 60's." Those were the carefree days and I smile to myself remembering my own reckless youth spent guarding people against Mother Nature, surfing at dawn and partying till two a.m.

"That beach is rough," he replies and we begin a friendly peer discussion of the dangers of being a lifeguard. We talk about the calm surf on the Brooklyn side versus the real tough Atlantic Ocean currents that line the Rockaways. It is a great surfing beach, that entire peninsula, and luckily for me, most of the locals never went swimming during my four years guarding the beaches. We both agree swimming is really a white man's sport. The blacks that live in the Rockaways rarely went swimming. The Latins are more open to the beach but more as a social venue and the Chinese are also no shows. Everything in NYC has an ethnic and racial slant.

My host was never a surfer but he knew many lifeguards who were die-hards. I knew I was reaching him when he offered me a little financial advice. "Make sure you have the city count your days as a lifeguard in your city pension." The link was secure.

"So what do you know about Mrs. Feinstein?" I ask, now that he's more relaxed.

He's smart and now he figures out why we have bothered him on this hot, sunny day. "I don't know her."

"But you were a good friend of the late Mr. Feinstein?" I ask.

He shrugs his powerful shoulders and responds, "We were friends and possibly he would consider me his best friend because Jack was well meaning but he didn't have many friends. Since his first wife died he fell apart." There is sadness in his voice.

"Did you know he had a bad heart?" I want to know how much information they shared.

"Yes, of course, and actually he was beginning to look a little better. Finding that woman actually did help him. He lost weight and his clothes were clean. There was a definite improvement." He nods his head.

"Did you know the sisters who lived with him?" What else did he see?

"Actually," he tells me, "we saw the sisters more than we saw the wife. We go to the Brighton Beach concerts practically every week and Jack would occasionally come with the two sisters. They didn't wait in line; we saved them chairs. Jack's wife didn't like the concerts."

Another common thread. "I have been going to those concerts since I arrived in America." Now Mr. Bernstein and I have made a real connection. "I work security at those concerts now." Maybe I know Bernstein from the concerts. Of course with clothes on he may have a very different appearance. I don't want to stare too hard, but he and the wife must be part of that regular, reliable group of early arrivals.

"Yeah, we're there with Jack most Thursday nights."

What a small world is this place called Brooklyn.

"So how come the wife doesn't go." I need to keep him on track.

He doesn't seem to know, just shakes his head. "She was really missing out on some fun. Those concerts were the highlight of Jack's life. I mean that's how little he had going."

"So if she didn't participate with him going to these concerts how well did they get along?" I ask watching for some indication about what's really going on with this relationship.

He turns his head in a lackadaisical type of shrug. "The truth," he says and I am listening.

"He's a lonely guy. He meets her in one of those restaurants in Brighton Beach. You know." Of course I know. "He is good-hearted; don't let anyone tell you differently. So he feels sorry for her and he takes her into his house; not only her but also these two sisters. Who may or may not be her sisters. And he wants some payment, not money, you know." Actually this I don't understand. "So he presses her for sex." Now we're getting close to the truth. "But with all that heart medicine he can't get it up.

He tells me this in real despair. I feel sorry for the guy."

"Is she a willing partner?" I ask, because this is central to the relationship.

"Actually," and he moves closer to me; discussions like this require a certain intimacy, not suited for idle ears. "He told me almost in tears that she loathed him." Two people have now used this same word.

"And this produces tension?" I ask.

"Listen," I'm all ears as I place one foot closer to Mr. Bernstein's tanned body, "I don't know if this is true, but he tells me that he watches her have sex with another man." I want to smile but that would be unprofessional.

Mr. Bernstein dips his head a little closer; his personal space has evaporated, we are standing close together. "One of the sisters has a boyfriend and," he stops, "He threatens his new wife about calling in Immigration and having her green card taken away unless she and the sisters have sex with his guy and he watches. That's what gets him off. He tells me, and again he liked to boast about a lot of things, that he even has the girls do it together. Now, I don't know if any of it's true."

"Kinky stuff," is my best cool response. I am filtering and processing the information. Is he a boastful liar or his ordinary home a den of depravity?

I have to know more details, more facts. "Who is the boyfriend? Where can I find him?" An investigation thrives on names, places, dates, and times. I need a description—is he tall, thin, white, black? What is he wearing? Where does he live?

"I don't know his name, another Russian. I saw him only once with the sister named Masha, you know, the taller blonde sister." One of those pesky American expressions, if I knew would I be asking you.

We both turn as Jimmy and Mrs. Bernstein return with a tray filled with tall glasses of ice tea and cookies.

Jimmy winks, and we eat and drink. I feel like making a toast in honor of the deceased but of course that would be rather tasteless. Let's congratulate our hosts because the investigation now proceeds with motive since we have kinky sex, immigrants praying at the shrine of the green card, and a boyfriend to meet.

We thank the Bernsteins for their hospitality and as we drive back to the station we start discussing the case.

"So what did she tell you," I ask Jimmy. They were together for a long time in the house. Jimmy can be very charming with the ladies, especially the older ones whom he compliments about their house decorations, the color of the drapes, or a picture on the wall. He's a master of the small talk; that's what makes him so effective as a political animal. He will move up the ranks because he knows what to say and when to say it. My father instructs me to try and emulate Jimmy's moves, but it's not in me. I'm too much like my mother. When it comes to politics we breathe fire, not cool, blue ice.

"He's a pig and kept the wife as a sex slave. He deserved to die. Her words not mine." Jimmy flashes one of his gorgeous can you beat this smile.

I just say out loud, "What about the sisters?" We need to know more about the three sisters. With the Chekhov names of Irina, Olga and Masha—they must think we are stupid. Do they imagine that they are capable of committing the perfect crime?

"Mrs. Bernstein likes the sisters and the two of them went to those concerts you're always talking about. Doesn't know the wife well. Most of what she knows about the wife is from the sisters. They told her about the deceased's demand for conjugal rights."

"Did you compliment her on the furniture?" I snicker and he smiles.

"It was hard to keep a straight face, but I did tell her I love the decorative dishes hanging on the walls." His mouth opens wide and he laughs quietly while shaking his head.

"But she is a valuable source," he turns serious. "Saw the deceased every Thursday night during the summer. And when the late Mr. Feinstein visits them at their house, she makes excuses to leave. Mrs. Bernstein did not like the deceased and only occasionally socialized with him outside of the weekly summer concerts."

Jimmy takes out a stick of gum; it's cinnamon. I can smell the strong, sweet scent from several feet away. Chewing on cinnamon sticks helped me kick my nicotine habit. I don't usually chew gum but I am drawn to the flavor. I take the piece Jimmy offers.

Jimmy has more. "It seems they got married in church. The Bernsteins weren't invited because of the inter-faith thing. Feinstein knew that the Bernsteins wouldn't approve, especially Mrs. Bernstein. And why did they get married? Because Immigration was after her." That is a path to be investigated.

I tell Jimmy what I know. "So, is this worth continuing to investigate? Now we have a good reason for them to be very happy he's dead and gone."

"OK, maybe you got something here." He acknowledges my dark Russian instincts and admits," We can keep this case open."

Of course, it could still be nothing more than coincidence that the guy drops dead from a heart attack even if he makes his wife perform sex acts with another man and with her own sisters. My guess if there's any truth to this we will also find videotapes of the group sex. I've never been with vice, but from what I know about human nature, if this is what gets him excited he'll want to keep these memories for posterity. Immigrants, Brighton Beach Bandshell concerts, Immigration, and kinky sex—this is a case.

I'm eating dinner with my parents. A glass of strong, clear-colored Russian vodka and a kosher hotdog smothered in dark sauerkraut and deep yellow mustard. This is why we left Russia, so we could sit in the backyard of our own single-family house eating kosher food.

My mother heard from the nosy neighbors about the death of 'First-in-line, Jack.'

She hands me a bowl of grapes. "So what's with that case? I think I know who he is, or was, fat and sloppy looking. Is that the guy?"

"I shouldn't talk about my cases." I always say that to my parents and then share.

So I give them a few details about the wife as sex slave and marrying in church. The Feinstein's next-door neighbor has broadcasted through the entire neighborhood about the heart attack.

"Pig, that's the right term," my mother responds indignantly. "He deserved what he got." My mother responds predictably; hers is a typical woman's reaction to the case. My mother and Mrs. Bernstein have reached the same conclusion. Unlike the more sympathetic Mr. Bernstein, the women don't accept the lonely part as an excuse for depravity and indifference. For us guys, sex is sex; you get it wherever you can find it.

My father isn't judgmental. "A green card is a powerful seducer. People will do many questionable actions to be able to stay and work in this country," he adds.

"A man shouldn't be able to force a wife to do anything against her will." My mother is not finished criticizing the morals of the deceased. I didn't share the part about the kinky sex with the other man and the sisters.

"Immigrants pay a heavy price to work in this country." My father hears stories about Eastern European women who are tricked into prostitution because they are so eager to leave the former Soviet Union and come to America. "Things in these countries are very difficult for many people, especially women." He extends his arms forward as if he were delivering a mathematics lecture. The only thing missing is a piece of chalk. We, his eager students, give him our exclusive attention.

My father adds, "I bet those women are not actually Russian but Ukrainian." My father, the detective, always is thinking. "Don't just check with the Russian Orthodox Church in Bensonhurst." We all went to a wedding of one of my father's co-workers in that magnificent church. "I'd check on the Ukrainian Orthodox or Ukrainian Catholic churches first." He has a good point.

"You know there's a beautiful Ukrainian church in the Catskills. Maybe they got married there." Another good lead; I should consider engaging my father in more of my cases.

"You're going to the boss' house," and my mother is on to a new pressing matter; she has extended enough energies on the Case of the Russian Lady.

"Wait," and she returns to the house. She re-emerges carrying a tray with a picture of Jerusalem's Wailing Wall. On the tray are three tall glasses of hot tea and six small cubes of sugar on a plate. It can be 100 degrees outside but a Russian can drink sweet, hot tea all year round.

"First, you must pick up flowers for your date and the woman of the house," my mother tells me.

Flowers for my date, I don't think so but I'll let my mother continue because what's the point of interrupting her.

"Do you know what she will be wearing? Maybe a corsage would be nice," she adds.

"Momma, this is a Bar-B-Q; we aren't dressing in formal wear. What should I bring to eat?" I answer perhaps a little too harshly. Then I bow my head slightly to show that I don't mean to be disrespectful.

"Chocolates, bring the Lieutenant's wife chocolates and flowers," she answers, disregarding my comments.

"And I will make you something special to bring," she adds, and my father and I look at each other and grimace. We both know that my mother is a notoriously lousy cook.

"I'll make my famous vegetable goulash," she says, and we both nod our heads because it's one of the few things she successfully prepares; it's simple and healthy, her criteria for a good meal.

My mother was never a good cook or a great housekeeper. It wasn't only that she was busy being an engineer—a working wife and mother in Russia was a typical pattern. It was the time she was absent from us. There were the days she languished in Soviet prisons or on hunger strikes or committing other acts of public protest. These were the activities that defined her life in the Soviet Union. It was my father's mother that actually helped to raise me while my mother was gone. Some of our Petersburg neighbors were afraid to speak to any of us. The KGB followed me to school. Their job was not to be inconspicuous; they meant to be intimidating and school children kept their distance, but not Vasily's family.

Her status as the daughter of the Hero of the Battle of Stalingrad did keep her from the worst harm, but she was not immune from punishment by the Soviet authorities. She didn't escape all injury and some she inflicted on herself.

Her last hunger strike was unforgettable. Since the time of the ancient Greeks, people have expressed their political displeasure by publicly starving themselves. The Soviet authorities were acutely aware of all of my mother's acts of disobedience. They were conflicted. If she died by her own hand it would be one less political pest to watch; however, political martyrs were dangerous symbols.

Crowds of people flocked to our small apartment in Petersburg. My mother had a hard-core group of followers or her devotees. My father considered them annoyances while my grandfather treated them as parasites.

Her Jewish dissident cause attracted international attention. Letters arrived from America in support of her protests. The Hasids sent matzo during Passover and Protestant religious evangelicals prayed for her in their churches. The World Jewish Congress wrote to President Reagan and Senator Jackson on our behalf. US politicians uttered her name on the floor of the US Senate as an example of Soviet religious intolerance and the evils of atheism.

But this time she had taken her hunger strike too far. My father was gravely afraid that she might actually succeed and starve to death. She was so weak. Some of her supporters were cheering her on but others realized this was serious. I was young, but not so young that I didn't see the danger.

My father could not reason with her.

"Anna, it is too much," he sat at her bedside trying to reason with her. The offers of broth were rejected.

She pushed them aside, "No, no, I must continue."

I heard my other grandfather, my Zayde who lived with us, whispered, "She is slipping away from us."

My father was desperate and he called for my grandfather, the Hero of the Battle of Stalingrad, who at that time was in Moscow. Despite his age, my grandfather was a valuable Soviet bureaucrat and official authorities sought out his counsel and advice. Even my grandfather knew that the Soviet Union was unraveling, and in those perilous times, at the highest levels of the bureaucracy, they sought out the old champions. They looked backwards to those who were there with Lenin in 1917 for suggestions on keeping the system alive. At his death, his dying words were affirmations of the communism that he watched grow, fester, and then implode.

My grandfather had no place in his life or heart for religion. But blood was more important than politics so when my father called, he immediately left his official business and returned to Petersburg.

The authorities knew he was coming. Our phone was tapped; we always heard the clicks on the other end. All our visitors were followed by the secret police, but my grandfather was not afraid of the authorities; he was not afraid of anything. My grandfather belonged to that long line of family Uncle Vanyas and he recognized himself in my mother.

He arrived at our apartment directly from the airport in an official Soviet government car. I ran down to greet him at the entrance to our building.

"Grandpere, grandpere," that is what I always called him, "I missed you," and I hugged him tightly although I was a teenager, it didn't seem strange or immature. At first, I wouldn't let him go.

"Sasha my boy," and he kissed me on the forehead. "Let us go see your mother. She outdid herself this time, um…?"

I wasn't a doctor but I knew something was terribly wrong. "She is very weak. I have never seen her like this."

He grabbed my arm as we walked up the stairs. "I have seen everything, everything in this life. But voluntarily starving yourself is truly idiotic. I have seen people forced by the horrors of war to starve to death, but only someone so pigheaded would commit such an act as a protest."

Neighbors were afraid of him as they were of the KGB. We were the building pariahs. As we continued climbing the stairs, neighbors came out of their apartments and stared. My grandfather ignored them. Eyes watched as we passed from one floor to the next.

"Mrs. Markov," he called out to the large woman standing by her apartment doorway. She worked for the Agriculture Ministry and was a government informer.

Mrs. Markov slammed her door shut.

As we approached our floor, I stopped my grandfather.

I couldn't stop the tears, which were followed by hiccups. "She's going to die, I know," I said as I wiped my nose with the back of my hand between spasms.

He held me very tightly and then cupped my chin. "Have I ever lied to you?"

I couldn't speak but I shook my head.

"I tell you, she will not die. I won't let it happen."

He took from his breast pocket of his imported suit a French linen handkerchief.

"Wipe your eyes. Don't show your father your tears."

I obeyed. He looked at my eyes and gently kissed each swollen lid, running his strong hand through my thick, wavy hair.

We continued our ascent to the cramped apartment.

The coterie of onlookers congregated in the small hallway near the bedroom. People stepped aside as he entered the apartment

"Leave, leave at once," my grandfather shouted in his booming voice, which age had not diminished.

No one dared to look him directly in the eye. He forcibly pushed them away from the doorway. My relieved father followed in the path he created.

"Out, now," and the crowd dispersed.

He sat next to her on the bed." Anna, can you hear me?" He was intimate with the signs of starvation.

"Anna," she looked more dead than alive but her eyes flickered when she heard his voice.

"Anna, you cannot starve yourself to death. I will not let you die." His voice cracked with emotion and his powerful voice dimmed to a whisper.

"Anna, I could not save your mother and baby brother from starvation during the war but I will not let you die." He made her look directly into his eyes by placing his hand under her chin.

"Anna you will not die," his voice broke. The sight of his dehydrated, rail-thin daughter diminished the booming tone. Two weeks of starvation can be fatal. Feeling out of control and overwhelmed by helplessness, he started to cry. It was not quiet little tears but violent shaking sobs of grief.

"Anna, look at me." He sobbed heavily, his words barely audible; his tears fell on her gaunt face.

My father and I watched, frozen in our shoes. We were reduced to feeble witnesses, unable to do anything but watch.

"Anna, promise me you will not die." His anguished voice filled with remorse for the harsh words that had recently passed between them over her politics.

He grabbed her shoulders and wrapped them in his giant arms cradling my mother.

"Anna, you cannot die. I will not let you die. I will save you." He buttressed her frail body in his arms and they rocked together.

"Anna, promise me you will not die. You must stop this nonsense now." His voice grew stronger and louder. They rocked together as if he were cradling a baby in his arms. Time lapsed although I couldn't say how long it was that they rocked.

Finally, my mother looked at her teary-eyed father, the wet tears covering her cheek and with all her remaining strength she said, "I don't want to die."

"You won't die, I will make certain. You wouldn't break my heart," he answered.

She nodded and rested her head against her father's strong arm. "I will live," she spoke with a stronger voice than before and we knew she was saved.

It took several weeks, but my grandfather painstakingly nursed her back to health.

Here she lives in exile in this new land, free to practice her religion and protest, but no more hunger strikes. That folly was never repeated. I looked at my mother bringing a tray of tiny desserts, which she had baked. Awful was probably an understatement of how they tasted. In America, she had remade herself from radical, uncompromising dissident to Anna, Homemaker, Wife and Mother. Her career as a brilliant inventor vanished and in its place was the mid-level corporate computer programmer.

My father tastes the small pastry. "Very good Anna; very good. Sasha eat one." He manages to smile with the light piece of crust resting precariously on the tip of his tongue.

I take one from his hand. I swallow one with the help of the tea. It is almost edible. "Delicious," I lie. Too bad our dog isn't alive to finish our plates; he never complained in ten years and since he didn't die of food poisoning it's never been fatal to eat her culinary creations.

As we sit around the patio table, for no particular reason, my mother reaches and takes my hand and then grabs my father's hand. I instinctively take my father's hand. We sit, the three of us, our hands and spirits joined together.

"A toast," she says.

We raise our vodka glasses and exclaim to the world, "L'chayim," to life.

CHAPTER 5

It is still night. The darkness surrounds me, but I am never afraid. As a child, I welcomed the shadows. With my acute eyesight, like a cat I am. Few things can hide from my sharp gaze.

I rise earlier than usual because I don't want to be rushed. Concentration and calm composure is required to meet the challenge I have assumed. I dress for the heat of the day. The summer weather begs for a white, cotton, short-sleeve shirt. Protocol demands that I wear a tie, but on my feet are black sneakers in case I have to chase some bad guys.

Cool, always cool in the face of danger that is my modus operandi. Let the sweat of my underarms be the only visible sign of my tension. Evil is before me, but the goal is to save a life and avenge an injustice.

Through my open windows I hear the early stirrings of the gulls. I stare out and there is one eying me. First, he attends to his daily cleaning ritual of plucking his feathers by burying his head into his chest, loose feathers flying into the air. They are picked up by the sea breezes and simply float away. I watch the feathers drift past me, carried out to the sea.

A light tapping at my door, "Can I come in," asks my mother.

I open my door and there she is in her multi-colored robe. A modern, female version of the Biblical Joseph is how to describe my mother's attire.

"You're up very early. This is a big day?"

I nod.

"Something dangerous?"

"My job is always dangerous," I reply without hesitation.

Unexpectedly, she wraps her thin arms around my waist and presses her head against my chest.

"I love you, and I am very proud of what you do," and she kisses me on the edge of my jaw, the farthest her neck will stretch.

She squeezes me tightly and says, "I'll get you something healthy to eat, to keep you alert."

As she moves towards the door, I call out to her, "I love you," and my smile is warm and tender, a child's devotion to a beloved parent.

"My Uncle Vanya," she gently shakes her head and laughs. "Your grandfather would be proud," she says, as she closes the door.

I assemble the team at the station house at 5:45 AM. Reassuring is my voice as I direct them. Confident are my decisions to place my people in the right spots around the buildings, but never so arrogant that I dismiss a better suggestion. We are willing to use Albert as bait because our real catch may be the Surfside Gardens killer. Just like doctors, we make life and death decisions. Everyone knows his assignment. Jimmy provides my backup. Lewis and Murphy patrol the key entrance points. Two former colleagues from the SWAT team, Carty and Graham, agree to participate. I assign them positions on the roofs of the buildings. EMS parks an ambulance one block away, in case we need emergency medical assistance. The uniforms stay in the background. We move stealthily into the projects on foot; each one of us stakes out his specific piece of ground. It's an operation reminiscent of the exercises I practiced endlessly during my Army days. At this moment, I am grateful to the US Army for my training.

I am packing armaments from my varied experiences: an Army pistol, a SWAT rifle, my police revolver, and a knife for hand-to-hand combat. Preparation is the key to success. A plan, a team to follow the plan and materiel sufficient to meet the unpredictable are required.

I am stationed at my post. I rest against the building, waiting for Albert's arrival and then the unknown. Jimmy is within my sights, diagonally across the courtyard hidden in the shrubs. No one is stirring. Perfect. Every ten minutes each member of the team radios me to confirm any activity or lack of.

The gulls sense danger and they stay away. I don't see a one. It's just us humans ready to kill each other that are here this early morning.

The minutes move slowly. I snack on the food my mother prepared as I wait. Like an owl scanning the ground for anything moving, I keep my eyes peeled looking for action. The slightest rustling of the leaves sets my heart racing. To prevent my legs from cramping, I shift the weight from my left one to my right one. I squat and flex my toes. I use the building as a prop remembering the skills I learned as a young ballet student in Petersburg. The concrete wall is my ballet support. I position my legs and bend my knees, slowly, concentrating and visualizing my goal, a captured Red Roy.

"The fat man is arriving," I hear on the radio. The uniforms have dropped him off, following the plan.

"Get ready," I tell the team as we synchronize our watches.

Our star witness waddles into the apartment complex pathway, ambling towards his building entrance. Undoubtedly, his mind is focused on breakfast.

Only two other people are walking in the courtyard and they are thankfully oblivious to our presence. The loiterers and idle youth who park themselves on the benches calling out obscenities to the ordinary folk are missing. It's too early for them to be stirring.

Albert ignores everyone. He steps with gusto towards his apartment, thinking about food. I can see his lips moving as he talks to himself probably about his breakfast menu.

Carty speaks from his position on the building's roof. "Red head at one o'clock."

"Get ready and don't wait for my personal OK." I remind him of the order.

Within a minute, we all see Red Roy approach the courtyard. His skin has an unnatural, whitish sheen. Could be our bad guy is an albino. My eyesight isn't sharp enough for me to look into his eyes to determine the color, but the man is a killer.

He calls out to Albert," Fat man," and Albert turns. I can't see Albert's face from my position but fear has paralyzed him. He doesn't move. He's too clumsy and massive to run and hide.

Before I actually see the gun, I am momentarily blinded by the sun's reflection on the metal object.

Nanoseconds count. I scream, "Po…lezce, stop."

Red Roy turns his head towards my voice and his gun goes off. I hear Albert cry out, but I don't look at him. I am in assault mode, my target, Red Roy. My rifle is pressing against the top of my shoulder; my finger is on the trigger and I charge like the Light Brigade in the poem. I run faster than I thought possible, wings take me as if an invisible angel is holding me above the ground. This is truly a race for life. With my index finger resting steadily on the release, my feet dash across the asphalt, my blurry shadow the only trace of my existence.

At the moment that I see Red Roy raise his arm, his revolver pointing towards me, I crash into him with the full force of my rifle. The action produces a swift reaction and throws him off his feet, his revolver flies into the air. But I can't stop myself hurling forward as my feet keep rushing onwards until I crash into Jimmy who braces himself as my shock absorber. I am a hockey player skating so fast that only the railing can cushion the power of my frontward movements.

Jimmy is pushed backwards by my frontal assault, but he remains standing, holding onto my arms.

"You could have gotten killed. Why didn't you just shoot the bastard?"

"No way, I wasn't in danger," I say with complete confidence. "My finger never left that trigger. If I thought he would get off a shot I would have fired. Besides," and I point to the building's roof. "Carty or Graham would have gotten the guy if they thought I was in trouble."

Jimmy shakes his head. "You like to live dangerously."

"Hey," I answer with a smirk. "Now I don't have IAB up my ass." Anytime a civilian is killed the Internal Affairs Bureau of the NYPD investigates.

On the ground, Red Roy is clutching his stomach. I must have caught him in his rib cage.

Murphy picks up the assailant's gun and places it in a baggie for evidence. It's possible forensics can trace this gun to other as yet unsolved crimes. Meanwhile the EMTs arrive with a stretcher.

Albert is crying, but more from shock and fright than a painful injury. The bullet only skinned his arm so the uniforms are searching for the stray bullet.

Red Roy is rolling on the ground shouting, "fucking, mother fuckers," to no one in particular while the ants crawl nearby. The scent of sweat also draws flies that hover over our supine assailant. A call is made for another stretcher. Murphy and Lewis stand over Red Roy laughing and kicking the souls of his sneakers. Helpless is how to describe his predicament, a killer reduced to a bad-mouthed, crying child.

"I'll check on our star witness," I tell the others as I walk towards Albert.

The EMT has him on a stretcher attending to his wound.

"Nothing but a superficial cut," says the EMT. He lets me observe him practice his skills at cleaning the spot where the bullet grazed Albert's beefy arm.

Albert watches the EMT attentively but then he notices me. "I got a boo-boo," he points with his other hand.

I slap Albert on the back. "You'll be fine. We'll send you to the hospital. They'll give you breakfast."

Albert quickly interrupts, "Breakfast. Yes, I got to have my breakfast. M...m...m."

I tell the EMT, "Take him to the hospital, we don't want him here." The EMT continues to apply the bandage and nods in agreement.

The black man that I met yesterday, wearing the Muslim cap, approaches me. I remain unruffled although neighborhood reactions to police activity are hard to judge. More people are milling around and the uniforms are keeping them away from the crime scene.

"You saved his life," and he points to Albert.

"No, I'm just doing my job," I cordially answer.

"No, you did more. I saw the whole thing from my window," and his finger points to a courtyard window.

His lips part and a smile emerges; he extends his hand. We shake and I childishly grin. Yes, this was for a job well done.

Another stretcher arrives and they roll the moaning and twisting Red Roy on to it. They're both headed to Coney Island Hospital's Emergency Room. We'll then arraign Albert on assault charges for his misadventures at Harbor House and drop the drug charges. Red Roy needs to be interrogated, preferably at the hospital while on morphine so we can get some interesting stories and maybe settle some unsolved crimes. He's worth so much more alive than dead.

Still carrying my rifle, I walk towards my fellow officers. Twenty police form two straight rows at the mouth of the courtyard.

"Hero of Harbor House, Perlov the Protector," I hear the mantra. My colleagues raise their arms, fists held high as they continue shouting, "Hero of Harbor House, Perlov the Protector." It is the new station house cheer.

At the front of the rows, I see the Lieutenant wearing his best blues and smiling broadly. He grabs me by the shoulders and shakes my hand. "Perlov, good job. We got arrests. Murder cases solved." Then he turns to the rest of the assembled, "Good work, all of you. The streets are a little safer because of your actions." He repeatedly shakes his head completely satisfied, his head bouncing up and down. He has an unusual way of pressing his lips tightly together when he's pleased, as if he were blotting his lipstick.

"Perlov," he almost whispers, "I expect you at my house for the Bar-B-Q. Doing a great job this morning is not an excuse for not showing up later."

I laugh, "I wouldn't disappoint your wife."

He gives me another slap, only harder, but the action is well intended; he's like a happy, rambunctious child. The station's murder statistics have immediately improved and the brass on Park Row will be very happy.

I meet up with Jimmy.

"So Hero of Harbor House, Perlov the Protector, we got several brownie points today." He beams a radiant toothy smile because we all know this is a team effort.

"Don't worry about the Bar-B-Q," he says. "This whole operation will erase any ill will about your date. The guys love a winning display of police power," Jimmy announces with total self-assurance.

"You bet," I quickly answer.

As I make my way back to the station house I see Carty and Graham.

"Thanks" I respond.

They are both beaming. "You looked like you were charging up San Juan Hill," Carty laughs and as a former decorated Marine from the Persian Gulf War, I take his comment as a compliment.

"We had that freak Red Roy in our sights continually. No way would we let you get hit. Hey, you think we want to make you a wounded hero?"

With tightly closed fists, we slam each other as if our fists were beer steins.

"The next round is on me."

"Go get them, Perlov the Protector." The two snicker like mischievous kids with a secret to hide. They will spend the next hour taking apart and cleaning their rifles. I don't miss the SWAT team for a moment.

After I complete some paperwork on the case, I have the rest of my day free except for my short appearance before the press. Of course, later there's my commitment to the Lieutenant's shindig. At this moment nothing can hurt me or dampen my passion for this job. Schmoozing with the brass seems a small price to pay to keep my father and Jimmy happy.

The Lieutenant's wife was fond of me. I heard that from Jimmy after the last Christmas party. I impressed her with my table manners. She liked the way I used a knife and a fork, especially how I cut my food in the European style.

I get constant ribbing by my station buddies about my elegant habits of rising when a woman enters a room, and always holding the doors for my female colleagues. There are always one or two female officers who protest my door handling technique but only initially. Eventually, they come to accept that these are entrenched habits from the old country and not gamesmanship.

"See you on the Island," Jimmy says, as we leave together after the press departs.

I didn't utter a sound before the local TV stations' cameras. The department press officer arrived late declaring, "The traffic was impossible. Everyone must be coming to the beach," so the Lieutenant handled all the questions. Despite the heat the Lieutenant's neatly pressed uniform remained unwrinkled. He was at his smiling, self-confident best. The press reaction was muted; we all knew that another equally evil bad boy will quickly replace Red Roy.

I arrive promptly at Roberta's apartment in Park Slope at noon. She lives in a lovely, century old brownstone. I have never been here but I am impressed with how she lives. The dull, natural colors of the building's front wall contrast sharply and magnificently with the brilliant flowers sitting contentedly in their pots by the front door. As I walk up the steps, I am drawn to the flowers' beauty and bend down to smell the fragrances.

I ring the outside bell and I hear her voice call out, "Yes."

"It's me, Sasha," I tell her.

"Second floor," she replies. Even police officers are cautious in answering their doors.

She is waiting for me by her front door.

"You look lovely," I say in total sincerity because she is stylishly dressed in denim and leather. Her white sandals are a welcome departure from our typical sturdy police shoes.

I hand her a wrapped package, which she immediately rips apart and opens. She almost collapses at her apartment doorway when she sees the Belgian chocolate.

"You certainly know how to make a great impression," she says and gives me a little peck on the cheek.

She doesn't invite me in and I don't ask. I see from the entranceway a golden-colored cat is lounging on a windowsill, contemptuous of humans. Roberta has in her left hand a colorfully wrapped gift, which I assume by its shape is a wine bottle.

On this gorgeous, blue-sky afternoon, we arrive at the Lieutenant's house at a decidedly New York hour—meaning we are stylishly one hour late. Every block in the development follows a convoluted path typical of suburban living so I have difficulty finding his house, but Roberta serves as my navigator. I have been here before but the path seems so illogical that it takes a great effort to find the precise location. Why can't suburban streets follow perfect right angles like they do in the city?

Lounging on the grass is a small band of partygoers drinking beer, smoking cigars and sitting outside our guest's house. The lawn is meticulously mowed, the edges perfectly aligned.

I see the guys eyeing Roberta, but she ignores their harsh stares and just smiles.

"Hi, guys," she says pleasantly. Roberta has been through this exercise before and she handles it with aplomb. It's at this moment that I realize how cruel most of my fellow officers are towards Roberta.

I spot Jimmy standing with old colleagues, guys he knows since his beginning days on the force. He gives me a slightly shrugged shoulder meaning my fellow officers accept my rationale for taking Roberta, but they do not approve. I walk over to Jimmy, put down my presents and give him a big, tight, Russian bear hug. His face lightens up and the frown lines on his forehead fade. I can't help myself; I got to do things my way.

Roberta and I ring the doorbell although the front door is open. The Lieutenant's wife greets us warmly. I hand her a colorful bouquet of red, yellow and orange colored, summer flowers. My mother insists that the flower stall on Brighton Beach Avenue around the corner from their house offers the freshest, most beautiful flowers for the best prices. As usual in these matters my mother is right. As a good, dutiful son I never tire of telling her when she is right. She doesn't like to hear if she is wrong.

I am a member of a select list of station house invitees; not everyone receives an invitation from the Lieutenant's wife. I'll be expecting one for her next Christmas dinner. She's probably thinking about who she knows that has an eligible daughter for such a polite, well-mannered young man. I won't burst her bubble yet and tell her my mother only lets me date Russian Jewish girls. It's possible, but not probable, that the Lieutenant's wife knows any Jews living in the middle of goyish Suffolk County.

After I gallantly hand her the flowers, I follow up with the candy. She is flustered and doesn't know how to thank me. Then I present my mother's goulash.

Her face is bright red, maybe it's embarrassment or the heat but more likely it's the wine. She has that fair, freckled Irish complexion. There's a little streak of redness in her cheeks, a result of broken capillaries usually a good sign of someone who likes their booze, straight up and frequently.

The Lieutenant's wife, whose name I actually forgot until Roberta said, "Nancy, it's so nice of you to invite us," as she offers the wine bottle. Poor Nancy has no hands left to accept our gifts.

We follow her to the kitchen. Nancy offers me a glass of vodka, and not any brand but good Russian vodka, which I graciously accept. Roberta requests a glass of red wine.

We do the obligatory shaking hands with all the people we

meet, inquiring about the children or the pets. Roberta samples all the food; just a tablespoon from each of the different bowls and dishes set out on a long table in the backyard. I am always careful what I eat out so I stick with the raw fruit and vegetables, nothing treife—forbidden—about these beautifully laid out appetizers. We both totally avoid all the salty, fatty snack food.

Nancy wants to please her guests and I can be a problem as she discovered at Christmas. I am not the typical male that she is accustomed to serving. I don't eat just any kind of food. I am picky in a very specific and unfamiliar way. Today at the Bar-B-Q she has Hebrew National hotdogs; the plastic packaging is left in a prominent position next to the grill to show me that the food is kosher. At Christmas, the main dish at the dinner party was roast pork—my favorite food to avoid. Jimmy had to explain I eat only tuna fish on the outside.

At this summer party, the Lieutenant is grilling fresh tuna and he tells me, "This is just for you." He enjoys being an amicable host. Being able to read people, the unspoken words, to instinctively know how to please them is the critical factor responsible for his ascent into the highest levels of the police hierarchy; he's a born leader.

As I chat and make small talk with my colleagues, I realize I could be good at superficial nothingness. I know how to shmooz. After services at shul, I talk to all the other congregants; this is not a foreign activity for me. I should always listen to my father and years ago attend these events. The outsider making friendly gestures to become more accepted by the power brokers, I do understand.

Walking through the house after eating, I wander into the kitchen. Learning at an early age to be useful, I dazzle the ladies with my clean-up talents. I attempt to help Nancy rinse out the goulash dish but she shoos me away.

"Dick, he's such a helpful and polite young man," I overhear her tell her husband. "Doesn't Charlie have a daughter around 25 who teaches in Queens?"

The two hours pass pleasantly enough, but I'm ready to leave.

I see Roberta talking to one of the Lieutenant's sons who is also a NYPD cop in Queens.

I catch her eye as she puts down her wine glass. My head jerks sideward, pointing to the front of the house and she signals me with her pinky finger. We look for our hosts to thank them.

"Oh, please come back, anytime," Nancy says; and she is entirely genuine. She gives me a tiny, wet kiss on the cheek. I can smell the wine on her breath. The Lieutenant enthusiastically shakes our hands.

Stuck in heavy traffic on the Long Island Expressway, Roberta begins to relax in my presence. She slips her feet out of her sandals and closes her eyes.

"I'm so glad you agreed to come with me," she tells me.

"Hey, it was fun. You need company just to drive in this traffic." I could close my eyes and nod off since the car cannot move; we are totally stopped in the middle of a pack of idling cars filled with people returning from Long Island beaches or visiting with friends and relatives.

Peering ahead, I quickly glance at my traveling companion. Roberta and I could become friends; we share common interests. She graduated from Barnard College with honors with a major in English literature. She's the only one in the station house that admits listening to opera and discussing Russian literature. I can't say that I'm physically attracted to her but she's a nice enough looking woman, a little broad in the shoulders. I'm accustomed to seeing beauty among the peasant women of my neighborhood; round, strong shoulders are a sign of both physical and moral strength. Her hair is honey blonde owing more to the bleach bottle than nature alone given that her eyebrows are a few shades darker than her hair. With a name like Sullivan what can she be but Irish—a daughter and sister of NYC policemen who make their homes in Breezy Point on the tip of the Rockaway peninsula only a few miles across the bay from Brighton Beach. It's Breezy Point, Staten Island or leave the city completely behind. Even their beloved Staten Island is changing. We Russian Jews are moving in, upsetting the established order. We open our own restaurants; store signs suddenly appear in another language, grocery stores start stocking black bread. It's too threatening so most Irish cops move to Long Island just like our Lieutenant.

The ties between Roberta and I extend beyond our cultural tastes. We go to New York Law School at night—NYLS is what the banner says on the building in Tribeca where classes are held. We have similar future ambitions although in her family being a cop is a revered occupation, but she enjoys hearing my stories about the police in Soviet Russia.

We travel slowly towards the city with thousands of others. I turn off the air-conditioning and we open all the car's windows. A gentle breeze manages to cool the car.

Roberta knows about my past life as a lifeguard and surfer.

"You got to come to my parents' at Breezy Point so you can surf."

"That would be cool," I say and despite my frustration at driving in endless traffic the invitation immediately changes my disposition. I can visualize myself on the board, sliding easily across the tops of the waves, above the foam, with the sun baking on my back.

"Oh, yes I like that idea," I can't suppress my eagerness. "Yes," I repeat and the words sound insistent.

When we arrive at her brownstone, she turns to me, "Would you like to come up and have some coffee and meet my partner?"

Partner. I think I know what she means, but I must look confused.

"My girlfriend," she clarifies.

I smile, reach over and give her a little kiss on the cheek. "Another time, but I prefer tea and of course vodka."

"I'm not out of the closet at the station or with my parents, but I know that I can trust you," she announces.

I shake her hand firmly but gently. "I am a man of total discretion."

After driving Roberta home, I returned to my parents' house with the empty platter; my mother looked very pleased with herself. I displayed the dish, showed it from every direction. It was completely empty. She was satisfied that her food had been well received, and therefore, my standing in the station house had improved.

I reported on my spying at the Lieutenant's house and the conversation between my superior and his wife.

"You have to nicely turn down any possible dates," my mother says to me while my amused father watches. "Unless she knows, heaven knows where, a nice Jewish Russian girl." My mother is pointing her thin finger at me, poking at my chest for emphasis.

My father is laughing quietly and shaking his head.

"Oh," she turns to me, "Vasily left you a note." My favorite neighborhood gangster is often a great informant; he knows everything going on in the neighborhood. My parents treat him kindly because the family ties are deep and long-standing.

Vasily and I attended school in Petersburg together, his family emigrated a few years later. His older brother Mikhail, the leader of the reputed Russian Mafia gang here in Brighton Beach was a soldier under my Uncle Alexei in Afghanistan. They both served in the Soviet Army unsuccessfully trying to tame the unruly Afghans. We doubt that the US and its Coalition will be any smarter, swifter or stronger than the armies of Mother Russia.

Mikhail returned to Petersburg after his military service to surface as a thriving entrepreneur able to take advantage of the new capitalist Russia while my Uncle Alexei was buried in some obscure grave in a barbarian country. My grandfather received Alexei's medals at a military ceremony, the generals proclaiming his was a great sacrifice, which was not in vain. It was not the Great Patriotic War but a stupid conflict. We all knew it was a lie but knowing that would not bring him back to life.

But for Mikhail the Soviet Army proved a great teacher and he left government service as an armaments expert and a master of guerrilla tactics. No criminal element or police department in America could ever match the brutality of the Afghans he encountered.

People talk although no one knows for certain where Mikhail gets his money. The local cops think it's the standard gangster operation—drugs and prostitution with a little extortion thrown in. I know it's not money from crimes of consenting adults. And he is not alone in his pursuit of outside business interests because his Brighton Beach Russian Mafia isn't the Bloods and Crips or some common Dominican gang. His Russian Mob is international in scope and operation spanning the globe searching for opportunities. There is not one Russian Mob in the New York area but several groups and while they know each other, unlike the Italian Mob, an integrated organization is not yet evolved.

Mikhail doesn't have mules running in the streets selling crack cocaine and pimping girls from the Ukraine on the sidewalks. His is a much more sophisticated enterprise. Even the Italian Mafia is moving away from violent shootings in getaway cars to running fraudulent telephone pyramid schemes to unsuspecting greedy investors.

My guess was that Mikhail made his first money while serving in Afghanistan, buying pure heroin from the local subsistence farmers. Using this as seed money, his next step was arms trading. Decidedly more lucrative and less personally dangerous, arms trading had a certain panache. Not all arms trading was illegal although it was always risky to sell sophisticated, expensive guns and rockets to gangs of rebels trying to overthrow a government.

Mikhail, the soldier and adventurer, didn't start out as an underworld kingpin, but the money was good and the risks limited. My Uncle Alexei saw what was going on but concentrated his efforts on taming the Mujahedeen, which the US government at the time was supporting. Unpredictable consequences resulted and the Mujahedeen morphed into the Taliban. Our friends become our enemies.

I read Vasily's note to meet him at the St. Petersburg Café that evening for dinner and drinks. I'm not hungry but I can't refuse an old friend. I would not think of telling Jimmy about my excursions with Vasily. He knows that I know these people just as there are Italian cops who know Italian gangsters. If you grow up in the same neighborhood with people, you can't help it if they turn to a different way of earning a living.

Vasily is a regular presence and a favored client of the Café so I am expected by the maitre-d' when I open the front door. The room is stylishly dark and I am ushered into a private room towards the back of the building. It's not quite like dining in a fancy restaurant in the new capitalist Petersburg, but it's the best there is in Brighton Beach. A bottle of vodka is sitting on the table. Vasily pours me a glass. We nibble on dense black bread.

"Have you concluded the case of the dead fat guy?" Vasily keeps track of all the comings and goings of the neighborhood.

"What do you know about the widow?" Since I last saw him in front of the Feinstein house, he's probably been checking his sources.

"Olga," he says her name so sweetly. Does he know her in an intimate way?

"Olga," I repeat like a parrot on view in the pet shop.

"Not Russian—Ukrainian," he says, between tiny sips of vodka. My father was right.

"Should she be a merry widow?" I crack a smile and watch for his reaction.

"She needed a green card and he was available. I don't think she'll be heartbroken because he's gone. But she is certainly not going to be a rich widow outside of now owning the house." Vasily has friends in public offices across the city.

"Did she ever work for you or someone you know?" What I'm really asking is, did she originally come here as a prostitute?

"She worked as a waitress, she's an educated girl," Vasily quickly answers. He frowns with annoyance at my assuming the worst.

He continues, "She's not one of those desperate, starving waifs who come to America from the Ukraine." I know the type that he is describing.

"She is just seeking a lucky break. The fat man was her lucky break," he adds in defense of her character. His dark eyes stare intensely at me; we both spend most of our days with the underbelly of society.

The uniforms have called me to crime scenes where I have found young women left stranded, abandoned and left homeless on the streets. They don't speak English and my job was to translate. How did they manage to find themselves in such unseemly circumstances? Many turned out to be Russian or Ukrainian mail order brides. When the new husband was unhappy with his non-English speaking, uneducated wife who couldn't maneuver her away around a strange new culture, he literally abandoned her. We have found these women in hospital emergency rooms, Prospect Park, one even dumped in front of a police station. The American husband wanted to dispose of them as if they were kittens to be tossed away and forgotten.

For Vasily and his brother, prostitution requires too much handling. There are all those small bribes to pay, AIDS and diseases to worry about, and an emotionally damaged workforce of dependent women. Why waste your energies on small potatoes when you can be selling small arms, rocket launchers, or plutonium on the international market. The Ukraine is an open invitation to high-level arms looting. If there's an escalating mob war, it's between the Ukrainians and the Russians over the leftover armament spoils from the dying days of the Soviet Union. Not only are there arms to sell but also brilliant minds, scientists and engineers, willing to sell secrets for the right price.

"Your Russian Lady, Miss Olga, was not a player, not a mover and shaker, merely someone trying to get by in a big greedy world," says Vasily.

The waitress brings us bowls of borsht and sour cream. I ate a few hours ago but I can't resist good Russian food.

We make friendly conversation as we sip our drinks. We have

a lifetime of common memories and shared landmarks.

"Hero of Harbor House, Perlov the Protector, that's what I hear they are calling you. It's good that you help those old people. Why should it only be your mother who saves the community?" Vasily has an enchanting smile, which he puts on to charm people. "I send all the old bubbes to your mother when they complain about Social Security or Medicare." He laughs.

Vasily and I are cut from the same cloth. He's taller but we are dark, thin and very Russian looking. You know that immediately when you see us. We could be brothers. You can't call us lanky; that belongs to the likes of American actors such as Gary Cooper and Jimmy Stewart. Lanky means thin and tall but with rounded surfaces and smooth cheekbones. Vasily and I are sharp edges; there are no smooth rounded patches of skin on our faces or arms, rather our features are composed of jagged angles. Our elbows and kneecaps are pointy and potential weapons if accidentally you happen to be jabbed by an errant elbow or caught in the shoulder blade by a kneecap. Our arms move in 90-degree angles rather than 360-degree circles. It's not that there's hardness in the pit of our souls, but rather like the wary wolf guarding the den we move cautiously, measuring our steps, watching for sudden changes in the air.

We ravenously dig into our meal. Vasily looks up and says, "I read in the paper," the local Russian language daily, "About the upcoming celebration of the 60th anniversary of the Battle of Stalingrad." And I shake my head, family history.

"Hail to the Heroes," he says and we toast our glasses, filled to the top with clear-looking vodka.

Vasily knows all the community news. "Putin himself, the KGB man, your mother's enemy, will lead the ceremonies." Vasily smiles admiringly, reaches across the table, and slaps me lightly on the shoulder.

"But your grandfather will be honored despite your mother's past activities. He will always be considered a hero of Mother Russia with and without a Soviet Union," Vasily remarks.

I'm listening with amusement, cutting my fish delicately as

my mother has taught me and chewing my food before I speak, "There is a national movement to rename the city Stalingrad again in honor of all those who died."

"Russians know how to suffer—Americans are such pussies. They go through 9/11 and think they are experiencing suffering," Vasily says in a reproachful and disdainful voice that echoes the sentiments of most Russians.

"We know how to spill blood and guts in a big way." I'm smiling, proud of a heritage that refused to surrender.

"To the Motherland," Vasily adds and our glasses make a clinking sound.

"Another toast," he fills my glass.

"To your Uncle Alexei who fought to save Russia from the savage Afghans."

I nod and loudly tap my glass against his.

"To your lucky ass, who got out of the Army just in time so you wouldn't become another number lost to the cesspool called Afghanistan," Vasily adds.

I drink heartily to that repose.

"I could have been in Iraq," I add.

"God has another purpose for you," he says as he motions to the waitress and she brings our tea.

"I have interesting information for you," Vasily tells me as he pushes the sugar bowl close to my hand.

"Yes," I take a sugar cube and place it in my mouth, on my tongue. I let the sweetness of the sugar absorb the hot tea as I drink from my glass.

"I have some news that may be helpful to your investigation of the fat man. You are looking for a boyfriend?"

It amazes me that he knows so much about what's going on.

"Masha, the tallest sister," Vasily talks and blows on his steaming glass of tea."She has a boyfriend, the pharmacy clerk at Gerstein's."

"A name?" I lean back against my chair, relaxing as if it was a Passover Seder and I was remembering that I was no longer a slave in Egypt.

"Vladimir Ratnov; he was a pharmacist back in Russia." Vasily doesn't smoke but he offers me a cigar. I'm not in the mood but it would be rude of me to refuse. I'm not a shnorrer, someone who takes greedily from others, so I can't just put it in my pocket and save it for later.

"And the third sister? Irina, what about her?" I ask and we both laugh.

"Yes, yes, Olga, Irina and Masha," Vasily is laughing so hard he is crying. We both read Chekhov's play together at school.

"These are smart girls," he adds. "Irina was a lawyer back in Kiev, now she studies to be a paralegal. Olga was an actress, a graduate of the School of Dramatic Arts and," he is still laughing, "Masha was an architect. Now she works for that pushy, heavy-set interior decorator with the overdone office off Coney Island Avenue." He laughs again and his whole face brightens up.

I smoke while he motions to the waitress. Here at the Café no money will change hands.

"You want something to take to your mother?" A nice gesture although my mother is not one to request a doggie bag.

"Maybe something sweet for my parents." And the waitress goes back to the kitchen.

Dinner is finished and we both stand to leave. He slaps me gently on the back and we embrace man-to-man, Russian style.

CHAPTER 6

I stroll into the station house and loudly shout my hellos to the desk sergeant whose eyes never leave his newspaper. He just waves to a familiar voice. My feet have wings and so I rapidly climb the steps, conquering two at a time. Business is waiting for Jimmy and me. Albert's arraignment is today, but I don't have to attend; and the information about my Russian Lady continues to trickle in, slowly, but from solid sources.

Taking a critical eye at my workplace ambience, it's OK. Our shabby offices have a nice lived-in feeling. Who cares if the paint is lead-based and peeling? The room cries out for a make-over, but police work doesn't stop because the amenities are lacking. The detective offices are located closest to the bathrooms, a sign of status in the squad room.

Jimmy is standing and reading reports. He is waiting for the drip coffee machine to complete its appointed task so he can grab the first cup. He might as well be watching water boil.

The phone rings and I answer. The desk sergeant tells me, "I got a Mrs. Holmes here, wants to see you."

I look at Jimmy, "Mrs. Holmes, name mean anything to you?"

He shakes his head, "Holmes, no. Certainly doesn't sound Russian, not one of your people."

an you ask her why she's here," I tell the sergeant.

hear mumbles and incoherent sounds in the phone receiver, and then he answers, "Albert Speer's grandmother."

"It's Albert's grandmother wants to see me," I tell Jimmy.

His head nods and he sucks in the humid air before he speaks, "Be careful, these grandmothers can be dangerous. I would have her searched."

I shake my head, "Come on," but Jimmy has experiences with irate relatives. I speak into the phone, "Sarge is she looking angry? Could she be carrying a weapon?"

He directs her to take a seat and returns to the phone, "Who knows. I doubt it. But, we'll search her purse. However," his voice deepens for emphasis. "She's a big woman. I don't think she'll do well taking the steps and we can't trust that stupid elevator." We all know the quirks of our ancient elevator.

I tell him, "Send her to the first floor interrogation room and I'll be right down."

Jimmy grabs my arm as I begin to leave. "Take your gun."

I follow Jimmy's instruction. Careful, it never hurts to be cautious. It's true that innocent looking angels can turn out to be evil and the tough-talking punks we see on the streets can be softies that just need a shoulder to cry on or a willing ear to hear their stories.

Entering the stuffy room, I meet Mrs. Holmes and true to the sergeant's description she is a large, rotund woman of indeterminate age. Your body changes more than its shape when you get so hefty. The skin loses its elasticity; folds of flesh hide the underlying beauty and just moving becomes an ordeal.

"Mrs. Holmes," and I sit down on a chair across the table from her.

Her forehead is wet, large beads of sweat are congealing. She dabs her face with a tissue. I watch a droplet form and fall unceremoniously onto the table. I stare at the watery amorphous shape. The harsh ceiling lights add heat to the room making Mrs. Holmes more uncomfortable.

"Let me get the air-conditioner working," I don't want her to pass out from heat stroke, but getting the erratic machinery to function is always more a promise than a certainty.

She fans herself with a leaflet; I can't quite read it but it looks like one of those promotional pieces from the Jehovah Witnesses.

She has my attention as we sit across the metal table and the cool air begins to circulate in the enclosed space.

"I come here to thank you," she says, stopping her fanning so I know this is her central mission in visiting me.

I'm not sorry I brought my gun since there could be a 'but' to the statement.

"You save my boy's life." She stops moving and looks directly into my eyes, searching my soul.

My immediate reaction, "No, no, I'm just doing my job, to serve and protect. That's why we're here." Its standard police jargon although I do believe it.

"My boy be dead if not for you," she nods her head with renewed vigor; the air-conditioner is working. "You stopped Red Roy. He's a bad man, a bully."

I don't want to bust her bubble and let her in on our plans to use Albert to smoke out the real villain, Red Roy. I add, "Albert's been a bad boy and he keeps bad company."

She keeps nodding her head, "I knows. Yes, Lord Almighty, I knows. I try but," her head is still nodding in a hidden rhythm that she alone understands.

"Albert has to go to jail for awhile. He runs with the gangs. We caught him with drugs and a loaded gun." I wait for her response.

"I try, but his papa dead, the drugs got him. AIDS. He my boy, but I couldn't save him. His momma is in jail. Drugs. They kill. I know. What can I do?" She speaks in a steady beat, and then she stops rocking. She bends her head as if in prayer. No prayers to God will save Albert because his fate requires human intervention.

"You know that Albert has been assaulting old people from Harbor House, the senior housing project in Coney Island, right down the road from where you live."

Her eyes remain staring at the metal table. I sense defeat in her every fiber although she is not a person who gives in readily.

"Albert is a big boy and he could have really hurt those old, frail people who weren't doing anything to him."

"I know. He's a little slow. He don't always understand."

"He called those old people kikes and told me that they had money in their mattresses." I display no emotion; my voice is calm and steady. "He said that they didn't belong here. So it was OK to take their money. Is it OK to take their money because they're foreigners?"

She rubs her hands, turning them around and pulling at her hanging flesh while her eyes focus on her tired skin. Shame could be seen in her actions.

"Do you know that he alleged that you told him that these old Jews were foreign kikes with money in their mattresses?" I pause and continue. "Those are my people. I was born in Russia and I am a Jew." Our eyes briefly meet and then she looks down at the metal table. She couldn't face me.

"Mrs. Holmes don't you think we can all live together? There's room for all our differences?" I am trying to be reflective and not judgmental although it is a strain to act so relaxed.

"Hm...m...m. What do you say?" My voice is friendly and conciliatory.

She manages a small smile, just the crevices of her lips open. "Yes, you right. I told that boy the wrong things. I don't think he would do anything. I'm sorry."

I bend my head low so it would be difficult for her to avoid my face. "Mrs. Holmes, I have faith in you, you can save this boy. It's not too late. Listen to me."

She turns her head slightly. I have her attention.

"You got family in the country, in the South?" She just nods her head and her eyes look across the table at me.

"Albert is going to jail for a year and we'll segregate him from the other prisoners because he's a little slow." The real reason is we don't want him to be killed as an informer.

"I'll recommend he get some counseling to learn to control his outbursts. No more knocking down old people." I am making progress; she is looking directly at me.

"But when he's out of prison, he can't come back to the projects. If you want to save him send him South, away from the gangs here. He can start again." I speak in a serious but sympathetic tone; my hand resting under my chin, my elbow on the now-cold metal table.

"Have you ever read John Steinbeck's novel 'Of Mice and Men?' "

She shakes her head, "I don't read so good."

"You get one of your grandchildren to read it to you or see the movie. Because Lennie in the novel is a gentle giant with uncontrollable urges and the end is tragic. I don't think you want Albert to end up like the character Lennie, an unintentional murderer." I reach across the table and I take her hands in mine. We hold hands for a minute in silence. No one speaks, we are hardly breathing.

Then she speaks, "You a good man Detective Perlov. It was good I come to see you. I will do just like you say. Yes, I will," and slowly we let our fingers slip from the tight grip.

I help Mrs. Holmes to her feet and we depart, probably never to meet again.

"So how did it go?" Jimmy asks with curiosity when I return to the second floor.

"I'm still alive," I laugh. "She wanted to thank me for saving Fat Albert's life."

"You didn't mention the fact that our plan was to use him as bait?"

I slap him lightly on the back.

"The Lieutenant wants to see us," he tells me.

We walk briskly down to the Lieutenant's nicely painted office to get his OK before proceeding. We wind our way down the maze of closed offices belonging to the brass until we are standing in front of the Lieutenant's door.

Jimmy knocks softly.

"Enter" we hear, and we do.

As I am entering the Lieutenant's office, I button my suit jacket and smooth down a few stray hairs with my hand—a habit, like so much of human behavior.

"So what's with the dead guy in the house? Do we have a cause of death so we can close the case," he asks as he looks at our faces for signs of success or uncertainty. The Lieutenant is my kind of man. He looks you right in the eyes when he talks. No evasiveness, no eyes wandering all over the room or examining his nails or brushing off a few loose strands of hair from his shirt. No, the Lieutenant talks and shoots straight.

"Yes and no," Jimmy starts to explain.

"It's a heart attack, " I add, " but we still need to continue to investigate because we have some interesting little facts worth pursuing." The Lieutenant is listening but his face indicates impatience. "Is it a homicide?" If it is a homicide we could lose the case to other detectives. The brass assumes because a guy gets the title of Homicide Detective he knows, or lately, she knows, everything. We know plenty about solving cases and making convictions.

"No," Jimmy immediately says. He also doesn't want to lose the case to the two jerks sitting near us in the squad room; we would move from primary to 'other' and no ambitious cop like Jimmy wants a case where he's labeled 'other'.

"No, but she could be a green card bride so there's a few more angles we want to look into," I add.

Jimmy glances at me and says to the Lieutenant. "Give us just a few more days. We want to talk to Immigration and the guy's sister is coming in from California for the funeral." We don't mention the sex slave aspect either because we also don't want the Vice Squad involved.

My partner assures the Lieutenant that this is not going to be a major crime investigation.

"Okay, just a few more days," says our superior.

Jimmy chats about the great Bar-B-Q and what a great chef the Lieutenant is around the grill. "And the flowers were just beautiful. I wish I had taken a photo for my mother." Jimmy is animated while he speaks.

I get up to leave and Jimmy is following me when the Lieutenant says, "Perlov stay a minute."

Jimmy gives me a gentle punch in the stomach and a wink.

Now, I'm uneasy. As the object of the wrath of the Soviet bureaucracy, I did learn at an early age from my family that an individual worker always should feel apprehensive when his comrade is dismissed and he is left alone with his superior.

"Perlov," the Lieutenant adjusts his chair to find a more comfortable spot to rest his muscular frame. Then he turns his full attention to me sitting on the edge of my chair.

"I know about you and Roberta," he begins. I am mortified. Jimmy may be right. I have embarked on a seriously wrong-headed, rebellious stance by going to the party with Roberta. I feel the beads of sweat accumulating on my forehead. My neatly ironed shirt is beginning to stick to my armpits.

"Perlov, you are an honorable man." The Lieutenant's face is stern looking but I don't see any signs of reproach in his eyes. Nonetheless, my heart is beating rapidly while I wait for the full measure of his message.

"You know I have four children and all of them started as police officers. The boys are with NYPD." Actually, the Lieutenant had never told me anything about his family and they were rarely present at the parties that I attended at his house. I met the cop from Queens. I have observed photos on the credenza behind his desk. Each child looked similar to the other siblings with those bright blue eyes and freckled noses. Two boys must have grown up sufficiently to be photographed standing next to young women, probably their wives.

"My daughter Cathy joined the state police force after college." I don't remember being introduced to a daughter named Cathy.

"Cathy is a lesbian," he tells me but I don't react and wait for the Lieutenant to make his point.

"I understand what you are doing with Roberta. You have

guts Perlov. I admire a man with backbone. Maybe it's because you're also an outsider—you know, a Jew and a Russian." The Lieutenant displays a small chiseled smile on his face. There is pain in that smile.

"Cathy loved being on the force, serving the community," not Jimmy's reason or mine for joining the force. "But it was her fellow officers who drove her away with their cruel so-called practical jokes and nasty snide remarks. She would tell me stories that I wanted to take those guys and punch them out." I can imagine an infuriated Lieutenant trying to protect one of his babies.

"She wouldn't let me do anything. Wouldn't hear of it. She warned me to back away." He has failed as a father.

"So one day she quit. I don't want Roberta to quit." I wonder how much of this story Roberta knows but I would not inquire from the Lieutenant. If Roberta learns to trust me then she may share more of her story.

The Lieutenant leaned into his desk and stared into my dark eyes. "I have my eye on you, Perlov. The brass said you were trouble because you wanted out of the SWAT team, but I can understand how after awhile being asked to be a hired killer can be wearing on one's soul." I always suspected I was not one of the chosen ones in the eyes of the Deputy Commissioner.

"You're good; I have told them that you are someone to watch. The murders at the project very good, got the bastards and no real blood is spilled."

I can't suppress my grin.

"Perlov, you can be a pain in the ass with cases. You have to know exactly what happened. Actually that's good for the department. We have a tendency to want to put a quick fix on cases so you're here to remind me not to go too quickly. Time is necessary to analyze all the pieces." I could feel the warmth of his smile.

"Anyone in power loves a bootlicker, but a sensible person with good ideas is most valuable." I have to prevent myself from snickering; but I sit immobile and just watch his eyes. I think the reference is meant for Jimmy but there could be more than one in the precinct.

"You have a future Perlov. I know you are a man of discretion." The Lieutenant is finishing as he begins to reach for his phone.

"That's all," he says.

"Thank you sir," I rise from my seat and close the door behind me.

This day is going so splendidly, we even have time to return to the Case of the Russian Lady. We can pay a shiva call to the house of the grieving widow. It's only appropriate because it gives us time to meet the late Mr. Feinstein's sister who is arriving from California to attend the funeral. I learn from the funeral director at Weinstein's that the sister will remain in NYC for the traditional period of mourning.

"We have a shiva visit to make," I tell Jimmy. He prefers wakes held in funeral homes, which are more impersonal than visiting people in their homes. We don't expect any overly demonstrative appearances of grief, but death can bring out the unpredictable in people. Guilty parties can break down during these intense periods of grieving. If the guilty speak we want to be witnesses.

It's cloudy but still terribly hot and sticky. A typical triple "H" day: hot, hazy and humid, but I am wearing an appropriately dark, somber suit for the occasion. Jimmy doesn't own such an outfit. Our plan is to speak with the deceased's sister and if possible out of the hearing zone of the widow.

We pull up on the street several doors from the house. We don't want to make any obvious display of our presence. As I get out of the car, I spot an old woman, slightly hunchback, struggling to pull her large, plastic garbage bags to the curb for tomorrow morning's trash pick-up. I cannot help myself so I saunter over to her driveway.

"Can I help you?" I ask, bending down so she can see me.

I remember that the uniforms mentioned an elderly woman living across from the deceased. Even if her eyesight is not very good any more she is probably the neighborhood's eyes and ears.

She is the Neighborhood Watch.

"Who are you?" she asks.

I open my suit jacket and point to my badge pinned to my belt. "Detective Perlov."

She looks at the shiny metal object and eyes me with some suspicion. I know that look—it's not the exclusive purview of the new immigrant.

"We're just visiting the neighborhood." I move my head in the direction of the Feinstein house. "I understand the late Mr. Feinstein's sister is here." I don't wait for a response. "You know the Feinsteins?"

"Perlov," she looks into my face. "A Russian?" she asks.

I have the look and of course the accent hasn't disappeared. "Yes."

She searches my eyes. "A Jew?"

The top button of my shirt is open in this heat. I slip a finger under my loosened tie and under my tee shirt to pull out my gold Star of David.

She sees the object dangling around my neck and smiles reassured.

"You know Yiddish?"

I nod with appreciation.

You know the expression, "Gehokte leyber iz besser vi gehokte tsuris."

"Chopped liver is better than lots of chopped troubles." My father's mother had taught me Yiddish as a young child. Such a beautiful language, Yiddish; it embodied expressiveness and the frailties of mere mortals. So many words described our failings as human beings. The words communicated the fatalist mentality of one of Europe's most persecuted minorities. It was no accident that Yiddish, which looked like Hebrew and sounded like a guttural German belonged to the Jews of Eastern Europe. It was from knowing Yiddish that I became so easily fluent in German.

"The Russian people know tsuris, but they are pushy people," she tells me. I wait for her to finish; this is a common openly uttered complaint by other Jews. The goyim probably say much worse comments. "And clannish," she adds.

I have heard this before and she continues to speak in her accented voice. "I'm Hungarian and they say we're clannish."

She doesn't want to let go of this thread. "I go to the JCC and your people, chutzpah," she pokes me with one of her gnarled fingers in the middle of my chest, the highest point she can raise her arm. "Your people, always want to be first in the swimming pool, first to get on the bus, always," she adds the last word for emphasis, just in case I am somehow missing her message. "Chutzpdiker."

But I'm not annoyed. This nosy, little lady could prove to be invaluable to my investigation.

"Actually, you ask anyone in the neighborhood to be honest and they will tell you that we old people are grateful to have you Russians here. You don't know what it was like back 30 years ago with the colored taking over. I was sure we would be driven out. Now it's safe again because your people starting arriving in the 1970's and changed everything. For the better," she has a warm smile.

"Do you know the Feinsteins?" I want to lead her back to my purpose.

"I have lived here 50 years. My beloved Manny, may he rest in peace," she closes her eyes for an instant, "He bought this house after my youngest son, David was born." She sinks back into her memories of long, lost days. "Sol and Sylvia moved into their house later that year."

I need to know who are Sol and Sylvia. I have this confounded look on my communicative Russian face so she says, "Jacob and Susan's parents." Maybe Jack is Jacob.

It may be obvious but I must ask to be certain. "And Jacob is our late Mr. Jack Feinstein?"

She nods, "He was such a nebbish as a child and he turned into a farbissener," which means a bitter, vengeful and hurtful man.

"Jacob, now he's big and fat. What a mess he became not that we ever thought he would grow up to become a rocket scientist. A goyisher kop." I know that the expression translates loosely into English as a 'gentile's brain'; but it really is an insult for any Jew's intelligence to be compared to that of a gentile.

"But in the last few years he got awful. First Sylvia dies and then his lovely wife Irene, all within a few months. Such a tragedy—you shouldn't know from it." She cringes; her face turns into a tight little ball.

"His sister Susan, now that's a different story. She and my Gloria were always good friends—last summer Gloria, my son-in-law Max and my beautiful grandchildren visited Susan and her family in Los Angeles. We're practically mishpocheh." I am afraid we will be standing in her driveway for an hour as she elaborates on the intertwined family histories. I have to parse out what is relevant and important to the case.

"Jacob was in the Army. Vietnam. Were you in the Army?"

I nod. "Yes, US Army stationed in Germany."

"My Manny was in the Army during the war. Such terrible things he saw. He actually was one of the guys who liberated the death camps. During the war, he met Russian Army soldiers, even a few Jews. Tough people you Russians. The Russian soldier didn't speak English and my Manny didn't speak Russian but they talked in Yiddish about the fighting on the Eastern Front." She sighs deeply; hundreds of years of history rest in that hushed moan.

She continues without hesitation. "My Manny and I owned concession stands on the Boardwalk," waving her hand towards the beachfront only a few blocks from Brighton Beach. "Not here, we didn't want our customers visiting us in our home. In Rockaway, we owned a knish and hotdog place and a miniature golf course."

I raise my eyebrows, "Um. I know Rockaway I used to be a life guard there."

"We had our place on Beach 33rd Street, but that was years ago. What's happened to the Rockaways. It's the city's fault bringing in the colored and the welfare. What a disgrace." She is shaking her head and muttering something I cannot hear.

"What about lately? What's with the new Mrs. Feinstein?" I inject my questions once again.

"She's a shiksa, but a nice girl. I don't think she's really a Russian, probably Ukrainian and they are real Jew haters, but she's different. She helps me take out the garbage." She stares down at her plastic garbage bags.

"I remember how lazy Jacob was even as a boy. His father was a hard working cab driver up at four in the morning working fourteen-hour days to put food on the table and send him to college. And Jacob was a zhlub. I can still hear him dragging those metal garbage pails down the driveway. The sound those pails made as the metal scrapped against the concrete. He woke all the dogs in the neighborhood." She shakes her head in absolute disgust. "In those days, we didn't have rat problems because we had those metal pails, nothing could get in, but those lazy sanitation workers didn't want to pick up the cans."

"Do you know whether the current Mrs. Feinstein was home the afternoon he died?" I try to get her thinking about my issues but I speak in an unruffled tone of voice.

She looks me in the eye with unease. "What are you asking?"

"I just wanted to know if she was out of the house that afternoon. Did you see her leave?" I ask self-effacingly.

I can feel that she is ill at ease talking although I am trying to make her comfortable telling me things she might hesitate to divulge to a cop. She likes the blonde girl and is not fond of the dead man. She can't avoid talking, she loves an audience to talk to and I am her man for the moment. Now if she would just tell about that afternoon.

I wait patiently for her response. "The four of them left around noon," she says. The four of them, I'm thinking; but I don't want to interrupt her immediately.

"I thought they were going out for lunch. Jacob rarely went out for lunch. The only thing he ever did regularly was go to those concerts in the Bandshell. He would wait for hours on line even in the rain to see those concerts."

Then she glares at me. "I've seen enough cop shows on the TV. You don't think she had anything to do with his death?" she responds with anger.

I disregard her tone of voice and ask in a soft voice, "Four people?"

She can't help talking. "The three sisters and the tallest one's boyfriend, the boy from the drug store."

She gives me a zetz in the arm. "He had a heart condition. You shouldn't be thinking anything else."

Now I do have a dilemma because the timing makes it only possible, certainly not definitive that she and the others are present as he is dying. The coroner can't pinpoint an exact time of death.

"Were they gone long?" I have her eager to convince me that I shouldn't be thinking in a malevolent way.

"They were gone for awhile. They must have been shopping because they came back with bags. Then a few minutes later I hear sirens and there's police and an ambulance."

"Did the boyfriend come around a lot?"

"They're all pretty girls, they should have boyfriends. You shouldn't be thinking anything bad happened."

"Do you know how Olga met Jack?" I use her given name.

"She was a waitress on Brighton Beach Avenue. He was lonely and she needed a green card. It served everyone's purpose."

"Did they live like a married couple?" I ask, and she immediately understands where I am heading because marriage carries certain obligations and responsibilities.

She wiggles her deformed finger in my direction. Her arm can't reach to my face. "You have a dirty mind. Nu. Did I look in their bedroom windows with binoculars?"

I look at her innocently. "You know how people act with each other when they're close. Were they happy together? Did they hold hands? That's all I'm asking." I have on my good boy, cherubic look.

"She was probably a good shtup, but not a kekaivch." These are good Yiddish words for the act of fornicating and a whore. "He wanted something in return," she replies but her anger subsidies.

She repeats her earlier statement. "They were out all afternoon."

"Thanks very much," I give her one of my cards. "If you remember anything interesting please call me."

"You live in the neighborhood?" she asks.

"My parents do, off Brighton Beach Avenue closer to Ocean Parkway. It's where I grew up."

"Do they go to one of the shul's here?"

"Yes, the little one on Brighton Beach Avenue."

She looks me over from head to foot. I can see that I have her approval. She knows that I'm doing my job so if she thinks of something she will call me.

I smile and wave as I walk across the street to the Feinstein house.

Jimmy is already inside the house. Earlier as we are leaving the car, I place a yarmulke on top of his shaygets blonde hair with those flirtatious baby blues. The door is open all day and most of the evening so anyone can walk in and share in the mourners' grief. I walk in. No one asks who I am or why I am standing in the living room.

The widow is sitting on the couch her two sisters surrounding her. Another woman is sitting on a small wooden seat; I assume this is the deceased man's sister. In keeping with Jewish custom, the immediate family of the deceased sits on a hard, simple seat to welcome visitors. Our widow is clearly not a Jewess. She may be in mourning but she is not sitting on a shiva box. I spot Jimmy talking to a casually but well dressed, tanned man leaning against the dining room wall munching pretzels. Jimmy's eyes tell me to approach.

"Let me introduce you to my partner, Detective Perlov," Jimmy turns his body from me to the man leaning against the wall. "This is Mr. Lenny Stein, the brother-in-law of the deceased."

The man grips my hand firmly as we shake.

"Unexpected," I ask the man, "Mr. Feinstein's death?"

"A heart attack waiting to happen," he answers and shakes his head with revulsion. Here is a tan, athletic man who probably plays tennis or golf, maybe he works out every day at a gym, talking about a man whose only outside activity was attending concerts at the Brighton Beach Bandshell on Thursday evenings during the summer.

"When was the last time you saw him alive?" I hope I'm not repeating Jimmy's questions.

"As I was telling your partner," he says without any annoyance about the repetition. "Jack visited us last winter for a few days. He actually looked better than I've seen him look in years." He pauses and a mischievous grin appears on his face.

"It must be the new wife. A real looker," he chuckles and we all smile the good voyeurs that we are wondering about the two of them together.

"Did your sister approve of the marriage?" I ask while Jimmy is staring at me, so I know this is a question he wants to ask Mr. Stein.

"What can she say? We're 3,000 miles away and he's over 21 so he makes his own decisions." He raises both of his hands in the air for emphasis.

"Was it love at first sight?" I ask the man as his eyes drift towards the widow sitting motionlessly on the couch, attentive to his wife's talking. She does not see us or she pretends not to notice us.

"My guess, as much as a zhlub that he was, he wasn't a total schmegegge. He knew she wanted a green card and she must have known there was some price to pay." Mr. Stein has the markings of a deal maker. A man who handles situations, solves problems, gets things done for a price. Everything has a price.

He turns towards Jimmy who had been staring at the widow, who is now conversing with her sister-in-law. Her eyes are resting on Mrs. Stein's face, but I can see that out of one corner of her eye she catches the three of us talking. If she is nervous about our interviewing her brother-in-law there's no indication. She just keeps talking and then waiting her turn to speak.

"Of what interest is this to the police? You don't think she's responsible for his death?" Mr. Stein asks.

We have bubkis for a case, but Jimmy acts cool. "It appears that Mr. Feinstein died in the house alone so each case like this needs some kind of investigation." It's a good fib, not an accurate picture of police procedure. Jimmy can lie well and he knows how to talk on his feet—keep the suspects guessing how much we know.

I get out one of my cards."If you think of anything interesting give me a call." He accepts the card and returns the favor and hands me one of his gold embossed cards—venture capitalist, a true American phenomenon.

We want to interview the sister, but we can't appear too aggressive while she is sitting shiva. We're not looking for a police complaint. However, she is due to depart soon and return to her home in California; and there would be no way we could justify or convince our superiors to let us fly out to California to interview her. I walk into the kitchen hoping to waste some time and maybe catch the sister on her way to the bathroom. Jimmy walks towards the back of the house.

"You a friend of the widow?" a small woman eating a deli sandwich asks me. I can't be certain what kind of meat she has on her plate—maybe corned beef or it could be pastrami.

I spy beef tongue on the platter. She must see me start to salivate. "You want a sandwich?" she talks with her mouth full of food, specks of meat dangling from her upper teeth.

"I know the widow, yes," I answer as she points me to the bread and mustard. I assume it's Kosher, who else eats beef tongue?

"You a Russian?" she speaks before swallowing.

"Um," I nod as I take that first bite of delight.

"Are there other Russian friends here?" I ask knowing that her antennae can quickly pick out any of my fellow countrymen among the visitors.

"Her sisters," and she gestures with her hand as if she were patting a big dog. "Sisters, they don't even look alike. They're blonde. They look like Polacks to me."

She gets up close to me. "You, you are a Russian with Jewish blood," she points at my nose. I don't think she is complimenting me but I don't feel offended.

"How's the widow taking all this?" I finish chewing and swallow before I talk. My mother would hold down my jaw with her hand if I ever speak with food in my mouth.

"Jack was such a zhlup. After his mother died and then his wife. This one," and she points to the doorway leading to the living room. "She just wanted a green card. There's no money here. This house," she looks around the 1950's-style kitchen. "This house hasn't been maintained since Sol died. God knows maybe ten years ago." She looks at the food on the counter as if distracted by such an opulent display.

She returns her attention to me. "Sylvia and Sol they should rest in peace. And poor Irene." She nods between wiping her mouth with a plush, expensive paper napkin. The napkin even folded is twice as large as the old woman's face. The wrinkles of age and history are etched on her immigrant face.

"Are you a relative of Jack's?" I ask her as I finish my sandwich and although I am tempted to take another I feel a little guilty about being a shnorrer at this house.

The woman takes a good look at me. "You ask a lot of questions. Who are you?"

I'm caught and I don't lie as well as my partner Jimmy. "Detective Perlov," and I show her my badge attached to my belt.

She's short enough that the badge is easy for her to see. She stares intently at the metal object. "A cop, what are you doing here?" she looks at me with surprise but not suspicion.

"Poor Mr. Feinstein died here alone so we always investigate." I'll try Jimmy's story.

She gives me a harsh stare; she doesn't believe me.

As I am attempting to make up a more convincing story, Jimmy walks in with Mrs. Stein.

"Mrs. Gerstein." The old woman puts her skinny arms around Susan Stein. My presence is no longer important. A few moments later Lenny Stein strolls into the kitchen.

"Mrs. Gerstein," and he gives her a hug.

Gerstein, the drug store is named Gerstein, must be the widow of the original pharmacist. I know from living in the neighborhood that a man in his late 50's currently runs the store, probably a son.

"Detective Perlov," and Mrs. Stein extends her hand and we shake. Mrs. Gerstein is secure in my presence if our hostess is extending a sign of acknowledgement.

Within a few minutes, Jimmy and I are alone with the couple. Mrs. Gerstein finds someone else she knows and they start talking, wandering into another room. We all gravitate towards the kitchen table and sit down.

"Detective Sutton has explained why you're both here, the formalities of finding a dead body in the house," the deceased's sister says. Jimmy weaves a good story.

"My brother had a big heart, that's why he welcomed Olga and then her sisters."

Jimmy and I watch her gesturing about her brother's good intentions. Mr. Stein gently squeezes her hand.

"The Immigration was not satisfied with them just marrying at City Hall. He said they were calling him, telling them to go to Federal Plaza and meet an Inspector to discuss the marriage. So they recently had a church wedding here in Brooklyn. No one was invited so I don't know much about the specifics," she adds. Her husband puts his arm around her shoulders.

"Do you know what the widow will do now?" I inquire.

She shakes her head and laughs. "We are not close, but I don't think she really knows."

"Did she mention returning to Europe?"

"I doubt it." She looks at my inquisitive face and says, "You should ask her these questions." She's right.

We offer our condolences and we start walking towards the front door. But I stop. I walk into the living room where the widow is talking to one of her sisters. I stand in front of them. I bend my head and say. "Our condolences," pointing to my partner. Jimmy gives a toothy smile. "Perhaps when your period of mourning is over you can all come by the station house. We just have a few questions." I spot the boyfriend from the drug store. "Maybe your friend, who I understand was with you the day your husband died could also come by."

She doesn't answer, but Irina does, "We'll be there."

CHAPTER 7

It's the middle of my investigation, the clues are slowly coming together but an important family event supersedes all my work. An obligation must be fulfilled; my presence is required elsewhere for a few days. Mother Russia calls its faithful to return to celebrate the bravery and courage of its citizens.

In this modern world, the immigrant can truly stand in two worlds. The old country is not that far away, planes take you back in 10 hours. Emotionally, viscerally, my mother has never entirely left Russia. She is after all a survivor of the Battle of Stalingrad and the daughter of the hero of that historic battle.

My mother had gotten a personal invitation signed by President Putin to attend the 60th anniversary commemorating the defeat of the Nazis at the Battle of Stalingrad. My mother, the Soviet dissident, was reluctant to return for an official purpose, but she had received a personal invitation. Could she disregard the government's belated grand efforts to honor my grandfather, the Hero of the Battle of Stalingrad? She couldn't simply toss it in the trash so she tried to hide it in a spot where it would be forgotten until it was too late. My father knew her tricks and retrieved it. For days they stared at the invitation. It was a very official looking document, celebratory in its appearance with the gold border and fine black lettering.

With the time approaching, my father just bought three tickets without discussing it further with my mother. He had hoped that my Uncle Boris would fly from Berlin to join us, but my uncle was stubbornly anti-officialdom.

The presence of a family member was required. We all owed it to my grandfather and his large role in that momentous piece of Russian history. One million Nazi soldiers under General von Paulus faced one million Russian soldiers under the command of Field Marshal Zhukov. What a battle. Historians later reported that more than 200,000 soldiers were wounded or died, and three-quarters of a million civilians were killed including my mother's mother and her baby brother.

My grandfather, Dmetri Aronovich, became a hero of the Battle of Stalingrad by chance. He rose to the rank of Colonel because he was still alive in 1942. Stalin, the crazed, ruthless, paranoid autocrat had managed to kill off hundreds of his officers in the 1930's, always fearful that they would rise up against him.

His job as civilian administrator was a task for a Solomon because the Red Army and the German Army were fighting hand-to-hand combat in the streets of Stalingrad in the middle of a typical bitterly cold Russian winter. My grandfather managed to keep the population from starving despite the fact that it wasn't possible for food to be trucked into the city. Then there was the problem of the civilian population freezing to death as the Nazi Army pummeled the buildings, the electrical lines and the power plants.

In the morning, the Nazi Army rolled into the streets and captured sections of the city. During the night, the Russian Army aided by the civilian population retook those same streets. This continued for months. Hitler ordered General von Paulus never to surrender. Eventually, the Russian Army surrounded the German Army and began to squeeze the enemy into a smaller and smaller circle inside the city and the Germans surrendered.

Some 90,000 German soldiers were taken prisoner, and rightfully feared for their lives since word had spread across the eastern front that the Nazis had murdered millions of Russian prisoners of war. After the war, Russian historians, later verified by outside scholars, reported that the Nazis had murdered more than three million Russian POWs. The Nazis learned how to organize the gassing of the Jewish inmates at the infamous concentration camps in Poland and Czechoslovakia by experimenting with mobile gas vans using Russian POWs as their first test subjects. Jewish Russian POWs were most at risk of immediate extinction and there were hundreds of thousands of Jewish Red Army soldiers on the battlefront.

The authorities would not attempt to hold an anniversary celebration during a frigid, cold Russian winter although the battle was fought in the bitter weather. So they postponed the celebration until the ground was soft and small buds on the trees could make an appearance. There we were, the three immigrants, back to the blood stained fields for the 60th anniversary of the Battle of Stalingrad, the defining moment of my family's recent history.

And Vladimir Putin was at the front of the line of dignitaries, smiling and shaking hands with the veterans and survivors of that ghastly battle. Most people defined battles by hours maybe days. Not Europeans. We created battles that last years. Only the last great European land war engulfed millions of civilians as well as armies in battles. No, of course, I was not there; but it was an intimate part of my personal history. My mother was only a small child but the death and destruction permeated her very being. Sixty years later and she remembered that monstrous time when the ground shook from the huge guns firing inside and outside the city. The Battle was a part of me as surely as the skin that covered my body or the muscles that gave strength to my form.

Stalingrad was never a beautiful city, not a St. Petersburg where I grew up or a Moscow, the center of the Soviet Union. It was a vital city to the Red Army and the survival of all the Russian people depended upon our Army defeating the Nazis at that moment in history.

You no longer can find its name on a map. It existed as a metaphor for the sacrifice of a nation during a war that destroyed all boundaries between military and civilian life. One of the first things Khrushchev did when he assumed his dictatorial reign was to de-Stalinize the Soviet Union. He began by renaming Stalingrad, Volgograd.

When we visited for the 60th anniversary there were veterans and nationalists promoting the idea of reverting back to the name Stalingrad. Never the original name, the city lived with that name only 25 years. Stalin himself had it named in his honor during the grip of his rule in the 1920's. It was why Hitler wanted to occupy and destroy its inhabitants. There were the oil fields in the Caucasus and the city stood as the gateway to those rich resources, but actually that was only of importance to Hitler's generals and ministers. Hitler wanted it destroyed and occupied because it bore the name of his rival for ultimate and absolute rule of the European world.

And here we were visitors to the country of our birth. Strange and surreal it felt as we came to bear witness and rejoice in the sacrifices of so many others. The new democracy called Russia had much to learn from America and its supreme ruler was at the helm of the ceremonies.

Putin stepped forward to place the wreath on the tomb of the Unknown Soldier and my mother stood at his left side. Another survivor of that infamous battle stood unsteadily on the right. Old and wrinkled, it was his patriotic duty to be present at this anniversary because rapidly they were dying out. Soon there would be no survivors, only historians to write about the battle.

Those months had sucked the life out of my mother's mother. Too weak from her initial injuries during the opening Nazi bombardment, coupled with a lack of food and proper shelter, she succumbed to an eerie stillness one night. My mother's baby brother was totally defenseless against the elements, without mother's milk and a warm body to cover his fragile little frame, and so too did he seek relief in death. My grandfather the Hero was able to save only his two older children—my mother Anna and her older brother Alexei.

Tears slowly rolled down my mother's face as she assisted Putin in placing the flowered wreath upon the cold granite statue. It was only fitting that the tomb should be solid and stoic as were the people who fought and died on the streets of the city during those horrific months. It was a lifetime of sacrifice compressed into less than a year; for hundreds of thousands of soldiers from both sides of the war as well as civilian women, children and men—it was their graveyard. Most had to wait until the frozen ground had softened so they could be buried.

My mother introduced me to President Putin.

"My only son Fyodor Ilich Perlov," was what she said to the Russian President. It was my real name but when I came to file papers for US citizenship, I chose my nickname Sasha. In America, you can re-invent yourself, so in my new country I called myself Sasha. To all my American friends and colleagues, I have no other name. Sasha was a childhood name, which my grandfather gave me, and my mother always called me by that name. Only when she was very angry with me she reverted to my given name and then I knew I have committed some major gaffe.

Mr. Putin was a man who had spent his professional life learning about the frailties and flaws of human beings. It was these characteristics that a good spy used for the state's advantage. Torture was useful as a tool of intelligence agencies, but the clever intelligence chief manipulated one's own failings and indiscretions to gain information. This was far more effective than brutal coercion and intimidation.

The President gently held my mother's gloved hand in his and patted it lightly. I carefully watched his every movement.

Then he put his arm around my shoulders and hugged me.

"You are always welcome here in Russia." His words sounded so sincere. Was it possible that all had been forgotten? Russians don't forget. We were honoring people killed 60 years ago and the wounds seemed so fresh.

When my mother began her protests against the state for its

treatment of Jews in the Soviet Union, it was never her ultimate intention to leave the country. Influenced by her father's deep devotion to the state and his position in Soviet society, she wanted only to change the status quo. It became obvious with the arrests and imprisonment of other dissidents that a tolerant Soviet society was not possible.

My grandfather repeatedly told the Soviet authorities that there was room for openness and while religion was indeed the opiate of the people, an adaptable Soviet system could support religious freedom. They never listened until it was too late and the system disintegrated before their eyes. A few were able to re-emerge from the ashes to become powerful new forces in modern Russia.

For my mother, Putin would always be an enigma; he was a master spy and an object of suspicion who was instructed to find and root out anti-Soviet meddlers. However, she remained ambivalent about him because he was the first Russian head of state to have a good relationship with Israel. That relationship was worth a great deal in my mother's eyes and he knew it. He wanted to win her over so he continued to talk softly to her.

"We need courageous blood here in the new Russia. New blood ready to commit to our new society," he said as he playfully slapped me on the top of my shoulder.

"You can make a difference here," he said to me as I listened warily. He knew that in the depths of my mother's Russian soul there still lay a patriot. It was her anger that took her away but perhaps there was a way to persuade her to reconsider. Her return would be a great psychological advantage for Putin and his political friends.

"It's not that I would suggest that you give up your new citizenship, but maybe you would be willing to visit more often. Look at the new Russia. See all the things that have changed," he sweetly urged us. "Join me in creating a new country."

He stood close to us. "I want to allow all our former Soviet citizens who left, for whatever reasons, to return. I'm thinking about instituting dual citizenship. Like the Israelis. You can belong to the country of your birth and a new land. The Motherland needs you."

Russia needed its former citizens to help ease this volatile new country into the future. Jews had throughout history been vital to the success of Russia. The Soviet Union was founded with the help of the Jews who had suffered under the heavy heel of the Czars. Now Putin wanted to bring back many who left with their knowledge about markets and new technologies.

As my mother edged away from the President, an old woman emerged from the crowd. The woman was wearing a medal on her coat. It looked similar to the one my grandfather wore on special occasions.

She moved forward walking around the wooden barricades that had been placed next to the Unknown Tomb to keep the multitudes from getting too close to the President. He was mingling with his people, but there were limits to his friendly demeanor. Russian politicians were learning and imitating American master politicians. You wanted to be close to your voters, but power demanded respect and a sense of distance.

The woman was approaching my mother. She was an old woman but lives spent in sacrifice were hard to pinpoint with an exact age. A peasant-looking man accompanied her, years younger, probably a son.

She blocked my mother from moving ahead. She stared in a rather rude but typically Russian way. We are a people totally lacking in subtlety and obfuscation except for the spies and the politicians. She stood completely in my mother's path; it was impossible to avoid the stranger.

"You don't remember, you were a child, but I am Veyeny Sudensky." Her hair was mostly white, but traces of gray could be seen and around the very ends a few dark brown strands of hair.

My mother did not signal that she remembered the woman, but she waited patiently for her to finish her introduction.

"I was a telephone operator during the Battle; I worked with your late father. I was on his staff," and she smiled broadly. You could see most of her teeth in that smile. A few were missing on the bottom but she showed no embarrassment about their loss.

My mother's facial expression did not change; she still had no memory of this woman. She glanced at the younger man.

"This is my son, Yuri." The young man extended a hand and my mother reached forward to meet his in midair.

My mother introduced my father and me.

"It is about time that our sacrifices are acknowledged and remembered by the government," the old woman said. My mother nodded her head in agreement and was ready to move on. This woman was not letting her go. "Your father was a great man but during those times how we hated him. We who were defending the Motherland had so little to eat." Her face grew stiff and a new wrinkle appeared as she recalled 60 years ago. She had a story to tell and we were to be her audience.

"There were moments that I didn't know which side he was on. We were all starving, no heat, no electricity, we ran out of coal. People were burning their furniture, books, anything to keep warm in burned-out buildings." She sighed deeply and took a moment to catch her breath.

"You were so young, but I saw you many times in those months." She placed her hand on her chest and seemed to lose her balance but just for a moment. Her son was standing right behind her to offer support.

"But he never let us give up hoping that we would prevail. He screamed at us to stop complaining and just keep working. If we didn't defeat Nazis we would all surely die." She shook her head and my mother continued to watch her, interested in the story. This survivor was a window into another time that my mother was forever marked by but certainly couldn't remember in any detail. It was all just blurry images, uncontrolled fires and loud noises, trembling ground, rivers of brown mud where streets had once been.

"And he was right. He was always right about what he did. If we all had eaten more or burned more coal we would not have lasted through the winter. We would have all died and the

Nazis could have walked over our dead bodies to claim the city." She paused, and this time my mother's eyes widened, actively engaged in the story.

"We understood that when he pushed us, he pushed himself harder and he worried every moment whether we would survive, if anyone would survive." The tears began to inch their way down her cheek. Her son, sensing his mother's every expression, handed her a tissue.

"We knew that if the Red Army did not defeat the Nazis, we would all be dead—all us Jews. We had heard about what was happening along the steppes." She nodded her head and the tiny droplets of tears fell on her coat.

"People deny they knew, but everyone knew what was going on. I am from the Ukraine. For us the Red Army was the last redeemer. We fought with every ounce of strength because otherwise we would certainly all perish." The temperature was dropping and the wind started to shake the trees. Spring was never warm in Russia.

My mother was tired of standing in the cold but her eyes remained fixed on the old woman's furrowed face. She still did not know this woman but her story was important. She glanced at my father and me while the woman spoke because her story was really meant for the three of us. To remember the dead and never forget was the reason for surviving.

"Your father was not a religious man but he was proud of being a Jew. He told us this might be our last stand. And there were plenty of Jews in Stalingrad fighting. But we weren't fighting for the Soviet Union or even Mother Russia; we were fighting to preserve the Jewish people. Hundreds of thousands had fled from Lithuania, Poland and Ukraine days before the Nazis pushed eastward. We all knew what happened to those left behind. Murdered. Murdered in their hometowns. People whom we thought were our friends and neighbors assisted the Nazis. Shot in the head; men, women and children. The healthy men escaped because they were fighting in the Red Army. Cattle were treated better than the Jews."

My mother reached out and touched the woman's bare hand. She suddenly leaped towards my mother and embraced her. My mother didn't move; she allowed herself to be enveloped because the emotion was so pure and raw.

Springtime in Volgograd was still cold even though it was mid afternoon and the sun was bright yellow. My mother wanted to hear this story, but not standing in the cold, so we wandered towards a restaurant to escape the weather. The Soviet Union was gone but its lingering traces remained in forgotten cities such as Volgograd. The clubs and fancy shops existed in the hundreds in Petersburg and Moscow but not in the hinterlands.

The five of us sat down in a shabby café, and were served hot tea and cakes. The steam from the five cups blanketed our space and when you bent your head to take a sip the others at the table became invisible—sweetened tea and cloudy memories.

The old woman began where she had left off minutes ago.

"I was happy that you came. I was hoping someone from your family would be here. I had read about your brother Alexei, his obituary was in the papers all over the old Soviet Union. We traveled from Kiev where we now live. This is an event that cannot be forgotten. Never." She looked at us for agreement and each one of us nodded.

"It was after the war, it took years before I could admit that without your father's draconian measures we all would have been dead. So today, I can thank his daughter for saving us. At the time we wanted to mutiny against him but we knew to save our energies to kill Nazis."

We needed something stronger to toast my grandfather. My father called over the waiter and he brought us five glasses and a bottle of vodka.

"To Dmetri Aronovich, the Hero of Stalingrad," said my father and we all toasted our glasses in the damp, cool Russian air.

"And we knew he was fair." She leaned over and touched my mother's cold hands. "You suffered, your mother and brother taken from you." She paused to take a sip. "You and your father sacrificed much for the war effort. He could have gotten extra rations for your mother and skirted the rules. Found precious medicine for your brother that was assigned to the soldiers, but not the Colonel. He was fair to a fault." My mother breathed in deeply at the mention of her mother and baby brother lost in the endless dying during the Battle of Stalingrad.

"And honest. Above all, he was an honest man who would not tolerate bribe taking by his staff." Her eyes opened wide and she began to laugh, not a hearty laugh but the strange outburst of a child caught in a frightening situation.

"His orders were that no one could take any favors or money or silver for extra rations. People were trading their coats for food. He warned all the soldiers. Women would sell their bodies for an extra piece of bread, but if he caught any of us taking a bribe he would personally shoot them in the head." Her memories reached back.

"I remember when he brought in one of the officers who had been sleeping with a few women and giving them extra coal. Your father took his pistol from his belt and placed it to the man's head. We thought he would simply scare him but he pulled the trigger. We all gasped. We were too shocked to move. I stood there with my mouth open. The man's lifeless body lay in the middle of the room. The blood was all over the place. Fortunately, I was not told to wipe it clean. Two soldiers dragged the limp body away." She stopped to catch her thoughts.

She wiped her forehead with a napkin. "Blood, we could never escape, but to kill your own. People were constantly dying and bleeding. Soldiers were shot; the bombs killed children. There was no place safe in the city from the war. No place." And she shuddered; the tiny hairs of her arm stood erect.

"But your father had a purpose in what he did. He was the man with the plan to save us. And no staff officer ever took a bribe after that. The word got out. There were black market activities going on but not by any officials under the Colonel's command."

At the time, my mother didn't really understand her own mother's death. One day she was no longer around, but there were people to take care of her and Alexei. Her father kept them near in his ever-moving headquarters after his wife's death. Nothing in the city during the Battle was permanent; the people lived in a constant state of temporary living.

"I remember you as a small child sometimes hanging onto your father's leg. He would be dragging you around the room and you would be giggling. I don't think you had any understanding of what was going on. Children adapt so quickly." My mother and the woman held hands across the table in a tight grip.

"I was young at the time, 19, and too busy to think about much more than survival. Killing Nazis, that's what we planned, and keeping Russians alive. My large family was from Ukraine and only my brother and I survived war. The Nazis shot them to death in early days of eastern assault." It was a history of the war that few people know about outside of Russia. The Poles and Ukrainians purposefully had amnesia about those years.

"Now I am living in Kiev. I returned with my grown children and grandchildren ten years ago. We have a nice Jewish community perhaps 100,000 strong. The synagogues are again filled with people on Sabbath. And this time, we are not quiet when we even sense that authorities are fingering Jews, we collectively scream. You must visit."

My father piped in, "I am a Ukrainian, born in Odessa. I hear that even in old Odessa Jews are trickling back." The old woman shook her whole body in agreement.

"The shtetl is returned to Ukraine. There's actually a group called Association of Jewish Communities of Small Towns of Ukraine with religious schools, music and dance ensembles. It's not same as 100 years ago but neither Nazis nor Stalin have annihilated us," she said with pride and vigor. "We have Hasids to thank."

The Hasids with their emissaries have been instrumental in bringing back Judaism and the religious experience to the countries of the former Soviet Union. They are the Jewish equivalent of Mormon missionaries only seeking out Jews who are not living an observant life.

Then she returned to the source of her pain. "It was so long ago, but there are things that stay with you lifetime, they can't leave you. You try to forget but you can't. I worked for your father and he was hard man but times were hard." She sat back in her seat and all eyes were on her. She had other revelations to share.

"What riled him more than anything else was thought of any of our people—Russians—collaborating with Nazis. There was time when some gossip filtered in about Russian women giving favors to Nazi soldiers in exchange for food or some trinket. Oh, your father. That was scene."

As if in a trance, she left this world for 60-year-old reminiscences. Her eyes were lost in a memory as vivid today as when it occurred. "He gathered up all his staff, which was dangerous in those times. If bomb came and killed us all what would happen to all vital planning. So we knew it was important." She was back in the underground headquarters, buried deep in the earth, and a 19 year soldier.

"He stood on a desk, high enough so no one would miss any of his words, not being particularly tall man. He said to us, 'it has come to my attention that perhaps people have grown so desperate that they are cavorting with enemy for a few crumbs of bread.' Then he stomped his foot on desk. And he was wearing his heavy boots so desk shook in fear."

I pictured my grandfather's anger; how his face grew so beet red with emotion that you were afraid the blood vessels would explode. I have personally witnessed that righteous indignation, which he displayed when my mother's political activities defied Soviet authorities. My grandfather represented Soviet officialdom.

The old woman continued with her story about my grandfather. "I remember that night, standing and lecturing us on that sturdy desk in that bitterly cold, half-lit room. He said 'if anyone learns of man, woman or even child giving aid to the enemy. Anyone. He, Colonel Aronovich, will personally cut their throat. The Ukrainian sluts and their miserable men, they give comfort to the enemy in return for favors. Those Lithuanian swine that hated Russians more than the Nazis, they give comfort to Nazis. That just proves how stupid they are because Nazis turn around and enslave them. We will never give comfort to enemy.' His exact words. I remember them completely. I can't forget because then he spoke of Nazi soldiers surrendering. 'Kill them, cut their throats' he told us. 'We will not give our meager rations to those Nazi bastards or waste precious bullet on them.' " She was tapping the table with her fingers.

"Someone asked him about respecting human life even during a war. And his response was clear. 'There are no conventions in this war. The only thing I understand is dying and I will never give up food meant for our people to these Nazi bastards who would kill everyone—man, woman, child that they found. Death is too good.' " The frown on her face produced more wrinkles.

"He said to his officers, 'Rape is one thing. If we find any Nazi forcing himself on our women then we cut off his balls and let him bleed to death in snow. And our women, if they go near one of these beasts, I will kill her myself.' And we knew he meant every word." She looked at my mother whose face was stone; this human rights activist was unmoved by stories of Nazi deaths. She may have heard some of these tales before from others. I was not shocked because at school in Petersburg, our teachers spoke of the bestiality of the Nazis.

"Your father was hard man but we would never have survived without his strong hand. It's a wonder that we did survive and so many of us. You have much to be proud of—yours is family of greatness."

She turned to me. "Your family sacrificed much for our survival," and she turned to my mother. "I heard that your father married Natalya Stumkoff after the war. She worked with us and was wonderful with all children. We had orphans to care for."

Thinking about her stepmother opened up raw wounds. My mother dabbed the corners of her eyes with her white handkerchief. "She was always good to me and I loved her like a mother. She died before my father."

The day had turned too emotional for my mother. She could

not relive any more powerful memories. My father and I noticed her right hand, the damaged one, shaking involuntarily, a sign of fatigue.

We stood and my father paid the bill. The old woman embraced my mother.

"We may meet again," and I thought yes, it's a small world.

"Who knows the next time could be in America," she said. We all shook our heads in agreement.

We left the next day for Petersburg where we spent a few more days visiting old friends and the cemetery. A Jew spends more time honoring the dead than the living. The circle of our Petersburg friends had decreased dramatically. All our immediate family had emigrated. We were more likely to meet old neighbors in Brighton Beach or Israel than in Mother Russia. There were stories of émigrés who changed their minds and returned to Russia. None of our circle had changed their mind and fled to the Motherland. Some went to Israel first and then found a home in America. A few settled in America and then emigrated to Israel to fulfill the Biblical prophecy.

The transition from immigrant to citizen is never an easy process, except for the very young, even in an immigrant-friendly country like America. My mother's soul is forever linked to Mother Russia—too many memories. I am in a different category. I am young enough to look back in twenty years and feel a slight tinge of nostalgia for the Motherland, but no longing to return.

As invigorating as it is to be back in Mother Russia, I realize how much I love the New Jerusalem. The Old World stands for the past and its thousands of years of torturous history. Then there is the New World—unlimited possibilities—life, liberty and the pursuit of happiness. What an American concept - the pursuit of happiness. No Russian would ever identify that idea as an essential item for a Constitution.

As we board the plane to return, my brain weighs the challenges of my Case of the Russian Lady. What about my

Olga and her two sisters? Why did they come to America and what did they expect to find? Who did they leave behind? The memories—what memories does she cling to? What secrets does she hide? Is Olga, my obsession, a calculating murderess or a helpless immigrant? Do I really want to know the truth? Do I really want to know what really happened? Would I prefer just loose ends.

CHAPTER 8

So as I am unpacking my suitcase from my short vacation in the Motherland, I get my new assignment directly from the Deputy Inspector.

"Putin's in town, Perlov, so you will be part of the security detail," he commands on the phone.

And naturally I obey so instead of immediately working on my Case of the Russian Lady, today, I put on my dress blues as a NYC police officer to provide security to Vladimir Putin, President of Russia, while he meets at the United Nations in Manhattan. Mr. Putin and I are practically buddies.

The irony is not lost on my mother. "Guess what I'm doing today?" I laughingly report.

"No idea, I hope it's not dangerous," she responds as a concerned mother.

"No, I am assigned to protect President Putin when he comes to the UN," and I can't contain my glee.

I hear my mother chuckling on the phone. "Life, what more can I say," and then she reminds me of my other responsibility. "Don't forget to make a reservation at a nice restaurant when you take out the good doctor," she instructs me.

I am putting serious thinking behind my plans for my first

evening of dining with another newly minted American citizen from the Motherland. First impressions matter so it has to be special. When I get a break during the day, I'll call her and tell her I am back in the country and so our postponed date can resume a week later than originally planned. Dr. Marina and I have much in common; my mother has a point about the importance of a shared history and values. Marina understands that inner tension between the "new" with its unlimited promises and the familiar "old" with its millennium of stories and genealogy.

I take a good close look at my image in the mirror as I prepare for leaving my apartment to meet the day's challenges. "I am looking mighty smart," I shout out loud to the air-conditioner, which is breathing very hard, gasping for greater voltage as it attempts to cool my bedroom. In the evening, as I lie in my bed in my Kew Gardens apartment, I can hear my upstairs neighbor's cranky, old AC dripping droplets of condensed water on my new machine. Drip, drip, drop, it goes all night. Living half my life in a cold land has not prepared me for the summer heat of NYC. I will never enjoy sweating. The sticky residue clogs my pores and produces a throbbing red heat rash.

Despite the humidity my dress blues are immaculately pressed. My mother is always offering to be my laundress but I never trust her to successfully complete the chore. Her domestic skills never were in the baleboosteh category. She spent too much of her time chained to fences protesting official Soviet directives, on hunger strikes, and editing underground newspapers. A prodigious letter writer, she filed countless complaints with the Ministries. She occupied a prominent position among Mr. Putin's files of Soviet citizens to watch.

Living as I have in two worlds, I like to present myself as someone who can manage all possibilities, to be ever resourceful, never undone by unexpected circumstances. This requires a certain appearance. I am vain but not a peacock. Jimmy spends hours on selecting his clothing, picking out the right cologne and buying the newest shaving gadgets on the market. My aim is to project an aura of self-confidence, which is not achieved with the simple selection of the right color tie or the shape of a cufflink. A master defines himself by how he holds his head, the volume and tone of his voice, the crispness of his speech.

If I'm not a handsome man in a movie star type of way, I'm still an object of interest. I see women glance my way trying to appear inconspicuous. I don't disturb them or even hint that I realize what they are doing. I am enjoying their attention. My mother says I have a face of character, an introspective, intellectual air about me. In America, this is not always a virtue.

It's important today that I craft a particular appearance so I check the mirror to make certain my tie is perfectly straight and that I haven't left any unshaved stray hairs on my face. Being as dark as I am, I don't want the slightest hint of a five o'clock shadow this early in the day.

I am one of a handful of New York's finest fluent in Russian; United Nations security requests my assistance when Putin is in town. I have done this duty once before and I feel honored to represent the police before my former countrymen. When the United Nations' General Assembly meets in early fall, I return to my role as a sharpshooter because every steady eye with an unflinching hand is called to duty when all the dignitaries from all over the world are in New York. It's a great opportunity for every crazy with a political point of view or some fanatic nationalist from a country no one can even pronounce to become an instant celebrity by shooting a President or Prime Minister. Security is kept on high alert and I find myself not in dress blues but back in my SWAT uniform perched on a building watching for anything shiny, presumably metallic that could be a gun, rifle or knife among the crowds. I scan the roofs of all the nearby buildings looking for someone with an instrument of death. Technology has made our jobs only more difficult. I can't see from a high vantage point plastic explosives or dynamite strapped to a martyr's body. This day I play a more diplomatic role, not as a hired scout and killer, but as a resource that the American Secret Service can turn to for cultural and linguistic assistance. I am ready to begin my appointed task; I take one more look in the mirror and brush a few stray hairs with my hand.

Before I leave the room, I concentrate, staring out the dirty windows of my apartment. What are the other chores for the day?

"I need to call Marina," I say out loud to the bird perched outside on my air-conditioner. That task is now embedded in my brain.

The bird talks back to me. "Squawk," it replies indignantly. I eye the black, feathered creature and feel myself drifting, my thoughts ambling along to a different place, an open meadow near my grandfather's dacha. I am a youth again, thin and strong. The sky is alive with buoyant black-colored birds. A slender blonde woman skips through the high grass of summer. "Olga," I scream to my companion, the crow.

"I will call her in for questioning," I yell to the silent apartment walls as I slam the door closed.

I arrive at UN headquarters long before the dignitaries or the crowds. We receive our instructions on where to stand and photos of some possible crazies or political dissidents who may be among the people milling around the periphery. And we wait. The waiting goes on for hours. I'm lucky that where I am positioned is out of direct sunlight. It's hot again today but almost bearable; at least I'm not forced to wear a heavy bulletproof vest or a covered facemask like the guys in riot gear. NY's finest is prepared for all possibilities. The Chechnya conflict is bringing out protesters to Mr. Putin's visit. It's a conflict far away and unfamiliar to most native-born Americans, but our loose borders enable a determined martyr a guarantee of glory by blowing himself up and taking lots of innocents with him. We even carefully watch the women because lately young females are also seeking martyrdom.

Finally the dignitaries start arriving. We hear on our walkie-talkies that Putin and his American hosts have left their cars and are heading our way. Mr. Putin walks in front of me surrounded by American officials as I stand in line, shoulder to shoulder with my fellow officers, creating a human chain so nothing can get near him. I think I spot on his left side Mr. Powell, the US Secretary of State and a black woman near his right, perhaps Condoleezza Rice. Then he suddenly stops. He looks back and his eyes lock on mine.

He turns and retraces his steps. He faces me. "Fyodor Ilich Perlov," he says loudly and all eyes turn to him and then towards me; the Secretary of State stares my way.

I leave the line and move towards one of the most powerful and methodical minds in the world.

He says in English. "Officer Perlov, grandson of Dmetri Aronovich, Hero of Battle of Stalingrad."

I stand ramrod straight and salute. "Yes Sir."

He moves closer to me and extends his hand.

I hesitate, but then shake his outstretched hand. I realize once again that he is a short, compact man, but physical strength and brawn have little to do with power in the modern world.

In Russian he says to me, "It's nice to see you again." His eyes scan my uniform for indications of rank, valor and places I have served. As a former security chief, he recognizes metallic and cloth displays of status or belonging.

"I hope you will be returning to Russia soon. We do need you just as I mentioned. What was it—less than a week ago?"

"Of course," I answer although it's questionable when I will return and certainly not to Stalingrad in the near future.

"When I saw you last at the memorial for your grandfather and all the others who sacrificed so much for the Motherland, I told you that Russia needs bright, young people and new ideas." He has an intense stare as he sizes me up. Do I have my grandfather's resolve and dedication?

He doesn't wait for my reply. "A police officer, an agent of the state just like your grandfather and uncle." He touches ever so slightly the sleeve of my uniform.

I nod and quickly glance at the others watching us speak as if we were old acquaintances, which we are in an odd sort of way.

He points to the insignia on my chest. "A marksman?"

It must be a universal symbol. "Yes," I reply with a brief motion of my head.

"Your uncle started as a marksman in the Soviet Army. I'm sure you know that." He is making a courteous attempt to engage me in a cordial conversation.

In fact, my grandfather gave me one of my uncle's medals after he was killed. I kept it wrapped in its fine box lined with velvet.

"Your family has sacrificed much for Mother Russia. I hope that this new country that you have embraced understands what you are capable of doing in its name." His tone is so genuine that it's easy to forget his autocratic and authoritarian hold over my native country.

"Did your uncle teach you to shoot?"

"Yes, I was his best student," and I can't suppress a smile.

Our eyes are caught in a knowing embrace. We have much in common, more than the others that surround us.

"Send my regards to your mother," his thin lips smile broadly.

"I will tell her of our meeting," and I look deeply into his eyes. This man is an enigma; unquestionably a patriot, but should I forget and forgive his past deeds towards my family.

Our President Bush has told the nation of looking with affection and respect into those small eyes, and seeing the man's generous soul. This can't be the same eyes I am looking into because I see a domineering and ruthless, black Russian soul. This is a man who respects power not money or materialism, but raw, cruel, and absolute decision-making prowess. It is a Russian soul as old as Peter the Great and only more nuanced and subtle than the Premiers who ruled during Soviet times.

"And your Uncle Boris, I missed him in Stalingrad. Is he here in NYC?"

"No, he lives in Berlin," and suddenly I am stricken with fear and anxiety. Have I put my uncle and his family in danger? I can never tell my mother what I just did. If only I could retract those seemingly innocent words. To release personal information to a former KGB man can still lead to treachery. Will the new security apparatus send out agents to track down my mother's brother in Berlin?

I remain still and retreat into myself for a second so I can mask my apprehension. I have become such an American that I readily divulge information without being prodded or threatened. It's not safe to be so free.

The American Secret Service and NYC police brass stare at me following our conversation's body language if not understanding what we are actually saying. President Putin moves on, having gained new information.

I return to my position on the line. An American Secret Service man whispers to one of the NYPD brass. I can't hear what they are saying and his body is facing the Inspector so I can't see his lips.

Shortly after a Police Deputy Commissioner walks up to me. "Friend from home?" he asks with a smirk. He may be one of those who knows my file and my days as an unhappy SWAT member. Perhaps he knows me as the Russian Jew in the department, an outsider, an interloper who will never be accepted. My first impulse is to spit into his face with its hanging jowls and puffy lips. But I like my job too much so I control myself. The Uncle Vanya in me wants to strike out against those who are antagonistic towards me, but I am learning composure.

It's impossible for native-born Americans to image the vast journey my family made from Russia to Brighton Beach, USA. I sometimes gaze into the mirror and imagine myself back in our apartment in Petersburg. Since our arrival in America, we have returned to the new Russia infrequently. Other Russian immigrants travel freely, often visiting family and friends. We don't have many living people to see in the new Russia. There are a few distant relatives in Odessa, which is now part of the new country called Ukraine. It's the same corrupt place only the crime wave has accelerated. The dead wait for our occasional visits—my grandfather, the Hero of the Battle of Stalingrad has forgiven us for leaving the land of our birth. My mother has told me so. In her dreams my mother, the true descendent of Uncle

Vanya, the Cossack, with a direct line to the Biblical Joseph, sees her father. He doesn't approve, she tells my father and me, but he understands.

I am in deep thought. My mother in her multi-colored robe stands before me; she has more dreams to report.

"Detective Perlov, Detective Perlov," a voice says… Someone is speaking.

"Perlov," I hear a voice calling my name. I feel the sweat on the back of my wet neck. I look down at my blue uniform. "Perlov," I don't know how long someone has been calling my name. A man approaches that I don't recognize.

He moves with deliberation and control, weaving between the barricades. You can see the outline of his muscular chest through his short-sleeve, dress blue police shirt. He is someone who respects his body and expects admiring glances.

"Perlov," he stands in front me and blocks my path. "My name is Tommy Sullivan, Roberta's brother." I gaze at him, but his face is unfamiliar although I see the family resemblance, another pure Irish face. The police department has become a multi-colored melting pot except that the best positions are still held by the Irish and their direct descendents; the Sullivans, O'Malleys, O'Connors still dominate the upper echelons.

We shake hands. Roberta has more than one brother belonging to NYC's finest.

"It's nice to meet you. How did you know who I am?" I ask, thinking he may possess extraordinary police powers.

"A guy pointed you out," he moves his head in the direction of some of my fellow officers milling, still watching the crowds. He waves to an officer wearing the stripes of a sergeant.

"You're a known guy Perlov. A Russian Jew from the 60th. You got a rep," he is laughing with that big, pleasant grin. It's a friendly expression although not every one of my fellow officers who refer to me as the Russian Jew is as benign. I am hoping my new moniker, 'Hero of Harbor House, Perlov the Protector' is circulating among my colleagues on the force.

"Say, Roberta tells us you're a beach guy." Roberta is spreading news of my talents and hobbies to her relatives. I'm flattered that I can serve as her model friend.

"Why don't you and Roberta come to our little compound in Breezy Point? Not exactly like the Kennedys, but a bunch of us have homes right next to each other. It's a great place Breezy Point."

It does have its own reputation. What my mother calls anti-Semite country. Breezy Point, it's a great name, a fortress city at the tip of the Rockaways with great beaches, simple houses and a real sense of community among its many police and fire families. You don't leave; you marry and bring your bride to Breezy Point to live. I'm wondering if brother Tommy and family think I may be potential Breezy Point material. They must be desperate if they're considering the Russian Jew cop.

"I'd love to come." I do long for an invitation since my lifeguard days in the Rockaways. "Can I bring my surf board?"

Tommy looks at me and then whistles. "A Russian surfer," he looks incredulously at me. "You're really a surfer?"

"Well, I won't win any competitions, but I love to surf. I have a board at my parents' house in Brighton Beach."

"Hell, yes," he shrugs his shoulders. He has my partner Jimmy Sutton's shrug. "Roberta says you only eat fish? Maybe one of us will get lucky and fish up dinner for you. Any fish you don't eat?"

Roberta must be doing a lot of talking about me.

"I don't eat shellfish." I tell him. I don't want any surprises like the pork roast at the Lieutenant's Christmas party. He has that questioning look.

I add, "You know shrimp, lobster, clams" and he nods.

"You mean you don't eat lobster? I know Jews who eat lobster." And there are many, but not me.

Does he want to make me feel embarrassed? But I'm proud of my self-discipline?

"No, but there's a lot of other things to eat from the sea."

My feet are anchored to the concrete; I do not retreat.

"We do a lot of fishing; my brother and cousins all have small boats. Do you eat bluefish?"

Since he's offering me a menu of possibilities I add, "How about fluke, it's summer and I know they are running."

"Yeh, so you like bottom fish."

Jews love the scraps, what others leave behind. "My favorite," and I smile.

He swings an arm around my shoulder. "We'll get along just fine. My father likes a guy who knows exactly what he wants."

I need to ask Roberta what she's been telling her family about me. I am a man of discretion, but it seems I have unknowingly become an actor in a Pirandello play—someone's reality and another's illusion.

I was going to my pocket to check my Palm Pilot for my next available free afternoon when one of the lesser brass approaches.

"Perlov," he says and looks at me.

"Your Lieutenant is looking for you to get back to the 60th. You got a news conference to attend—something about protecting old ladies in Harbor House."

The Lieutenant, the publicity hound, has arranged for the press to pounce on the station. This will be fun, but I have no transportation to get me back to the station house. I took the subway from my Kew Gardens apartment. It's much faster than hassling with the traffic and finding a parking space.

"I need a ride." The deputy commissioner's bootlicker looks around for someone to be my chauffeur.

He finds a uniform that has time on his hands since the crowds, while not friendly towards the police, are not hurling bottles at us. Potential suicide bombers did not make an appearance today so it will be safe to let two of us leave.

Tommy and I depart with a handshake.

"OK, we'll set something up in the near future. My mother wants to meet you. You being a cop and also going to law school like Roberta. The same law school as Roberta. Happy coincidences," he tells me. I like to surf and I want to see Breezy Point, but this is taking on a life of its own.

He manages to slap me on the shoulder as we move in opposite directions. I must have irresistible shoulders yearning to be slapped because I always find myself on the receiving end of someone's hand.

Duty calls me and I hop into a squad car illegally parked near the delivery entrance, behind the main Secretariat building. My driver puts on his siren and lights; and reluctantly cars separate and create an aisle for us to speed through on our way to South Brooklyn.

After standing for so many hours, it feels good to sit in a police squad car and be chauffeured to my next destination. I could get used to being driven to my next event. Despite my mother's ideas, a future as a bigwig in the police department has its allure. Once I learn how to effortlessly schmooze and become a real tuchis lecker—ass licker—I'm on my way to the highest heights of officialdom. We Russians gravitate towards power and position, not tangible objects such as cars and clothing.

As I drift into a hazy dream, his face appears—the master manipulator, my new friend President Putin. I am jolted awake.

"Hey are you OK?" my squad car host asks. "It was a good thing you're wearing your seat belt. I thought you'd fly through the windshield."

I shake my head, "I was nodding off and then I remembered something;" Putin's face. Am I a paranoid? Get real, I tell myself, this is post-Soviet times. Still I won't mention to my mother about how Putin knows where Uncle Boris lives.

Here I am sitting in a police car and a member of this commanding force. I am called to this assignment because of my expertise at finding potential martyrs, at least ones that speak Russian.

Still, I try and remember every word of today's conversation with Putin about my Uncle Boris. How can I put this right? Does danger lurk even now from the Motherland? It's difficult not to be suspicious; it's in my nature. I have the perfect personality for a policeman on the street—believe nothing that you see, always suspect the worst.

My police companion talks amicably about the Yankees and the farm team in Staten Island. I know very little and care even less about baseball, but I want to be friendly. "The Yanks are sure to be in the World Series again," which I say effortlessly and without a hint of knowledge.

"Steinbrenner can buy anything. Money matters in baseball," my traveling companion says. Money matters in America, period.

As Jimmy explained it to me, if you were born in Brooklyn before the mid-1950's you had to be a Brooklyn Dodgers fan. Then the treacherous Dodgers moved westward following Horace Greeley's declaration 'Go West young man,' deserting Brooklyn with the result chaos and ugliness, as poverty and dysfunction arose on the former hallowed grounds of the Dodgers' playing fields. Since the Dodgers and Yankees were always archrivals, that left the morose Brooklyn Dodgers fans rudderless. So lo and behold a new messiah arrived, the New York Mets emerged from the ashes, but there was no place for them in Brooklyn to play. They relocated to Queens and Shea Stadium. Brooklyn baseball fans formed a new allegiance with the New York Mets. A Brooklyn boy can't be a Yankee fan.

I ask my driving buddy, "Where are you from?"

"The Bronx," he says proudly, "but white people can't live in the Bronx anymore, except for Riverdale, and there are too many Jews." I don't know if he knows I'm Jewish, but then he's probably not constrained by political correctness.

"My family moved out to Jersey twenty years ago."

My eyes glance out of the car and I see the familiar sights of Brooklyn. We are inching closer to my destination. Even with the lights and sirens we are stopped on Brighton Beach Avenue. These Russians will not make room for a police car. We wait with the cab drivers, truck-delivery boys, and the other polluting cars under the overhead subway tracks. The sounds of the squeaking, braking trains cannot be escaped. The gulls flee the grating sounds.

I don't like air-conditioning in a car, too artificial, so I open the squad car's window. That's when I see her walking on the crowded street. I stare and to my surprise she spies me, maybe sensing my presence. There she is in my neighborhood, our neighborhood. The bond is preordained; no amount of good common sense can separate us.

She stops walking, turns and directly faces the idling police car and me. Those stunning, large blue eyes, the color of a Caribbean sea, meet mine. I try not to blink. I don't want a nanosecond to go by without my being able to draw her in. She stands in front of the rusting post box; the official brown container is screwed into the curb. Resting her upper torso on it, she concentrates on me. We are ten feet apart. The light changes and my driver moves on. She remains standing, attached to the immovable, concrete sidewalk. People stream by her, but she stands alone. I turn my head and stick it outside the window so I can continue to have her in my line of vision. She is still watching me. Olga, she will not leave me.

As the police car turns into the narrow lane where the 60th precinct rests, she is out of sight but certainly not out of mind. We arrive at the station house on West 8th Street now in the middle of gridlock as police cars and TV satellite trucks angle for the limited space available on these tight streets. I see the Lieutenant walking towards me with his unwavering stride. I leave the reliable hands of my police chauffeur and thank him for the ride.

"The press arrived early and I have a pain in the ass from the Commissioner's office hanging on my heels." I look at the controlled mayhem that awaits us.

"I don't want you to speak unless someone asks a question I can't answer," which was fine with me. I respected the Lieutenant's need for total control; he was the power here, another Irish cop up from the streets that made good. There was a whiff of scandal a few years back, but he managed to pin the blame on one of his sergeants and since then it had been clear sailing to the top. He assumed the mantle when the former Irish Lieutenant retired three years ago.

Jimmy is standing regally on the top step of the station house stairs dressed in one of his expensive and well-tailored suits. He doesn't show any signs of perspiration despite the rising temperature. He is cool as ever. I'll let him stand at the Lieutenant's elbow while I stand inconspicuously in the background, outside the camera's range. It's a photo opportunity for everyone with enough stripes on their uniform. I see the Commissioner's press lackey pushing to the center of the makeshift podium. It is always interesting to watch these two. I place my money on the Lieutenant being the spokesperson for the Department and the press boy left putting away the microphone after the conference.

The Lieutenant gets to the microphone first. "Ladies and gentleman," he tells the assembled, a mixture of TV reporters and the print press. We don't get any Internet types here in Brighton Beach; nothing too dazzling or cutting edge about finding bad guys and bringing them to justice.

The Lieutenant speaks of our valiant efforts and the cooperation of public affairs. It's mandatory good politics to make-believe we cooperate with other divisions in the department. Since 9/11 some of us feel a slightly greater level of mutual aid with our fellow officers in other locations.

"Let me introduce the detectives who led the operation, Detectives Sutton and Perlov." Jimmy swung his arm out as if he was catching a fly pop up with one bare hand and smiled to the press with those baby-blues sparkling in the heat and sun. I moved closer to the podium and cracked a small smile. When my picture appeared in the Daily News' Brooklyn section tomorrow, I wanted my mother to remark about how earnest I looked. A public servant should take his position seriously. I had no intention of running for elected office.

"How did you find the thug," asks one old timer TV reporter who is just hanging on to his job. After Brooklyn, there's only retirement left.

Before I can make a comment the Lieutenant replies, "Good police work and cooperative citizens." The guy is going to ask a follow-up question but a young, pretty, female TV reporter on her way up the broadcasting ladder of success is asking about the evidence."What did the forensics team find?"

The Lieutenant doesn't reveal too much to the press and certainly we don't want to link a mentally challenged thug to a triple murder.

A Russian language reporter from the Novoye Russkoye Slovo, the only Russian language daily, asks in Russian, "Will the families of the victims be compensated by the city?" A typical Russian response to a public tragedy—where's the entitlement?

The Lieutenant can't respond and of course the press lackey is speechless so my Lieutenant pushes me forward towards the microphone. I know the reporter; we see each other on the streets. In the past, I have allowed him to quote me as an unidentified police source. He reports for a newspaper no one else in the department reads. He smiles at me and I respond with a shake of my head. I move up the step to reach the appropriate official level.

The Lieutenant whispers to me with the press guy hanging on his shoulder, "What did he ask?" I tell him with the press guy leaning on my shoulder so he can overhear the conversation. The press guy is wetting his dry lips, waiting anxiously for the right moment to spring into action. He asks me, "Does the guy speak English?" I know he does, but he asks the question on purpose to see how the brass responds.

But I don't get to answer. The press guy can't leave without saying something; he has got to get his words out. "The City Council has created a Victims Compensation Fund and the families will be compensated." He is proud of having edged out the Lieutenant for a word. The Russian reporter scribbles some notes. I expect to get a call later.

I am about to slip back into my discreet role as observer of the political scene when I see her among the crowd. It's Olga, in the rear, watching the proceedings or may be just watching me; I glimpse her face. When did she arrive? Our eyes meet. Jimmy also captures her radiance in his sight. She observes the press conference, standing beyond the press among the congregated people on the street. Jimmy winks at me and places his hand on my elbow. Our reunion is inevitable. It's destiny, which I can't escape.

I lean towards Jimmy. "I should go after her and set a time for her to come in for questioning. Perhaps right now."

Jimmy shrugs his shoulders and smirks at me, "Go."

I easily slip away from the makeshift podium; the officials are not interested in my presence. Then I feel my arm being pulled. I am in someone's grasp.

It's Gleb Pakhalina, the reporter for Novoye Russkoye Slovo. He firmly holds my arm. "Tell me, what is Putin doing at the United Nations?"

I look at him in astonishment. I am thinking Olga and he's talking Putin.

"I was covering his appearance at the United Nations today. I saw you with him. I really came to this press conference wanting to talk to you and hoping you would be here."

I am dumbfounded. Since when am I in a position of authority? "I have no idea."

"Listen we know each other for years. You can trust me. Is there a deal being discussed about Chechnya?" He releases my arm and stands in a casual stance with his hands in his pockets.

I am flattered that he thinks I know anything about a visit by our family's former adversary. "Really, I know nothing. I am only called to provide security."

"But you were shaking Putin's hand."

"How did you see that?" amazed at the man's stealth. I am thinking we were invisible and away from probing eyes.

"I have press credentials." He proudly points to an object hanging around his neck. "I saw the two of you from a distance as he was walking into the main building."

He shifts his weight from one leg to another and he gets real close to my face. We're not worrying about personal space. "Grandson of the Hero of Battle of Stalingrad you can trust me. I won't attribute any quotes to you. No one will know." His round face exudes eagerness like an earnest young student trying to impress the teacher. "Remember, I interviewed your mother when you all returned from the Motherland after the 60th Anniversary of great battle."

"Yes," I am smiling; my mother didn't tell me their exact conversation; only that the article doesn't reflect her precise words.

I add, "You would think that now that the newspaper is part of a global network, you would have some idea about why he is in New York." His paper was recently sold. In an irony only a Russian can truly appreciate, his long-established paper, which was started by Russian immigrants 100 years ago, was bought by a Kiev-based media conglomerate.

He laughs loudly and heartily from the bottom of his gut. "It's a wonder I still have a job," he said, wiping his forehead with the back of his hand in a silly pantomime gesture. One of the first things the new owner did was fire most of the veteran reporters. A former Soviet apparatchik, raised on the business principles of a state-dominated economy, the new owner quickly adopted the heartless capitalism of America, and cleaned house.

"No, we hear rumors, gossip," he laughs. "We got an official Russian government response, so that's why I'm interviewing you." He's standing so close to me that I actually feel the ends of his long curly hair touch my face.

"And I find it interesting speaking to your mother, the fiery Soviet dissident was so nuanced and diplomatic about your trip for the Anniversary. Where's the fire eater of yesterday? She had nothing to say about Russian politics or the US involvement in Iraq."

I know my mother has changed; we are all entitled to a personal metamorphosis—this is America, the land of new opportunities and new beginnings.

"My mother is almost 65. She's getting on in years. What do you expect her to be another Emma Goldman?" My mother's devotion to all things political had often led Russian Americans to compare her with Goldman, the passionate Russian-born Jewish anarchist of the early twentieth century. The American government later stripped Goldman of her US citizenship and deported her back to Russia where she died. My mother had always found the comparison unflattering. She was a model dissident in the Soviet Union. Now she was a model citizen in her adopted land.

"All I hear about your mother is praise from the old bubbes, thanking her for her letter-writing to the Social Security authorities. No more hunger strikes and lying down in the middle of traffic like in Soviet times."

"She's tired. She loves being an American." I rightly defend my mother from her critics and there are some in the émigré community who think she is too passive.

"I can tell you about solving the murders in the Coney Island project. Are your readers interested in those crimes?" I change the subject.

His body turns away from me. Rocking on his heels, he says, "Who cares if the shvartzers kill each other in Surfside Gardens or O'Dwyer Homes—a few less thugs."

I frown but he ignores my expression of disapproval.

"We do care about the bubbes at Harbor House." He squeezes the flesh on my arm and says, "Hero of Harbor House, Perlov the Protector."

I feel my face redden. "Where did you hear that?"

"Oh, I have sources."

I know there are no other Russians working at the station house. There are immigrants for sure. The Mexicans clean the floors and toilets. A Guatemalan keeps the grass outside looking green and healthy. None of the cops are Russian. The civilians come as far as Westchester but none of them speaks Russian. These are not his sources of information.

"Yes," and I wait.

"I hear. You're the only Russian in the place but where do the officers eat and spend money. At the delis, the luncheonette around the corner, they buy coffee and their newspapers in the neighborhood."

He smiles widely, and his uneven and yellowed teeth overwhelm his mouth. "The police are not like at home in Mother Russia; these guys have big yappers. They talk. I overheard one cop at the newsstand, holding a baseball glove, hailing the Hero of Harbor House, Perlov the Protector."

My reputation expands and grows daily.

We are surrounded by police but totally ignored by them. We are speaking a language no one else understands and culturally we stand in a different universe.

Pakhalina gently places his arm around my shoulder. "Let me tell you what I know."

I give him my absolute attention. And he continues, "Mikhail Davidovich," which is Vasily's brother as well as the real surname of the charismatic, Russian revolutionary Leon Trotsky, my grandfather's first mentor.

I always wondered if Vasily was related to Trotsky, but I never asked. I don't know why I never asked.

"He and his brother Vasily were spotted vacationing in Sukhumi," the capital of the breakaway Georgian state of Abkhazia. No one in the NYPD cared about a breakaway Georgian province. But it had magnificent beaches and a fabulous reputation as a highly desirable vacation spot for Russians. The Czars and the Soviets loved those beaches. My grandfather took us there on a holiday twenty years ago.

"I hear that the Davidovich brothers are heavily involved in providing the Abkhaz fighters with arms, with the tacit support of the Russian government." It had been reported that Putin and his government clandestinely backed the rebels even allowing the Abkhaz populace to claim Russian citizenship.

"How do you know what the Davidovich brothers are doing a continent away?" I ask although perhaps the newspaper's new owner has good worldwide contacts.

"Just luck. I was back in Russia for a month visiting my cousin and he suggested we go to the beach at Sukhumi. I saw them, without their families, enjoying some cruise." He taps the side of his head. "Something is up; Mikhail is not some Moishe Pipik"— Joe Blow. "The brothers are not typical tourists. My cousin knows the second mate. He told us it's all hush-hush." Pakhalina hasn't a 'goyisher kop'; he's insightful and quite capable of putting the pieces of a puzzle together.

Does Pakhalina realize Vasily and I are old friends from Petersburg or is he just blindly trying to impress me by offering secrets? What's the reporter's motivation? He wants something.

I know Vasily and his brother just returned from a vacation in Russia but these details are tantalizing bits of information. As one of NYC's finest, I don't need to know if they are smuggling arms in the hulls of tourist boats anchoring at the harbors of Gagra or Pitsunda in the breakaway Georgian province of Abkhazia. However, I am naturally curious.

He can see on my demonstrative face that I am pleased that he is sharing his knowledge with me. "So you will let me know anything interesting you learn about Putin and the United Nations?" Pakhalina hands me his card although I already have one in my wallet.

"I don't know anything but I will let you know if I hear anything." We shake hands and my eyes return to the fading crowd. I watch the reporter as he walks back to his office.

I scan the street, only a few stragglers milling around. Olga is gone. My call will wait another day.

I'll call Marina.

CHAPTER 9

Before I leave the station house for the day, the Lieutenant stops to thank me for my help at the press conference. I make no mention of my discussions with Gleb, but if the Lieutenant has any information about Putin, I expect him to share it with me. Then I will repay the favor with Gleb.

"That son-of-bitch," he says referring to the press lackey. "But what can you do, the brass forgets what it's like on the streets. Good job," and he slaps my shoulder.

"What about the fat dead guy," he asks. I can feel his impatience as his eyes follow my breathing. "Have we closed the Case of the Russian Lady?" He needs his top detectives for more promising cases, which will garner him rewards by the brass. Not a selfish man, he always shares the glory with his officers.

"Loose ends," I tell the Lieutenant; we still have loose ends. The case isn't closed; it is creeping towards a resolution, inching closer to an ending, but still loose ends. The facts remain murky.

The Case of the Russian Lady is only teasing suggestions. The cop in me says we don't know what happened. Was she present as he lays on the stained carpeting dying? Did she walk away from his cries for help? Did she glance his way as she slammed the door shut? Did the three sisters linger at the back door discussing what to do? Were the sex slaves moved to an unholy act of omission?

"We're almost ready to close the case," I say.

Motive. We have plenty of motive—a green card without having to submit to unnatural sex acts. Russians are not Scandinavians. We are prudes. Being forced to perform group sex is more than embarrassing, it's spiritually denigrating. These women might do almost anything to avoid being the objects of such depravity. I don't discuss anything about these aspects to my Lieutenant.

With the birth name of Fyodor, named as I was after the Russian writer Dostoyevsky, I must search the innermost desires and motivations of my potential suspects. What were they thinking at that exact moment when the crime was executed? Even the impulsive, in fact, even the mentally retarded, all have a moment of bursting neurological energy that moves them conclusively towards a fateful criminal action. Cases involving the mentally ill were the most fascinating. The deranged have vivid minds with abundant ideas racing through their brain cells at the moment they cross from law-abiding citizen to criminal.

So my beautiful suspect was thinking something. It may not have been a pre-meditated plan. What should I do, she must have asked herself? Conscious thoughts mixed with her basic survivor instincts, learned from being an Eastern European immigrant, certainly created a dilemma in her mind. Whether she weighed her actions and considered the full consequences, I'll find out. It doesn't matter if the official case was closed or I kept it alive through sheer stubbornness, I must know what happened on that day. The case waited another day. Before sleeping as my head rested against my pillow, her image returned, her face, those blue eyes the color of the great sea and all its mysteries.

I need no alarm clock; I just know when it happens. The sun rises; I am awake, for my redemption is at hand. A new day brings and with it new opportunities in this New Jerusalem. I can be reborn, join the forces of the righteous and fight evil. I am an agent of Hashem, the Holy One, who loves those sinners that seek the true path. I am ready to investigate my Russian Lady. In the depths of my dark Russian soul, I feel she is somehow linked with my redemption.

Jimmy took the unmarked car; he was driving in from his home in Bay Ridge. I take the subway downtown to lower Manhattan and the Immigration offices located in the main Federal Building in New York City. Cops don't generally like to travel subways or buses. They don't want to meet the ordinary Joe or Jane because public encounters were unpredictable. They may be drawn into an activity far from backup or fellow cops they knew and trusted.

For me, it's the start of an adventure the moment I head down those steps as I take the "F" train into Manhattan from my apartment in Kew Gardens. The unknown is what I seek. Since I'm wearing a suit people don't assume I'm a cop. While I'm waiting on the sweltering platform for the subway to arrive, I open my suit jacket. Now depending on how I'm standing or leaning against the platform wall, my gun can be visible. People glance suspiciously at me and back away. I always smile, and try and look friendly. I'm mingling with the people I'm paid to protect.

I move from my air-conditioned subway car onto the scorching platform and up the stairs into the muggy summer morning. All these federal buildings are named after some former government official, usually a Senator from the state or a revered member of the House of Representatives. This building is no exception. It's a block wide and within spitting distance from ground zero, our national tragedy. It's an ugly, nondescript government building where tens of federal employees hang around the entrance puffing on the last of their cigarettes until they are forced to return to a smoke-free environment.

Immigration does have a special dislike for American men and women who are willing to sell their name on a marriage license since the fastest route to a green card is marriage to an American. The petitions of foreigners seeking green cards by marrying Americans are scrutinized carefully. For the right price there are dozens of Americans willing to sell their name on a marriage license. The going rate is $10,000. Love at first sight is not a concept immigration officials accept.

Marriage scams escalated since 2001, when a change in federal regulations resulted in thousands of foreigners rushing to City Hall for that precious marriage license. The lines wrapped around the marriage license bureau at 1 Centre Street. The food vendors were jubilant about the new business during those curious weeks. They may have been witnesses to a crime as the same American stood waiting on line with a series of different foreigners. Their responsibilities didn't extend to reporting the unusual only making certain that the food they sold didn't poison any unsuspecting customer. Besides many of these food vendors were themselves illegal immigrants, hungry for a green card.

Our assigned immigration bureaucrat, Tony Adams, is a nice fellow. He is open about sharing information in his files. He is without guile probably because he's too low in the hierarchal food chain. This is our first meeting since all our previous contact has been by the phone or through the ubiquitous e-mail.

We see a figure rise from a maze of partition walls after Jimmy says, "We're here to see Tony Adams."

A man moves from his cubicle towards us. His clothes are rumpled and his white shirt frayed around the cuffs. The Salvation Army would reject this donation. He offers us a chair and a cup of coffee as we sit in his cramped, messy cubicle; space is at a premium in lower Manhattan. "So guys, you're looking into the Jacob Feinstein—Olga Moisseyev marriage. I got the file but I don't need a file. I remember them." He smiles at us, his crooked teeth showing. "You met the widow?" our fellow public servant asks with a light laugh.

Jimmy immediately likes this guy. "Yes we have," and my partner whistles.

"Yeh," Mr. Adams' smile gets broader and you can see the cigarette stains along the ridges of his teeth.

"Beauty and the Beast," he adds.

Yes, a totally apt description. I give Mr. Adams credit for his wolfish imagination.

"We did wonder about the arrangement," speaking as one of the members of the immigration unit. "They came in together. He is, oh, forgive me, I don't want to speak ill of the dead, but he was a fat slob although he wore a suit and tie that day. He was busting out of the shirt. She is beautiful. Great legs. What a picture. She is blonde and thin. He was big and ugly."

He looks down at the file and his fingers skip over some of the pages. He glances at a particular page for a moment.

"We can't chase down every American who decides to marry a foreigner for questionable reasons. I mean how much time is there in a day. Give me a break." He takes one sheet of paper from the pile.

"Yeah, we are always suspicious. I mean we're like cops in a way. But we save our energies for the big cases. You remember the woman who married forty-four different guys. Now that was a case worth pursuing." I did vaguely remember the story in the newspapers.

Jimmy is yawning; undoubtedly a late night with Lori and his increasing boredom with sorting through government bureaucracy. The action is missing; and in Jimmy's police world of tracking down the bad guys and chasing down cases, this case is developing into one routine bore. If we could find photos or videos of group sex then I would have his complete attention.

Adams picks up the paper and checks it one more time. "She said they would get married in church." He watches Jimmy stretch his arm muscles and then crack his knuckles one by one. The noise I find absolutely grating. The Immigration guy just observes in admiration so impressed with Jimmy's dexterity.

"Where did they get married? Do you have a marriage license?" I ask.

"Yes," and he passes a piece of paper in my general direction. The paper floats in the air; we watch it sail on the streams of forced air from the air-conditioner and it lands in my hand.

"They got married at City Hall but then after we called them in for an interview, they got married by a priest."

Jimmy turns his attention to fixing his tie. He sees his reflection in the glass window. The cubicle has a great view of the city since we are twenty stories up. Not bad amenities for a government worker.

"Can we get a copy of this paper?" I inquire and the man dutifully leaves his chair and heads to a copier machine.

Jimmy turns towards me. "So what's the purpose of all this? Are you looking to cap off your diplomatic skills by joining Immigration? Why are we here?"

I am about to answer when the man slips back into his office and hands us the paper.

"Thanks, we may be in touch," I say as we exit.

The tipping point is about to be reached for Jimmy and this case. If I am to retain his interest we need to find the links with the sex slave aspect of the case.

"Listen," Jimmy says as we approach our unmarked car, "I don't care if we go looking for some Russian Orthodox priest somewhere in Brooklyn and ask a few questions, but really what have we got?"

"Bubkis, that's what we got," I reply. Jimmy understands what the word means since he's learning bits of Yiddish by working with me.

"I mean if you want to see her," then he gives me his mischievous eye.

"Do you think we know what happened? And motive. What about the group sex. Think. Were the three sisters thrilled with that part of the housing arrangement?" I urge him to consider.

"Alright, maybe, just maybe, there is something here. Do we know if anything really happened or was he just a fat slob boasting to a friend? Um...m." Jimmy removes his suit jacket and places it very carefully on the back seat of the car to keep it from wrinkling in the heat.

"Amuse me," I plead.

"We'll probably never know what happened because I don't think she was there when he died. I don't think there's anything here," and he shrugs his shoulders. "But if you want to waste an afternoon, I don't care. Sometimes your screwy ideas have developed into something and besides we have nothing else to do."

Jimmy takes a look at his reflection in the outside side mirror. "I'd rather be driving around in the streets in an air-conditioned car than stuck in the station house with those useless fans."

I read the church documents. As my father suspected, she is Ukrainian and they didn't get married in a Russian Orthodox Church but a Ukrainian Catholic Church. I have the address. We're headed to the church to question the priest who married them when we get the call.

Jimmy talks on his cell phone for a few minutes, mumbling responses. "We are wanted back at the station. The Lieutenant has a case for us," he tells me and he begins to whistle. "The Sarge didn't say much but it could be important. We are needed immediately." A small smile appears on his face. I turn the car south. My case will have to wait.

The Lieutenant has his back to us when we enter his office. Then he turns to speak to us like Moses to the repentant masses, wandering the desert in search of truth and enlightenment.

"I need you, Perlov and Sutton, to work on this. We got a problem because the Deputy Commissioner has a problem. His problems are our problems." We always hear this line when the brass in Lower Manhattan is feeling political pressure from some citizens group or an influential contributor, who thinks a case is absolutely vital to the protection of the public's safety. We proceed with great speed like the time a cute, little white child from the Upper East Side was reported missing. We were all involved, even us guys from Brooklyn South.

"Someone or groups of people are committing all kinds of

vandalism against Jews in Brooklyn, so I offered you," he points to me.

Being one of the few Jews in the Department, I have done anti-Semitic bias crime investigations in the past. Jimmy was with me the last time and we solved that baby. It looked like the Lieutenant wanted us to pair up again.

The cases are complex and there's a lot of chasing around looking for a different breed of criminal. Jimmy likes these types of cases. There are lots of people to talk to because it's rarely one isolated incident. When we do well, there's great publicity and public notice. It can be frustrating because there are so many leads and unless it's a bomb or a shooting, few clues. But if we get the culprits, everybody loves us. We walk on water. This could be our golden messenger.

We have had a string of great cases. A normally unsuccessful investigation of a mugging case led to the solving of a major murder case. If we succeeded in getting the culprits on the bias cases, we were looking at promotions; the Lieutenant's reward a corner captain's office when the old man occupying the seat retired.

Was Brooklyn awash in anti-Semitism? We were brought on now because the cases, after months of supposed police investigation, remained unsolved. The politicians were screaming at the Mayor and the Police Commissioner, so the Chief of Brooklyn South told all his field commanders that the criminals had to be brought to justice. Tires were slashed in Borough Park. Congregants arriving for morning prayers in Midwood found swastikas on the synagogue. Apartment buildings near a neighborhood synagogue known to be home to Jews with large numbers of Holocaust survivors, awakened to find swastikas on the building wall facing the street.

"Your assignment is to focus on the Borough Park case. I doubt there's a connection among all these cases in different parts of Brooklyn but stay alert to the possibility. Find the bad guys and bring them in," says the Lieutenant as he looks directly at me. "Your people need you, Perlov the Protector. Get those bastards."

I remembered the last case. "And if they're fellow Jews?" I raised the possibility that finding the truth brought unexpected results that the politicians hated but citizens accepted because human nature had a dark, self-loathing side. How else can a neo-Nazi Jew be explained?

"Find the culprits—it doesn't matter who they are. Clear your calendars, put everything on hold. Start immediately," he barks at us.

We start by assuming there's a relationship among all the incidents. Organization is the key; we begin by studying the patterns if any exist, plotting the crimes by census block, questioning the victims, assembling the names of potential witnesses and from that hopefully will emerge a list of suspects. Hunting down criminals is hard work.

The case is launched. "Can we get some visual aids here?" I ask Jimmy.

He turns and heads downstairs. I hear him yelling, "Geary, do we have a blackboard somewhere?" Geary, the new department softball hitting champion, will do anything for us. He is convinced that his game is significantly improved by repeatedly mouthing softly, 'Hero of Harbor House, Perlov the Protector' while at bat.

Geary and Jimmy carry a dilapidated old schoolroom blackboard up the stairs and gingerly place it near our desks. It squeaks in the shrillest voice as Jimmy pushes it across the floor. I feel my teeth ache as he moves it closer towards me.

"Okay, now we need a big map of Brooklyn so we can locate exactly where our vandals have struck. Patterns, we're looking for patterns." I tell my partner.

Jimmy understands the importance of a detailed map so he heads to the top floor where we hide the computer geeks.

The blackboard, probably a reject from nearby P.S. 100, does come equipped with pastel colored chalk and a worn but functional eraser.

I'm writing on the board when Jimmy returns with a large street map of Brooklyn. We are putting our tools to use. Luckily the map has a Styrofoam backing, which is perfect for our use.

The files are delivered from the other precincts as well as the one from the uniforms who are investigating the apartment house in Brighton Beach.

Jimmy pins the map to the blackboard with thumb tacks, and I tell him the addresses. He knows his Brooklyn. I watch in admiration because he is a born cartographer; his knowledge of even the smallest lanes that cut through the borough is legendary. He finds each address and gives the brightly colored push pin a nudge into the map. We now have a pictorial representation of our many crimes.

"Okay what do we see?" I ask out loud and begin pacing. "The crimes are spread all over the map." I fold my arms across my chest, staring at the map. "Any similarities beyond the obvious? They happened in predominantly Jewish neighborhoods and they are directed against Jews? What else?" I wonder about these inconsistent and scattered clues.

Jimmy stares at the map and looks for patterns. "Right. Something in the geography? We have four cases. Two are in Borough Park. Both of these occurred on main streets. The synagogue is in Midwood and on a small street. The defacing of the apartment house in Brighton Beach is also on a little off-street."

"Nothing obvious yet," I add.

We both like to think out loud when we are planning out an investigation. We just talk without finishing sentences or thoughts. Anything in our heads is said. At school, they would label this a brainstorming session, but pragmatic cops just see it as thinking out loud—no wrong answers, no one spared suspicion, no need for sense because most petty criminals are not logical beasts. Separate the facts from the possibilities and later think about the probabilities.

I write on the board the locations of the events and the crimes.

So we have two separate reported incidents of tires being slashed in Borough Park.

"Why is this a bias crime and not simply vandalism?" I stand with one foot resting on the other as I speak. I can stand in this awkward position for hours. Ballet lessons in my early years in Petersburg have a practical application in police work.

"Nothing makes this a bias crime except it's in Borough Park and lots of bearded Jews with long, black coats live there," Jimmy responds, sitting at his desk.

"Let's read the files and see what the uniforms uncovered, if anything." Jimmy hands me the first file on the tire slashings; and he opens the second folder, and starts reading.

"There were 36 slashings on the first incident and 18 on the second," Jimmy says as he repeats the information handwritten on a single piece of note paper stuffed into the file.

Instantly, I know this is significant. "Well that's interesting because 18 has an almost magical connotation among Jews. Eighteen is the good luck number so maybe there is something here. And of course 36 is double 18. Jewish people often give money presents or donations to charity in increments of 18." Probably no one else in the station house knows this fact since I am the only Jew. But the criminal knows this fact.

"So this means the criminal is a Jew?" Jimmy says as he looks up at the worn blackboard.

"I don't know, but it is not likely a random decision." A Jewish neo-Nazi suspect, that's what I'm thinking. Maybe a Jewish convert to Islam is responsible. It's probably some stupid kids but they have to have some Jewish knowledge. Eighteen is not a haphazard number to choose.

We both continue to read the files for clues, searching for answers where there are none. We will need more information than these skimpy files provide. Walking the streets, talking to strangers, canvassing the neighborhood will lead to answers.

"What about the instrument. Do we have a forensics report on what did the cutting?" I ask.

Jimmy looks through the investigation forms. The police department has forms for everything. "I don't see a thing; I'll call the lab to ask if forensics worked on the case and if they have any information."

The best weapon of destruction is a box cutter, effective for slashing anything including faces. We once had a case with a model whose face was slashed with a box cutter. All the plastic surgery in the world would never remove those scars. A jilted lover was responsible; he was filled with hate, without a hint of mercy or pity. Love can be twisted; never discount its power to inflict pain. Our Borough Park tire slashings could be the work of a Jewish stalker, leaving his victim a veiled threat. The vandalism was annoying, but meaningless to everyone affected except the intended victim who immediately recognized the clear and threatening intent of the action. I was thinking a man but why not a woman.

Unexpectedly, my mind suddenly drifted to a particular woman. Love, no, lust was on my mind. My Russian Lady and her fat dead husband, what kind of love existed between them?

"How about a box cutter?" My brain returns to the tires.

Jimmy has one in his desk and takes it out so we both stare at it. I grab it from him and feel how dainty it sits in the palm of my hand. So small, but so dangerous is this piece of metal and plastic.

I'm fascinated with the potential of box cutters. As the preferred weapon of criminals intent on serious maiming, nothing compares to a box cutter. And for slicing necks. Nothing does a more effective job at cutting a throat than a box cutter, small and easy to hide in a pocket. It's no wonder that the terrorists used them on 9/11.

"The kid weapon of choice would be a nail," I advise. Available and completely ordinary, a nail just requires a quick visit to Dad's tool chest.

"How about knives," Jimmy shouts. Yes, knives are useful weapons for all types of crimes, and they come in so many varieties in terms of size, shape, different handles, angle of the blade. If it is a knife, it is probably the kitchen variety, and therefore too difficult to trace. A good investigation doesn't neglect any of the pieces.

"Witnesses, do we have any witnesses?" I ask. They are often unreliable but essential for most cases.

Jimmy searches the notes of the responding uniforms and notes a few scribbled names. He pulls the page from the file and lifts it towards the ceiling light. He squints as the light hits his blood-shot, tired eyes. "I can barely read this but I think I got a name or two. They ought to give those uniforms handwriting lessons. What sloppiness."

If there's one thing I can say about my partner, his handwriting is beautiful. No one who reads his notes would have any trouble deciphering any words or numbers. Addresses, he is especially careful with when writing reports.

"Do we have telephone numbers?" I inquire as I take a piece of chalk in one hand.

"No, but we have addresses. We can get a clerk to look these things up." Civilians do many grunt functions for the police department. It's not that we're such expensive employees to handle computer search and find functions, but our training is too job-specific to waste on such mundane activities.

"How about the victims? Do we have the names of any of these people or at least license plates for the cars?"

Jimmy searches. "It's incomplete but it looks like we have a few license plates. I can have someone track down the names and addresses. What are you thinking?"

"Maybe, just maybe, we have a few victims who didn't discard their damaged tires. Now we have some evidence. It would be particularly important if we have a tire from the first batch of 36 slashings and a tire from the second group of 18. Is it the same person or persons? If it was the same cutting tool? Right?"

Jimmy is shaking his head. I know he likes where I'm going. "Okay, and then?" he poses the question.

"That new technology the Commissioner is boasting about, wouldn't this be a perfect use for the new DNA lab. Couldn't we call this a property crime?" The Police Department has established a new DNA lab through the Medical Examiner's Office to investigate property crimes. The magic part of this new technology is using just tiny bits of DNA, less than a dozen cells instead of the 100+ necessary for murder cases. Let's join the cutting edge crowd. The Lieutenant will like this and since it's been tentatively labeled a bias crime no one will protest the use of valuable department resources.

"You think we will find something after so many months? And DNA from these crimes would come up on our criminal database?" Jimmy is right to be skeptical since only violent offenders or major crime figures are currently logged in the system.

"We can try because murderers and rapists start with petty crimes. Could be our tire slasher has since moved on to more serious activities. Or maybe he's not a kid, but an adult criminal with a vendetta to settle. We're not likely to find the instrument he used to cut the tires, but the tires might have a few smudged fingerprints."

"Yes, this has a more promising feel to it." Jimmy smiles with delight; he takes out a pack of cinnamon gum from his pocket and hands me a stick. I can smell the tangy flavor the moment I see it. The silver foil packaging cannot mask the scent. It's Jimmy's present to me for providing a case we can really get involved with and not a hunch about a Russian Lady watching her pig of a husband die of a heart attack.

"Okay, so what do we know about the Borough Park incidents," I repeat to myself as my partner watches me; and then he reiterates the threadbare facts that we know at this moment.

He starts with the obvious. "Right now we have shit," he answers quickly. "The guys at the 71st did a crappy job of getting info. But if we find a few tires we might have some evidence. Yes, the magic of science has real potential here."

"Our brethren at the 71st were not paying enough attention because they assumed it was childish vandalism, but just maybe there's something else here," I reflect out loud while Jimmy shakes his head in agreement.

The phone rings and instinctively Jimmy picks it up. "Sutton here."

I am concentrating on the blackboard.

"For you; I think its Mrs. Chervony. I can't understand what she's saying," and Jimmy hands me the receiver.

"Hello Detective Perlov," and I recognize her voice and we speak in Russian.

I hang up the phone. "She wants to see me." I'm reluctant to leave my partner to scramble through the limited and incomplete pieces of evidence.

"Go, I'll get help from the computer geeks on any crime reports and make some calls to the 71st about names of victims. I'll ask about witnesses. I would like to call the FBI and see if we can get a few morsels of info from those squirrels. Perlov the Protector, your people need you."

I walk to her apartment; it's only a few blocks from the station house. It's hot today, but I don't take off my suit jacket. If my gun, sitting comfortably in its holster, is visible to people in this Coney Island neighborhood, they immediately respond negatively to my presence here. Tempers flare in the heat and I don't want any excuse for trouble.

I ring the building bell and straightaway notice the new security video cameras. I doubt the camera's picture is perfectly clear but it's enough of a deterrent to keep any bad guys from hanging around these apartments. She rings me in and I walk down the corridor. I notice more cameras. The politicians came through with more money for security. There's even a small camera in the stuffy elevator.

She is waiting for me, standing in front of her open apartment door. I walk towards her small frame.

"Detective Perlov, I'm so glad to see you," and she grabs my hand and shakes it forcefully.

"Come in, I'll make some tea," she says enthusiastically. It's more than 90 degrees outside but it's never too warm for Russians to drink hot tea.

A stocky and well built man of middle age, with a full head of dark hair freckled with gray, stands as I enter the room.

"My son Grigori," she smiles widely at the mention of his name.

"Sasha Perlov," I answer.

"Sasha," he says questioningly. "That's your real name?"

"Fyodor Ilich, but in America you can be anything you want to be."

He laughs jovially. "Yes, in America, you can remake yourself. You start all over beginning with a new name." He pumps my hand as we shake.

I take off my jacket. No one in this room will be uneasy with my visible gun.

"Grigori, put on the air-conditioner for the Detective." I don't object since the ocean breezes cannot cool this room today. The air conditioner hums quietly, quickly bringing relief. It probably is only used for special company like the good silver and the best China tableware, precious like presents from long lost relatives.

"You got the criminal who assaulted my mother?" the dutiful son inquires.

I nod my head. "A stupid black kid from the projects." Then I point to my head. "Not much up here."

"I beg my mother to move in with us. Move to Staten Island, but she's a stubborn old woman, probably why she's lasted so long." She kisses the top of his hair.

"I like it here. The ocean is right at my door. I stroll on Boardwalk all year round. There are few bad apples. But I have my protector," and she reaches over and squeezes my arm.

"You're good man, Detective Perlov. These old people depend upon you to protect them from the colored." He sighs. "I can't get her to move. It's difficult to get her to visit. You would think Staten Island is other side of world. I mean we have plenty of Russians there now. Stores and restaurants right in my neighborhood. She's just stubborn." And he smiles, and she takes his hand in hers. We hear the kettle whistle.

Her son helps her bring the tea to the table next to the sofa. "Will my mother have to testify in court." We both turn to look at his mother. She is ready; her hand is locked in a tight fist.

"No, it's not necessary because the kid confessed and he will be sentenced by a judge." I will not divulge the part about using Albert as bait to catch some real criminals.

"Will it help if she went before the judge and described what happened," he asks.

I think about the convergence of two distinct cultures in the courthouse. The accused stands with his public defender lawyer arguing for mercy. After all, he's of limited mental ability and has had a rocky start in life. Maybe his mother's drug addiction affecting his mental abilities. Then there is the old immigrant victim, small and defenseless. The court and judge represent the scales of justice. But where is the justice? Can the punishment ever equal the crime? Albert steals only a dollar but he inflicts great psychological pain on an innocent woman who is struggling to find peace in America. Yet Albert is himself a victim, a little brain is trapped in a bear's body.

"He will be locked up in prison, and the streets will be safer. I can assure you both of that." I answer with confidence although I don't know which judge will be assigned this case, but none of them will let this act of callous incivility go unpunished.

"Those colored kids are dangerous. I tell my mother to be careful when she shops or goes on Boardwalk. She doesn't listen." We look at the small woman who is disobedient because she demands to live an independent life. In America, there are freedoms unthinkable in Soviet Russia. The new Russia, despite its introduction of courts and law, has given birth to wanton criminals just like those who haunt the alleyways of Coney Island.

"When we arrived, we had nothing. We got help from Jewish Family Services for six months. So I started my own business," Grigori tells me. He's following a popular path for immigrants.

"I know Russian Mafia here. That Mikhail, the young boss, I met him when I started my business." He is proud to make the acquaintance of a Russian gangster.

He moves closer to me; we aren't concerned with personal space. "When I arrived I needed some capital. Where could I go? No friends or relatives here with any money." He winks and clutches my arm. "So I go to someone I know has money. And he treated me well."

He sucks in his lips and makes a soft smacking sound. "Could I go to a bank? Who wants a bank to know so much about you. Right?" He wants my concurrence with his decision and I'm not certain how to respond. As a police officer, I cannot be recommending that citizens use the services of gangsters. I say nothing but nonchalantly shrug my shoulders.

"I saw him today. I stopped on Brighton Beach Avenue to pick up some food for my mother. He was standing in front of Russian grocery. I walked right up to him." Grigori points his finger in the air as he demonstrates his familiarity with the local celebrities.

I don't tell my hosts how much closer I am to Mikhail and his brother Vasily. I listen.

"Now my business is thriving," spoken by a proud, successful immigrant.

"I still don't like banks but I keep checking account." He gently slaps my shoulder.

His story continues. "I was engineer in Russia, but there was no place in America for electrical engineer trained in systems not used here. And my English wasn't good. So now I'm importer. I make good living for my family; I give money to my shul and charities that assist immigrant Russians." He smiles at his very pleased, beaming mother.

Grigori looks intensively at me; I can feel the heat of his perspiration. "I asked Mikhail why his men couldn't provide security for the old people at the senior housing."

I wait for the answer.

"He told me that it's your job," and he gently jabs me in the arm. "Mikhail tells me that the police are responsible."

"It is our job," I quickly add. "You pay taxes for me to be on streets protecting the community. And I see new cameras in buildings that politicians promised." It's an election year. The police are trying. "We have more undercover and uniform cops on Boardwalk during daylight. Things are not perfect but it's under control. Our greater physical presence scares off most would-be petty assailants."

The cameras must scare off Vasily and his brother's men. I know they would like to be seen as a positive community resource, but not if his people's faces or bodies are caught on film by police. The FBI and NYPD are building cases against the Russian Mob, but the information remains inconclusive for the American courts. Informers are few because nothing the American authorities can threaten will equal the punishment meted out by their fellow Russians. Torture is not forbidden by Russian organized crime figures.

Mrs. Chervony edges closer to me. I can feel her hot breath from the tea, "You are good man. You come from fine blood. I told Grigori that you are grandson of Dmetri Aronovich, Hero of the Battle of Stalingrad." She taps my arm lightly and sinks back into the comfort of the soft sofa. "Stories, I tell about those days. Sometimes I don't think grandchildren believe me. You had to be there to fully comprehend. It's like trying to understand what it was like to survive concentration camps. People can't really understand suffering. The human heart doesn't want to believe." She sighs.

Her son places his heavy arm lightly on her shoulder. He knows these stories.

She pats my hand. "I would like to meet your mother. I was only simple citizen during those hellish days but I want to thank her for her father's brave actions on people's behalf and," she smiles and squeezes my hand, "to thank her for her wonderful son who continues in family tradition."

I blush from her gushing praise, embarrassed for the entire family. "Oh, she doesn't need to be thanked."

The old woman is insistent. "Yes, yes, I want to meet your

mother. I didn't realize who she was until my son said something."

Grigori shifts his weight in his chair and looks directly at me. "Anna Aronovich; that's a name some Russian people know. The fiery Jewish dissident, Russian Jews seeking emigration in the 1970's and 80's know that name. What is your mother doing now here in America?"

"She became Anna Perlov, corporate employee and loyal naturalized citizen." I respond with a wily smile.

He sips his tea slowly then says, "She also is remaking herself? Yes?"

"Yes, she is out of the spotlight. She only writes letters to local politicians on behalf of her fellow Russians, mostly seniors who don't understand English."

"No more hunger strikes, underground newspapers, or public displays of civil disobedience?" he asks.

Mrs. Chervony interrupts, "What for? This is good country."

"Everything is perfect in America," her son responds with a slightly sarcastic tone, not harsh, but still critical.

I defend my mother as a good son should do when she is criticized. "Really, she likes it here. And I guess more than anything, she got tired. She's older and she just wants to enjoy her new life." I sometimes marvel at my mother's uncritical acceptance of American life.

He puckers up his face like a succulent pig on a goyish dinner table. "I guess she's entitled to little peace."

"A good Russian, she's suffered enough," my tiny hostess adds and gives her son a hearty zetz on the arm.

He hardly feels the impact.

"I want to invite your mother to tea," the old woman says in a firm and adamant tone.

I protest; my arms rest across my chest in an unthreatening act of defiance. "No, no, it's not necessary."

"Yes, it's important to me," and she is very solemn for a moment as she waits for me to give in to her request.

I shrug, too weary to argue. "Of course, I'll tell her to call you."

"No," she stops and pauses; we all wait patiently, "Please give me her number and I'll call her."

I write down on a notepad my family's phone number. My people can be quite demanding. Hero of Harbor House, Perlov the Protector, has to capitulate in order to keep his free-thinking fiefdom happy.

My mother will be flattered and Mrs. Chervony will be a most gracious hostess thanking the entire family for past deeds as well as my notable future actions. Uncle Vanya, the Cossack, was also remembered for his good deeds—family traditions are carried forward in this New Jerusalem.

CHAPTER 10

When I return to the station house, Jimmy is ready to begin the investigation. The computer geeks were able to match names and addresses. We now have a short victims list.

"How did it go with Mrs. Chervony, Hero of Harbor House, Perlov the Protector," he grins with that sweet, boyish smile that reduces the ladies to mush.

I give him a quick, playful zetz.

"Did she bake you cookies," his smile is even wider.

"No," and now that he mentioned it, I'm surprised she made no offering.

"Okay, let's get back to real business," and he's grabbing his linen suit jacket and heading for the car. I tag along.

I admit, I am not paying attention. My mind is on a nice dairy-rich pound cake or big, raisin cookies with the edges burnt, just slightly.

I get into the car without thinking and Jimmy, the navigator, directs me to Borough Park.

"This one is supposed to be an important person in the community," Jimmy tells me.

I nod and drive. My attention is divided between the car in front of me and scanning the people walking on the sidewalk.

Always looking for bad guys is the way we approach our job, try and prevent crime. Although there are many critics of the police department's focusing on quality of life, petty crimes, most citizens appreciate the positive results—crime is down. The city is safer and cleaner, and everyone is benefiting, especially those folks trapped in high crime areas such as Coney Island.

This assignment is interfering with my Case of the Russian Lady. I prefer investigating her and her relationship with her fat, dead husband. There's a crime there; I just know it. Still I am an obedient minion and so I go, and maybe something interesting will develop.

I spot a stocky guy on the street and my mind drifts to Mrs. Chervony's son Grigori. It's not him; the man just reminds me of Grigori and I wonder about his relationship with Mikhail. How much do I really want to know about the brothers' business? I prefer to remain dumb and blind although I listen to the gossip and search FBI alerts about Russian organized crime.

Vasily, his older brother Mikhail, and their entire family were part of a small circle of friends back in the Motherland. They were one of the few in the neighborhood who were not intimidated by the Soviet authorities. Vasily and I were close growing up. Fingered by our teachers for being Jews and unafraid of being identified with the label, we bonded. Discriminating against Jews was only one example of the absurdities of the Soviet system. After all, Russian Jews were the heart and soul of Soviet communism. People like my grandfather had fomented and spread the gospel of communism in those early days. He went to his grave a committed Communist. And how did the Soviet regime thank those tireless Jewish devotees; by creating a new category of subversive called the Jewish dissident, which the KGB hounded and sometimes imprisoned.

As I drive, it's clear I am heading to a unique New York City neighborhood. You know immediately when you enter the Borough Park enclave. I see the women in their long skirts and covered heads pushing baby strollers surrounded by lots of little heads following behind. I can't picture myself the father of ten.

Jimmy tells me to stop; this is the address. There's no point searching for legal parking on these congested streets. I park by a fire hydrant.

It's only then that I recognize the building.

"What's the victim's name," I ask Jimmy.

"Rosenberg," he says.

It's a common enough name in many parts of Brooklyn.

"He's expecting us?" I inquire with a truly surprised look on my face.

"Yeah, he seemed eager on the phone to meet with the police." Jimmy stares at my flustered face.

"Does he have the tire from the attack?"

"I didn't ask. He was so pleased that the police are actively pursuing the case and wanted to meet with us." Cooperation with the public is what we need to break cases; I understand Jimmy's enthusiasm.

We announce ourselves to a young Hasid at the door. I know enough about Borough Park and the man we are about to meet to know we are in Lubavitcher territory. This old, sturdy building belongs to the neighboring synagogue. This is where the business of running a major Jewish institution is located. Our young man is courteous and ushers us into Rosenberg's cluttered study.

"Rebbe Rosenberg," I address the man sitting behind the desk. I know him, does he remember me. I call him rebbe, a Hasidic term for a rabbi with a following and as a sign of respect. The Rabbi doesn't stir from his chair. Jimmy walks behind me. The man gestures and we sit down in the two chairs facing the bearded man.

"I am Detective Perlov and," pointing to my partner, "Detective Sutton from Brooklyn South."

The Rabbi pushes his glasses up his nose, closer to his deep-set, brown eyes; heavy dark bags form half-circles under them.

"Perlov?" He looks intently at me, examining my face. His eyes first concentrate on my almost ebony, dark eyes. Then they travel and focus on my angular nose. I feel his gaze while his eyes progress across my cheeks and down to my dry lips. I feel his absorption with my very being.

I nod my head.

"Perlov, we have met. You are a relative of Anna Perlov?"

"Yes Rebbe, I am her son."

Now his face lightens and he smiles at us. It's been a few years but obviously he remembers me although we met only twice. There are many who come to seek his counsel and assistance, in matters large and small. My mother's case is worth vividly recalling. Her desperate pleas for help and her tears of despair during that initial visit immediately softened his heart. Who, she asked herself day after day, could she turn to for help in her complicated and difficult project? The Rebbe's organization is always soliciting money and used cars so she tells my father, why not them. The Lubavitchers are everywhere in the universe and the most visible Hasid sect to outsiders.

The rabbi asks, "How is your mother?" The question is filled with genuine interest and concern.

"She is well." I answer knowing that this man performed a Herculean task for my mother, which she can never forget. He is a man in her daily prayers. For his sake she is more observant although she still doesn't believe in God. It is the least she could do for the man responsible for bringing my mother's project to triumph using his worldwide contacts. I think he found it a challenge. If the Lubavitchers perform these tasks for this anguished, desperate woman then surely keeping Judaism alive in the former Soviet Union is a simple undertaking.

"Retzd di Yiddish?" he asks me if I speak Yiddish. Most of my mother's conversation with the Rebbe is in Yiddish.

"Ich farshtey a bissel Yiddish," I answer him that I speak a little Yiddish.

He is going to start to speak in Yiddish, but I say, "Rebbe for my partner's sake, can we speak in English?"

He nods.

I need Jimmy to participate in the interviewing and if we speak Yiddish and I translate, he will lose the nuances of the mamaloshen, the mother tongue of Eastern European Jews. But by speaking English, we begin the investigation together and nothing will be lost in translation.

Two sets of ears are important in interviewing a victim, especially since the case is already old, if not totally cold. We are fishing for information; we have few leads and no suspects. You always miss something even if you take notes, but a second person can catch the lost mumbled words, the body language, sounds whispered or words spoken under one's breath.

"You are one of the victims of the tire slashings?"

"Yes, my old car was attacked?"

"The case is getting new life. We have been assigned to look into acts of vandalism against Jewish property in Brooklyn," I answer and Jimmy nods his head in agreement.

"Perlov, a good name and a fine family. What an accomplishment. Right?" He is thinking back to my mother's request and smiles with deep satisfaction; I nod my head in agreement.

"Yes, I can feel that you will find the no goodniks." He extends his arms across his desk as if he is making a benediction, visibly more comfortable in our presence. His shoulders relax and he slouches in the chair.

"Yes, if someone will find them, it will be you," he says with complete confidence. "Your mother is a fighter. She digs in and doesn't let go, so will you." He taps his clutched fist against his heart and points to me. "I feel it here," and he gently strikes his chest. "Hashem has brought you to us."

I offer him a reason to feel so secure. "We have had some success a few years back finding a criminal who was defacing synagogues," I tell him.

"Who were these criminals you found the last time?" He eagerly asks.

Jimmy answers. "It turned out to be a young Jewish kid, looking for a little excitement. He was the one who found the graffiti. Like a firefighter who sets fires."

I purposefully fail to mention the kid's Neo-Nazi fascination.

"A goniff," the Rabbi answers angrily. Jimmy doesn't need a

translator. The Rebbe's face turns beet red; rage fills him.

"Let's start with this case," I suggest. The case gets older each minute and we are in short supply of any solid facts. We need to learn does anyone actually know what happened? Are there witnesses who have not come forward?

"Do you still have that tire?"

He shakes his head, "No, no," he rubs his chin covered by his long, dark beard. "I gave it to the man at the service station when he replaced the damaged tire."

"It's OK," I say with coolness and poise. "Which station?"

"The one owned by the Dominican a few blocks down the next street."

"You remember the name?"

He gives me a shrug. "Names, I don't always remember names."

Jimmy knows Brooklyn, we will find the place.

"Do you know anyone else who had their tires slashed over that two day period?"

He scratches his forehead with his hand while the dark curls fall, covering his eyes. I notice his long, straight fingers, so beautiful; clearly they belong to a man who doesn't do manual labor. He labors at his books, writing, discussing and arguing the finer points of the Talmud.

"I have to think. I'm sure someone from this shul also had their tire slashed. You think if I had saved the tire, it would have helped?"

"We'll see, but maybe the station still has it. Could be others from the neighborhood went to him."

"I could have gone to Sears to replace that tire, but I like to buy from local businessmen."

Forensics helps if we can locate a tire, but cases are built on people who see things or hear gossip or rumors about the culprits. Criminals love to brag about their crimes to their friends or co-workers or to impress a girl. We find many bad guys because they have big mouths. In Coney Island, occasionally we find bad girls, desperate drug addicts or prostitutes who commit violent acts but it's the guys we usually watch. That's why I'm having difficulty convincing Jimmy that my Russian Lady is potentially a suspect and responsible for her husband's death. Shock is how to describe a case when we discover a wife actually is responsible for killing her husband. Motive is the key. We easily believe that a husband can kill his wife because there's another woman. In fact, the gentle sex is more than capable of committing a murder or hiring someone else to do the killing.

However, young men are most likely to commit vandalism. Truly shocking would be the reaction of everyone, including the police, if we find the culprit here is a woman. I press our victim, "You will inquire at shul if there are other victims?"

"Yes, yes and I will ask if they still have the tire," he adds, understanding that I need his assistance if we are to crack this case.

"Who do you think did these terrible things?" he inquires while tapping his fingers on the desk.

"We're taking a fresh approach," Jimmy puts a positive spin on our mission. We have no leads and, if not for politicians clamoring for justice, the case would lie dormant for years until someone confesses or a friend or acquaintance squeals.

I tell the rabbi. "We mull over two tactics." I sit closer to the Rebbe's solid wood desk crammed with religious texts and endless sheets of loose-leaf paper scattered across the surface. "On one hand, we assume that the case is not a random property crime, but specifically targeted against Jews. We consider the possibility that a variety of similar acts of vandalism here in Brooklyn are part of a larger conspiracy." I extend my left arm across the desk with the palm showing to demonstrate our logical approach. I don't initially mention the fact that 36 tires were slashed the first time and then 18 the next time since I don't yet know what it means. The Rabbi knows the significance of the number 18 but it may cloud his responses to us.

"And then we take the opposite position and assume it's a series of malicious acts without any religious overtones." The

Rabbi is studying my face. As he listens, he strokes his beard. Religious men such as the rabbi do not shave.

Jimmy reaches down by his chair and pulls up his laptop computer. "I like to use the computer to take notes." He moves quietly to activate the machine; it's a new toy from Lori.

"If we assume it's a series of organized actions then who is most likely the culprit?" I watch the Rabbi's face while he watches my face and Jimmy's hands on the computer keyboard.

"If we were living in France, I would suggest unemployed, angry, alienated, and unassimilated Muslim youth born in France but whose parents came from North Africa," I say. The Rabbi has many contacts in France and he is familiar with the organized acts of vandalism and anti-Semitism committed by Muslim youth. Besides the great European cities, Lubavitchers have people posted among the small and dying Jewish communities in North Africa and Asia.

I continue. "But here in Brooklyn, most of the Muslims are employed, hard-working people; Turks and small numbers of other Arabs. We have Lebanese and Syrians, some Egyptians but many of them are Christians. We don't have large numbers of alienated Muslim youth."

The Rabbi agrees and nods his head. The Rabbi knows the innocent can look guilty and the guilty appear as cherubs.

"But we will start checking the Mosques because maybe the conventional wisdom is wrong. It takes only a few terrorists to do a great deal of damage. September 11th taught us that." I didn't want to bring it to his attention but a Yemeni cleric was arraigned in federal court in Brooklyn on charges of funneling money to Osama bin Laden from his Brooklyn mosque.

Rabbi Rosenberg says to me with concern painted on his face, "Be careful and check out that mosque with the terrorist cleric who gave money to bin Laden. Who knows how many are involved; as you say it takes only a few dedicated zealots. We keep track of his activities." It should not be a surprise what he and other Hasids know about hostile groups here in the New Jerusalem.

Jimmy and I will have to work with the Feds if we intend to look into a connection between terrorists and mosques. If the Lieutenant's so eager to get this solved then he will have to intervene. Those cagey bastards, you would think we were working on opposite sides of the law.

"Jimmy and I will be visiting the mosques in Brooklyn and Queens. We look for the new zealots. Many American Muslims are in fact America blacks—they converted. And there's Africans now living in NYC. Remember the shoe bomber, that guy Reid from England, was a black convert. When we start, we don't eliminate anyone. We look at all possible angles even if at first blush it seems illogical."

The Rabbi is following my lips and then shifting his attention to the sounds coming from the computer laptop.

I continue. This was the same logic we applied a few years ago on our other case. "Say it's not Muslims. So who else would be responsible for a series of anti-Semitic acts? The next logical group is white supremacists and Neo-Nazis. There aren't many members in NYC, but just like the foreign terrorists it doesn't take many people to make mayhem. The Police Department does track the Internet sites of these groups. The Feds are also concerned about these groups because some FBI agents are still concerned they didn't get all the culprits in the Oklahoma City terrorist attack. It's possible there are some native-born, white crazies with a terrorist cell here in NYC."

Jimmy types as if he's taking dictation. He wants to test if it makes a cop's routines more efficient; certainly the notes will be more legible than the handwritten scribble for most cops, although Jimmy's handwriting is impeccable.

Then we move from the lethal groups hiding undercover to the most obvious villain. Motive, the first rule of police work—motive.

"Rebbe could all these tire slashings around the shul be personal. Who do you know that has a grudge against you or the congregation?"

The Rabbi shakes his head. "No one. This is not about me or the shul." He adamantly rejects that possibility, but Jimmy and I know from police experience that the most likely vandalism suspect is someone who has a personal score to settle. It can be someone who you don't even know has a grudge. It doesn't matter that we are discussing a reported hate crime—a vandalism culprit is usually someone from the neighborhood who knows where to strike the vulnerable places. It takes a criminal with knowledge of the neighborhood to know where and when to strike. The ugly possibility is that the criminals are members of another nearby Hasidic shul or the worst possibility is that the criminal is a member of this shul, a crazy kid.

"No, no it's someone out there who hates Jews," the Rabbi is firm in his belief.

Jimmy and I have no proof to support any assumption of guilt so we just continue.

"Just play along with me, placate me. Has there been any rupture in the community? Have there been any arguments? Has anyone left the shul unhappy about anything? Have you received any threats even ones you consider idle words said in anger?"

The Rabbi wants to reject my questions, but he's listening.

"Don't we all want the truth?" I say with passion as I strike my fist against my heart.

"Nu," the Rabbi twists in his chair, reluctant to disclose incriminating information about a personal relationship. Then he sits up straight in his chair.

"Tell me, who did you have heated words with?" I plead.

"I don't want you harassing him," he pauses. "Moishe Glickenstein recently left the shul because of something very stupid."

Jimmy and I wait for the reason like two dogs eager for a treat. "There were some bad words about the finances of the shul."

Jimmy and I know that one of the prime motives for crime is money—a bad feeling about the almighty dollar is classic motive. Then there's the general malaise prompted by a lack of it. For some people, there can never be enough of it no matter how much they have or control.

"Yes," Jimmy asks.

The Rabbi describes a common issue among people who belong to a large organization where only a select few hold all the information, especially about finances. Do we smell a scandal over someone pocketing money? I watch my victim. This cop's gut says it feels like a power struggle. The ever-reluctant Rabbi gives us Moishe's address and phone number.

The Rabbi is apologetic, "When you speak to Moishe tell him from my heart that we want him back. We have nothing to hide."

"What else, can there be something more?" I implore.

He shakes his head.

We have a potential lead. "We will be back in touch," I tell the Rabbi. "It takes time to sort through the foreign influences but I'll call you next week and let you know what's happening. You will call if you remember any more names and please ask around other congregants or neighbors?" I pause and then add, "And if Mr. Glickenstein has a change of heart, I'll encourage him to call you."

The Rabbi replies, "Fun dein moyl in Gotts oyeren," from your mouth to God's ear.

Then on impulse because I can't always control these sparks of genius, which may turn to dreck—shit:

"Rebbe, a favor if you please."

He sits up in his giant leather chair. "Nu?"

"My parents will be celebrating their 40th wedding anniversary after the High Holidays. They never had a proper wedding. Would you be willing to perform a religious ceremony on their 40th anniversary?"

He doesn't hesitate for a second, "It would be my honor, my young Mr. Perlov, an honor."

As we leave Jimmy looks my way. "So what's with this guy, what did you call him?"

"Rebbe is a Yiddish word for a rabbi, but it means more. A rebbe is the social and spiritual leader of a Hasidic community.

He acts almost like an interpreter between the people and God."

"Who is this guy? You seem to know him pretty well, right?"

"He is an important member of this religious Jewish community here in Borough Park. When my mother got this idea in her head, a real bobbe meyseh, to re-locate the graves of her relatives and rebury them in the Jewish Cemetery in Petersburg, a truly crazy idea, he was the one my mother went to for help in how to do it."

My mother is the true Uncle Vanya, the Cossack, in the family. Once she gets an idea in her head, no matter how meshugge, no one can dissuade her from pursuing it. From living with her I understand how young dreamers leave their hometowns and go off to Hollywood to become movie stars or singing stars. Obstacles, barriers, hindrances, doubters; all are irrelevant. Clear thinking and common sense have no part in these obsessive dreams.

One morning my mother came down from the bedroom after tossing and turning most of the night. She announced that she had a dream—my mother was our family Joseph—her dreams foretold the future or her interpretation of what was to be. In her dream, her brother Alexei, dead and buried in a soldier's cemetery in Afghanistan, where he was killed fighting for the Soviet Army, told her he was so lonely and cold. He cannot find peace. He was buried far from friends and family; his body rested alone in a heartless, brutal land. He had sacrificed everything and he wanted to come home. 'Please bring me home,' he told my dreaming mother.

She announced to my father and me that she will find a way to bring Alexei's grave home. But home was a problem. We were living in Brighton Beach. At first my father and I thought she wanted to bring his body to America to be buried here, in a land he never saw nor ever expressed a desire to visit in his lifetime. During the next few weeks as she slept in a continued state of unease, the ideas began to form and crystallize.

Yes, she announced one morning, she will bring his grave

from Afghanistan to the Old Jewish Cemetery in Petersburg. My father's first mistake; he sighed a breath of relief—hoping she can now sleep in peace, which my mother interpreted as approval. Then there was no stopping her. My father was thinking how difficult it will be to move the body; fearful it must be badly deteriorated after so many years.

After all my uncle was killed, assassinated, murdered by a cruel and savage people masquerading as religious zealots in the late 1980's during the closing days of the war. It would always be a worthless ten-year war that only added to the final demise of the Soviet Union. In those days, the Soviet military authorities simply abandoned the dead. They buried them in a cemetery, but were not going to worry about what happened to those bodies. If the crazy zealots desecrated the bodies so be it—another sacrifice of the Russian people.

In my mother's mind, that sigh and the other gentle words spoken by my father were signs of encouragement instead of caution against a wild idea that had no promise of ever being realized. People have a habit of misjudging my mother's determination. Her own father made that mistake on countless occasions. So my father found himself in the same situation. In her new, comforting dreams a fuller image of what bringing the dead home meant was forming in her overactive brain. The dream grew from locating Alexei's grave to reburying it back in Mother Russia. My mother had never visited the grave in Afghanistan, only my grandfather had placed a stone on the marker. While we knew where the cemetery was physically located, we had no idea after ten years if the bodies had been left undisturbed. Would we be able to find his gravestone? Meanwhile, the Soviets abandoned the country and within a few years the Taliban emerged to continue a long stream of authoritarian Afghan rulers. In this case, their hatred of the infidels actually worked in favor of the plan because it provided a good excuse to remove a dead infidel Russian out of hallowed Muslim land.

Not satisfied with Alexei's new internment arrangement, she started to conjure up a bigger picture. When my family left in haste from the former Soviet Union, my grandfather, the Hero of Stalingrad, had just died. We left as quickly as possible because of my father's fear that the Soviet authorities might retaliate against us without my grandfather's protection. It was my grandfather's personage that we counted upon to save us from more serious harm caused by my mother's political activities. There were people in the Soviet bureaucracy, rivals of my grandfather, who wanted to lock her up and throw away the key. The Soviet Union was inching towards its demise, but influential people unknown to Americans still were calling the shots and they had a thin tolerance for dissidents like my mother. A certain group of Soviet authorities were by this time happy to get rid of her. It was this small group that ushered us out of the country. Initially, my mother viewed coming to the New Jerusalem as an act of going into exile, as she called it. Later she began to appreciate life in the new world and she was reborn as Anna Perlov, happy corporate worker and bourgeois American citizen.

But she missed her father. So why stop with Alexei's new internment. She decided that she wanted to exhume her father from his grave in the Heroes cemetery to join Alexei in the Old Jewish Cemetery in Petersburg.

The idea was actually taking definite shape although how it was to be accomplished was still unknown. But my mother never feared the logistics involved in implementing her ideas. It was left to my practical, methodical father to find the solutions. Then, several weeks later in the middle of the night, we were all awakened by my mother's screams. Her piercing sounds could have roused the dead, which is what she said happened. Her dead mother's bruised and bloodied face appeared in her dream. My mother couldn't possibly remember the woman since she died in the great Battle of Stalingrad when my mother was two or three years old. But she insisted that it was her mother. There was one cherished and treasured faded picture from the 1930's in the living room. So instead of sending her to a psychiatrist, my father listened patiently to her story about the dream. Now we had to rebury not only my uncle and grandfather, but we must add her mother and baby brother buried in Stalingrad. The scope of the challenge was formidable but my mother was certain it was possible. That's when, in tears, her hands clinging to her handkerchief, she went to visit Rebbe Rosenberg to seek his help. My father and I tagged along certain that the rabbi would discourage her from this narishkeit—foolishness.

As we sit in the car, Jimmy putting in his notes in the computer, asks. "So?" he waits for the story.

"What's this story about?" Jimmy already knows we are a family with lots of stories to share.

The story is too complicated to repeat in any detail. Besides to describe how all this happened would only add to the impression by goyem that Jews belong to a worldwide conspiracy.

Jimmy stops typing and turns to face me. "And?"

"My mother wanted her father to be buried in a Jewish cemetery. A functioning one didn't exist until after the fall of the Soviet Union. And she wanted to bury her mother and baby brother killed during the Battle of Stalingrad in that same grave site. And her first idea was to get her older brother Alexei, killed fighting for the Soviet Army in Afghanistan, exhumed from the military cemetery where he was buried and let him rest next to his father."

Jimmy rests the laptop on the car's bench seat, and listens attentively. He loves my stories especially when I sprinkle them with Yiddish expressions. As a boy his grandfather would tell him stories about Poland—the bad, cruel days under Russians rule, the time of the nasty communists. Jimmy's grandfather conveniently forgets the days when the Nazis occupied Poland. Those stories he doesn't tell.

"You have no idea what a task this was," I shake my head thinking about the intricate details, the plans and the waiting; I only know the surface facts. My mother's many visits to see the Rebbe, the layers of government bureaucracy and the calls at all times of the day and night. One government official agrees and then more complications.

"So the first question my mother asked was, who could make

this happen?" I point my finger at Jimmy. I panic for a second; I am becoming my mother—that's her typical hand gesture when she's excited.

I return to my story. "Sensible people said it was impossible but nothing would deter her. It was then she made what turned out to be a brilliant move by contacting Rebbe Rosenberg."

What I failed to include in my description was the fact that he was an important player in a vast Hasidic emissary movement with tentacles throughout the former Soviet Union as well as places as diverse as Finland and Croatia. Their accomplishments often defied logic or good sense; it was just the group to work with my mother. In cities and towns, small ones and major metropolitan centers throughout the former Soviet Union, you saw a Hasidic presence. Rebbe Rosenberg used that network to win the support of government officials in the new Russia, but the bribes paved the way. His fellow Hasids went repeatedly to the Russian authorities asking, begging, pleading, and handing out favors to get officials to move on the internments.

"Months went by and nothing. Then suddenly there's movement on my grandfather's internment. Again, months go by and nothing but government stalling, more action, followed by months of inaction. Patience, the Rebbe tells us."

Jimmy is resting his elbow on the dashboard and his head is cradled in his big, powerful hand.

"Rebbe consoled my mother weekly, assuring her that, in the end, Hashem would ensure success. God was on our side."

It was a most surreal experience. "The phone calls would come from the far corners of the world and always at an inconvenient time as we were eating or going somewhere. Plans we made were dashed because she then had to call a dozen more people. Updates. My mother waited, tense and uneasy for those updates." I think back. "Russian voices sometimes in hushed tones called and left cryptic messages on the answering phone. Bizarre is how to explain it. We never knew what to expect."

I sigh and shake my head. "Afghanistan would prove to be the most difficult part of the grand scheme. But even there Rebbe

Rosenberg found contacts among the Taliban before September 11th." I picture shadowy figures with guns running through an abandoned graveyard.

"How they actually were able to bring out the body from hostile territory remains legend. The zealots had a certain respect for infidel holy men with money to spare."

"So how did they do it?" Jimmy demands to know.

"With a shmir, a bribe, is how they accomplished it, and unrelenting patience and persistence. Rebbe embraced my mother's desire to have her loved ones reburied in the Old Jewish Cemetery in St. Petersburg. It became a personal mission. Her dreams were a sign from Hashem, God. And they made it possible."

Jimmy crinkles up his nose in admiration. "Wow. I love it. What folks to have on your side."

"We made progress on my grandfather only to learn in Volgograd that the officials were reneging on their promises to exhume my grandmother and baby uncle." I shake my head in wonderment at the accomplishments of a dedicated team of Hasids on a godly mission.

"A Hasid in Israel knew someone in Moscow that had a cousin in Volgograd. This was how convoluted the process was." My mother was comforted by her nightly dreams. It was not prayers or tender words but her nocturnal visions of the family together that gave her the most comfort during the years of starts and stops. My mother was the true Uncle Vanya, the Cossack, who dreamed the visions worthy of the ancient Joseph.

"My mother will be forever grateful to Rebbe and his colleagues."

"She should be, was it expensive?"

My father to this day only whispered about the costs because money was nothing compared to eternal peace even if my grandfather was an atheist. And as for my mother's belief in God, well it was a good thing Judaism permitted many ways of viewing the Lord.

"It cost thousands and thousands of dollars but to my mother, money could never be a deterrent. How does this act of righteousness compare to spending money on a new car or a second home."

"And did you give a party for this guy? After all that he accomplished."

"No, our home wasn't Kosher enough for him to come to dinner."

"Wow," says Jimmy, shaking his head in disbelief, "this deserves a party. It's good you invited him to your parent's 40th anniversary shindig."

I return to the case dearest to my dreams, the case that consumes my daydreaming, "What about meeting with the priest?" I ask Jimmy.

"Come on Sasha, do I have to kick you in the head. Now we have something to really do. You want to continue with the dead, fat slob case, go ahead and bring in the three sisters for questioning. I'll support you but keep it for another day." Jimmy stares intently at me.

Will I be satisfied? Can I wait another day?

"Okay," I spit out the word reluctantly giving in to Jimmy's demand, "so do we head to Glickenstein's or find the service station?"

"We'll save hunting for the tire after I know the names of all the service stations in the neighborhood. We can get one of the geeks in the attic to locate all stations owned by people with Hispanic last names. Let's talk to our potential suspect. A guy with a grudge. I love it."

We arrive at Glickenstein's characterless office in a small building in Williamsburg, unannounced. We are not expecting him to flee but surprise is a good police procedure. There is no receptionist or secretary to introduce us or escort us so we just walk around the floor until we find an office with his name on the wall, next to the door.

At the entrance, I announce, "Mr. Glickenstein, I'm Detective Perlov and this is Detective Sutton from the NYPD." We produce our badges.

He is visibly shocked. His jaw drops and hangs open; flies could jet in and out undisturbed. We stare at each other, no one is blinking. He makes no friendly gesture so we just walk into his corner office.

The size of his office indicates that he is a top life insurance producer. My father, the life insurance actuary, is my teacher about all things to do with the insurance business. Certain physical attributes such as the size of an office are highly recognizable symbols of success and an important part of the professional life of an insurance agent. My eyes drift and circle the room. He has awards from life insurance organizations framed around the walls of the office. Million Dollar Round Table Award winner is the ultimate sign of success. He has four plaques nailed to the wall.

"Mr. Glickenstein, we are investigating the tire slashings in Borough Park," I tell him. Jimmy and I are standing since he has still not gestured for us to take a seat. The office décor is presentable but certainly not elegant considering his wall awards indicate a highly successful insurance agent.

"We are talking to all the community leaders. Do you have any suggestions for us? Any leads we should pursue? You still live in the neighborhood?" We hear no sounds, his mouth is still open.

"The police department is very interested in finding the culprits." I am still not invited to make myself comfortable so Jimmy and I stand like mischievous schoolboys being punished by the teacher.

His mouth remains ajar; he is motionless and eerily quiet.

Then he erupts. "Me, me," he shouts in outrage. His face is bright red. I'm concerned that the man is going to have a stroke. "Me, how dare you come here and question me." He starts frantically waving his arms. He stands and makes a menacing approach towards us, but we have no intention of starting a small war. We back off physically and just wait for him to calm down.

"Mr. Glickenstein, we are questioning every one for leads. Anything, even something small and seemingly insufficient could prove to be useful in this case," Jimmy says calmly.

Glickenstein's dark eyes stare at us intently while all of us remain standing. His indignation may be guilt or a cover-up; totally innocent people with nothing to hide don't express such rage. We have to figure out the cause of his wrath, that's our job. Motive—do we sense it's here in this display of fury?

His screaming attracts the attention of others in his insurance office so two men draw near us. In Yiddish, he is screaming words about us, complaining to the man closest to his door. Arrogance is the accusation. Police power and loss of liberty are mentioned. Since I understand what he's saying I could respond in Yiddish, but I refrain. Let him vent his rage while we appear to be totally ignorant about the nature of his ravings. He could utter something useful in Yiddish.

One man, big-barreled and neatly dressed, takes charge of the unfolding event. He attempts to quiet Glickenstein down while we just stand and observe.

"I am David Isaacs," he extends a friendly hand. We shake hands.

If I had been a woman police officer, Mr. Isaacs would not have been so friendly. I would not have expected him to look me in the eyes nor shake my hand. The differences between the everyday lives of men and women were steep. The Hasidim lived in an urban, modern city but they have managed to turn the clock back three hundred years. Since immigrating from the ashes of Europe after the Holocaust, they continued sixty years later to view America as the treife medina, the unclean country. It was not their New Jerusalem.

We are in Williamsburg, a Hasidim neighborhood although not the central location for Lubavitchers like Glickenstein. The Lubavitchers call other parts of Brooklyn home; close by physically, but customs and rituals apart. Isaacs could be a Satmar Hasid from Williamsburg; they are considered the most Orthodox of Orthodox, but there's nothing in the creed that prevents either making money or achieving material success. Their married women don't merely cover their heads, but shave them and wear a head kerchief. Jimmy often talks about the old style Catholic nuns who also shave their heads as a religious ritual.

"Moishe is just upset to think that the police would be questioning him. He's certain that this is an attempt to discredit him and his successful business. Where did you get his name?"

Jimmy blurts out, "Another community leader suggested we call on him."

"It's Rosenberg," Glickenstein screams in English.

We had never mentioned any names so we were immediately suspicious about the nature of his extreme agitation.

Isaacs puts his hand on the excitable man's shoulder. Glickenstein begins to calm down and sits. His face is still red but the deep color is fading; a slight pinkish tint is visible. We remain in the corner as he takes his seat. He is still not looking directly at us, but keeps his face focused on his colleague, Isaacs.

"Mr. Glickenstein, were you one of the victims? Was your tire slashed? We are looking to collect as many damaged tires as possible?" My tone is gentle although I am forcing myself to be civil. I know if this is a black man, we would haul him into the station for questioning, but we want to keep peace with the Hasids. The politicians need these people at election time.

Glickenstein refuses to look directly at us, but I approach. He refuses to speak to us. He gives me a steely stare. Something is wrong, but what it has to do with slashed tires will not be settled by this discussion. We may have stumbled into the midst of some religious, or maybe business, feud. Since we have no hope of getting any information or leads, it's pointless to stay.

"Mr. Glickenstein," I stand over his desk. "My card," and I drop it on his neat desk with the nicely arranged file folders framing the borders of the desk pad.

"Call me, if you can recall anything."

Mr. Isaacs leads us out the door. "Moishe is really a nice, gentle man."

"With a bad temper," Jimmy interrupts.

"I know that he seems gruff and mean, but things have been very strained between him and Rosenberg."

We stop at the staircase. "Why?" If the anger isn't directed towards us what's going on.

"It's a long story," Isaacs answers.

"We have time," Jimmy pipes up, and stands with his hands on his hips waiting for an explanation.

"Give me your card," he says to Jimmy, "I promise to call."

We leave his office, uncertain of anything about the case.

Jimmy opens the car door. "We did the right thing just leaving? I mean can you see the morning papers if we had to call for back-up and hauled his screaming ass to the station house. We are supposed to be solving this crime for the benefit of these people." Jimmy shrugs his shoulders as he slides into the front seat.

"I don't like to run off with things so tangled," Jimmy continues, as he sits moving his body in different directions, trying not to wrinkle his perfectly ironed pants. "We would need two squad cars of uniforms for back-up to get this guy into the station for questioning. The Lieutenant would not be happy."

"We could have stayed around and just pestered Glickenstein, but that probably would be a dead end." I agree with Jimmy. What would we have accomplished sticking around? We have no evidence to bring him in for questioning; just that he's hostile and uncooperative. He's guilty of something, but maybe not slashing tires.

Our best hope for now is locating Rosenberg's damaged tire from the repair shop in Borough Park. When we aren't facing loose ends, there are always dead ends to reckon with on the job. Still, I love being a cop. We could have used brute force to squash this guy but instead we decide on diplomacy. Cops are not simpletons or gross caricatures of brutality—at least not this cop and his partner.

CHAPTER 11

Chasing down a possibility that's the life of a detective. Who are these vandals? I must ask myself some questions. Solving crimes is what the citizens expect from us—we the public servants of NYPD. I am ready to perform my duty, always willing to test all the angles, push the envelope, as they say in English. Don't you just love that phrase? Can't you picture a giant envelope, the size of a living room wall, inching closer as you stand in the middle of the room, which is getting smaller and tinier by the second? I love this country and its magical language.

On this case of treachery and intrigue, Jimmy is completely with me. We are a team, two merged as one, devoted to finding the criminals and bringing them to justice. It's these kinds of cases that bring out the best in our team work. He rarely offers criticism in the beginning of our searching for the bad guys. He lets me pick at the edges, consider all the possibilities, test our brains as we sort through absurdities. Crime sometimes pays and we try to minimize any criminal's success.

At this moment, the vandalism case is nothing but suspicions and officialdom's assertion of religious bias. Money is always an excellent motive for criminal activity although slashing dozens of tires doesn't make sense. I can't picture any Hasid slumped over the curb gutting tires, but logic never stops a criminal, especially if he's a hothead and really angry. We need to know the source of this rage. Then we need to get lucky and find a fingerprint. A witness might help, but no one has come forward.

"So what did you find?" I ask Jimmy, when I get to my desk at the station house. He's on the phone with the computer geeks in the attic locating all the service stations in Borough Park owned by people with Hispanic names.

It doesn't take them long to find a name, and off we are to discuss Rebbe Rosenberg's tires with Hector Diaz.

"Will our luck hold?" Jimmy's voice indicates uncertainly as I drive back to Borough Park. More ambitious than me, Jimmy is depending upon on our success on this case for that glimmering promotion. Some cases, appearing out of nowhere, are the pivotal ones.

I respond, "You don't really think we'll find a smudged finger print of Glickenstein's on a tire? Even if it's him, what is the likelihood that he's in the crime database?" I accept Jimmy's offer of a cinnamon gum stick.

Jimmy fixes his tie for our interview. "None, unless he's been convicted of some kind of white collar crime like insurance fraud. Although he's got a temper, maybe a domestic disturbance."

I let the flavor of the gum flood all the pores of my mouth, attacking all the strong odors of coffee and onions. "I doubt wife beating. Our luck will be truly golden if we can find any tire slashed during that time period. Like—why would anyone keep a damaged tire? "

We arrive in our unmarked police car, which everyone in this low-crime neighborhood knows is a cop car. Two strong looking young men are standing outside a brick building, which houses an office and the repair shop. There are no gasoline pumps or nice looking waiting room. This is a bare operation.

Jimmy announces us, "Detective Sutton," and he points to me, "Detective Perlov. Can we speak to the owner?" We show our badges.

"I'll get my father," and the tallest one goes inside the building and in less than a minute a small, muscular, walnut colored man approaches. He's wiping his hands on his dark green work pants.

"I am Hector Diaz, the owner of this shop. What can I do for NYC's finest?" There's not a hint of sarcasm in the voice, just a friendly citizen willing to help. Jimmy nods his head; we like this guy immediately. In a true sign of appreciation, Jimmy offers Mr. Diaz a stick of gum.

"Thanks," he says reaching for our offering and gingerly taking the stick with the two fingers not stained black by oil and machine lubricants.

"We're looking into a rash of tire slashings on and around Brooklyn Avenue," I say while I wipe the sweat off my brow. It's hot.

Mr. Diaz is alert and friendly. "Hey, guys, come inside; it's air-conditioned," and he waves us into his office.

His English is understandable but heavily accented. He speaks slowly, considering each word. "Water?" He offers us a bottle of water.

The room is comfortable so I decline, but Jimmy takes his offer. "Thanks."

"Those tire slashings maybe two months ago, you guys just working on it now."

"You know, murders to solve, rapists to lock up, so we're just getting to it at this time. Anyone bring you in some slashed tires?" Jimmy inquires.

"Yeh, I got at least two, maybe three, tires."

"You still have them?" I ask. Jimmy winks at me; we're almost holding our breath waiting to learn if lady luck is running strong.

"Yeh, funny you ask today, because I am about to get rid of them."

"You keep damaged tires for two months?"

"I got a woman, an artist here in Brooklyn, who uses the tires to make I don't know what, but she comes to pick them up every few months. I expect her later today."

We are happy cops, our smiles wider than the Atlantic Ocean.

"She pays me to keep her tires for her art work. Are the police going to pay me for the tires?" Typical immigrant response, what's in it for me?

"Yes," Jimmy and I both answer instantly. We don't want a few dollars to impede our investigation. We'll take the money out of our own pockets if necessary.

"She likes tires that are slashed?" I was mystified but never shocked at what people collect. Certainly, I was not a modern art expert. But I saw the controversial art exhibition at the Brooklyn Museum of Art a few years back. The last mayor was against the exhibition so naturally my mother had to see it, and dragged my father and me along for the experience. It was less an artistic occasion than being part of a cultural experience. I rated that exhibition high on a real Big Apple happening. Painting with cow dung didn't rate as art in my limited experiences as a culture seeker.

"No," he shakes his head; I could see the scars running along the side of his face. "She has me keep any damaged tire I get. When I collect 25, she comes here and looks at my pile. She takes what she wants, pays me nice for my trouble, and I sell the rest for pennies at the recycle plant."

"Can we see what you have?" Jimmy asks, as he finishes the bottle of water. He looks at the empty plastic container and hands it to Mr. Diaz. Our tire man has a great right arm and successfully flings the bottle into a cardboard box labeled 'recycle.'

"It tastes good in the heat," a thankful Jimmy responds.

The owner laughs and he directs us to the back of the building.

"You from DR," Jimmy asks.

"No, do I look that black, I'm from El Salvador."

"Someone said you were Dominican. No, that's what we were told," I answer defensively.

"You," pointing at me, "You are an immigrant."

"Yes," I answer proudly and straighten up my shoulders.

"Eastern European?" he adds.

"Russian," I reply with a big smile.

"From Brighton Beach?" he asks as we wind around the building, which is much larger than it seems from the street.

"Of course, my parents still live there."

"American citizen yet?"

"Yes, after I served in the US Army I became a citizen."

"Me too American, me too," he walks a little faster; his step is a little higher. "Just this year. Me, the wife and the four boys." I notice one of his sons following us.

"Your people did a good job in Brighton Beach. What a mess it was becoming. Immigrants are remaking this city. It's us," and he points to include me in his statement. "We are making this city better."

Jimmy agrees and nods his head. "It's one big melting pot, New York City," Jimmy adds in a mocking tone.

"Americans, especially those blacks born here, don't know what a treasure this country is. They don't appreciate it. The West Indians, I like them, maybe not the Haitians." He crinkles up his nose. "I'm a Catholic, but I don't go to church with Haitians. I like to pray with my own kind."

New York City is a segregated melting pot. It is enclaves, designated blocks, certain streets, sometimes whole neighborhoods, of people from different parts of the globe. The Big Apple is a remarkably cosmopolitan place but people stay with their own kind. The next generation of immigrants ventures out, exploring the unfamiliar, and rarely with their parents' permission.

We enter the room with its neatly piled stack of damaged tires in varying degrees of disrepair and different sizes. "This one looks awful. Your buyer is interested in ones so beaten up?" Jimmy says, kicking at one damaged tire.

"I never know with her; it doesn't have anything to do with the damage. She touches them all, rolls them on the ground, and studies the tread. I don't understand, but she is an artist and, I understand, a successful one." He rubs the top of one of the tires as if it were an amulet.

"I like her. I got four sons and two are good with their hands. They will stay with me in my business. The youngest one is a dreamer, he likes to draw, and I showed her his school drawings." His smile is serene; the boy, an agent of God, who brings pride to the family "She tells me he has a talent and she has him going to the Brooklyn Museum on Saturdays taking art lessons. She is very kind to my family. If she didn't pay me, I would help her." The world has too few good hearted people.

"Can you identify the tires that were slashed two months ago?" Jimmy asks incredulously.

"I know the one from that Rabbi—the slashed one. Strange, those Jews with the hats and dark suits they wear even in August. But good customers and very pleasant. I never talk to the women. If one comes in, I tell the boys just give the ladies a receipt and take the money. No nice talk." He stares at his son, who nods in agreement. Mutual respect prevails among these inhabitants of Borough Park, although not all is so peaceful with other residents.

He gives me a wide smile. "People like me and those long beards have lots in common here in Borough Park. I go to church every morning, I take my boys. I see the bearded men with the little boys following every morning—they go to pray. Family is very important. And we both need large apartments. We don't like those developers who come in and want to tear down all the old buildings so rich kids without any morals can live here. I got four children, they got maybe 10 kids." A look of determination is etched on this pleased immigrant's scarred face.

"Which one belonged to the Rabbi?" Jimmy says placing his nicely polished designer shoe on the smaller pile; he wants to skip the small talk and find the evidence.

Mr. Diaz understands immediately. "Tito, give me a hand," and the smaller son comes quickly.

"I mark it," the father tells us, "in case the Rabbi needs it for insurance claim."

How thoughtful. And sure enough, there it is. Tito moves to take it from the pile but Jimmy's arm stops him. He takes out a

231

pair of latex gloves. "If you push these away, I'll take this one."

"Any other you remember was slashed?" I ask, amazed to see our first real evidence in the case. Is it God, lady luck or some other force that smiles on us this sweltering, sunny day?

The shop owner stands completely still while he studies the three piles. He touches one tire after another with just the very tip of his fingers as if he is calling to unseen spirits to help pick the right one.

As I watch this small, nimble man maneuver through his vast holdings of tires, I consider the nature of knowledge and its link to success in this New Jerusalem. As immigrants, we both understand that success in America is far more fluid than in our native lands. Formal credentials are only of limited value. My own parents and family are proof that golden-leafed diplomas from the Motherland are meaningless here. Yet Mr. Diaz has a skill that has value without credentials.

When I arrived, I read Allan Bloom's book "The Closing of the American Mind" detailing what an educated person should know. I became an ardent fan of Bloom's. He was influential in my choices of reading materials. I soon learned that the New Jerusalem was a land of unlimited possibilities but with little regard for intellectual pursuits.

The man with the agile hands quickly sorts through the damaged property to find the treasures. "That one," and he picks out one that looks new.

With Tito's assistance, Jimmy manages to grab the tire from the pile and pull it out. "We now have two specimens for the lab to examine."

"Do we have a third," I squat looking at the neat piles.

"Yes, one more. Can you wait? When my artist comes she looks here at this pile first." He points, and then he spreads his arms as wide as the wingspan of a giant eagle. "We look together. I tell her it's for the police she will understand, but I don't want to touch anything until she sees all this."

We are satisfied with these two tires. "Great," and I hand him my card. "Call us if you find it."

Jimmy writes a receipt for the tires and hands it to Mr. Diaz. He asks me, "You think I look Dominican?"

"Does it matter," I answer. "I could be from the Ukraine or Latvia rather than Russia, but do people in America make a distinction? Spanish speaking immigrant that's you. Hard working businessman, good American, that's what counts."

He nods. He extends his hand to shake mine, but his black, oil-stained hands make a visible contrast with my pearly colored, clean hands. We both notice our differences. I slap him gently on the shoulder and he smiles.

Yet we know there's that link that binds us together— immigrant, foreigner, and outsider. How the native born vacillates in its attitudes towards us. It's almost schizophrenic— they depend upon us to invigorate the country, yet they arc anxious and suspicious of us, envy our success. I wave at him and his sons as we leave.

We are driving to the Medical Examiner's Office in Manhattan on the same property as Bellevue Hospital, located on the East Side in the mid-20's. There's where we will drop off our prized evidence, two slashed tires.

"This rocks." Jimmy is set to aggressively pursue the case; I can feel his radiating energy. "It doesn't matter whether it's a bias crime or a case of personal revenge by Glickenstein. We get to use the best of the city's forensics. Hey, this is a beautiful case." Jimmy starts humming a Beatles song, "Yellow Submarine," one of my mother's favorite tunes. Her collection of Beatles albums is expansive.

How Russian dissidents loved the Beatles, early transmitters of anti-establishment mores. My mother inherited her initial collection from my grandfather, the Soviet official, who confiscated them from college students and political dissidents in East Germany. My grandfather often visited the Soviet satellite country; despite armed guards and electric fences, new ideas filtered into the place. East Berlin was especially porous.

As Jimmy repeats the chorus for a third time, I park in the space reserved for official use.

"I'll take them," I put on my latex gloves and carry the tires, one in each hand. "I don't want you to get that pretty suit dirty." Jimmy nods in appreciation. His suit costs more than my entire wardrobe.

The new lab director, Matt Tannenbaum, greets us as we enter the old, dilapidated building. It's a good thing that defense lawyers don't get to see where the materials are analyzed. The city will break ground on a new facility sometime in the future so we use the best and finest equipment that technology provides in this decaying facility.

"What do we have here," asks our chief investigator. "This is part of a property crime?"

"Higher profile," Jimmy responds with a strong and forceful voice. "We got a potential bias crime. Attacks against Jews in Borough Park. High priority."

Tannenbaum signals for another lab coat to retrieve the evidence. He doesn't want his clean white coat to be dirtied. He has a public image as important scientist to protect.

"And what are we looking for?" He stands a distance from the evidence and points to the two objects.

"We are hoping there maybe some fingerprints of our attacker on one or both of the tires," I explain in a dry and authoritative tone.

"You think I will find a match in our database. Should we be thinking Interpol?" He motions to another white coat that emerges from the shadows to listen to his boss' command.

"We may have international terrorism," he tells his underling.

Jimmy winks at me. This is getting bigger by the second. Despite our earlier impressions of working with Tannenbaum in his former, less important role in the Medical Examiner's Office in Brooklyn, he is our hero at this moment.

"Yeh," Jimmy quickly answers. "We're investigating every angle. I got the FBI on this," a small lie.

Jimmy has been frequently calling the FBI and they aren't ready to acknowledge our existence. It isn't necessary to answer his calls, a mere detective from Brooklyn South.

"Can we watch what you're going to do with the tire," Jimmy eagerly inquires.

Tannenbaum looks at us with contempt. "You have your jobs finding the evidence and we have our jobs analyzing it. Would I ever ask to ride in a police car, chasing criminals in a dark alley?"

"Why not?" I answer and receive a probing glare by Tannenbaum that is meant to pierce my brain. It's the scientist's equivalent of knocking me in the head.

He walks down a corridor and disappears. The two lab coats follow, each holding one of our prized tires. We hear a powerful voice from deep in the recesses of the ancient building. "I'll call when we find something."

I love his confidence; not 'if' but 'when.'

"Snotty son of a bitch, but if he gets us something, hell who cares." Jimmy is satisfied.

Although it appears on the surface that our Hasid insurance agent may have something to hide, we have to consider everything. Instead of a meaty hate crime case it could merely reflect a personal grudge. Still, Jimmy's contacting the FBI about activities at the mosques in Brooklyn. We have a strategy for working with our federal colleagues. First, we contact the FBI and ask for assistance. After they stonewall us for a week, we get the Lieutenant to use his influence with the NYPD brass on Park Row to get their cooperation. We have our own computer geeks checking the Internet for white supremacist sites when they're not following pedophiles. There are more NYPD officers who speak Arabic then all the fed agencies combined. We can turn to our own if there's a mosque connection.

"Interpol." I whistle, "This is going to be very nice." Jimmy rewards our good fortune by pulling out two cinnamon sticks of gum.

"This could be very rewarding for all of us," Jimmy says, pointing back to the building housing our evidence. "Good for the Medical Examiner's Office and great for NYC's finest. A real win-win."

I head the car back to Brighton Beach. What a day for the daring duo; but, driving in our nicely air-conditioned car in the middle of thousands of cars, my mind wanders to my same obsession. Those eyes; lust is in my heart or perhaps it's centered on a different organ.

"We should bring in the three sisters just for some routine questioning," I try to seem nonchalant.

I can feel Jimmy's breath; he's so close to me while I'm driving that if I turn my head, I'll be smelling the cinnamon on his tongue.

"You're nuts. We have a real case to pursue with potential glory written all over it and you still got the hots for that treife woman." He says the word correctly and my partner fittingly grasps my motivation; he knows me well.

"Your Yiddish is getting very good," I commend his accent.

"I learn quickly," he answers with a snicker.

"We have unanswered questions. It's my duty as an officer of the law." I quickly defend myself.

"Do what you want, but don't let it interfere with this case." There's an edge in his voice but not anger. Jimmy is after all a man who loves women; he understands obsessions.

We get to the station house and I call the widow's house. I hold my breath while the phone rings. My heart is beating faster as I listen to the constant ringing in my ear. My heart goes thump, thump; I feel it expanding with each throbbing. My pulse is racing, beads of sweat appearing on my forehead. I wait. Then Irina answers; I immediately recognize her voice. I can't sound out the word Olga so I speak to Irina.

"It's Detective Perlov." I wait.

"Yes," and she pauses.

If she is surprised to hear from me, she gives no indication.

"We would appreciate it if you and your two sisters stop by the precinct. We just have a few questions to settle the case." I can't bring myself to use the first person, but refer to my actions as we.

"Okay," she says in a curt voice in her heavily accented English. I know she doesn't trust me. Some of that suspicion is instinctive, derived from her former life in the Soviet Union. On another level, I feel that she reads my heart and knows my interest in the case goes beyond Jack Feinstein's death. But I am a police officer and I could be trouble for her and the others. Immigrants don't pick fights with American authorities, especially now that they think they are sitting pretty, protected by Olga's status as the widow of an American citizen.

"When is it convenient?" I ask calmly although my heart is pumping wildly.

"Masha and I work so it has to be in the evening or on the week-end." I agree to an evening next week.

Then I hear the phone slam down on its receiver. I continue to hold my phone. Our conversation is finished but I don't want to end it. I hear papers rustling and I see a nosy Jimmy making exaggerated motions with his arms.

"Good-bye," and I release my grip on the phone although no one's on the other end.

"So? When does she come by?"

"Next week in the evening."

"I'll be with you; I don't trust you alone with her."

My pulsating heart slowly lightens and my breathing is almost normal. I'm disappointed. I never even got to hear her voice.

Jimmy dials the feds and he gets a real voice on the other end. He signals me by tapping on a pen. His face is a smiling Cheshire cat. There maybe a hint of cooperation. They are interested in the case of the slashed tires. Jimmy doesn't say a word about Glickenstein to the feds. He wants to run with the case, find out more about what the feds know about the Arabs and Muslims in Brooklyn. I try to look enthusiastic, but I am thinking of her. I have days and hours to wait; in the meantime, I reach for the phone and dial Dr. Marina to discuss our dinner date.

I am engaged in my own conversation when Jimmy starts making a scratchy, irritating noise with a scissor as he drags it across his metal desk. Then he loudly clears his throat and I look up to find Officer Roberta Sullivan standing patiently by the side of my desk. Jimmy gives her a hard stare, but she's not intimidated by his glares. She is accustomed to more vitriolic actions. She uncomplainingly waits for me to finish the call.

My dinner plans with Marina are set so I put the phone receiver down and look at her.

"My brother Tommy says he met you at the United Nations security detail," she says to me.

"The family resemblance is clear," and I smile at her. Out of the corner of my eye I see Jimmy repositioning his body in his chair. I hesitate to face him. I know he disapproves of this conversation or any with Roberta. He's protecting my image with the other guys in the station house. His intentions are good but they're just not the way I want to operate.

"Are you interested in visiting the family compound at Breezy Point this week-end?"

I was expecting an invitation after meeting Tommy. "Yeh, can I bring my surf board?"

She shakes her head in disbelief. "A Russian Jewish surfer, what next. Sure." She sees Jimmy's continuing discomfort and a few other eyes staring at us. "We'll talk later," she waves. "You registering for class tonight?"

"No," I call back to her, my fellow night school law colleague, "probably tomorrow morning before I check in here." I could do it on-line but then I miss chatting with the other students about what's a good class and what to avoid. Roberta is very helpful in steering me towards the best professors and keeping me away from what the catalogue describes as a terrific class only to be disappointed by a dry and boring teacher.

She's gone. Now I face Jimmy's scowling face. "What's the matter with you?" He gets up and gestures for me to follow. We head downstairs and outside. This is a serious conversation if it requires such privacy.

"You are really nuts?" He doesn't wait for me to answer. If I didn't know him so well, I might feel threatened by his aggressive approach. He stabs his index finger against the side of my head. His polished nail makes an imprint on my flesh.

"You going out with her and all the guys see you together." He stamps his foot on the ground. "Forget the chivalry shit. Man, this is serious."

He is not waiting for an explanation. "You got a date with that Russian Jewish doctor. And you can't get that blonde with the nice tits and ass out of your mind. That's why we're still chasing down that case. The fat slob died from a heart attack while she was out shopping with her sisters." He takes a breath but he's not expecting me to answer.

"I mean, come on Sasha, you ass, you're looking at trouble from two directions. We got to close that case. Forget that Russian merry widow. I'm no fool; I see how she looks at you." He's shaking his head and walking in little circles.

"And Roberta, what's the matter with you? You want to bed that dyke for a reason. You got something to prove. I mean that's not like you. Fuck a dyke. Just tell me what you're after? I don't get it." He stops. He's standing in place, not moving or gesturing, just waiting. He's exhausted by his tirade.

"I love to surf. I mean Breezy Point. When were you last at Breezy Point?" It's such a simple motivation, but at first, it's lost on Jimmy.

"Surfing, why don't you go to Robert Moses State Park? Surfing!" He's moving again in little circles.

"It's nothing. The merry widow, well, I don't know what's got into me but it's because she's so forbidden. I mean so treife. I can't explain it even to myself." I'm now joining him walking in little circles; we look like schoolboys on a treasure hunt.

Jimmy gives up. "Let's get upstairs and check with the computer geek Zimmer, and see what he has about terrorists and mosques in Brooklyn." He is still shaking his head and I hear in a low voice, "surfing, surfing, idiot."

I got a date so I have a good excuse to leave while Jimmy and the computer expert review announcements from the feds on people and places to watch. Terrorists in Brooklyn, why not here, where did those 9/11 mass murderers live? Neighbors who seem ordinary, friends you think you know well, relatives who are the pillars of the community, all commit crimes. Martyrdom, now that's a real motivation for crime. If it's not common here in America, we certainly have a history of crazies or zealots who assassinated Presidents, killed members of Congress and attempted to murder our highest officials. So why not Muslim terrorists in Brooklyn, it's possible and in my dark Russian heart, I know that good people have hidden desires that lie in the deepest recesses of the soul, invisible to all around them and sometimes unknown even to them. Then one day an unforeseen event triggers this mighty force and everything changes.

Marina lives with her parents in Brighton Beach not far from my parents—a good Russian Jewish daughter. My mother insists that I stop by their house before I pick up Marina so she can inspect and make certain I look presentable. This is not simply any date.

Since I work so close it's very convenient to keep a wardrobe in my old bedroom with the nicely ironed clothes hanging in the closet. This is still my real home, where I am most comfortable. I pick out a casual outfit from my closet since I intend to take her to the St. Petersburg Café and it's not necessary to wear a suit. It's summer and the night is sweltering. No deodorant will keep me from sweating. Russian women like men who look and smell like men, none of this pretty cologne or after-shave. But I shave again to eliminate my five o'clock shadow, which sneaks up on me by early afternoon and makes me look too sullen.

I go downstairs and my mother says, "You look very nice," and she reaches over and kisses my cheek.

"Have fun," and my father slaps me on the shoulder in a good-humored, man-to-man kind of way. We know that you don't have to be a big lug to be manly.

I drive the few blocks, parking in her driveway; street parking is difficult in this congested part of NYC. A single visible mark of materialistic status in Brighton Beach is to own a home with its own driveway, no parking on the city streets for the Lublins. It's a clear night although the stars are rarely visible from the street with so much neon and lighting. We will be able to see the stars if we venture onto the beach. And that is part of my plan—dinner and a walk on the Boardwalk and a stroll on the beach. It's illegal after sundown but no one obeys this rule. In a country that is ruled by law there are always exceptions. That's why I love America because in the New Jerusalem, the law is just like the English language, filled with exceptions; there are endless laws, rules and regulations that are disregarded. They are rarely discarded or eliminated, just ignored.

I find myself being greeted by Marina's father. He's not a big man but he has a forceful and commanding manner. Like most Russian men, he's the boss of the family and, unlike most immigrants, he approves of my profession.

"You carrying a gun," he asks, as he waves me into his house. I am his guest and so I remain respectful even when the questions seem so silly.

I open my thin, cotton jacket as I enter the house and there in my holster sits my Glock. I wear the jacket only to hide my gun from inquisitive eyes.

"Fine piece, but too expensive for my tastes," and he shows me his cheaper firearm. To demonstrate its legitimacy, he shows me the permit allowing him to carry a lethal weapon.

I can't image that there are many real dangers lurking in the shadows of Brighton Beach but he is in the diamond business. I can't quite figure out what he does, but I know he weaves his way through the District on Manhattan's 47th Street. He is clearly not a Hasid and they dominate the diamond district although lately there are Asians who are renting booths. I try not to be suspicious or ask any questions. Our relationship is still in the delicate, unfolding phase so it would be impolite to get too personal about the family business.

I know something about her mother because she is a colleague of my father's and it's because of his matchmaking that I am in this house—a family connection. Naturally, if my father is involved, the intended must be a Russian Jew, not just Jewish, and definitely not a Russian or Ukrainian Christian. My father eats lunch with her mother every day, but he never asks questions about the family business. He knows only what Marina's mother tells him. I will ask Vasily about the family business—if it's lucrative or the least bit shady then he will know through his connections.

Her mother shakes my hand and we all assemble at the foot of the staircase. She looks beautiful as she gracefully walks down the steps. Her smile is radiant, someone with a good heart. Russians are capable of possessing these gigantic hearts of compassion. In a woman like Marina, the gloominess that hides in all of us Russians is buried deep inside and only makes an appearance when the times are punishing. May she never experience those tragic moments, which force a cold, hardened heart to emerge. We Russians know that tragedy seeps through our collective bones, deep in our very marrow, bringing on a darkness that others cannot fathom. But we are in America now; in the New Jerusalem there are limitless opportunities.

I want to kiss her but I am shy in front of her adoring parents. They are investing much in their only child. Although the family appears to have accumulated riches in the new land, gauging by the furnishings inside of the house and the luxury cars outside, their souls and dreams wait for an unknown future. Their legacy is their child, a precious being who ascends to the highest heights of status in America through her education as a physician.

Her parents linger in the doorway but we make our way out into the summer night. Inconspicuously, I let my hand drop close to hers and she reaches for it. Although we are almost strangers, there is an immediate bond. We hold hands the way the young do in their early courting days. The skin of her hand is warm and the physical attraction is strong. There is an arrogance and certainty about her, which her physician training reinforces. I like that about her. She walks with confidence, back straight, eyes looking ahead. She doesn't hesitate when the light turns yellow but charges across the intersection.

We desire each other, but there is a progression to follow. First, we eat dinner. And within ten minutes we are standing in front of the restaurant. I am cordially welcomed in the St. Petersburg Café because I am known to frequent the restaurant with Vasily. We have a quiet table in a corner so that just the two of us can hear our conversation in this noisy place. She knows this place and she is impressed with the obsequiousness the wait-staff shows towards me. The waiter doesn't exactly fawn over me but he is very attentive. He pulls out the chair for Marina, handing her a cloth napkin, presenting one to me. His eyes center on my face and occasionally drift towards Marina as he repeats the specials of the day. I am a person of importance, at least tonight.

We order. She doesn't wait for me or seek my opinions about what to drink and what to eat. She knows exactly what she wants. Our fingertips touch as she extends her arms across the table. Her nails are cut short so as not to snag the latex gloves she wears treating her patients. Her head, topped with great dark, wavy curls, moves with her shoulders. This is the woman I will marry.

"My mother said you are working on the hate crimes here in Brooklyn," she tells me. My father obviously mentioned the case to his co-worker. He had called me at work in the late morning to check on my dinner plans.

"If it really turns out to be a hate crime," I don't ordinarily give away too many police secrets, "but we may actually be investigating a more routine case of revenge or twisted misunderstandings." I don't want to share further and she doesn't ask more about the case.

"I saw your picture in the paper after those murders in Coney Island projects," she announces with enthusiasm. Jimmy is so right about the illustrious publicity that we would garner from the case.

My respect for Jimmy's sense of priorities increases with each case. He has the right instincts when it comes to determining what is worth pursuing. He doesn't always display the best judgment in dealing with the people we are pursuing nor does he ever care about motivation. He wants to solve the cases as quickly as possible and be able to pick our cases. We are moving to that point in the station house pecking order where we can actually choose our cases.

"Are you a hero?" she asks with a buoyant smile, her tiny dimples showing.

I modestly reply, "No, actually we got a tip that lead us to the murderer."

The drinks of vodka arrive and we toast to our futures, which will include our blossoming relationship.

"Are your days and nights of blood and gore as fascinating today as when I saw you in the hospital?" I ask.

She reaffirms her love of being in the Emergency Department, "it's the most exciting part of medicine." Then she pauses. "I first thought I wanted to be a surgeon but unless you're willing to spend years in highly specialized residency programs with some cutting edge technique, plain vanilla surgery gets old fast." She takes a sip of her drink, savoring the moment, swooshing the potent liquid around the insides of her mouth. It's where I hope my tongue finds itself later in the evening.

We share an appetizer. She tells me, "I couldn't eat so much."

She turns from the food to a question. "Do you wish you were back in the Army fighting in Iraq?"

I don't censure my words, "It's the last place I want to be."

She watches me intently, examining my face, the frown lines of my forehead and my high cheekbones. "If I was still in the Army, for sure, I'd be a sniper picking off Iraqis from rooftops." I shake my head. "You peer through that rifle barrel and it's so crystal clear you can see the blood after a good shot. And if I get him in the head, the power of the gun creates a hole big enough for you to put your arm through. No thanks." I take a short sip.

I recall my cop days as a SWAT member. "The one thing that is magical is being on roofs even if it's only a couple of floors higher than the people on the street. Being elevated—above the rest, it's a strange deifying feeling. Like you have command of all the surroundings, I like that about being a sniper—I'm God looking down on my sheep."

The main dish arrives and we compliment each other on our choices. She lets me sample the goodies on her plate. At first I do so gingerly. "Oh, take a bigger piece," and she cuts a big piece and points the fork in the direction of my waiting mouth. I chew slowly remembering my mother's instructions.

Women seem to like to see men eat even if they aren't the cooks.

We change from drinking vodka to sipping wine, such a bourgeois act my grandfather must be cursing the family.

I don't see him approach until he is standing over my shoulder. Usually, I am more aware of my surroundings, but I'm caught in life's basic needs—eating and thinking about sex.

"Shalom," Vasily says and smiles at Marina. I introduce her, "Dr. Marina Lublin," and I touch the sleeve of his shirt, "Vasily Davidovich." She carefully looks at the smiling stranger.

He points to his brother Mikhail and his well-dressed wife; another young woman is sitting at the table. "Before you leave I have some information to offer," he says in Russian and slaps me gently on the shoulder. Now I have another reason for finishing dinner in a timely fashion.

The waiter refills our water glasses. He quickly takes away the empty dinner plates. "Should we eat dessert here or catch something on the Boardwalk?"

"Later," she replies, and I get the check. The waiter watches me sign the credit card receipt and then, as I stand, he pulls out Marina's chair as she rises.

I slip by the side of Vasily. The men at the table stand and we make the appropriate introductions although I know his family and the young woman is his fiancée Tamara, a fellow Russian-born Jewess. Marina enjoys being introduced to people she personally doesn't know but recognizes; the local celebrities. I am careful to introduce her as Dr. Marina Lublin.

"I'll walk you out," Vasily pushes his chair under the table and leaves his dining companions.

Marina excuses herself and goes to the ladies room.

He whispers, "That fat zhlub Feinstein, he was an evil man. I have something for you to see. Nothing can be gained by keeping this case open. God did you a favor." I listen and he continues. "The word on the street is that you are after the people responsible for those tire slashings. I'll put out my antenna and see what I find." He puts his arm around my shoulders. "Tomorrow we meet at the green grocer." There are two on the Brighton Beach Avenue strip, but I know which one he means, certainly not the Korean. I wave good-bye and we leave the restaurant.

"You know the gangsters?" She is laughing as we step onto the cooling concrete sidewalk.

I smile, "We're practically mishpocheh. Vasily and I are boyhood friends, classmates in Petersburg." I don't tell her that on the streets of NYC we keep our distance for the sake of appearances, although as a Russian Jew she understands that the ties that bind us are much stronger than the English language labels that separate us—gangster and police officer.

The Boardwalk is filled with summer walkers escaping the heat of their apartments and houses. The summer breezes are sufficient to keep the bugs away and the temperature tolerable. Holding hands, we walk among the crowd and as a man walking a big dog approaches, I take my arm and place it around her waist. I reach over and kiss the side of her face. I can smell her perfume; it's not Olga's scent; stronger, more French. Russians with the slightest materialism seek out expensive European names and labels.

I guide her down the wooden steps to the sand. I slip off my loafers and remove my socks and feel the sand's coolness. She watches the joy on my face and she copies me. I help her by supporting her body while she removes her pumps. She wiggles her bare toes into the sand and laughing she says, "It feels so good." I kiss her lips. In my lifeguard days, as a college student, the goal every summer evening is to get a girl underneath the Boardwalk. My intent is no different tonight, but my moves can't appear so crude.

The moon is bright and we hold tightly to each other. I bend my head slightly and kiss the top of her head, then her temple and her lips. She opens her mouth and I feel her tongue. Our tongues dance together in the moonlight.

"Do you want to go back to my apartment?" I ask between kisses to her face.

She nods her head. We are practically running off the beach having managed to quickly put on our shoes. I stuff my socks in my pocket.

We head towards her parents' house. We are about to get into my car when her father appears at the front door. He gestures for us to come in. He is not going into the house alone.

Marina starts laughing. She slaps my thigh gently. "Next time."

"Next time, we'll go to Queens for dinner." And I smile at her father. He closes the door as we enter. A bottle of vodka is on the table and Russian sweets.

CHAPTER 12

Despite my disappointment at not having Marina all to myself last night, it was a very pleasant evening, The first and certainly not the last. I knew my partner will be eager to know more, demanding me to share.

When I arrive at the station house, Jimmy is busy on the phone checking out our terrorist leads. He is totally animated, gesturing with his arms, hands; his shoulders swaying as he listens to an invisible voice on the phone. I see a big, wide smile on his face. He raises his thumb, a sign of victory.

His ear remains glued to his phone, but he whispers, "So, so what happened? Did you score, at least get to first base, a little kissing?" and he returns his attention to the phone.

I turn a pinkish red and smile.

"Yeah?" and he points his finger towards the ceiling listening.

"It was very nice," I sheepishly answer.

"No bedding her but it's early in the game," the knowledgeable one replies.

I just laugh and the redness intensifies.

"The FBI is willing to share some limited information with us about the mosques in Brooklyn," he excitedly replies.

Who would think that Brooklyn would be a hotbed of terrorist

248

activity? On the phone they invite us to their Brooklyn field office to see surveillance videotapes. We're not trusted enough to hear the wiretaps. The times are a' changing, radically since 9/11. The FBI and the federal prosecutor's office actually talk to the NYPD.

The Jewish High Holidays are two months away; the early fall begins the 10 day period starting with Rosh Hashanah, but the police are worried. They don't have any hard intelligence; no wiretaps or videotapes indicate that anything is brewing. Still the police are hearing concerns from Jewish politicians, who are listening to their constituents. Should Homeland Security activate a yellow alert or orange and what do these colors mean? My family asks me those questions and I don't have any real informative answer. I go where I'm told.

We have stumbled into potential glory. Fate had linked me to terrorists and given me the responsibility to protect all the people, beyond my Hero of Harbor House, Perlov the Protector fiefdom.

The Lieutenant has never been happier. He stops by our desks. "How's it going boys, finding those bastards?"

Jimmy gives him the thumbs up.

"Protecting Jewish lives and property from terrorists is our number one priority this fall," and he slaps me on the back. The physical impact is mild, but the noise is loud enough that all eyes look at the three of us.

I observe my fellow detectives in the squad room; there is envy and jealousy in the room. I feel its insidious odor radiating from the pores of their skin. I don't gloat but I am filled with self-confidence.

If only I could concentrate on the case. Terror cells. Jimmy and I are going to receive special training to learn how to detect terrorists in our midst. I volunteer to learn Arabic since I speak fluent Hebrew; how different can the languages be—Israelis and Arabs come from the same place. I should be ecstatic; the ambitious outcast is being granted permission to enter the inner circle of police strategic planning.

Still today, my mind is on women—all the women in my life. If not for these women, I could direct all my energies into the case—a greater grandeur I will never find in the police department. But my mind is adrift. Olga, I can't escape that face, those eyes such perfect symmetry. If only I am granted just a touch. Is she a murderess or an innocent immigrant victim? Why am I the only one who cares?

Of course, Marina is now a part of my life. I must call and thank her for a wonderful evening despite the ending, more amusing than satisfying. Another time awaits us; maybe during the weekend, if she is available. She is definitely marriage material and I think I would like to settle down.

Above them all, the center of my universe, is my mother, not an ordinary woman although in the New Jerusalem she appears normal. She is a martyr, a Soviet dissident, a victim of a torturous judicial system. Among her native-born work colleagues she seems mild-tempered, a good grunt, they would say, willing to work extra hours for no recognition. We know better. And I am her mama's boy. There's no point in escaping or ignoring that fact. I need to work with my Aunt Tatiana on finalizing my parents' 40th wedding anniversary party.

Yes, I can't forget Roberta, my police colleague and fellow law student. We need to talk about what she's telling her family.

My salvation in all of this is the beach. Surfing can take my mind off of any problem. Participating in frivolous but physically demanding activities is my best reaction to stress. I have plans to arrange with Roberta about visiting the family enclave in Breezy Point. There's not much time to practice my moves and regain the tricky balance required of a good surfer; even an amateur needs balance. I don't want to look like a complete novice if I have to put on a show for strangers. Be prepared, my father's motto to live by.

After work, I'll drive to the Rockaways to practice. With just the aggressive sea gulls for company, the beach will belong to me if I take the board to the middle of the Rockaway Peninsula. There are no sun worshippers or swimmers on this section of the beach, despite the summer heat wave.

Decades ago, Rockaway had been the summer home to thousands of working class city residents from the crowded Bronx, Washington Heights and central Brooklyn. The families rented bungalows to escape the asphalt and apartment heat in the days before effective air-conditioning. A city treasure of sand and dunes, a magnificent oceanfront was left to hungry, feral dogs. Four legged creatures were my greatest danger when I cycled the ten miles of the Rockaway Boardwalk. Abandoned by neglectful bungalow owners who set the buildings on fire to collect insurance money in the 1960's, the land had retreated and returned to a natural state.

Then there were the city housing projects that jutted out of the sandy landscape. Ugly monuments to old ideas; they stood alone, a curious sight seen from the air. Just like in Coney Island, a concentration of the poor live in ten, fifteen, and twenty story buildings, isolated from the middle class mainstream. In the Rockaways the isolation was twofold—social and physical—the peninsula was far from the rest of Brooklyn and Queens with Jamaica Bay in the center; city officials rarely visited since not enough people voted.

My partner is focusing on terrorism and I'm plotting how to leave the station house early to practice my surfing when I hear the phone ring and the sergeant tells me, "Call on one."

"Perlov?" I recognize the voice but I can't immediately pinpoint a name.

"Tommy Sullivan," he quickly answers.

"Sure," I reply with relief. At least I don't have to pretend. He and Roberta may look very similar, coming from the same womb, but their vocal styles are totally different. His words spew out with force and power. Tommy doesn't parse words nor does he think about what he's saying—let the words fly. Now Roberta, she considers every word. They don't tumble out of her mouth.

"Yeh, Tommy, nice to hear from you."

"Listen," he says, and of course I am listening. Why do people always say listen? Do they think we're all so distracted we can't take the time to hear what the other person is saying. It's like saying—hey, remember me, the one talking to you.

"What about Saturday to come out to our place?"

This was one of those very rare weekends during the crime-ridden summer time when I had a complete weekend off duty. I promised my mother that I would go with my parents to shul on Shabbes, the Jewish Sabbath. But that left the late afternoon for surfing and Sunday for Marina.

"What time?"

"How's around noon?"

I don't want to explain my religious commitment or being a mama's boy trying to please a demanding mother who views her future by the accomplishments of her only son. "I need to wax the board so how about 2 PM?" That's a believable lie.

"Great, I'll tell my mother. In case we don't get lucky and fish a fluke for you what else should my mother be buying? Not a meat eater?"

I'm not really an observant Jew. I don't wear a kapi, yarmulke, on my head nor do I refrain from any work on Shabbes. But I try and keep the dietary practices. It's important to me, but I don't have a sensible explanation why. I never eat non-kosher meat, not even during my Army days, peanut butter and jelly, tuna fish and egg salad everyday during my years of military service. A Jew is required to follow the rules because they represent religious doctrine; the foundation of being an observant Jew is discipline. I haven't studied other religions but I'm sure that all fundamentally require discipline and the unquestioning acceptance of doctrine. An observant Jew follows the 613 commandments. Life is made simple. Something in this black Russian soul yearns for the simple—the black and white—the absence of gray.

I tell Tommy, "Well there are always Hebrew National franks. And I do love tuna fish."

He laughs. Jimmy can hear the laughter and looks askance at me. He knows I'm talking to Tommy Sullivan.

"Good, it's set. I can pick up Roberta."

"No," I say, in a chivalrous moment. "I'll pick her up and we'll be there around 2 PM." As I hang up the phone, I see my partner's face.

Jimmy can't contain his displeasure. He points the pencil at me. "Be careful. It's a good thing for you that it's Tommy Sullivan inviting you. He has a good rep as a cop."

I don't respond immediately. I wait and then add, "Surfing, remember, it's the surfing and the beach."

Now I must get away later in the day and practice my surfing skills. If they're going to feed me then they must be expecting some kind of demonstration. I'm not your typical blond, blue-eyed surfer boy.

Meanwhile Jimmy and I have hours to waste, waiting, always waiting. We wait for the FBI to get back to us with a time and date to visit the field office. Jimmy is content to work with the computer geeks scanning the Internet for racists and extremists.

Jimmy reads some Web site information our trusty computer geeks put in front of his face. I don't want to interrupt but I have a question. "Listen, my friend." Here I am, adapting to what I dislike, following in line. Jimmy looks intently at me. He is listening and knows I am seeking a real favor if I'm using the word 'friend.'

He reaches over the desk and taps the tip of my nose with his pencil. "I'm listening."

"What about questioning store clerks on Fulton Street about the three sisters? I could go downtown and pass around photos of the four of them, which we got from Immigration. You like Juniors; we could buy a nice cheesecake for your mother."

His face is rapidly turning red. "No. No—not me and not you." He slams his open hand against the desk. He should be more careful; he needs to protect those boxer showpieces. A few eyes glance our way but we are known for being demonstrative.

His eyes meet mine. "Please get real." He stretches his arm across the desk and pulls me closer by yanking on my tie. "We have an important case. Possibly, this is the most important of our young careers. Just call them in for questioning and hope they don't bring in a lawyer." I am released from his powerful grip.

He fixes his own tie. "No more trips across the city. Call them in and question them. I doubt you'll get a confession but I'll support that."

I'm not surprised or angry. I know he's right. Surfing. Focus my mind on surfing, I tell myself.

I'll slip away and visit my parents where my surfboard is lovingly stored in their garage, wrapped in a hardy canvas cloth. I expect them to be home on a hot, sunny summer weekday. Now is the time when they take their well-earned vacations from their corporate masters. There is no dacha in the countryside to idle the days away, no second home in the mountains away from the city smog, no time-share in the Caribbean. The extra money for those luxuries was spent on a cemetery plot in Petersburg. A vacation means extended weekends at their Brighton Beach house, blocks from the soothing ocean. I can smell the salt air from every corner in their house; at very quiet times, you can actually hear the surf pounding the hard sand. The masters of the neighborhood are the aggressive gulls whose frenetic shrills command the skies. My father claims the droppings make great fertilizer; he scoops up the green slime with a special little shovel and places the oozy liquid in his garden.

Stopping by my parents at this time of the day, I'm hoping to catch a free meal. I can discuss the bias case with my eager father. He considers himself a model, modern Sherlock Holmes. Methodical and always logical, that's a good description of the guy except when it comes to my mother. Love is not rational.

"Hello," I call out and walk in. My mother is always forgetting to lock the doors. After so many years worrying about police raids in the Soviet Union, where locks are worthless, freedom means keeping your doors open. She reads press reports about the decreasing crime all over the city including her insulated neighborhood. Never a hot bed of criminal activity, now this neighborhood is virtually crime-free except for an occasional burglary.

"Sasha my boy, Sasha," she swings her arms around me and kisses my cheek.

"Hungry? I'm entering the chicken soup contest again, so come in and sit. You will be my first judge." We walk into the delicious smelling kitchen. My mother never gives up. She is unlikely to win even an honorable mention as a cook, but that doesn't stop her from trying. The prize recipe winner gets a free trip for two to Israel, sponsored by the National Jewish Outreach Program. If she intends to return to Israel for a visit, she'll have to buy the tickets herself.

I sit at the table.

"Where's Papa?" I ask as she pours out the soup; a sample from each of the two different pots. She hands me two dishes with presumably different recipes for chicken soup.

"Taste." She watches me take up my spoon.

"Papa is playing chess with Lev. Should I call him?" Lev, a fellow Russian Jew, and my father's favorite chess partner only lives a block away.

"No." I taste the first soup. It's actually good. Practice is making my mother a better cook. "Good," I tell my eager-looking mother.

"What are you going to get for Papa for your anniversary?" Forty years is an important milestone in a couple's life.

She sits down close to me. We are co-conspirators. "It's a surprise." She doesn't know the surprise I have arranged for their anniversary.

"Nu," I ask.

"You're come with me and I'll show you."

I expect to go upstairs to the attic or maybe the basement to see the big surprise.

"Natalie helped me." Natalie is an old Russian Jewish friend who has achieved true American success and now lives in Scarsdale, a wealthy northern suburb, which has become home to the newly rich Russian Jews.

"I took the Metro North and she picked me up at the station, and we drove to the country, some place called Salem, like the place with the witches." That was Salem, Massachusetts but why complicate my mother's story.

"I picked out a little boy." I hope my mother was not adopting a new son from the Motherland or some other place in the former Soviet Union as a surprise for my father.

"He's so cute and when I take him home permanently, they will cut his ears and his tail." Now that was making more sense.

"What breed?"

"Another Rambo, but a puppy."

My father's greatest desire when he arrived in America was to own a dog. He missed having one all of his adult life living in small, cramped apartments in Moscow and Petersburg. As a child in Odessa, he had a dog and long memories of walks with his favorite pooch on the beach. Brighton Beach was called 'Little Odessa' not 'Little Moscow' or 'Little Petersburg' because this new Russian Jewish settlement was on the sea just like my father's birthplace.

Natalie was living in Brighton Beach when she told my father about her dog rescue group, helping people to adopt dogs that had been deserted by their original owners. My father was mortified that dogs were killed because they could not find homes. Natalie owned a miniature schnauzer and was a part of a schnauzer rescue organization. She found us Rambo, a three year old who barked too much for his first owners. To my Papa, barking was a sign of protection; he was our watchdog. They were devoted to each other—Rambo and Papa, walking on the Boardwalk in all types of weather. Rambo eventually settled down and barked only at strangers, which was exactly what my father wanted from a trusted canine companion.

Less than a year ago, Rambo went to the happy hunting ground, his physical body buried in the backyard.

"He's only 5 weeks old, but I want you to see him. Not much of a barker so far but he likes to sit on your lap. Papa will love him. He can sit on his lap while he plays chess." Rambo sat on my father's feet as he played chess. All his fellow chess players always brought the attentive, protective pooch a dog biscuit. Lev often joked about the name Rambo. How could a dog owned by Russian Jews living in a Kosher home have such a name? My father's response, "Rambo is an American name and we live in America." This New Jerusalem offered so much promise.

"You'll go with me and see him in a few weeks. Shss, not a word to Papa. I want this to be a surprise. Natalie will pick him up and bring him down for the party."

She returns her attention to the soup. "Essen," eat, I am told.

I obey.

"What's going on with the tire slashings? You went to see Rebbe Rosenberg," she says with a giant smile, so pleased with my reaction to the soup.

Between sips I reply, "He says hello."

"A good man."

I wipe my mouth with a napkin. "What do you know about a Glickenstein, originally from the same shul as Rosenberg?"

"Oh," she shakes her head with a sigh, "That's a story."

"Nu," I'm waiting.

"Essen," she pushes the other bowl towards me, "which one do you like better?"

"What's wrong with Papa as a tester and judge?"

I knew the answer. "He's never critical. Everything is good with him."

"Glickenstein and Rosenberg," I repeat; she smiles that special, mischievous look of hers; it's the one that makes her tiny dimples appear and the years fade away.

"Yes, yes, what a scandal," she laughs, and a throaty sound is uttered.

"About money and the shul?"

"No, no better than money—love and sex."

I'm all ears, "Yeh."

"This is what I hear, all gossip so I can't tell you if this is true."

"Nu?" I answer with great anticipation.

"Rebbe Rosenberg's sister is married to Glickenstein; I think she's the oldest sister. Now that I don't remember," and she pauses to think.

I make little circles in the air. I'm waiting not too patiently for the real sensational material.

"Glickenstein is a very successful insurance agent with an office in Williamsburg," she continues, but at her own pace, slowly.

"I've been to his office," I quickly reply.

"Why? Has this something to do with the tire slashings?" she asks with her mouth slightly twisted, as if she was hearing a shocking tale.

"First you tell me your story." We make little compromises.

"From what I hear, Rebbe's sister wants a 'get' and Glickenstein refuses." A get is a Jewish divorce approved by a Council of Rabbinical authority. Without a 'get' a rabbi cannot remarry an observant Jew. A Jewish man can easily obtain a religious divorce while a Jewish woman must seek permission from her husband before the rabbis will grant her the divorce. Some husbands refuse, making the process very difficult. A religious Jewish woman can obtain a civil divorce, but a religious divorce matters just like it matters to certain Catholics that they obtain permission from the Church.

"Any reasons?" I say, while leaning towards her.

"Gossip, it's all gossip, but I hear there's another woman," she practically whispers.

Surprise overwhelms me; unconsciously my eyebrows rise and the corners of my mouth turn up. "Nu, what else? Any idea who is this other woman?"

"Younger, I hear a young woman. Poor Rebbe's sister, she has eight or nine children," my mother empathetically says.

"Why does she want a divorce?" I ask, my hands folded on the table eager for more dirt.

"The news has gotten out and she's embarrassed but he doesn't want a divorce." She leans closer as if to tell me an even bigger secret, but there's no one else in the house.

My mother wets her dry lips with her tongue, too much sun. "With a little shmir, her brother will eventually make it happen, although the costs both in money and reputation will be steep. Maybe in his heart, Rebbe wants to see the couple reconcile."

Then my mother twists her mouth in an unflatteringly way. "Money is involved, I think," she points a finger at me. "Glickenstein doesn't want a civil divorce because he doesn't want any lawyers looking into his insurance business. He thinks if she can't obtain a 'get' then she won't pursue a civil divorce."

"But isn't the Rosenberg family involved in all kinds of businesses in Brooklyn. The sister has money." The family is philanthropic and receives favorable coverage in the Jewish press.

"Yes, but there's something not kosher about all of it." My mother knows better than I do; she has her own sources.

She pauses, and then adds, "Very messy and upsetting to their community."

She is watching me eat, looking for any sign of my favorite soup. She continues her story, a pensive expression on her usually animated face. "It's very interesting about this sister. The Rosenbergs are known for their Talmudic scholars but also they have a very successful nursing home business in Borough Park and maybe other parts of Brooklyn."

"And?" I ask between sips.

"The sister runs the business. The father left her in charge. You would wonder with a family with a few sons, why did he choose her?" and my mother nods her head in amazement.

"Maybe she's the one with the brains, the shrewd one who likes numbers," I offer a plausible explanation.

"I first met her at the mikvah years ago in Borough Park, but I don't know her more than just to say good yontif. It's just interesting."

I nod in appreciation.

"And what were you doing with Glickenstein? Why did you go to see Rebbe?" she asks, as she observes how much soup I am finishing.

"It started as part of an investigation of the tire slashings. Is it a bias crime? Who knows, so I have a list of community leaders in Borough Park and Rosenberg's name is first on the list."

I have my mother's undivided attention. Her hands are resting on the table with her chin tucked on top of her slightly deformed fingers.

"I spoke to Rosenberg," I tell her.

She interrupts, "He recognized you?"

"Yes, so we talk about the slashings and then this could be nothing more than some stupid kid or someone with a grudge. I ask is there something personal. Anyone leave the shul unhappy."

She is back in her adoring attentive mode.

"He tells Jimmy and me," I continue.

"Jimmy was there also," she exclaims with a shout.

"Yes, he's my partner, we were together," I add.

"A goy on the case," she responds, mystified with the decisions of the NYPD.

"This is standard police procedure. You go investigate a case, two partners. One happens to be a Jew and the other is a goy, a gentile, a non-Jew. OK?"

"Fine, so?" and her hand beckons for more information.

"As we are winding down the interview, Rosenberg tells me that Glickenstein had a misunderstanding about the shul's finances. Don't harass him I'm told." I have been hoodwinked.

"A good move, he's cunning. How do you think he managed to get my brother out of that hellhole, which we stupid Americans are back in? Smart and a little devious," her head bobbing up and down.

"So, I go to talk to Glickenstein and he explodes, says Rosenberg is out to ruin him."

"He's known to be hot tempered," she lowers her voice. "Gossip mind you, but I heard from the mikvah ladies that Glickenstein has hit his wife. But he has managed to find love with a young woman. Remember it's only gossip. Supposedly one of the new teachers from the girls' school of the Yeshiva." She smiles.

"Money can be a curse, but love and lust…?" I laugh and snicker. For a fleeting moment her blue eyes pass before me.

My mother sits in her own thoughts.

"You should know," I answer.

She reaches over and gives me a klop, smack, on the side of my head. "Be respectful."

The scandal of scandals of our family was my father and mother's love story. A brilliant, young aspiring mathematician, living in the hinterlands in Odessa, was sent at age 16 by the Soviet authorities to Moscow. My grandfather, a high-ranking Soviet figure, took him into his apartment to live with the family while he studied at the best university in the Soviet system. My mother, four years older, was his mentor. They attended the same prestigious university although they don't attend the same classes. She was a graduate student studying engineering and he was the flowering theoretical mathematical genius who will garner great recognition for Soviet academia. They spent many hours together. My grandfather would remark later about how it was his responsibility for the mess; too many hours together.

My mother was known as a woman of fire and passion. People forget that the passion extended beyond ideas and philosophy. They thought of her on hunger strikes and protesting, spending months in a Soviet prison that the authorities publicly label a mental institution.

Before there was protest, her life was filled with an irrepressible love. These two star-struck lovers lived in the same apartment; they spent their days studying and the nights engrossed in each other. How could they remain platonic colleagues? My mother twenty-four, and already engaged to a fellow engineering student, eloped with my twenty year old father. Only the personal and persistent intervention of my grandfather prevented my father from being sent back to Odessa on a freight train. He managed to move the entire family to Leningrad, now known by its former name, St. Petersburg. My grandfather persuasively argued to the authorities that my father's genius should not be lost because of a romantic indiscretion. Stalin was dead; long live clear thinking.

"Fresh, my Uncle Vanya, the Cossack. That's you." She takes her crooked finger and pushes it against my nose.

I smile, big and broad. She loves me just the way I am because we are one and the same.

My mother is today a fountain of information. If not for her gossip, I might be stupidly looking for a suspect in the wrong place. Even the righteous have devious sides.

I had another reason for visiting—my original reason.

"I'm going surfing after shul."

"On Shabbes you go surfing," she replies with indignation.

"Am I so religious? I work most Saturdays." Sometimes she just likes to protest.

"I'm thinking of testing it out maybe later today. I'd like to head to the Rockaways, but it could be Coney Beach if I have no time."

"And who and where are you going surfing with on yontif?"

"I'm going to Breezy Point," I quietly tell her.

"Anti-Semite country. What's wrong with you? Jew-haters you go to visit."

"Remember Roberta, my colleague from the station. Her family lives there. I'm going with her," I inform this impetuous woman."

"You got a nice Russian Jewish girlfriend, you need a cop girlfriend," her voice is sharp and critical. "Are you trying to tell me something?" she asks me with reproach. "That lovely doctor is the daughter of a friend of your father."

"No, no, Roberta's not a girlfriend, just a friend. You know she's the one I go to law school with."

"Friend," I see my mother's concern. "Treife, you were always attracted to the forbidden."

"Friend, just a friend," I try and explain to closed ears.

She stares intently at me.

I give her my best smile. I'm your baby boy and you love me. I see her face soften. "Don't you think we are cut from the same cloth?" then I laugh.

She can't stay angry. She leaves her chair and wraps her arms around my shoulders.

"Uncle Vanya, the Cossack, that's you," and she plants a kiss on my head.

My cell phone rings, I can feel it vibrate against my waist. I don't recognize the telephone number calling, but I answer. Informants and people in the community will call from pay phones to remain anonymous.

"Hello."

"My friend," it's Vasily calling from a pay phone on the street. We communicate through pay phones on the street.

My mother is staring at my phone. I speak Russian so she knows it's not someone from the police station, probably a voice from the community.

"Nu?" she asks, after I make plans to meet Vasily in two hours.

"Vasily," I tell her.

She doesn't need any further explanation.

I finish my meal. It's too warm and muggy outside for hot tea. I would like a tall glass of vodka, but I'm still on duty. I must find the time to practice my surfing skills. The vodka must wait.

Returning to the station house, I mark time by filling out forms and finishing old paperwork. I am anxious to meet Vasily, but the minutes move slowly. The FBI keeps us waiting. The lab report from the Manhattan Medical Examiner's Office on the tires is still being processed. I don't really expect much, but the possibilities are exciting.

The advantage of being on the street, driving a squad car or even walking a beat, is there's less time spent waiting. You're busy doing something. Of course, then you're stuck with constantly meeting the public. The shopkeepers always have complaints about the city government. The old people complain about the thugs on the streets. The black kids look at you with suspicion. You know half of them in Coney Island are carrying weapons or drugs, but you can't just stop and frisk them. The neighborhood would be better off if they didn't live alongside so many old, vulnerable folks.

I spy the tag team of Murphy and Lewis and wave. We are all pals since the capture of Red Roy. The place festers with rage and discontent. The Brighton Beach enclave with its old and young from places and with names the average New Yorker can't pronounce that's my responsibility.

The Hispanics in Coney Island are mostly immigrants; some are hard working illegals that are afraid of the police and unlikely to commit crimes. Their sons and some of their daughters do get drawn into the gang life. The viciousness and macho territoriality is a huge headache for Murphy and Lewis.

Once the black gangs ruled the streets of Coney Island but now they have competition from the Dominicans and Mexicans. Luckily for Jimmy and me, we were never perceived by the brass to possess too many empathetic skills in dealing with troubled youth so the cases belonged to the tag team.

Ambitious cops take different routes to success. Vice and narcotics are the familiar paths to glory but working with the gangs is another choice. I do things differently and Jimmy sees potential in our path. Since 9/11, terrorism is the dance card.

I glance at my watch; it's time to meet Vasily. I tell Jimmy that I'm off to see a community member. Jimmy rarely joins me because he knows I'll be speaking Russian or Yiddish. As an immigrant, I know how disquieting it is to listen to a conversation in which you have no idea what is going on.

"Go, your people are calling you," he says, as I head down the station stairs.

I arrive precisely on time and walk into the store. Vasily is eating an apple in the back of the store. The owner recognizes me from the neighborhood. He knows I'm a cop but, unlike in the old country, I am not here demanding my weekly bribe. I visit only to buy his produce, refusing free samples, although I am willing to accept a discount, especially if it's for my parents.

Vasily waves and I approach him. He is carrying a handful of apples in his big hand and he offers me a bright, red one while he munches on a yellowish-colored one.

I take a bite and the juice from the fruit drips down the side of my mouth. I don't have a napkin and I begin to wipe the trailing liquid with my fingers. Vasily hands me a paper napkin.

"Good," he says.

I smile and wipe my sticky face.

He nods for me to follow him to a back room. We walk through the doorway and instantly it's cooler. A gigantic air conditioner, lodged between a wooden shelf and the ceiling of the room, is pumping out cold, dry air into an area where the fruit is stored.

There is a table and a few old wooden chairs in the room along with row after row of neatly lined up crates of fruit and vegetables. It's cool without being frigid, quite bearable in the summer heat.

"Sit," he says in Russian and I obey.

"Your mother and father are good?" he continues.

"Very well," I answer and take a seat on the hard chair.

He offers me a small bottle of cold, freshly squeezed orange juice. I take it and pull off the aluminum foil top.

"I know you are still looking into Feinstein's death. The widow said something to the old woman across the street, and she's a good gossipmonger so then someone tells someone else and I hear."

"Yes," I say between small sips, nodding my head in agreement with his statement. We understand each other in ways my fellow police officers cannot comprehend.

It was Mikhail who chased down the brutal Afghan bastards and their treacherous allies responsible for the bomb that destroyed my uncle in the fading days of that merciless war of attrition. Eventually, the bankrupt Soviet Army withdrew to be replaced by the Americans. Two Russian Jewish boys who were mislead into thinking that the ten year war against the Afghans was virtuous. Together they owned a drawer full of medals.

"Feinstein was a bad man. You wouldn't think so if you just saw him."

I've been waiting for this story since last night when he first broached the idea.

"Nu? What, what?" I ask with more impatience in my voice than I want to express. I am losing my tolerance for implied hints of evil doing.

"He made his wife and the others do awful things."

I am still waiting, these are just teasers. She didn't look like her husband beat her. I never noticed any bruise marks, at least, not on visible skin.

"Sex," Vasily says with a contemptuous sneer. I hear the sounds of an aggrieved party seeking justice. I am part of the legal system. My job is to provide people, not necessarily with the truth, because that doesn't bring solace, but with fair punishment.

I open my hands in a gesture of expecting more. His slowness indicates a tale of such ugliness that he must prepare me.

Vasily takes a deep breath and a sigh comes out. "He made his wife have sex with the others."

I don't indicate that I had also heard the rumors. "Group sex orgies?" I answered in a clinical fashion, as if I was investigating a sex crime where we detach the description of horrific acts into just mere words.

"More," he adds and pauses. Time moves very slowly when the storyteller has to take a moment to gather his thoughts.

I don't say anything. I wait for his next sentence, but my eyes are wide with anticipation.

"Feinstein couldn't do it;" the reason for Viagra. "So he had Olga and her sisters kiss and fondle each other and to add to the mix, Vladimir had sex with the three sisters while Feinstein watched."

Now I interject my police knowledge of the case. "We know he had large quantities of Viagra in his system on the day he died. A tox screen, which we ordered the lab to perform, indicated that this was the probable cause of death. The drug can, in certain susceptible people, trigger a heart attack."

"He got off—watching—with the Viagra." Vasily's face intimated abhorrence as if he had swallowed a bitter and poisonous piece of fruit.

"A good motive to kill him or at least let him die if he has a heart attack." I nod my head. I am such a good actor; I remain detached to the story and the players. "What's your angle in this?" I have to know.

"My friend," Vasily says, "I like to keep things nice in our neighborhood. You want a pervert like that fat zhlup humiliating our women?" He raises his voice in indignation.

"A kike, that was what he was," Vasily turns his head and spits on the floor.

"And how do you know what happened in their bedroom?" I know there's more.

He quickly answers. "Vladimir brings me tapes. Feinstein had the activities videotaped. He wanted to sell them."

"How do you know it wasn't Vladimir's idea—the taping and everything?"

"I know because I called Feinstein. I spoke to him. He wanted to put the tapes on the Web and charge money."

"Why did he have Vladimir come to you?" I ask.

"He heard I have connections," my friend replies.

"Yes, you do so what did you do with the tapes," and I am holding my breath for the answer.

"Bad quality and I don't want these four innocents being humiliated," he quickly replies.

He took in a deep sigh. "I know Vladimir's mother. Would you like to have people know you did terrible things because you think you have no choice?"

"And why did they do it if it's so sickening?" I ask the obvious.

"Feinstein, the kike, threatened them. Told them he would have them deported. Immigrants, you know. They are afraid of such things," he indignantly responds.

"And where are the tapes?" I ask although I don't want to know, but I must know.

"I have them. I want to give them to you," he says.

Interesting gift he is offering. "Why?"

"Because we are pals. I know you have an interest in this. Vladimir tells me you have that look in your eyes when you see her. Treife of course. You should be careful, but I have no interest in them. I'm not a pornographer," he adds nonchalantly.

That was probably an honest answer.

"There are many things we don't do for money," he tells me.

The 'we' must mean the family business. Russians are really prudish although I know there is a growing and insatiable sex trade out there in the big, bad world. Russians and Ukrainians are part of the sex trade industry; not my Vasily.

"The shvartzers parade their women in the street in Coney Island and call that a business." He spits again and fixes a hard gaze at me. I don't doubt his personal revulsion. He's not finished differentiating his family business from other illegal activities stirring in the larger community.

"The Spanish, they run those drugs and unlike the shvartzers they manage not to sample the product too much. Bad business selling on the street. Not a sound long-term business proposition. Too dangerous; Mikhail and I want to die old men."

Then he adds, as he repositions his body in the hard chair. "Pornography is a big business. But if we are going to profit from people's perversions, we can't depend on poor quality, grainy tapes made by amateurs using scared fellow Russians. No good. Feinstein was a pig, not much better than the niggers and spics from Coney Island."

"Destroy the tapes. I don't want them," I tell him without hesitation.

"Do you want to look?" he asks with a voyeur's wink.

"No, destroy them. I agree we should not cause any embarrassment. They have gone through enough." There is a part of me that really wants to look at her naked body, but I quickly put aside that impulse. It is a powerful impulse, but I can control it, if I never possess the tapes. Then I stare intently into his dark eyes; I could be looking into my own eyes.

"What happened that day? What do you know?" I must know exactly what happened that day.

"I don't know, no one was there. When Vladimir says they were out shopping and eating, I believe him. They were not there when he died."

I should be satisfied but I know in my dark Russian heart that something is missing.

"What else did Vladimir tell you?" I demand.

"Isn't that enough. The fat man is dead and no one should be crying. You think Feinstein's family wants to read about this in the tabloids? Let it die with him," he breathes in deeply, letting the air out slowly.

Where else can I go with this case? I'm so torn. Is something to be gained by digging up this dirt and publicizing the sleazy tale of a pervert who uses his wife to make pornographic movies to sell on the Internet? I'm still not satisfied.

Vasily drops his arms to his sides. "I want to make you aware of the consequences?" His tone isn't threatening, merely a statement of fact. "All actions, including supposedly good ones, have consequences."

I don't argue with him as we stand and I take my leave.

I shake hands with Vasily as he hands me a perfectly round, dark-red plum. I put it in my pocket. Is the story finished? Do I forget it all and go pursue terrorists? The news is suffocating and I unloosen my tie.

My soul aches for purification to clean away Feinstein's dirty business. What better way than to go surfing in Rockaway. The fresh, salty water will cleanse my thoughts. I cannot forget her but I must go on with the terrorism case. I have a promising career to protect.

I return to my parents. Can I slip into their garage without alerting them? It's a good thing Rambo is gone off to the happy hunting ground to forever chase squirrels, run aimlessly in circles, and fetch sticks. I sneak around to the back of the house. It looks like no one is home, the garage door is as usual unlocked and my prized protection stands waiting for me. I leave undetected.

As I drive along the Belt Parkway, with my trusty surfboard balanced across the back seat with the front and back ends sticking out of the rear windows, I blast the CD player with Beach Boy sounds. Beach 90th Street is surfing heaven in NYC. I expect no one on the beach. If the waves are especially powerful, I may encounter a few other surfers in the ocean.

Parking is never a problem. There are no late stragglers on this beautiful beach. It's empty. I stand on the wooden Boardwalk planks viewing my kingdom for the day. The waves are pretty puny so it's all mine. Where else but in the Rockaways could you find such a priceless treasure so neglected and forgotten by most of the public.

This winter I will take the plunge and buy one of those two-family homes, only a hundred feet from the beach and the Boardwalk. I'll sell my Kew Gardens co-op and get a loan from my father. A two-family house, I can handle that and rent the second unit. I want a house of my own. I can keep my surfboard and bicycle in the garage. Yes, I've decided this is where I belong, not in a house in densely packed Brighton Beach or in an apartment in crowded Kew Gardens. Here, there is space—redemption awaits me. I'll rise each morning to pray as the glorious sun appears from the darkness, filling the void in my heart as I wait for love.

My company in this neighborhood will be the few other brave urban homesteaders buying these houses. The infrastructure, forgotten for years by the authorities, is in need of major improvements. But so what—this is a new world waiting to be rediscovered. My home-owning neighbors and I will share the immense bareness and open space with the nearby residents of the surrounding low-income housing projects, who never seem to enjoy lying on the beach, swimming in the powerful currents, or walking on the rotting Boardwalk. If we come in enough numbers, we will change the landscape, maybe even improve the performance of the dismal schools in the Rockaways. I may have to give up riding the subways since, even when the trains are running, the commuting time is beyond my tolerance for mass transit.

I don't need a wet suit. I dive into the surf and feel the foamy salt on my bare skin. My mother says it is an elixir ridding your body of every pain and ache. The bubbly brine attaches to the skin's pores and squeezes out the hurts, physical and emotional. I paddle out and wait for the waves. Here is my redemption. My women can wait.

CHAPTER 13

It is not often that I accompany my parents to shul for Saturday morning services. The walls of the low-slung building, right in the middle of a major commercial strip, aren't too soundproof. But it's where we have been going since coming to America. It's not that regular attendance is changing my mother's mind about God; she doesn't believe and my father is scientifically dubious but they are regular worshippers.

Today is a special Sabbath service following Tisha b'Av, an observance of the destruction of the two Temples in Jerusalem more than two millennium ago. Jews spend much time celebrating the dead and destruction. I love it; it's so Russian.

We walk together in the rising heat and humidity; my father holds my mother's hand and he places his arm lightly across my shoulders. He's a short, trim man with a powerful and forgiving heart.

We greet people we know outside the shul; my mother walks alone to the women's section while my father and I join the men. The women live their separate religious lives, not allowed to touch the Torah or read from the scriptures. The men dominate the entire physical space; here men are supreme. My mother, the radical dissident, doesn't question the rigidity of the rituals.

Tisha b'Av is a significant but largely ignored Jewish holiday. It's only the truly observant and children in Jewish summer camps that retell the story and observe the specific rituals associated with this holiday because of its timing during the summer season. People have more immediate concerns; vacations, trips to the beach, Bar-B-Q's. Observant Jews will fast on this holiday from sundown to sunset. My father doesn't permit my mother to fast; too many days spent in prison and on hunger strikes.

It's a 25 hour commemoration of mourning; in the evening at shul we recite the Book of Lamentations, which scholars say is from the time of the destruction of the First Temple. This is followed the next day with a general mourning for all Jewish death and suffering including the Holocaust; and for my mother, prayers for the 20 million Russians, Jews, and gentiles, dead as a result of the Great Patriotic War, as we Russians call World War II.

Many Jews, even those who are not observant understand Judaism as a religion of duality. A good Jew follows two overlapping paths because they ultimately lead to the same goal. First, there's the individual's personal closeness to God. A righteous individual follows the endless rituals of religious life in order to grow closer to God. Then there are the required ties to the Jewish community and the larger world community. Yom Kippur, is considered the holiest of holy days, the holiday where the individual asks God's forgiveness for personal acts of sin and evil while Tisha b'Av is the quintessential expression of the Jewish community's asking for God's forgiveness for its collective sins. My mother finds consolation in honoring Tisha b'Av.

The Sabbaths that precede and follow Tisha b'Av, the Sabbath Hazon (Vision) and the Sabbath Nahamu (Console) are my mother's favorites. Last Saturday at shul the rabbi read from the beginning of the Book of Isaiah. In those prophetic passages, we are reminded of our evil and transgressions; and a week later on this Sabbath Nahamu, we hear hope from Isaiah: "console, console my people, says your God. Speak tenderly to Jerusalem, and declare to her that her term of services is over, that her iniquity is expiated." (Isaiah 40:1-2)

The Book of Isaiah is what draws my mother to these particular services. Isaiah promises us that deliverance from exile is imminent; my mother lives in perpetual exile. She is awaiting redemption, but she doesn't think she'll find it at the coming of the Messiah. I see redemption every sunrise as I stand on the Brighton Beach Boardwalk, a new dawn, a new day, a new opportunity to be good and, of course, always many chances to sin.

A male member of the shul stands on the bima, the pulpit, reading the prophet's words. After having a quiet cry, I see her dabbing the inside of her eyes with a white hanky; my mother is ready to leave. We don't wait for the Oneg Shabbat, a small meal after the services prepared by the Sisterhood ladies.

As we walk home, I remind my parents of my plans for the day. "I'm going surfing." I want them to move a bit faster.

"After services you go to that goyish place." My mother shakes her head in disapproval.

"I got to first go and pick up Roberta."

My mother stops; her heels dig deep into the concrete. "You go to pick up another woman."

I'm going to be late. "Roberta is not just any woman but a fellow officer and law school colleague. And more important, she's gay."

"She likes to have fun?" my mother says and I can't tell if she is being coy.

"That too." I don't want a long discussion. I quietly add, "She's a homosexual."

"Gay," my mother repeats the word and I don't see a hint of impishness.

"Yes," says my father, in an understanding tone. Although I can't be certain what part he understands—my being late or Roberta's sexual orientation.

"We are friends, just friends. We work together and go to school together. Men and women can be friends. Nothing more."

Both my parents stare at me. They have friends of the opposite sex so the concept can't be totally foreign; it's part of their working lives but something is not registering.

"What does Jimmy say?" my mother replies.

"He doesn't like to interfere with my social life." I tell a small untruth. OK, maybe it's a lie.

My mother isn't buying my rationale. "You're not telling me the whole story."

In frustration, I scratch the back of my neck with my hand. Time is escaping and I'm standing on a hot sidewalk, stuck in the middle of a major philosophical argument with my parents.

"Here's the deal." I liked that phrase; the first time I heard it was in a movie about bank robbers. I gently placed my hand on my mother's slightly bent shoulder. "The police department isn't fond of homosexuals so I play the role of a male friend of Roberta's. She's a nice person and a good cop. I'm trying to help out."

Pretenses, now my parents understand that concept; the slipping and sliding people do to get by in an imperfect life. That's a wonderful phrase—slipping and sliding, I first heard that on television's "Saturday Night Live" about the first President Bush.

My mother's frown softens. "Okay, you go but be careful." Protecting the virtues of someone that is a victim of the system, this is clearly something that she can relate to in her imperfect world.

It's not easy to find parking in Park Slope and I worry about leaving my surfboard unprotected. It is mounted on the roof of my ordinary sedan, but is it safe? My suspicious policeman nature tells me, 'No.' The safest action to take is to park in front of a fire hydrant, with my official police sticker prominently on display. I glance back once more as I climb the steps to her apartment.

I'm unusually tardy as I ring the doorbell; once again, I instinctively bend down, admiring the flowers on the front stoop.

"Come on up," I hear Roberta say. I could just suggest she come on down and we get started; we are late, but I'm curious so

I walk up the stairs.

"I have no presents," and I show her my empty hands.

She reaches over and gives me a peck on the cheek. "Your coming here is the best present."

I follow her into the apartment and resting on the ledge of a big bay window is a fat, orange cat, stretching; what contortionists are cats, something to be admired. And their contempt for the very humans who feed them, a very independent species those cats; I prefer the panting obedience and servitude of a friendly dog.

A slender, dark-haired woman of about thirty approaches us.

"Julie Eckstein," she says, as she extends an open hand towards me.

"Sasha Perlov," I reply, as we link hands in a playful gesture.

"Sit down," Roberta points to a big, soft-looking chair. A large, pink triangle flag is draped across the mantle of the fireplace.

I recognized the symbol of gay pride, which was taken from the armbands that homosexuals were forced to wear during the Nazi reign, pink for queers and yellow six-point stars for the Jews. The Nazis, master propagandists, isolated and categorized all non-Aryans using the state media to convince the populace that these people were truly enemies of the state. The Soviets tried to force labels on their enemies but were not as successful as the Nazis. The educated people in the former Soviet Union figured out that political dissidents like my mother were neither mental patients nor actually enemies of the state unless ideas were dangerous.

"Hot tea?" She knows we are running late but she isn't feeling any need to rush. I relax and let her instincts be the guide. After all, it's her family we're going to visit. The afternoon is still young and I have hours to surf. But I do worry about my exposed surfboard.

"No," I shake my head.

"Vodka?" she smiles.

"Too early even for a Russian." I reply, although a small glass of wine did satisfy my thirst at shul at the conclusion of the service.

I lean back into the cushiony, bouncy chair to observe Roberta's partner. A few freckles follow the outline of her high cheekbones. They make an attractive couple, one dark with long, wavy hair and the other with her short blonde shag.

"So what do you do?" In America, that's the first thing you ask people. Here a person is defined by what they do to earn money. Status is wrapped around money. Among Russian intellectual dissidents there is mistrust about the value of money. Yes, it's a useful and necessary commodity, but does it deserve such a defining significance.

"I'm an Assistant Professor at Brooklyn College," she answers promptly and with clear satisfaction.

"You and Roberta went to school together?" That was the perfect place to meet a future mate. I was never too successful while at school, but then I wasn't trying too hard.

"Yes, we went to Barnard together." I know Roberta had graduated Phi Beta Kappa from the school in upper Manhattan.

"An English teacher," I knew that Roberta was an English major at Barnard College.

"I'm a criminologist."

I have a look of surprise. "Hmm. You should be teaching at John Jay." That's the City University of New York college known for its criminal justice curriculum.

"I'm in the Sociology Department." She edges closer to Roberta, creating a protective or perhaps possessive gesture with her body. "Did you study sociology at college?" she asks me.

"I was a psych major so I took a few sociology classes and one or two anthropology courses." I smile thinking back at my aimless college days. I could have done so much more, but what the hell, my life is still in its formative days.

Ms. Eckstein is very interested in me. Her gaze isn't harsh but it's intense, and I sense an air of mistrust. What are my real motives in accepting this invitation from Brother Tommy?

"I tell Roberta, practically every day, that she should quit the police force, go to law school full time, finish, and then do something more rewarding. She can stay in public service and work in the prosecutor's office or for legal aid."

Roberta shrugs her shoulders in an off-handed way; I hope these discussions are merely Julie's idle thoughts.

"No, no," I say emphatically. "Roberta is a good cop; we need more just like her; we can't afford to lose her." The Lieutenant will be disappointed if I fail him. She must stay.

Julie gently grabs Roberta's arm, pointing her finger at me. "She has to go through a lot of crap and it isn't worth it."

I tap Roberta's knee while staring at Julie. "She's a born cop. It's in her blood. We need smart people like her, but sensitive," I wink at the two of them, "and at the same time, calm and unafraid. For a Catholic school girl, she's plucky." What a great word, more English than American.

Roberta is enjoying our talking about her rather than engaging in a three-way conversation.

I don't like to point at people while I speak, my mother's preferred gesture, although the impulse is strong at this moment. "It's not easy to be a cop. You get to see all kinds of ugliness. You're always on edge looking for something suspicious, not quite trusting what you see." I look directly at Roberta who nods in agreement.

Her back straightens as she speaks. "I decided to be a cop because I wanted to help people. It's a wonderful feeling when you can find a lost child, recover stolen property, even," and she hesitates for a moment, "bring relief and a sense of retribution to a family who has lost someone to a murderer." I don't interrupt. However, in my cop's mind, a typical woman's response to being in law enforcement; it's not my rationale.

I look directly at Julie. "You want to understand the messes people create for themselves but not get too close." I thought about the opportunities that were offered to me. "I made a point to stay away from Vice and Narcotics. The temptations to sample the product are so strong and the lure of the contaminated money; money, so much money." I remember the suitcases of cocaine and unmarked hundred dollar bills that pass through the evidence room.

"Roberta calls you the fearless one." Julie glances at her partner and then back to me.

"I like the sense of danger that's why I'm a cop. I don't want to throw my weight around and impose my will on others. I don't really want to help people. I like being on edge; it's what I miss about not being on the street."

"So why not undercover Vice or Narcotics." Julie, the criminologist, prods and provokes, not happy with my first response.

"No, I don't want to get too familiar with the filth. You can't walk away from those squads without getting a little dirty yourself. It's not fear of being shot but fear of being tainted. Although among the rank and file, everyone knows that's the quickest way up the promotion ladder."

Roberta is ambitious. Being a cop is important to her and we discuss our futures as cops with law degrees; she can't walk away, the pull of police work is too great. She knows I am also an ambitious cop.

"Sasha, you should study for the sergeant's exam. It's not like you would actually double your studying time because of law school, it's actually complementary." Roberta has suggested this in the past.

"You have this family tradition to uphold. I like what I'm doing and I'll get promoted my way, working my type of cases. You have a vision of a ladder straight up to the top. Me, I'll take the circuitous path. I started working with immigrants because no one else speaks the language. I moved to bias cases because I'm a Jew, which now is leading me to terrorist cases. It works for me. It's the uncharted course."

Julie is watching us. She will not be able to pressure Roberta out of the police force.

"Smart," and I tap the side of my head with my index finger. "We," and I point to Roberta, "we are smart, and, despite popular impressions, the department needs smart people. Brawn is cheap and available, but smart and resourceful is a valuable commodity.

Don't think the brass doesn't think that way."

Julie the criminologist doesn't agree. "And the police don't encourage brute force?"

Defending my job feels like I'm defending my mother. "No, that's the exception to the rule. The police have been doing a much better job of weeding out the psychopaths."

I edge closer to my two women. "Listen," I'm fully assimilating the words I disparage, "the real reason for overreaction is fear. Cops who are afraid cause trouble." I watch them watching me with interest and attentiveness.

"Rookie uniforms arrive on the scene, and even black and Hispanic guys who haven't grown up in the ghetto, get nervous in the housing projects. These are dangerous places; but when you're scared, you think there's a bad guy with a gun at every corner, waiting for you on the elevators, stalking you on the roofs." I move even closer to them to make my point. My shoulder touches Roberta's; I am entering her personal space.

"These aren't all bad people. Most of the residents of the housing projects are good people, not really smart or well educated; they don't know how to manage the system. Still, they deserve our protection because they are frightened of the few bad apples that live in the buildings or hang around."

Roberta agrees. "Yeh, you're right. But those smelly, commonplace buildings can feel like traps." She and I once detailed the perils for our law school classmates. "But some of the dangers can be avoided. The Housing Authority has to make certain that all the bulbs in the building are working and that there are no blind spots. Use mirrors in the corners. Make the elevator buttons tamper proof. Put in emergency signals in the buildings that connect directly to the police department. More cameras would work." We move out of our huddle.

I'd love to continue this conversation but I check my watch. "It's fun talking shop but it's getting late and the good surf is getting away. And I'm worried about my surfboard tempting a bad guy."

Julie shakes my hand. I feel her suspicions fading, maybe not disappearing. "It's great to meet you. We should have dinner," she says, looking me directly in the eyes. Her gaze is softening.

"Sure, I would like that. There are some great eating places here in Park Slope," I respond, as I stand so we can leave.

We make our departure and leave Julie and the purring cat. I take two steps at a time to quickly reach the street. Roberta is racing down the stairs, right behind me. I hold the front door open for her. My car looks undisturbed and we climb in for the ride to Breezy Point.

"Roberta," and I want to be careful what I say, "what have you been telling your family about me? I figure they must be desperate if they consider a Russian Jew as potential boyfriend material."

Roberta starts laughing. I try to drive and yet glance her way. The tears are rolling down her face.

She gives me zetz, a small poke. "Sasha, you are a good sport," managing to spill out the words amid the laughter, tears, and the hiccups.

I can't avoid smiling and shaking my head.

As she catches her breath, she squeezes out a few words. "I know I'm a coward; I should be more honest with them."

"Like, Roberta, do they come to visit you in Park Slope? You take the flag and hide it; make believe you're sleeping in some other bed."

"You're right, I live a lie. It's just hard. Wait till you meet my family."

"I guess," I say, although since I don't hide the fact that I'm a Russian Jew, it's not like I really can be empathetic.

I'm ready to dismiss the subject since the day is so gorgeous, much too beautiful to waste on half-truths. A mile from the sea and the salt air is pungent. We both unconsciously breathe in the heavy moisture as we drive over the Marine Park Bridge, making our way towards Rockaway and Breezy Point.

She pokes her head out the car window. I hope she's not going to throw up, but instead she starts whistling. I also love the feel of the salty breeze whipping through my hair.

Roberta is not finished with our discussion. "What do the other guys really say about me?" she sheepishly asks.

Honestly is the best response. "I mean, like, Roberta, they all say you're gay so what's so awful about admitting the truth?"

"It's not the squad room that's so frightening, it's my parents."

"Hell, they can't be so dumb. I mean your brothers are on the force, don't they hear gossip or rumors?"

"It's not the same as saying to them, I'm gay." Her voice gets tighter. "Sasha, you are a real pal. And don't think I don't appreciate what you are doing for me. You have always been polite to me and treated me as an equal."

"Roberta, you can't believe that you're brothers and father will desert you if you come out as gay." I know that whatever differences there were between my grandfather and mother regarding Soviet politics, he would never have knowingly allowed anything to happen to her or any of us. Could Roberta's family be so different?

I hear no answer so I let the sea air and the images of food on the grill, surfing, and the brilliant sun rule my thoughts.

We arrive at the gated community and the guard lets us enter since he is expecting us. It looks like any surfside community with houses of many varieties, but very few of gigantic proportions, mostly three or four bedroom houses sitting snugly, next to one another, block after block, surrounded by the Atlantic Ocean. I could fall in love with this community. The sea and me; that's the plaque I would put solidly on my front door.

Roberta gets lots of kisses from her associated family members. There are the brothers Tommy, Timmy, Patrick, Brian; next I meet the wives and girlfriends Megan, Mary, Bridget, and, yes, a Miriam. We know immediately that we are the interlopers.

"Hello," and I shake Miriam's hand; I notice the gold Star of David hanging loosely around her neck. My impulse is to show her mine, but I need to better understand the terrain. This is a new world and immigrants know to quietly survey unfamiliar territory before making any rash movements.

Uncle Dennis introduces himself.

"A policeman," he takes my hand in his meaty hand and surprisingly gently shakes it. "A fireman in Bushwick," he tells me with satisfaction.

Father Sean and Mother Ginny are all smiles.

"Nice to meet a friend of Roberta's," and she immediately offers me a glass of clear liquid. "Russian vodka," she tells me.

I accept the offering. I pride myself on being a good guest even as a child in Russia. The mothers of my few friends would always call my mother and compliment her on my fine manners.

I see the Hebrew National package near the grill. The gulls are eyeing the package but Brother Tommy scoots them away with his long, strong arm. They will wait patiently for the humans to let up their guard. The winged scavengers know that people have limited abilities to focus.

"You've done good, Detective," I turn to face Brother Timmy.

"Which station house?" I ask him, and he tells me.

Soon my brother cops, young and old, surround me. "I didn't think it was a good idea for my daughter to be a cop. It isn't ordinarily dangerous since the crack cocaine epidemic killed off so many, but I worry." Father threw his freckled arm across the shoulders of his little girl. She smiled while he pulled her close to his burly chest. The brothers all nodded.

"Sasha, is that what people call you?" Mother asks, as she moves into the center of the circle and the brothers form a protective, larger circle around the women.

"Where did you learn to surf?" Father inquires.

"Right here in the Rockaways."

Mother hands me a hotdog on a bun, smothered in spicy, dark, deli mustard and hot sauerkraut. I can barely open my mouth wide enough to consume one of my favorite foods. Brother Timmy refills my glass to the top. They all watch me eat and sip my vodka. I feel like a trophy wife.

"I like Jewish cooking," Mother tells me. "Is your mother a good cook?"

I could lie but I instead I say, "She's always working on improving her chicken soup."

Mother's sweet, approving smile, tenderly urges me to eat. "I read chicken soup actually helps with colds and flu; it's not just an old wives' tale. I gave it to Roberta and the boys," and her radiant smile includes all of them, "whenever they got sick as children. I didn't make my own, just opened a can of Campbell's, but it works."

I'm finishing my hotdog, wiping my mouth with a napkin, trying not to look too messy in front of my admirers. Tommy is already preparing me another.

"I wonder who discovered its value as medicine?" Roberta asks, and everyone looks at me.

I know the answer, but I don't want to appear too much like Al Gore, the know-it-all. "Maimonides, the Jewish philosopher and physician is reported to have written of the healing properties of chicken soup," I casually respond, as I wait for more food.

"A great man," adds Patrick, "they named a hospital in Brooklyn after him. He must have important patrons."

I think for a brief moment before speaking. "Yes, although he's been dead almost 800 years. But for Jews that's nothing," and I loudly snap my fingers. "We live to honor the dead."

Father hands me a steaming hotdog just as scrumptious looking as the first. Tommy offers me a can of beer. I don't have enough hands and besides I don't ordinarily drink beer. I shake my head at Tommy.

Father has a pensive look when he speaks, "The Irish love a good martyr." He is temporarily distracted. "Why have peace when there are a couple of centuries of martyrs to honor with bombs. A martyr's funeral is something to behold."

Commonalities between the Irish and Jews, this is a new one for me.

I don't finish my drink. It's never prudent to go swimming in the tricky Rockaway currents if your reflexes are diminished by alcohol. You have to be acutely aware of all the smallest ocean motions.

No one minds as I prepare myself, rubbing down the board with a special lotion. I feel their eyes on my back as I walk through the sand with my trusty board resting on my head. I swim out on my board. Roberta and the brothers join me in the surf. I'll never win any surfing competitions but the tension between balance and daring quickly returns.

I move from my belly, to my knees, and then on my feet as the wave propels me towards the shore. I am surfing. The waves are several feet high and I take advantage of the momentum. I glide on top of the wave as the salty foam follows behind my board.

On shore, Father and Mother clap as my board coasts just above the broken shells and dark green seaweed towards them. I stand with my board in triumph. Timmy grabs me under my armpits while Tommy holds on to my ankles. Roberta is screaming encouragement to them. They toss me from side to side as if I was a rope and then fling me back into the sea.

I'm laughing as I splash into the choppy ocean waters. I get back on my board and swim out to catch the next great wave. It's not Hawaii, but I could die at this moment a satisfied guy.

I think for a moment of my own funeral. Then she appears— my Olga, my obsession. No, I'm not ready to die without knowing what happened that day. I feel the wave under the board and I get back on my knees.

An hour later, I am thoroughly exhausted. I accept that glass of vodka and a third hotdog. I look at the raw clams sitting in their shiny shells, but I politely refuse. Watermelon and steamed corn I ravenously devour.

I lay down on my board on the family deck. I can't move. Food, fun and surf have drained me of any energy.

I must have fallen asleep because slowly I become aware of something gently poking at my arm. I look up and see Roberta standing above my comatose body.

"Have I been a bad guest? Was I snoring?"

She laughs that hearty laugh of hers. Out of my sunburned eyes, I see brothers Tommy and Timmy.

"Hell no," Tommy says. "We appreciate a guy who knows how to enjoy himself."

Mother has another hotdog for me. Another hour passes with meaningless chatter mixed with a little shoptalk. I feel this bond with these strangers. I never felt as welcomed as a cop.

I'm still a little sleepy as Roberta and I prepare to leave, but Timmy offers to take his sister home since it's on his way. I accept his proposal. Does she invite her brother and his girlfriend in for a drink? Do they meet Julie?

I'm driving across the bridge with the goal of crashing at my parents' house and just collapsing on the lounge chair out in the back. My cell phone is ringing. It's Marina.

She speaks rapidly in Russian. "There's a crazy mix-up about the schedule at the hospital so I don't have tomorrow off. I do have a few hours now." Her brisk verbal delivery doesn't dawdle to take a breath. "Instead of calling my father and having him pick me up, I thought I'd give you a call. We have to cancel tomorrow. I wish they were more organized here." I hear her condemnation and visceral disapproval. "Hey, do you have time for a meal and some conversation?"

"Of course, I'm on my way."

She's waiting at the Emergency Department entrance. Ambulances and police cars surround my car making it difficult for me to get close to the door. I show my badge to the EMS driver and he lets me maneuver around his vehicle.

I stop the car and before I can get out and open the door for her, she's jumping into the passenger seat of the car.

"Where to?" I ask.

She doesn't hesitate. "Let's try something by your place."

"Okay," and I turn the wheel and we head north towards Kew Gardens. I'm thinking, does she have a plan?

As we drive, we talk. "What are you interested in?"

Out of my peripheral view, I see her turn her head towards me. "Besides you?"

Do I like this much candor? My skin is getting hot.

"Kosher Moroccan," I suggest. "We can park my car in my co-op space and walk to the restaurant."

"Papa won't be able to pursue us," and she laughs. It is a nice, spirited but suggestive laugh.

When we arrive at my co-op, I just have to ask. "Do we do take-out?"

"Let's not be too rushed," she says as she takes my hand in hers.

And then I release an energetic, boisterous laugh.

The restaurant is crowded and she is on a schedule. My mind and hormones are considering the take-out when a waiter seats us at a table.

We listen to the waiter's recommendations. I eat here on a weekly basis and know the menu by memory. The owner, an Israeli of Moroccan ancestry, recognizes me and he comes by our table; we chat in Hebrew.

I spent six months in Israel before actually emigrating to America. That was a common practice among Soviet Jews in the 1970's and 1980's. As an adolescent, I was a quick study, as they say, and I rapidly became conversant in Modern Hebrew. But my mother was never persuaded to stay in the Land of Milk and Honey. She had her heart set on the New Jerusalem. The ancient one was too caught up in wars and fighting. She was tired of struggle.

I tenderly take my Marina's hand and gently massage her fingers. We order a Moroccan drink. I couldn't possibly have much more and stay awake.

She tells me, "It's the anniversary of our arrival in America."

I glance at my watch, which has a day of the week and date on it.

"And does your family celebrate it?"

She sucks in some air. "Not really; my father considers it our destiny to come to America."

I shake my head. "My grandfather's death prompted our departure. I was this pimply-faced kid and I didn't want to leave Petersburg. I was used to the anti-Semite slurs. I had my friends and classmates. There was the swim club." I stop to reflect. "I hated my parents when my father announced one night we were going. And I mean we left, like in the middle of the night."

Marina grabs my hand and holds it tightly. "Why?"

"It would be years before I understood. I was a self-absorbed adolescent."

"So are we all," she says, encouraging me to continue.

"My father was afraid; really afraid something would happen to my mother and maybe all of us. As soon as my grandfather got very ill and it was clear he was dying, my father started acting strangely. I caught him whispering to people on phones in public places. He would be strolling on the street and a complete stranger would walk alongside of him and stuff a piece of paper into his hand."

Marina was eagerly following every word I said.

"People heard that Russia was changing and Gorbachev was talking reform, but my grandfather had enemies and my mother had many enemies; and it was totally uncertain what would happen to the Soviet Union."

I wrap my hands around her sturdy, powerful fingers. "My father knew my mother would never survive another stay in prison. He worried that I was in danger and his parents who lived with us might be arrested."

I paused, remembering those crazy days. I felt a grimace forming on my face and the earlier fun was fading from memory. Our family had many tales of sacrifice and intrigue.

"If my grandfather had died in 1992, we would never have left the Motherland. We would have been a part of the new Russia."

"You can always go back and live."

It was beyond her understanding that my mother, the daughter of the Hero of the Battle of Stalingrad, deserted the Motherland.

"Not now, never now. We have fallen into the intoxicating grip of democracy. How can you go back and live under a repressive regime when you have experienced freedom of speech and freedom of the press. You can't go back and be happy. And my mother is too tired to go back and fight Putin. If we had never left, we would not know about these things. It's one thing to visit as a stranger and a tourist; it's another to live as a citizen of a free nation."

"It must be hard to be a son in such an illustrious family. My father was one of hundreds of government engineers and my mother a physician in a country where the majority of physicians were women. They waited out the chaos and then left out of frustration with the crime and corruption."

The hot, steaming food arrived and we held hands while the waiter placed them on the table. "You didn't really hate them?" She asked.

"Of course not, but I couldn't articulate how I felt so like an immature kid, I did stupid things to get back at them. I was first in my class in Petersburg. People called me the future Great Russian philosopher-poet. In America, I did OK at high school and well enough at college, but never did I rise to meet their expectations of the boy genius."

She bent her head and kissed my fingertip. "You're still young with so much potential yet to realize."

"Yes, yes, I agree. I wrote angry, belligerent poetry when I first arrived. Then I abandoned all poetry. But now I think about starting again."

She straightened up in her chair. "I wanted to go to the Berklee College of Music in Boston and be a jazz violinist."

"Hum," I say and stare at those fingers. "A jazz violinist?"

"I studied violin since I was four. And when I made the request to go to Berklee my father had a fit. He said if I wanted to study classical violin at Juilliard that was OK. Nothing wrong with a violinist in the family, but jazz."

She makes an impish gesture with her face. "I could have lied and gone to Juilliard. They have a jazz program, but I'm not the liar type."

"How did you get interested in jazz violin? What is it? Like country music is something people know."

"It was all by accident. As my father likes to say—it was

destiny. My father found a recording of Joe Venuti's, one of the first and greatest jazz violinists, and I fell in love with the sound."

"It's how my mother discovered the Beatles, by accident, when my grandfather, sent to East Berlin on Soviet business, confiscated early Beatles' albums from the home of a dissident. He brought them home to her but never expected that their sound and message would become her anthem."

"At Berklee, there's a class devoted to jazz violinists like Venuti and Stephane Grappelli, Jean-Luc Ponty. Names most Americans don't recognize but in Europe these are more familiar. One of the reasons I wanted to come to America was to study at Berklee." If she is disappointed, there is no hint in her voice.

"You have to play for me."

"Oh, I will. I'm good. I don't know why but the sounds just connect." Her enthusiasm is infectious. I am eagerly looking forward to a performance.

This is a new Marina, the jazz musician. How cool.

"So it's a hobby for relaxation after a day at the ER?"

"Well," and she edges a little closer and pushes the plates to the side, "actually, I was drawn to the ER for more than the excitement. I do love the spontaneity of the work. It is what draws me to jazz—the improvisation. The central connection between the music I love and the ER." A tune comes into her head and I see her fingers moving on the table as if on the strings of a violin.

"At the ER, the hours are regular. You can get stuck with the midnight to seven AM shift but it's a predictable schedule. No one calls you at home at all hours because of a problem, no rushing to the hospital. So I can perform gigs at some of the little clubs opening in Brooklyn and then maybe Manhattan."

This is the secretive side of Marina. "What will your father say?"

She has a mischievous twinkle in her eye. "That's the great part. I got him investigating these contract firms that place residency trained ER physicians in hospitals. My father is a first-rate entrepreneur. America and Father were meant for each other.

He sees this as a business opportunity. He wants to create an ER physician company for me after I finish my residency. We'll have other doctors working for us. Then I can play." She slowly nods her head up and down, very proud of her scheme.

She's a cunning woman. I love her. "Does he know the real motivation for your interest?"

She grins a wickedly, devilish smile. "Of course not, but after it's done he'll go along. Business, he'll love it; he'll be creating a viable money maker and I will practice medicine between gigs."

This is a woman with a plan. After we drink our tea, I check my watch. "Do you want to see my apartment?"

"Certainly," and I ask for the bill.

On the street, I snuggly wrapped my arm around her waist as we saunter to my apartment, only a few blocks from the restaurant.

I am newly energized; the image of my bed dancing in the center of my bedroom. I hope she isn't too neat because I haven't been paying much attention to the apartment's order and cleanliness.

My cell phone loudly rings out, 'Answer, answer.' It demands to be heard.

I sigh before answering, the life of a cop. It's Jimmy. "Yeh, what's going on?"

"Where are you," he asks.

"I'm in Kew Gardens on the street."

"Alone?"

"No, I got Marina with me." She's listening and screams near my ear. "Hello Jimmy."

He answers back, "Hello Marina, I look forward to meeting you. Am I interrupting something," he asks in his naughty voice.

"Not quite yet."

"Good, pick me up at home in Bay Ridge. We have a date with Matt Tannenbaum. He called me, all mysterious. It must be big because he's not one of those workaholics. He's a city worker who works on the clock."

"Okay, but I have to get Marina back to Downstate."

I put my phone back on my belt where it rests along with my badge. "Police work never stops."

She smiles and kisses me on the cheek. "There will be many more opportunities," and she pinches my ass.

Startled, I jump a foot into the air, and then turn around and kiss her on the lips.

"Interruptions, so many interruptions," I mumble to myself.

Marina steps out into the street looking for a cab, but I insist on driving her back to the hospital, otherwise her father would be angry.

"It's out of your way," she keeps insisting.

"No, it's on the way." That's a lie, but I still need to make a good impression on her parents.

Jimmy and I arrive at the Medical Examiner's office and Saturday night is certainly not a slow time here. People are running in all directions. We're surprised to see Tannenbaum personally come to greet us.

"Guys," and he's actually smiling.

Jimmy and I wait for science's messenger to tell us the news.

"Come here," and he beckons us with his finger; we obediently follow our Pied Piper.

"I'm so glad I thought of Interpol," says our expert.

Jimmy raises his eyebrow and my mouth hangs open.

Finally Jimmy speaks, "Tannenbaum," and he pulls at the ME's elbow, "hold up."

"Let me hear this again," and both men stare at each other. I am a curious observer.

I speak. "Interpol?" I repeat the word.

"This started as an investigation of slashed tires in Borough Park and we're discussing," Jimmy pauses, "international terrorism."

"Guys, guys," Tannenbaum is an excited kid, "follow me," and we practically race to keep up with our scientist.

The old offices of the Medical Examiner have had a fantastic face-lift. Institutional gray has been replaced by neon yellow. We enter a room filled with scientific instruments.

"Look at this, I mean look at those marks." We stare at the smudged fingerprints magnified a hundred times.

"Now," and he turns to a photo on the shiny, metal counter, "here is our tire slasher."

It's a face only a mother would love, with its droopy eyelids, puffy lips, and a scar near the chin.

"I can't pronounce the name," says our ME, allowing for a small flaw in his resume.

I look at the sheet.

"He's a Russian. A mob figure and could have links to terrorism. Seems the old crime distinctions are fading." Tannenbaum is bursting with energy.

I pick up the photo and carefully read the name.

"He's not a Russian."

Tannenbaum pulls the page from my hand. "You doubt Interpol?"

I don't want to deflate Tannenbaum's unusual enthusiasm.

"It's not a Russian name," I reply. The old Soviet Union was comprised of many people who were not Russians.

Jimmy is standing with his hands on his hips. "Why would a mob guy on Interpol's list be slashing tires in Borough Park?" Jimmy asks in amazement.

Tannenbaum pushes his index finger into Jimmy's chest. "You guys are the police. Find out. I'm from the Medical Examiner's office. I found you the evidence," and he is beginning to show annoyance.

And so we leave with a copy of the grainy photo and the urgent question of why a guy on Interpol's list is running up and down streets in Borough Park slashing tires.

"Are we lucky we got such a high profile criminal or is this the beginning of a giant headache?" I ask my partner.

He slaps me near my shoulder blade. "Think positive. Who knows where this will lead."

"I'll call my contacts tomorrow and see what I can learn about this guy," I reply.

CHAPTER 14

Our tire slasher's name appears on an Interpol list of people of interest to international authorities. I don't know yet whether that's official double-speak for a terrorist or a member of organized crime. Startling results is what we tell the Lieutenant. How did a religious bias case evolve into an international case with organized-crime links or terrorists?

It's Sunday, our rare scheduled weekend day off, but Jimmy and I are busy at work. We are checking all NYPD files to see what we can learn about the name pulled by Interpol.

In walks the Lieutenant. He's a man of the streets, never afraid to mix with the grunts. Sundays, evenings, when there's an important case brewing, he is with us.

"Sutton and Perlov, what a case," he tells us. We stand to greet him and he slaps our backs with zest although blunting the impact of his blow.

"What do we know?" he enthusiastically asks.

"It's Sunday and we can't get too much information," Jimmy answers.

The Lieutenant whistles and Jimmy shakes his head in agreement. "What have we stumbled into this time?" our boss says, and we concur by nodding our heads in unison.

"Later. I'll go out in the street and see what I can find out," I reply, and the two men stare eagerly at me. I am expected to know about all things Russian.

"Do we have any outstanding warrants for him in New York?" the Lieutenant wants to know.

"We have nothing in our computer database but that doesn't mean something isn't brewing. We got to get to the FBI." Jimmy adds. "You know how they treat us, but now we got a few contacts. So tomorrow, I'll be calling around." Jimmy is working hard on securing us FBI contacts. He simply never lets a bureaucrat's answer of 'no' stop him from pursuing a lead. He's the Rottweiler dog that bites into a bone and refuses to release. I admire his tenacity; it complements my natural inclination to be suspicious and my compulsive need to know all the facts.

"A Russian crime figure?" The Lieutenant again starts shaking his head in disbelief.

"Maybe a terrorist," I say. "In today's modern world of bad guys the two often intersect. Organized crime in Europe exchanges Afghan heroin, peddled by terrorists, for guns. It's a possibility."

We all know that we have staggered into unknown territory and we certainly have no idea where this will lead.

The boss says to his loyal vassals, "I have a contact at the Organized Crime Investigation Division. I'll give him a call and see what he knows. He's a good guy and owes me a favor from years back so I'm confident he will share info with us." The Lieutenant makes a note in his date book.

"Is this Russian living here in the U.S.?" my Lieutenant queries me.

"We don't have a local address. He's believed to be living in America but no real clues where." Since I am the authority of all things remotely Russian, I suggest, "This is not a Russian name. The face and the name are not from the Motherland; my guess is he's from Central Asia. It doesn't mean he isn't operating in Russia because he probably is from the former Soviet Union, but from one of those Muslim places. He's got a name no one can pronounce and he's probably from a place no one can pronounce."

"Check your contacts," he orders me.

And I, his obedient underling, respond, "You know I will."

I call Vasily from a pay phone near the Brighton Beach Boardwalk. "Can you meet me at our usual beach spot?" I ask.

He responds, "Be there in an hour."

True to his word and as punctual as I am, we take our seats on the bench.

He offers me a plump nectarine. As I bite into it, the juice runs down my face. Always ready, he hands me a paper napkin. "Delicious," I say.

He takes another one from his pocket and we spend a few minutes quietly eating our fruit.

I slip the photo on the bench seat and watch him observing the face.

"Anyone you know."

He stares at the photo, but doesn't pick it up. No fingerprints.

"Bukharan Jew," and he points his finger at me. "From your new neighborhood."

"Queens?"

"Forest Hills, maybe Rego Park, those parts of town."

"He's on Interpol's list. Russian organized crime? A possible terrorist?"

Vasily shakes his head. "This guy, Sherzod Sooltonov. I recognize the name." The name is labeled on the materials we receive from Interpol. "But if he's the one I think," his eyes return to the grainy photo. "It's hard to tell from the photo. Immigrant from Uzbekistan; muscle for those stupid Bukharan Jews in business with the scum Colombian drug dealers," he says with contempt. He pauses to spit in disgust on the wooden Boardwalk planks.

"Doubt he's a terrorist, but lately crazier things have happened." He pauses to wipe his face. "I hear the Colombians have ties to crazy Muslims exchanging drugs for rocket launchers."

He stares closely at my mouth and I gingerly touch my lips

with my fingers. A small piece of fruit rests precariously in the corner of my mouth. I brush it aside.

The distraction is over and he begins. "Stupid, just plain stupid. I wouldn't get close to those pieces of dreck if they offered me a billion dollars. No one is more unreliable. Money, that's the problem in America, so much whoring for money." Vasily pulls another piece of fruit from his pocket. With a small, silver knife he splits the plum in two and offers me the larger piece. I hungrily accept.

"What could be the possible connection with slashed tires in Borough Park?" The apparent link eludes my police mind.

"My guess, and I don't know anything specific, it was a warning and the intended party knows what for."

"I should be looking for someone in the Diamond District, probably another Bukharan Jew? Check the records of those living in a twenty block radius of the tires?"

"No, not necessarily. It could be a spic, some Colombian who suffers from loose lips, not likely a shvartzer. The Colombians don't play nice with the blacks. It's not likely a Hasid from Borough Park, although they're also in the Diamond District. But these Bukharans keep strange company. It's probably a scare move by the Bukharans or one of their Colombian partners against a tire slashing victim. Of course, I'm just guessing." He eats his plum.

"Appreciate any more info." I wipe my fingers on the napkin after finishing my half of the yummy plum. Cute word—yummy. I feel the urge to rub my tummy in wide circles.

Vasily nods his head. He will be looking out for me. His obvious distaste for all things Bukharan will help.

I remove the police documents and place them back in their large yellow envelope. I am about to leave.

He grabs my wrist. "And the fat man, Feinstein; is the case done?"

"My friend, my police antennae wants to know why you're so interested in the case." I would trust this man with my life but he's not revealing everything to me. Concealing secrets is what I sense in this dark Russian heart; I know my fellow Russians.

"They are nice girls and you need to spend your time on important police work."

"I'll be bringing them in for questioning and if I'm convinced that no one was present when he died, the case is closed."

"Good. I'll see what I can find out about our photo guy. You can check your other sources because the NYPD and maybe the FBI are checking on the Colombians." He rises from the bench. "I'll see you at the Seaside Russian concert?"

"Oh yes. I'll be working security. My parents will be there. Of course, they would never consider waiting on line for a good seat like the late Mr. Feinstein." Our fat man, first in line Jack, was a real character from the neighborhood.

Vasily laughs, small lines form around the curve of his smile. "I'll try and have something for you by then. My regards to your parents." He slips away.

I wait a few minutes, staring out at the ocean. It's calm; the restless sea commands its waves to simply lap the packed sand. A few bodies still linger on the beach while the scavenger gulls poke their beaks at the debris left by humans. Never gentle or passive, the gulls attack each other to claim the best scraps.

"Good bye," I scream to one who is eying my plum pit and any other remains. The scavengers leave nothing. Then I get back on my bike and cycle the length of the Boardwalk.

The next day and the days after, Jimmy and I spend our time walking the streets of Borough Park looking for anyone who knows any victims. We check the records about past crimes in the neighborhood. I am particularly interested in any assault cases. If this is meant as a warning, perhaps it isn't the first.

The Lieutenant's contact at the Organized Crime Division comes through with a few Russian or Jewish-sounding names. The computer geeks are working overtime trying to match any of those names with a Borough Park address. So far, there is nothing. So I am shifting to Vasily's angle of a Colombian name and the uniforms are searching for names by questioning the postal carriers. They know all about the illegals living bunched up together in these big, old apartments. Perhaps someone got a letter from Colombia. The Patriotic Act makes all these seemingly illegal invasions of privacy now within acceptable limits.

I ask the Lieutenant for assistance on the street. He assigns Roberta and her partner to work with a half dozen uniforms from the Borough Park precinct to walk the neighborhood. We still don't know what we are looking for but we are busy canvassing.

Jimmy and I debate whether we should show the photo of our Bukharan Jew to people in the immediate neighborhood around Brooklyn Avenue. But then we reconsider. If our victim is afraid this might push him, or it could be a woman, underground and totally out of our reach. We decide that our public approach should be on attempting to solve property crimes. With an overall decline in the crime rate, a sudden interest by the police in solving property crimes should be seen by the public as a reasonable police policy, which reflects shifting priorities.

I call Rebbe for the names of other victims. I never even hint where we are taking this case. He says nothing about Glickenstein. We are letting that diversion drop; we have no time to investigate grudge matches that may or may not have involved insurance fraud. The civil courts will be left to decide on the ugly divorce case. My mother, the gossip with contacts among Hasid women, promised to keep track of the Rosenberg-Glickenstein troubles.

We go back to our repair shop owner, Hector Diaz with news about our three tires. Rebbe's tire had no useable fingerprints. The second tire our immigrant owner retrieved was also without any valuable clues. And most unfortunate, the shop owner couldn't trace the owner of the tire with the important fingerprint. He thought maybe someone had just dropped it off at the shop.

I am so busy with my new important case that I almost forget that call to Olga to settle on a specific date and time. No one cares but me. Should I take Vasily's advise and close the case? Not yet; I'm not ready to end my tenuous ties to her.

Jimmy and I search for any lead but come up empty so I accept assignment on Thursday night for my usual off-duty security detail. Russian night at the Brighton Beach Seaside concerts brings former residents home as well as visitors from far away including my Aunt Tatiana, my father's sister from West Hartford, Connecticut. Saturday is her birthday and my mother is planning a big birthday bash at the restaurant Tatiana's on the Boardwalk. She will be staying with us for a few days so she can attend the Bandshell Russian concert. Her husband has an auto parts business to run so he won't be back in the old neighborhood until Saturday night. Her sons work during the summer for their father and together they will drive here for the celebration.

Of all my relatives, I feel closest to her. She is fervently religious; a true believer, Hasid material. She and God have a personal relationship. The certainty of her convictions, I admire. Everything is so clear. There is no questioning that God has a purpose for her and every day, morning, afternoon and evening, she speaks to her God.

And she's the best cook I know. I look forward to our visits; I can depend on her to cook something just for me. She makes a stuffed cabbage I love; my stomach starts crying out for a sample as soon as I walk into my parents' house and smell it heating on our stove.

I am dressed in my uniform for security detail. Russian concertgoers are a law-abiding group, but with dozens of politicians present, including the Borough President, the police must be out in large numbers. Who would try to hurt these low-level elected officials? I can't imagine. They are simply not important enough to attract terrorists, but I like the overtime pay.

Aunt Tatiana and my mother are sitting in the backyard talking when I approach.

"Oh, Sasha," and she plants a wet kiss on my cheek. "Do you smell the cabbage?" she asks in the mother tongue.

My tongue is wagging. I excitedly shake my head. "Yes, umm. Yes."

"Sit," my mother says. And I obey.

"I just started to tell your mother a story, something so

important." She clutches my arm. "You look so handsome in that uniform. Your grandfather always looked handsome in his uniform. And your Uncle Alexei," she deeply sighs.

"Anyway," and she loosens her grip on my arm, "I'm in the Crown," a Kosher supermarket in her West Hartford neighborhood that we all know. "I'm talking to the butcher and I see out of the corner of my eye a woman, followed by two big strapping young men." She sips her hot tea. The steam hangs in the air in anticipation. My aunt has a certain dramatic storytelling style, which she probably learned from my mother.

As a child, she was a constant source of entertainment to my cousins and me. Her re-telling of the Golem stories, the Yiddish tales that became the basis of the English Frankenstein legend, were so frightening, we hid under the covers as she spoke. She never raised her voice as a storyteller but the electricity she created as her pace quickened and the excitement built. Those were the best days back in the Motherland.

"I don't think much about this woman," my aunt continues, "although in the back of my mind, I imagine there is something so familiar. Where do I know her?" She sips and my mother rests her elbows on the table. This will be a long story.

"So I'm looking at the whitefish, and one of the young men that followed this mystery woman stands next to me. I turn and I am looking into the eyes of Alexei; the young man actually catches me under my arm as I almost faint, right there in front of the fish display. I tell him in Russian, 'I have a son your age.'" My skinny cousin Sergei, the Hall High School valedictorian bound for Harvard. "'What is your name' I ask him gasping for air and he says; wait listen;" we are intently listening to her every syllable. "'My name is Andrei Aronovich.' Hashem, in his infinite mercy, has brought me to the Crown that day so that I should meet Alexei's sons."

She takes another sip and my mother is speechless, catching mosquitoes with her open mouth. My face is a slab of motionless granite. We are in a state of disbelief and shock.

"Nu, what next?" My mother manages to say a few words.

"Then the woman comes around the corner and we look straight at each other. No one else existed at that moment. I don't remember who started crying first, but we're hugging and screaming in the middle of the grocery store aisle. I tell you, the people were staring. Two crazy Russian women; so what's new?"

My mother grips my Aunt Tatiana's arm. It's turning purple from the pressure, but if my aunt is uncomfortable she doesn't say anything.

"Nu, so," my mother can barely spit out a few words. She releases her hold.

"I meet the other son. It's little Aleksandr grown so big and strong." She pauses. I move closer to my mother and put my arm tightly around her shoulders for support.

"Hashem, great and merciful," my aunt is practically davening, praying, continues, "he has brought the family back together."

After my Uncle Alexei was killed fighting for the Soviet Army in Afghanistan, his gentile wife and two sons slipped away from the family. Then we left the Soviet Union and my mother has not seen or heard anything about them these past fifteen years. She had made inquiries but without success. They were not living in Moscow or Petersburg.

Part of the reason for my Aunt Marie's break with the family was my mother's harsh criticism. She blamed my aunt for encouraging her brother to stay in the Army and not retire. In my mother's view of family history, it was my aunt who enjoyed the military life and being married to a high-ranking Soviet Army officer. She was to blame for his brutal and untimely death at the hands of Afghan savages. His coffin actually contained body parts, scraped from the dirt road where the bomb exploded. If she had not urged him to stay in the combat zone, he would have returned to Moscow to a desk job. Hurts, so many bad feelings; angry words were spoken.

Aunt Tatiana might be right. Something—Hashem, fate, some spirit, brought her to that store at that moment; it was destined that they should meet so the hurts can be healed.

"You just stood in the store?" My mother asks. I see a tiny tear materialize in the corner of her eye

My aunt tightly clenches my mother's forearms. "I took her phone number. I mean we couldn't just stay there."

"Starbucks is next door," my mother adds.

"Listen," and we are listening, "I had ice cream melting. I had to get home; and I was in shock. I needed a little distance, but I called her as soon as I got home. She visited last night with the boys."

My mother rests her head on my aunt's outstretched arms. Then she raises her heavy head. "Is she still angry?" A damp spot was visible on my aunt's arm where my mother's face had rested.

"Time heals everything. It's so true; years and so much in between. She is eager to see you and Leonid, and of course Sasha."

My mother intensely sighs, her shoulders more slouched and bent than usual. "Where was she living? Not Moscow?"

"No, not in Moscow, in Siberia." My aunt tenderly strokes my mother's arm. "It's funny how things happen. After Alexei was killed, she went back to her mother in Siberia. And what happens. She meets another man, another Jew, an engineer with the Soviet oil company Yukos. They marry."

"More children?"

"No, just Alexei's boys. And they look so much like their father. I was struck dumb when I first saw the older one."

"She's lived all this time in Siberia."

"Yes, then her husband died; he left her a bit of money. He got in good when Yeltsin gave away our country's oil riches." In America more than a decade, yet my aunt still speaks of the Motherland as her country. "He was one of those lucky Jews who got rich with Khodorkovsky," the CEO of Yukos and whose father was Jewish. "What a sorry time. Those bastards gave away the store to a few cronies." The stories of Yeltsin's corruption, and who benefited when the Russian state industries were auctioned off, are legendary among Russians still in the Motherland and abroad.

"How did she land up in West Hartford?" I, who had been silent, ask.

"You remember her sister Elena," my aunt asks and my mother nods her head, first to the left and then right.

"No," my mother says.

"You know, that cute thing, the skater?" my aunt adds.

"I remember her," I reply.

"Well, she also married a Jew. Her husband died and he had a sister who had emigrated to West Hartford. So this year the two sisters made the plunge and left Siberia."

"She left her mother and didn't she have a third sister?"

"Her mother was dead and the other sister moved to Berlin."

The two women, who are ten years apart, shake their collective heads in amazement. I just watch. What a small world. I never thought I would see my cousins again. Harsh words; my mother has this tendency. My aunt, the healer, probably softens the way for my mother to approach.

"I brought you her phone number," and my aunt slips a small piece of paper into my mother's hand. "Later you should call her."

My mother didn't vacillate for a second. "Oh, I will. Maybe while you're here." They reach across the table and hold hands. "Just in case, I turn speechless," this is not a familiar posture for my mother.

"Did you say something about the re-burial?"

My aunt passionately shakes her head. "Yes, I did. I said you arranged to bring him from that hell hole to Petersburg."

"And," my mother cautiously asks.

Aunt Tatiana's dark, luminous eyes connect directly with my mother's watery ones. "She was pleased; thankful, and accepting that once again Alexei's family picked up the pieces. His death, so far from everyone, felt like unfinished business." As the women clutch their hands together, she continues. "When I told her, I heard in her voice, relief and realization that broken ties need to be mended."

My father interrupts their intense moment. "Anyone home?" he yells. Mrs. Chervony shadows him, followed by the old woman's son, and walking up the rear is a short, stout woman who I assume is Grigori's wife.

Mrs. Chervony had called my mother wanting to meet her and it was easier for my mother to invite the whole family to our home for dinner. After they could all attend the Brighton Beach Seaside Russian concert. My mother wasn't actually cooking; she was depending on Aunt Tatiana's goodies.

Mrs. Chervony's face lights up the instant she sees the two women. She immediately turns her attention to my mother. Although I haven't introduced them, my mother is said to closely resemble her own father. My mother rises to greet her guests.

Mrs. Chervony had been waiting decades to thank Dmetri Aronovich, the Hero of the Battle of Stalingrad. Since the colonel was dead, it was left to his daughter to receive the people's gratitude. Her son was more interested in meeting my mother, the Jewish Soviet dissident and inspiration for many Jews seeking to emigrate during the hellish 1970's and 1980's. Of course, they both wanted to thank me for bringing the old woman's brutish assailant to justice. Mrs. Chervony was laden with gifts. Grigori carried bundles as did his wife.

My father takes her offerings. The tiny woman wraps her arms around my mother as if they are long, lost friends. "Anna Aronovich, my God, Hashem smiles on us this day. All the years of suffering are forgotten. We meet."

My mother is overwhelmed by the day's events but she is unusually gracious to the old woman. "Mrs. Chervony, you didn't have to bring anything. My father would be honored simply to know how much you appreciated his service to Mother Russia." Actually his service throughout his lifetime was to the Soviet Union, but it has become unfashionable to praise the original American version of the Evil Empire.

Grigori and his wife wait to be introduced. Grigori steps forward and shakes my mother's hand. "I am Grigori Chervony and this is my wife Anastasia Smirnov." In keeping with Soviet Russian etiquette, Grigori's wife maintains her maiden name.

My father introduces his sister, "My baby sister, Tatiana

Perlov." My aunt always smiling, responds, "Hashem has truly blessed this day." Of course, Mrs. Chervony has no idea of what has transpired before her family arrived.

My mother turns to her hospitality duties; she is quite adept at being a congenial hostess since she often served as my father's official greeter during her younger days.

"Mrs. Chervony, you and your family are in for a marvelous treat. My sister-in-law has brought her famous stuffed cabbage and brisket for dinner." We can all smell the scrumptious odors emanating from the kitchen. My stomach is howling for nourishment.

The time is passing. My security duties are waiting, but I wouldn't think of leaving without eating my aunt's cooking.

I assist my father in bringing the food to our table outside. Despite her severe criticism of consumerism and wastefulness, we are using expensive, decorative paper plates because it's far too much trouble for my mother to wash dishes. In the New Jerusalem you learn to make adjustments in your thinking—be flexible.

We talk social niceties, but no one asks what anyone does for a living. Everyone present knows that one's training and schooling back in the Motherland doesn't necessarily have anything to do with how one is getting by in America. Their former lives are a fading memory; the New Jerusalem demands new skills for success.

The new immigrants have morphed into corporate employees like my parents or small business owners like Grigori and my Uncle Igor. Mostly Soviet-trained engineers, these men and women found their old skills obsolete in America. Grigori and Uncle Igor, Aunt Tatiana's husband, had similar backgrounds and now one was an importer and my uncle sold auto parts. Uncle Igor wasn't an automotive engineer but a mechanical engineer, yet he loved cars, especially American ones. So in this new land, he pursued what was once only a dream, restoring old 1950's American cars. He traveled to Cuba and other backwaters to find parts.

The past is never far away among the new immigrants. Mrs. Chervony says, "My grandchildren don't have any understanding of what happened during the Great Patriotic War. Everyone who survived those years was haunted by the experience." Mrs. Chervony is clearly an educated woman, someone who benefited from the old Soviet system. Her Russian accent is perfect and she speaks articulately, although she is yet to master this strange language, English.

Grigori is protective of his mother. She sits close to him; and lets him unfold the napkin, lightly placing it in her lap.

My mother remembers nothing from those days except the noise. "I was a child and my memory of my own dead mother is so sketchy. I think my recollections are really only based on stories my father told us and her faded photo, which I still have."

"Those days," says the old woman, "cannot leave me. At the strangest times, a car backfiring, a loud firecracker and I remember vividly the guns, Nazi ones and Soviet ones. And blood and dead bodies, horrible sacrifices. Nor should I forget. Just like the Holocaust, we must constantly repeat the stories so it is not forgotten by the children and grandchildren." The smells distract her and she samples my aunt's stuffed cabbage. "So good. Just the right texture and sweetness. Do you make your own gefilte fish?"

My Aunt Tatiana rarely opens a ready-made box or jar. "Fresh ingredients and patience is what it takes to make home-made gefilte fish. It's probably cheaper to buy jar from supermarket, but I couldn't do it." She gently taps her heart with her open hand.

We eat quietly for a few minutes, chewing with our mouths closed but savoring every morsel. "Back home," the oldest among us continues, "a schoolteacher asked me to address the class about living through the Battle of Stalingrad." She shakes her head and all eyes are on her.

"I spoke of your father," and Mrs. Chervony rests her hand on my mother's damaged hand. "How every morning the Nazi guns pounded the buildings and bridges. The fires raged and never were brought under control. They simply burned until there was nothing left to keep the flames alive." She sighs. "But your father kept us alive with literally grains of salt and chunks of bread. And moving, constantly moving away from the Nazi assault. We all rose up together, all Russians, despite our many differences, to fight the invaders;" she stops. We are her spellbound audience.

She strikes her chest with force. "Those bastards never understood how united we were. Napoleon was fooled and so was Hitler." It is frightening to watch her self-flagellation.

The tiny woman hugs the edge of the table. Her eyes move around so that they catch the attention of each of us. Despite her size, she is the centrifugal center.

"The flames of the fires danced so close to us as we ran night after night, from block to block, to escape the Nazi bombings. My sister and I had to carry my mother in complete darkness. She was so frightened but she told us repeatedly not to be afraid." We stop eating.

"The blazing fires were our only source of light. If a hell exists, it was there I saw it between the craters where once buildings stood." Her fingers grip the round curve of the plastic outdoor furniture.

"One night hurrying past the flames, I stood mesmerized at one particular spot while others rushed by us. My sister and mother tried to push me forward, but for those minutes, I was captivated by the allure of the flames. The colors were brilliant; it might have been a fuel station on fire."

She pounds her open hand on the table. We jump in our seats. "Pow. A bomb exploded and the people running in front of us were killed instantly; a few nearby stragglers were bleeding all over the street. The three of us were safe."

She shakes her head. "Yes. At that moment, I knew we would survive. Hashem needed witnesses to the atrocities to remind future generations of the horrors of Nazi barbarism." She continues to shake her head.

My mother reaches and takes hold of the old woman's arthritic hand. "It was a living hell, but I don't remember the fires except as places of warmth. I feared the noises." My mother's attention drifts to her feet. "I remember the earth always shaking. The pavement and my feet actually rolling up and down like I was on a small roller coaster. I always fell down and my father picked me up, and carried me through the streets. Later my father told me it was the hundreds of tanks moving through the streets."

My mother drifts to another time and she returns to us. "Decades later when I was visiting California and experienced an earthquake, I thought, yes, that was the feeling I remember as a toddler in Stalingrad."

"And the bombs exploding," Mrs. Chervony adds.

"Of course, the bombs. So many loud, thundering sounds echoing through the half-standing buildings. There were no nice sounds. No birds singing, not even dogs barking, because I guess people ate their pets."

"There were no rats left by the time the Nazis surrendered," the old woman adds. She looks at our faces to see for any of signs of disgust.

But we all had learned about the courage of our people during the Great Patriotic War from our Soviet schoolbooks. Our teachers never discussed that it was Stalin's fault for that mess in the western front. How unprepared we were for the Nazi assault. Hitler was our ally until he attacked us.

My mother's good hand just brushes the air. "Ess," she says.

We heartily ate our food, leaving the war behind for now.

I observe Grigori staring at my mother's damaged hand.

"Did you injure yourself in an industrial accident?" He shows us his left hand with the missing finger. I didn't notice it before in his mother's apartment.

"The old Soviet bureaucracy, the People's Party, never had an Occupational and Safety Department to protect workers," he sarcastically says.

My mother displays her hand. "No, a present from the KGB."

Grigori pulls back from the table, and angrily asks, "You mean that those bastards would even consider injuring the daughter of the Hero of the Battle of Stalingrad." He vigorously shakes his head.

He draws back to the table and stares at my mother's hand. Grigori is curious about my mother's injury, but not in a prurient way. Soviet dissidents often have injuries to exhibit as symbols of Soviet barbarism.

"What happened?" he softly inquires.

"They brought me in for questioning and somehow they knew I played the piano. I no longer can play the piano," my mother matter-of-factly remarks. "Finger by finger, one by one, KGB minions broke my slender fingers. The damp Brighton Beach air inflames my arthritis but despite that, I love living here because the sea breezes are so soothing and mild compared to Petersburg or Moscow." She enjoys being so close to a force greater than the Soviet Union, which consoles her; Mother Nature.

My father's fingers start pounding the table, at first quietly but then louder. Aunt Tatiana takes her hand and physically rests atop my father's fingers so he cannot make any motion. He does not speak but I also know the reason for his displeasure. My mother's injuries are not a subject he ever likes to discuss. Grigori doesn't notice my father's discomfort. "And what did your father do?" He goes on and my mother does not stop his inquiries.

My mother is willing to share her story although she quickly glances at my father's reddening neck. She inconspicuously places her good hand on his, squeezing his fingertips. It's okay to talk.

"My father never said a word to me. I heard through gossip and whispers that he hunted down the man who ordered this," and she holds up her hand. "He did what a distinguished military man does. He shot the man in the forehead so the son-of-a-bitch would see his enemy, face-to-face." My mother actually smiles.

"And the men who did this to you?" Grigori is waiting for the rest of the story.

"Again, I was not there but I heard from reliable sources. He found the two dogs. The one who watched, my father shot him in one knee. The man who hurt me, he shot him in both knees."

A look of satisfaction is on my mother's face.

"Crippled?" Grigori wants to know.

"Yes," my mother quietly answers.

"Good, very good," says Mrs. Chervony.

"What a father should do to honor his daughter," Grigori says. They all shake their heads in agreement except my father; but I find myself nodding in agreement. Is it any wonder that democracy and a rule of law haven't quite had the desired effect in modern Russia? American politicians don't understand the deep, dark souls of former Soviet Union immigrants. They like democracy, but strength is required; the people need a strong grip to control their vile impulses.

My Aunt Tatiana knows her brother. "Let's try my fruit salad and then there's cake," she eagerly changes the subject.

I excuse myself. I can wait for the dessert; there's enough for an army of ravenously hungry teenagers so I will get something later. "I must go on duty. But I'll see you all at the concert."

Mrs. Chervony grabs the edge of my sleeve. "Such a good boy," and she pinches my cheek with her small, strong hands. "He's a tribute to your family." They all smile and raise glasses of vodka in a toast to me.

"To Sasha, the Hero of Harbor House, Perlov the Protector," my mother says and the glasses clang.

"I'll join you for a drink after duty," and I wave good-bye as I hurry out.

The Sarge tells me where he wants me, which is exactly the same spot as last year at the Russian concert. I am the official translator and cultural attaché for the NYPD. My people usually stand quietly on line. They are accustomed to years of waiting patiently on queues. But I oversee my flock just in case someone thinks that in America you can bully your way on line. I stand watching the people supervise themselves.

The time passes quickly. There is one hour to go before show time. That's when most people start arriving. My parents have their spot on the lawn. I see my father and Grigori are dragging the beach chairs. My Aunt Tatiana and my mother wrap their forearms around Mrs. Chervony's arm. The daughter-in-law follows behind. A very Russian scene with the men in front, the old men and women being assisted, and following in the rear, the adult women.

My eyes survey the concert landscape. It's part of the job, searching the faces for a potentially dangerous malcontent, observing the bottles and silverware to make certain that they cannot serve as weapons or missiles.

It is then that my eyes spy them. I am betrayed. Who do I see? Why it's Vasily talking to Olga. If they do see me, they are ignoring me. Finally, she leaves his side and returns to her two sisters. The three women sit on the lawn on a blanket. Vasily returns to his seat, and his brother and family settle together in the prime center seats. None of these people wait on line.

After the comedian, a minor star back in the Motherland, there is a short intermission. I stand guard at the portable toilets so the lines move quickly.

At each intermission, the Borough President introduces the local politicians. It's an election year. Brighton Beach has yet to elect a Russian-American to any office although a few try, but they never receive support from either the regular Republican or Democratic parties. They run as independents without much financial resources or sophisticated advice. My mother is waiting for the right one to back. People have come to her to run for elected office, but she always refuses. She says, 'I am too old. Elections are for young people.'

People rush back to their seats as the singer and the band prepare to perform. The crowd rises to its feet to applaud as a well-known Russian group enters the stage.

I feel a hand brush against my sleeve. I turn vigorously and then I see his face. "Vasily," and he smiles. "I could have smacked you, coming up so quietly." He knows how to slip as slyly as a cat without a sound.

He laughs, "Sasha you wouldn't hurt a friend."

I look all around to see if anyone is watching us in the near darkness. We walk behind the portable toilets, away from the artificial light.

I have a question to ask, but I wait.

"Our Bukharan Jew is among a half dozen men ready to be indicted by the federal persecutor's office. Very hush, hush," and he places his finger against his lips. "Shss."

"For what?" I ask.

"Money laundering. Turning Colombian drug money into gold." He wipes his lips in disgust. "Greedy pigs to work with those Colombians."

"Where is our man?"

"I don't know. The FBI doesn't know, but I am certain you will find out."

"You think he's still in this country? Or is he back in Uzbekistan?"

"He's not there. These Jews are not welcome there, but he could be anywhere, but probably in Israel. He will eventually return here because he has family in Forest Hills."

I can't stop myself. "We are friends," I start.

"The oldest of friends," he adds.

"I saw you talking with the widow, Olga."

Vasily has a perfect smile. He could be a model for a toothpaste commercial. He is using the money he makes in America to alter the crooked, neglected teeth of his boyhood into something flawlessly aligned and white. I observe his sparkling teeth as he speaks. "She's a beautiful woman. Men talk to her. But she's very treife. You can look, make a little conversation, but you stay away. Right?" I see him winking in the near darkness.

I shake my head in agreement.

"If I hear anything about your Interpol guy, I'll let you know," he tells me.

I am about to leave when I feel his pulling at my sleeve. "Let me know what present I should bring to your parents' for their 40th wedding anniversary. Something very special."

I nod. "Of course," and I gently place my hand on his. We lock hands.

He slips away, back to his seat. I cast my eyes around me. No one is near.

Then I see her, alone walking towards the ice cream vendor. All interest is on the stage so she has to tap the window to get the man's attention.

"Vanilla ice cream bar, lemon Italian ice and a fudge bar," she tells the vendor in her halting English.

I quietly move towards her so when she turns to return to her seat, I am standing in front of her. She can't escape me.

"Which one is for you?" I ask in Russian with a wide smile on my face.

She returns the smile; she is not afraid of me. I don't see any tension, no constricted muscles along her forehead indicating stress or fear. "I like the fudge bar," and the smile grows larger.

I lean towards her. "I need for you and your sisters to come in for questioning so I can close the case." My voice is calm and soothing. "It's just formalities," and I lie.

She trusts me. "We can all come to the station tomorrow."

"Fine," I respond; and for several moments our eyes gaze at each other.

The drummer's sticks crash against the cymbals. It's another intermission.

We move away from each other.

CHAPTER 15

I can't sleep, tossing and turning in my old bedroom. I seek out the familiar comforts of my old hard pillow and the soft, spongy, layered mattress. My eyes follow the thin crack that runs alongside of the window, inching from the top of the pane to the ledge. The line isn't straight but juts out in unpredictable ways, just like life.

I listen for the sounds of the ocean from my corner room, but Brighton Beach in the summertime is too noisy even in the wee hours. Instead of soothing sounds, my psyche is jolted by the discordant noise of the remaining Boardwalk crowds. No doubt these are law abiding citizens, but nonetheless, ill-mannered Russians celebrating their new freedom to roam wild. There are no authorities to stop the merriment. I never expect to hear gun shots or screams of terror by innocent victims, only the drunken outbursts of late night party-goers.

My favorite companions, the gulls, are asleep not perturbed by either the unruly humans or by my moral ambiguities. I don't have to look to know that they are snoozing, their heads hidden in their feathers, as they sleep undisturbed in safety under the roof of our garage.

As I lay in my bed, on my back, with my eyes wide-open, I stare at the speckled ceiling. My father, the brilliant mathematician, is not an expert house painter, but he believes that everyone should passionately attempt things that might lead to failure. It is failure, he often would say, that leads to new thinking. My bedroom ceiling needs a more experienced touch.

However, my mother is totally accommodating. To her, his imperfect attempts are to be encouraged. Break out of the norms. Yes, that is my mother's motto. The rigid confinements of the Soviet system require that, as new adherents to democracy, we must seek out the different, explore our potential. Although she remains deeply displeased with my choice of a profession, I often argue with her that this is America. Isn't that her dream for me, to do the unimaginable? No, but not as a police officer; a poet, yes, I should become a poet. And I will do both. In America, it is the limitless possibilities that are so energizing. There is no time to sleep in this new land. There are so many things to be accomplished. One lifetime is not enough in the New Jerusalem.

My mind drifts among my women as I lay in the stillness of my room. Of course there is my mother. Marina. And I laugh out loud to myself when I think of our unrealized sexual adventures, the continuing tension as we think of new plans. Patience, I remind myself, is a good virtue; next time, everything will proceed much more smoothly.

Then there is the source of my dilemma. She is finally making an official appearance at the station house. And what questions should I ask her? Do I really want to know what happened that day? No one cares. Can it be that I alone am interested in finding out the facts of the day? Justice, what about justice? Punishment, can that mean anything? The minutes crawl by so agonizingly slowly as I lay in my bed, consumed by the need to know. I recognize it is an obsession, but it's what makes me a great detective.

Olga; I even say her name out loud to the walls. These 1950's masonry fortifications are my perfect audience; they listen but cannot speak. They hear my confessions of confusion, lust, and fear. Fear; what if she is guilty? Can I live with myself if I learn what happened and it is criminal?

Turning onto my stomach, I burrow my face into my pillow. I smell the delicate scent of the softener my mother uses in the wash. Sleep escapes me. It is her scent. That first moment we met, I locked onto her smell and can't let go. Unconsciously, I find myself kissing the cloth of the pillowcase because it reminds me of her. She is with me; can I be her protector and still be a seeker of truths?

When at last my friends, the gulls, make an appearance on the sagging electric line near my window, I rise from my bed. They greet me, squawking and complaining about a lack of nourishment. My father will hear their complaints and within an hour make an offering to the scavengers of the sky. But they are never grateful, just like us Russians. No matter what happens, we can never feel grateful. Survivors, that's what we are, and as survivors we always feel a little cheated by life, God, destiny, history. Czars, Soviets, the new Russia under Putin, just a continuum of power, they represent someone to blame for our troubles.

The birds are my dependable friends also serving as a reliable alarm clock. They don't spend their nights weighing life's choices; it's dawn so it's time to wake up and eat. Poking my head out of the window, their tiny piercing eyes meet my wide dark ones. There are no more excuses for my paralysis of doubt so I shower and dress. Ordinarily, cologne isn't something I use, but today I put on some expensive brand my mother bought for my father, which he gave to me. He never responds to the promises in advertisements, which claim that a splash of a sweet, smelly, clear liquid would improve his masculinity. According to my father, a man is never defined by physical appearance or shiny ornaments. A Russian intellectual from the tips of his highly polished leather shoes to the tightly woven gray cells in his inquisitive brain. The best dresser among his Russian friends, my father enjoys looking smart, but he never lets the superficial cloud his judgments about people.

As I slowly descend the stairs, I am met by my mother dressed in her colorful robe of many colors. Our modern family Joseph, who dreams of visions and speaks many tongues, greets me at the bottom of the steps.

"You look tired," she says as she grabs me under the arm and leads me to the kitchen for breakfast.

"I got a big day today," I answer as I suppress a yawn.

"It's that terrorist case. Can you believe what happens here in Brooklyn?" She shakes her head in utter disbelief. I have told my parents the outline of the case.

She is ambivalent about Bukharan Jews. More Asian than Russian, she also shares Vasily's lingering uneasiness about them, confirmed after I told her about alleged links to Colombian drug dealers.

Yesterday, when I originally broached the subject, her immediate response was, "Not Russian and not Jews. What Jews would work with such scum?" If history is any guide, I remind her that Italians and Eastern European Jews were allies in all kinds of dirty businesses starting with Prohibition. Here in America, you can create any alliance, even unholy ones.

"A good breakfast is what my big boy needs," she says, while kissing the top of my head. I eat ravenously, anticipating that I will need every fiber of strength and resolve.

The Sarge yells out to me as I enter the station house, "Perlov one of your people needs you," and he points to a solitary man sitting in the far reaches of the lobby.

I stare at him; he doesn't know I am nearby. He sits practically motionless, shoulders braced against a lone wooden bench, staring down at the old, abused station house floor.

"He said he must only speak to the Russian Jewish police officer. One of the black hats," and the Sarge's eyes turn in the direction of the large black hat worn by Hasid men.

I nod to my Sarge and walk towards the man who slowly turns to face me rising from his seat. He is middle aged with a small paunch but otherwise looking in good health and physically fit.

"Perlov the Protector," he says in Russian and extends his hand in friendship.

I don't recognize him. "You are?" I ask as we shake hands.

"My name is not important. Can we speak in private," and he motions to leave the station house.

He certainly doesn't look dangerous so I nod my head and we walk out the door heading, naturally, towards the Boardwalk.

"I always like to know to whom I'm speaking. Your name?" I gently pester him.

"Aleksandr Davidzon" he reluctantly releases his name.

We walk shoulder to shoulder silently staring ahead at the wooden steps leading to the Boardwalk. Our bodies move gracefully, together in step.

We find a bench and he quietly sits. I take my place within whispering distance and just wait. He must have a real story to tell so I give him time. I have a name so I will be able to fill in any blanks.

"The tire slashings," he finally utters and rests his elbows firmly into his lap, covering his face, the black hat wobbling on top of his head. "It's all my fault, all my fault, me, it's me," and he barks out a coughing cry of anguish. He presses his covered face against his body and all the time crying, "me, it's all me."

I bend my head so I can see the tears gushing down his face. "You slashed those tires in Borough Park?" I ask with incredulity since he hardly looks the part of the culprit.

He breathes in the sea air, stops and uncovers his face. "No, no," and his voice returns to a normal tone.

"No, so who's responsible?" I ask perplexed but patiently waiting for the facts.

"My son, my son," and the tears return as he digs his head into his chest, finally the hat falls to the floor.

I pick it up as he remains curled up in this convoluted, presumably uncomfortable position.

"Your son is responsible for the tire slashings. He was the one," I ask. Bad boy Hasid turns into a malcontent with delinquent tendencies.

The tears immediately cease. "No, no, he did not slash the tires," the father answers.

I am losing patience. "So what's the story?"

His voice wants to speak but the sounds do not come. I stare at his mouth, open but nothing comes forth. "Nu," and my displeasure is showing. Perlov the Protector has many more souls to protect.

"It's him, my boy, the tire slashings were a warning to him," the words return.

"Why?" I ask remembering Vasily's words.

The man suddenly grabs my hands holding very tightly to them. It's a mighty grip but I let him continue. The anguish escapes from his parched lips. "My boy did a terrible thing. It's not him, it was the drugs," and his grip is turning my hands crimson. Still I don't protest.

"Yes what did he do," and now I shake my hands free.

"He stole money from the Bukharans," and the man's head drops to his chest as he stares at his feet while the tears slowly travel down his cheeks dripping onto his lap.

I gently place my arm around his shoulders. "Where is your son?"

His voice clears. "Israel, I sent him there with some West Bank settlers. They will clean him up, change his life around. Return him to the good boy he is. The drugs, it was only because of the drugs."

"Where's the money?" My hand grasps his shoulder holding tightly.

The man's shoulder bends into my chest. He clings to me. "I gave it to the settler leader. Use that dirty money for some good," he says as I feel him shrinking and aging before me.

"The Bukharans will want the money back. You know that," I calmly offer the perilous truth.

"They can kill me but I don't have it. I sent my family to Israel. They already came to my apartment and tore it apart looking for it and found nothing," he is finally at ease and pushes back from me.

"I can protect you. We are the police. We are as eager as you to get dirty money and drugs off the street. Let me help you," I authoritatively inform him.

He instantly straightens up. "No, no, no," and he pushes me away. "No, I don't want the police. This is the way, Hashem knows the way."

"These are dangerous people who will not stop by just trashing your home. They will come after you," I coolly tell him but with strength in my voice and conviction.

"It doesn't matter. I am leaving for Israel. They can burn down the place. I don't care. We must start all over; it is our only way. No police," and he is adamant.

"I could start an investigation or prevent you from leaving the country just with this information," I deploy my heaviest police attitude; after all I am a member of officialdom.

"Perlov the Protector you would do this to your own people?" he stares into my eyes.

"No," and I shake my head. "I only want to protect you. If you don't want my help then go it alone. I understand," and I do understand. Then I look at him. "So why are you here? Why are you telling me this?"

"I don't want you to keep poking around at the investigation. There is nothing to solve. I had to clear my conscience before I left and you were the one I could trust. So just drop the whole investigation," and he wipes his nose with some crumpled up tissues.

His confession is over; he feels relief. And so do I. We rise to go our separate ways. I don't dare tell him how the investigation has grown into an international case with potential terrorist implications. Nor will I tell any of my superiors or even Jimmy the truth about the case. Not now when we stand to gain so much in our careers. Why spoil it with the dull truth that it was revenge for stealing illegal money from thugs. But now I know what happened, no loose ends.

The phone on my desk rings loudly; the table shakes in anticipation. The sergeant calls to let us know that our visitors are here. I tell him to send them upstairs. We're not afraid of having them walk around the station house, but the brass is very terrorist conscious so a uniform will accompany them. I signal for Jimmy to finish up with his caller. I know he thinks this is a total waste of his time, but when he sees the three sisters make their entrance, he remembers how much he appreciates feminine beauty. The drug store clerk accompanies them. One person stands out in front and the others follow, walking in a neat line. The obvious leader of the group is Irina.

The women are conservatively dressed in skirts and heels. Nothing is revealed, so my active imagination pictures what she looks like under the loose-fitting, white blouse and the pastel-colored, straight skirt. No one is wearing panty hose or stockings so their tan legs shine as they slowly move towards us. Our clerk is wearing a suit that hangs on his slender shoulders. He is the sole male in the group, but he is not the dominant force.

I stand, button up my suit jacket and approach my visitors. Jimmy remains at his desk and simply stares silently at our guests. I turn my head and look back at Jimmy staring at the women. His eyes start at their plaintive faces and move down, stopping at their breasts, traveling to their waists and wandering down to their sun-baked legs. Finally, Jimmy rises from his chair.

The tall skinny drug store clerk moves around the women and presents his hand; "Vladimir," he says, as we shake. Olga is looking at the floor; and then she slowly raises her head and looks intently at me. Our eyes linger and I feel that everyone in the room must know what I am experiencing; my feelings are so transparent.

Jimmy grabs his notebook and we walk towards the interrogation room. My fellow officers all look on as we shepherd the four of them into the dingy, windowless room. I feel their escalating jealousy. The best cases and now the best looking women from the neighborhood are under our control.

The room's hot air greets us as I open the heavy door. Crime has been in decline in the last week. The bad guys are on vacation causing turmoil somewhere else. The stuffy, claustrophobic room has been empty; sitting idly waiting for a case to emerge. Incrementally, the department has been updating our crime tools. They earlier installed small, partially hidden video cameras inside this interrogation room to complement the one in the downstairs room. The cameras are meant to provide documentation of our questioning. We like to use them to record confessions. I was glad we had video evidence when I questioned Albert Speer, Mrs. Chervony's half-witted mugger. It's more for the police department's protection than anything else. We don't want the defendant's lawyer alleging in court that we beat a confession out of the accused. For our Russian suspects the cameras remain off. There's no need for a trail of evidence; only I want to know what happened.

As she passes before my eyes, I force myself not to look at her, but to maintain a cool façade. Then I see from the corner of my eye that she is watching me and Irina is holding her forearm. Masha says nothing and merely follows the others.

The four of them stand together in the room casting glances towards Jimmy and I. We don't attempt any niceties. All eyes rest on Irina, the leader, who clearly does not want to be sitting in a tiny room in a police station.

I'm surprised to see the drug store clerk with the women. Still I maintain my police cool; clearly, he's part of the emotional support network.

The nosy neighbor had alerted me to the fact that he went shopping with the women. The first time that we met in Feinstein's drab house, Olga only mentioned that she went shopping with her three sisters. There was no mention of Vladimir; so many unanswered questions.

Loose ends; I hate loose ends. This case keeps me awake at night with all the questions whirling around in my brain. Is she a murderer?

"Can I know why we are here?" Irina asks; a deep frown marks her face.

I take the lead. I am in control by the very virtue of my being an official police authority. "Please take a seat."

I begin the interrogation in English. The four of them manage to sit cramped together on one side of the table. They arrange the chairs at such an angle that each body touches the edge of the table. They sit squeezed together like four sardines in a rectangular tin can. I wish I had a camera to record this class picture. Vladimir sits closest to the door while Masha, his reported girlfriend, sits next to him. At the other corner of the table, sits my Olga and Irina in the middle. I survey my four suspects.

In this normally warm room, I expect them to start sweating. During an interrogation, we purposefully keep the room warm. People feeling the heat do blurt out valuable information. Excessive warmth, closing skin pores, tightening collars, can bring on admissions of repressed guilt. I postpone putting on the air-conditioner. I am prepared for the heat and Jimmy is dressed in a light colored linen suit. He enjoys sweating out our suspects.

"We just have a few questions about the late Mr. Feinstein's last hours," I tell my wary guests.

No one shows any measure of emotion. They sit straight in their chairs, no sweat forms on any brow, at least not yet. There are no small, jerky motions common to guilty criminals. They radiate an aura of composure.

Jimmy is sitting in the corner of the room, behind the seated guests, as if observing a psychology experiment. He is the model of the observant evaluator. Silently, he waits. It's not often I see Jimmy as a picture of reflection.

The moment doesn't last. I see him pointing with his head towards the drug store clerk. After working together a few years, I read his signals. We know that we would be better off if we separate the clerk from the women. A foursome may be stronger than a single man and three women undergoing questioning, but Jimmy doesn't understand or speak Russian so he would not be an effective interrogator. And requiring Vladimir to step outside would be an intimidating gesture and may simply result in the women clamming up. They could demand a lawyer and we would not get any closer to the truth.

Jimmy hangs over the back of the chair, his arms wrapped around the metal.

"Why are you tagging along?" Jimmy leans over his chair as he asks the drug store clerk the question. His voice is unusually soft. The clerk wants to make certain that he accurately hears the question so he turns his body completely around to face Jimmy, hitting his knee on the table as he moves. If he is in pain, he makes no sign.

Vladimir is self-possessed, responding quickly but firmly in English, "I was with ladies so I think you want my story of afternoon." It's difficult to make the grammatical transition from Russian to the English language.

I place my arms on the edge of the table. "We called Mrs. Feinstein and her sisters because I have some unanswered questions as my partner knows," and my face moves towards Jimmy.

"I'd like to know precisely what happened. I like to picture in my mind the exact details of any event." It's as if I am a filmmaker working in slow motion as I reconstruct in my mind those last moments.

"Are some questions unanswerable?" my beautiful Olga responds in Russian. Her reliance on her native tongue is similar to many well-educated immigrants; they can understand English much better than they speak the new language even if they studied it at school in the Motherland.

I pause for a moment to digest and savor a hidden meaning in her question. Her words and phrases become instant texts worthy of study. A collection of her utterances is my Zohar, the celebrated Kabbalist book of hidden meanings and great messages. I shake my head like a shaggy dog. The very conceit of my even thinking her words equal to Kabbalist literature only reinforces the fact that my thoughts are treife.

But could there be more? Is her statement profound or simply something to divert my attention from the case? Then of course there are my raging hormones. I must hide my lustful feelings, and remain focused and authoritative.

"Maybe, maybe" is my poorly phrased best answer. The case still looms. "But I am fixated on reviewing the events as if I was present in the room."

Jimmy laughs under his breath. The suspects cannot see him without turning completely around so he hovers over them like a scolding seraph, God's messenger.

"So indulge me." I fold my hands together. I look as if I am praying although Jews don't normally fold their hands in prayer; they chant and scream and sing and lie prostrate on the floor during the High Holidays. Folding hands is a proper Christian display of religiosity.

"Let's repeat for my understanding, just what transpired that day." I speak in English and it appears they are all following my discussion.

Irina is concentrating. I observe the small, red capillaries of her eyes grow as she focuses, getting the timeline worked out and alert for my questions.

"We told you this before," she's annoyed but her tone remains civil. She doesn't want any trouble from the NYC police or me.

"I'm told that you're a paralegal," I ask Irina. I think Vasily is the source of that information about her occupation. He knows far too much about these women and Feinstein. Can it be that my pal Vasily is my rival? I force my eyes to return to Irina.

She speaks. "Yes, I am. I was lawyer back in Soviet Union."

"Without a real constitution or the rule of law did we need lawyers back in the Motherland?"

She actually laughs and I see an attractive smile; hers is a wide, smooth peasant face.

"Tell me again, when did you leave the house?" I say as the laughter fades.

The four first look at each other, turning their heads to face one another. You would think they are in a huddle, waiting for Irina to pick the next play. Perhaps they are using a secret code, I don't know. "We left about noon to go shopping," Irina reports.

"All of you together," Jimmy asks, touching the back of the drug store clerk with his solid, muscular hand. If the clerk is uncomfortable, he doesn't flinch. He looks straight at me. "Yes altogether," Vladimir answers.

"Where did you all go?" I continue my questioning while Jimmy observes the group dynamics.

Irina shrugs her shoulders and shakes her head. "Here and there."

"Here and there. If I go to the stores called here and there, will a clerk remember four people shopping?" I try not to soften my voice and my eyes scan the four faces before settling on Olga's blue eyes.

"Yes," the drug-store clerk answers, "yes, we visit many stores downtown and some people will know us."

"And you ate downtown?"

"Junior's we eat and we buy cheesecake for Jack," the widow replies.

"Did you shop and then eat or vice-versa." As I speak, I watch their body language. They are still sitting close together as if they need to keep warm on a frigid Russian winter day.

"We did both. We shopped and then we ate and then we shopped," Irina adds.

"So if we go to Junior's, they will remember the four of you?"

"They many customers, we eat downtown in afternoon," said Vladimir.

"And when did you return?"

"I can't say for sure. I wasn't wearing watch," Olga says in Russian, and then she adds in English, "four o'clock. "

"Then what," Jimmy asks, keeping his eyes on the back of Olga's head.

"I call Jack and nothing," Olga speaks to me in English.

"We called out his name a few times," Irina answers in Russian, "but we don't think to really look for him because sometimes he walked to Boardwalk when weather wasn't too hot." Irina seems to know the patterns of his behavior.

"Was the car parked in the driveway?" I ask although he may not have taken out the car very often.

"The car in driveway," he answers in English. The drug-store clerk turns to look at Jimmy.

"When did you discover the body?" I look at Olga.

"I found body," says Irina in Russian, "when I went into living room to catch early news."

"Who called 911?" Jimmy asks, without understanding her answer.

"I call," says Olga and turns around to face Jimmy. He understands her accented English.

"Did you check to see if he was alive?" I look from face to face for any reaction. No one is displaying any discomfort although the room is hotter. My suspects don't request that the air conditioner be turned on.

"I check pulse," said Vladimir, loudly in English. He demonstrates on his neck how he takes a reading to check if the man is alive.

I open my hands and look at the drug store clerk. Then I turn my gaze to Olga, avoiding Irina. "The thing that continues to bother me is that Mr. Feinstein, a known heart patient, who took lots of medicine," I say, pointing my finger at the drug clerk, "you know he took lots of pills since you work in the drug store where the prescriptions were filled."

Vladimir abruptly answers in an authoritative Russian, "I was pharmacist back in Soviet Union; I know all about heart drugs. We had modern pharmacology industry back in Russia." He's another émigré with a profession and a story.

"So you knew he took several medications for high blood pressure, high cholesterol, general bad plumbing," I inquire of my animated suspect.

"He had congestive heart failure," Masha unexpectedly answers in the mother tongue. The silent one does talk.

"So why did we find no evidence of heart medicine in his blood? A mystery?" I raise my shoulders in an exaggerated shrug as I finish my question.

"Sometimes he didn't take his drugs," Olga says sheepishly in Russian. "I told him—take your medicine," she adds in English, "He not listen."

She closes her eyes for a moment. "He not listen."

She slips her hand into her purse. There are no human security guards or metal detectors in the building. Jimmy moves closer to her chair and watches her hand move inside the purse. It's a big bag, and we all know that guns, knives, box cutters can be easily concealed.

She pulls out a plastic baggie filled with pills of many colors and shapes.

"I find," she says in English. Then she adds in Russian, "I found them under mattress. He was hiding pills. I don't know last time he took them."

So she wasn't a baleboosteh, not much of a housekeeper. My Bubbe, grandmother, would have found theses pills immediately while making the beds and airing out the bedding. Every morning she had this ritual. No one could have hidden such a vital routine from her prying eyes. Now my mother would have found the pills when she changed the sheets once a week. Weekly, she had my father help her to turn over the mattress. Both these older women would have forcefully confronted their husbands if they failed to take their prescribed medicine.

"So you didn't know he wasn't taking any of his medicine?" I inquire incredulously.

She quickly shakes her head and innocently adds in Russian, "No; if I had known he stopped taking his medicine I would have reprimanded him." She shakes her finger at me the way my mother does when I disobey. I'm thirty years old and my mother still treats me as a child. I love it.

My attention is back to my beautiful suspect. I let my eyes rest on hers as I try to decide whether she is telling me the truth. I continue to speak in English. "So he may not have been taking his pills for weeks?"

"Yes," she swiftly answers, and then adds in Russian. "It was only two days ago that we discovered these pills, hidden under the mattress, when Irina and I decided to remove furniture from bedroom."

How did this big, fat guy with a heart condition manage to hide these pills under the mattress.

"Where did he hide the pills?" I don't believe her.

"The bed has drape that wraps around the box spring, bottom mattress. That's where we found pills, scattered around entire perimeter." She confidently tells me in Russian while Irina nods her head in agreement.

"You never remove drape and wash it?" I ask in Russian, to make certain she understands my question.

She isn't self-conscious about her poor cleaning habits; her face is still a peachy, silk tone without a hint of red. "No, no," is all she says.

I take the pills and return to English. "I will have them analyzed by the forensics staff." Jimmy grins and shakes his hand in the air. He is ready to call this case closed. He shows his satisfaction by nodding and rocking in his chair.

But I am not finished so I speak again in Russian. "You just found them? You mean that you had no idea he was not taking his pills?" I look at her suspiciously.

At first, she tentatively nods her head. Then she looks directly at me, speaking to me in our mother tongue. "I never thought he would hide his pills. He was responsible man. And in America, people take responsibility for their own actions," and her voice gains strength and power.

I want to be certain that she understands so I continue the questioning in Russian. "What about the Viagra we found in his blood?" The four of them collectively blush, and focus their eyes on the tabletop. Russians are very prudish people and talk of sexual activity is embarrassing. She knows that I am intentionally pressing into forbidden territory.

No one speaks; even Irina is speechless.

Finally, after a long pause someone says something. "Yes," and Olga doesn't finish the sentence.

Vladimir gives me a hard stare. In Russian, he tells me, "I got him those pills because he wanted to perform his conjugal duties as good husband and he needed little assistance."

I continue to speak Russian to reduce the embarrassment. "He had a lot of Viagra in his blood."

"He needed lot of help. Those heart pills can really create impotence." Vladimir's face turns increasingly red around the cheeks as he explains the late Mr. Feinstein's medical problems.

"But I just heard that he didn't take his heart pills. So what gives?"

Vladimir continues to speak Russian. "The impotence can last and he may have overdone Viagra. You know," he is almost whispering, "he wanted to show his wife that he was good in bed."

Jimmy can see the discomfort on the part of all our guests. He enjoys seeing suspects squirming in their seats. He doesn't know exactly what I'm saying, but he can see the apparent embarrassment.

Then I go for the kill. I stretch my body across the table and, in Russian, whisper into Vladimir's ear, "I know about the tapes."

The drug clerk's shoulders drop and his mouth opens. I don't hear a word.

I am not certain if the three women heard anything so I repeat my message, "I know that the late Mr. Feinstein was making tapes."

Olga's warm gaze towards me turns to an icy stare. Irina purses her lips and straightens up in her chair. She is not going to be shamed. Masha reaches for Vladimir's hand.

"He was an evil man who threatened you all. I understand. I am an immigrant. I know what bad people can do to good folks." I don't smile while speaking but there is no tension or stress in my voice. I am calm and I hope reassuring.

"He was evil. He seemed nice at first; gave you place to live. Didn't ask for much. Maybe you cleaned house and cooked for him." I move my body across the table towards Olga but look at each one of them, pausing at each face for acknowledgment.

Only Irina looks me straight in the eyes. Vladimir is twisting in his seat so Jimmy places his strong boxer mitts on the man's shoulder. My partner doesn't understand the conversation but he knows I have struck emotional gold. The four of them are visibly squirming and for a criminal investigation that's a good sign.

"He made you do it, disgusting sex acts. Who could you turn to as you waited out getting those green cards?" I look for confirmation among my suspects. No one is talking or agreeing with my statement.

I rise from my chair and move close to Olga, kneeling next to her without having my knees touch the dirty floor. I gently place my hand on her exposed skin. "He wanted to sell them on Internet. Your own mother back in Ukraine could have seen them. Disgraceful." I nod my head and I am so close to her that a few strains of my hair touch her cheek.

The tears start welling up in her eyes. She closes her eyes tightly waiting for my next move. I have patience, resting on my heels, carefully balancing myself. Silence permeates the room except for her soft sobs. The others remain still like mannequins.

"Then good luck strikes and he has heart attack. God answered your prayers and instead of calling 911, you go out shopping. You go out to celebrate. He deserved it." My tone of voice continues to be calm and unemotional while my heart is racing with excitement and dread—what will they say.

There is an extended period of silence. No one moves. The stone faces of my suspects reveal nothing.

So what do I have here? Do I know what happened? Maybe at last I know exactly what happened.

She suddenly grabs my arm and practically screams, "No, no, we were not there. I swear on my mother's life, we were not there.

When we left that afternoon, he was in upstairs bedroom. He was quite alive." Her grip remains fierce. I see a tiny bit of mucus descending and resting above her lip. I reach into my pocket and present her a tissue, which she accepts.

Vladimir speaks in a cool, detached tone. "He was alive. He made us do terrible things that morning. Unspeakable things, but when we left he was breathing." He bends his head and Masha places her cheek against his shoulder.

Jimmy knows something big is happening but he isn't going to interrupt the flow of the interrogation to find out exactly what is being said.

"He didn't take his medicine because he wanted to die. He started watching pornography on Internet and that's what gave him bad ideas. He became evil. He didn't start out that way. It was dirty pictures on computer screen, they changed him. Then he didn't know how to stop himself. He was tortured man. We learned to hate him but he was alive when we left." Irina's voice grows more strident, "He was alive. We were not there when he had heart attack." Irina talks for all of them while the others nod in agreement. Her mother's life is not mentioned as part of her pledge of innocence, but she is insistent and firm. I don't notice the slightest crack in her voice. Olga wipes her nose with my tissue; her sobs become more intermittent.

We sit in complete silence. I look carefully at each face. Jimmy is watching me for a signal of what is unfolding

I am tempted to push them further, but watching my Olga sob fills me with remorse. How much more will be gained? I believe them.

They were probably not there when he died. Something awful happened of a sexual nature that morning but I don't really have to know the details. Feinstein was alive when they gladly left to go shopping.

"Alright," I say in English. Jimmy is alert to the interrogation winding down. I pause while the four of them stare at me. Their anxious faces are waiting for my pronouncement.

"I think I know what happened. I will take these pills," and I pat the bag. I pick up the evidence as if I'm showing off my prize. For the moment, the inanimate objects become the central focus of our collective attention. Jimmy is staring at the bag.

"We will have the crime lab examine them."

"Is that all?" a relieved Irina asks. She is anxious to leave and her chair's leg scratches the hard floor as she shifts her weight so she can more easily stand.

"I'll be in touch," I add. I hear an audible sigh of relief. I don't know the source, but it could have reflected their collective feeling of reprieve.

"Thank you all for coming in," Jimmy adds as they move from their cramped positions and start moving the chairs away from the table.

Standing, Vladimir again offers his hand and Jimmy shakes it.

Olga's eyes meet mine. I am staring so hard. Is she angry with me for digging so deep? I want to grab her and kiss her, offering my regrets, but it's my job to probe. I am a seeker of the truth. Instead, I step aside and let the four of them leave the claustrophobic room.

Once gone, Jimmy wants to know the details, "So what did they say? I know you hit a real nerve? It almost broke my heart to see her crying; Wow," and he slaps me on the shoulder. I smile and he slaps me again.

"The fat man didn't take his heart medicine but ate quantities of Viagra so he could perform his conjugal duties. Russians don't like to discuss their sexual habits. They didn't know we knew about the Viagra."

I have never told Jimmy about the existence of the tapes. I never wanted to share that potentially painful information about my obsession. Naked in front of a camera, how could I betray my Olga. Nor did I want to give away sensitive knowledge about Vasily. Jimmy only knew the rumors.

"All that squirming about Viagra?" Jimmy twists his lips in a skeptical grimace.

"Russians are prudes."

Jimmy shrugs his shoulders but he doesn't question my knowledge about my people. I am the Russian expert. Besides, he doesn't want this case to take up more of his time. And I am not someone who ever voluntarily leaves a case with loose ends.

"I wouldn't need any Viagra to perform my duties if I had a wife who looked like that." He laughs heartily and smacks me on the arm. "I see how she looks at you. Wait a few months and then call."

We leave the room. "So are you satisfied?" Jimmy demands. "Can we get back to a real case that might win us some glory, something important? Yes?"

"OK." When in doubt every foreigner knows the American word OK. If you can't think of anything, just say OK. "I know there's something else here." I press my fist against my chest. "In this dark Russian heart, I smell some intrigue. Trust me. I know my fellow former Soviets. But OK, we will move on because I feel certain that they weren't present when he died. A crime was probably not committed that day."

Jimmy just shakes his head as we get back to our desks. "Get her in bed and maybe she'll confess her sins," he tells me.

I have to let this go. There's nothing to indicate a crime, my partner is right. Officially, we close the books. "I will tell the Lieutenant the case is closed," I tell Jimmy as I walk towards the boss' office. The Lieutenant will be pleased that his two most promising detectives will now devote 100 percent to cases of real importance—terrorism and Interpol. I don't dare let them know the truth about the tire slashings because our Interpol thug may have committed more serious crimes worthy of our investigation.

CHAPTER 16

The Jewish High Holy Days passed without incident although the NYPD was prepared. For the first time in my life, I went to shul with a loaded gun in my holster. During the 10 days of Awe, I visited every synagogue in south and central Brooklyn, starting with our family's little shul in Brighton Beach.

Driving from one synagogue to another synagogue, it is my job to check security plans. There are cops in front of all of them, but I questioned the highest-ranking officer at each spot about their preparations. Could a car come barreling through the front door? Would a martyr with a bomb strapped to his chest be able to enter the sanctuary?

At each synagogue, I took a few minutes to step inside and observe the congregants praying. Then picking up a prayer book, I davened, prayed, for repentance, forgiveness and to ask God to inscribe me in the Book of Life for the next year.

In my official capacity as guardian of my fellow Jews, I traveled to Borough Park where I spoke to Rebbe Rosenberg. He congratulated my efforts and told me that Hashem would forgive me for riding in a police car on these holiest days, which required the observant Jew to only walk. My work was potentially lifesaving so I was permitted certain infractions of the rules.

The appeal of Judaism was that the observances were not totally rigid. We lived and practiced our religion in a world of nuances; a picture of gray, not black or white.

I reminded Rebbe that my parents' anniversary party was the Sunday right after Simchat Torah. It was a mere three weeks away before the big day. I was nervous.

"Oh, my young friend," he said as he placed his strong arm on my shoulder. "I couldn't forget. I will be there for the blessed event. Hashem willing." We did not speak about the tire slashings or of Glickenstein.

I knew the truth and what's more I understood human frailties. Even a religious man, basically a good man like the Rebbe engaged in imperfect behavior. He knew that Glickenstein was not guilty of tire slashings perhaps other sins.

I understood police preparation for an unexpected terrorist event but an anniversary party. What a revelation to learn there was so much to do for a party. I couldn't have arranged all the pieces without the help of my Aunt Tatiana, the consummate party planner. From her home in West Hartford, she ordered the food, table and tent rentals, and the flowers. From her earlier days in Brighton Beach, she was familiar with many shop owners and had her favorite vendors. She kept a Brooklyn telephone book as a reference guide.

My chief responsibility was the entertainment. I had to satisfy a wide range of tastes. For my father, it had to be classical music; my mother was easier to please and then there were the many guests. How could I guess what they all liked? Of course, Russian music was essential. Although not all the guests we were inviting would be former citizens of the Soviet Union.

One of our Brighton Beach neighbors was a relatively famous violinist back in the Motherland. Here he struggled. To put food on his family's table, he gave music lessons to the neighborhood children while his wife went to work as a music teacher in the NYC public schools. His dreams of concerts and recording contracts were dashed. He spent his mornings practicing for opening nights that never came and his afternoons watching snot-nosed kids attempt to master a grand instrument. Too few orchestras and too many émigré musicians were his problems. He was from Odessa, my father's home; naturally, I had a soft spot for him. I hired him to walk among the guests playing my father's favorite pieces. Since he already knew my father's tastes from their many shared musical moments, I let him make the musical choices. But to entertain all the others, I hired a deejay that knew both new and traditional Russian music as well as rock and roll, to please my mother. The Beatles had to be on the play list, starting with their earliest hits from 1962. A Beatle fan, who owned all their albums including the British releases, my mother searched eBay to add to her collection.

I knew what presents my parents had purchased for each other, but I was sworn to secrecy so I said nothing. I was good at keeping secrets—a man of discretion. My mother gave me the puppy supplies and a new crate for the newest member of the family, and I hid them from my father in the deepest recesses of our garage where even he could not find these treasures.

At every chance, my mother wanted to intercede with the party preparations.

"Tatiana, I must do something," she implores my aunt on the phone.

"Anna, you and Leonid, just show up. I love to do this. From my heart, I plan this event. This is my present to you. Hashem smiles on us," my aunt's religious mission.

"Something, there must be something I can do. You can't plan and then manage everything yourself," my mother is insistent.

"Yes, you're right. I want to spend some time that day as a guest. Yes, we need a staff to walk around with the appetizers and serve the drinks."

"Good, I'll hire some people." Then my mother thought out loud. "Whom do I call?" she asks my aunt.

"The banquet hall has extra waiters and bartenders. I'll give you a name."

So my mother was given her assignment by my aunt.

There was no sit down dinner planned, very informal, which was exactly what my parents wanted—no fuss. The arrangement was for guests to stroll around the backyard, sit at any table, eat little snacks on trays served by waiters and waitresses walking around, followed by people helping themselves to a buffet dinner.

I knew that the West Hartford relatives were bringing my Aunt Maria and my two cousins. She didn't say anything to my mother although my mother was anticipating their arrival. My Uncle Boris said nothing during his weekly calls about his coming from Berlin, Germany for the party. My mother was expecting his attendance but she wanted to say that she was surprised so she never pointedly asked him.

The only true surprise was my shocker, arranging for the Rebbe to marry them. I went down to the Lower East Side and purchased a ketubah, the Hebrew marriage contract. These are beautiful, hand inscribed documents, more pieces of art than a business contract. Beaming with pride, I secretly hid the scroll-like parchment paper in my apartment closet.

Marina and I constructed the huppah (marriage canopy) and kept it hidden in her parents' garage. We actually picked out the canopy material from a catalogue and it was sent UPS to Marina's house. Her father bought four wooden poles from Home Depot for our little project. Each edge of the cloth was tacked to a pole. Four people would carry the big sticks and the bride, groom, rabbi and I would stand under the blue and white canopy for the actual wedding ceremony.

My parents' major charge was to select the guest list. With my aunt listening in on the phone from West Hartford, we evaluated each potential guest. We all decided that fifty people was a good number for a party. There were many little cliques to consider. Relatives were easy, but what about the different circles of friends and how about acquaintances. Should we invite non-Russians? It was quickly decided we had to do so. Although it is an effort to speak English at such a gathering or translate from Russian back to English, there were simply non-Russians that had to be invited. My father, the politician, wanted to invite his boss; and he wanted me to invite not only Jimmy and his family, but also the Lieutenant and his wife.

"It's important for your career. They may not accept and probably they won't understand most of what goes on but still it behooves a subordinate to issue an invitation to the boss. He has kindly invited you to personal events in his own home. It is the polite thing to do." My father ends by staring directly at me.

"And your career? Is there a reason to invite your boss?" I ask my father.

"He has always been nice to me. He's a goy but it will be good for him to attend a Jewish affair," my father's logic. My mother agrees without questioning the rationale.

Then to irritate my parents, I ask my mother, "Are we inviting your boss?"

She has become a good corporate associate, but she says with a big smirk on her face, "No need; I'm retiring next year."

So we have the list. Every party has to have a list. List making is not one of my strengths, but I am charged with keeping the names, checking off all those who decline, calling those who don't RSVP. I am assigned the task to go to JFK Airport to pick up the imaginary relatives from Berlin.

My father's family from Staten Island is coming. My Uncle Viktor and his wife are far too busy in their travel agency to assist in the day-to-day preparations, but they arrange and purchase my parents' 40th anniversary honeymoon package. It is a three-week tour of Mother Russia and with some mighty arm-twisting, Uncle Viktor arranges for my Uncle Boris to join my parents in Petersburg. Aunt Tatiana knows about this arrangement, but purposely fails to mention it. This is another secret.

I am told by my Uncle Viktor, "Hush, hush. Together they would all visit the Old Jewish Cemetery where now everyone lies in peace."

No one says anything about Aunt Tatiana's discovering Aunt Maria and the boys—Andrei and Aleksandr. Six unnamed people from Berlin and three unspoken names from West Hartford are included in the emerging list.

While we are preparing the list my mother shares her dreams with us. Aunt Tatiana is fascinated with these visions; according to my aunt, my mother doesn't recognize the true significance of her dreams, Hashem is speaking directly to her.

"You are an instrument of God," Aunt Tatiana tells us on the phone. I think my mother just has a vivid imagination. My father, the agnostic, replies, "Anna has always had these dreams. They are a source of inspiration." And headaches.

One night before the celebration the dead visit her. "Alexei," she tells us. "I see him in his military uniform so strong and handsome," her mind drifting as we intently listen. I can hear Aunt Tatiana breathing on the phone. The seer speaks.

"We are all standing by the family gravestone in the Old Jewish Cemetery in Petersburg. My father is there in his military uniform, the one he liked to wear on May Day for the parade in Moscow. Those were the days," and her voice speaks from another place.

"We are all together; the family is one again," and my mother smiles at us. Aunt Tatiana somehow knows of this smile, perhaps the hint of her inner contentment is in my mother's voice.

"It is wonderful feeling," my aunt says. My aunt and I know about the planned rendezvous at the cemetery, but presumably my parents are ignorant of this forthcoming event. It's sometimes spooky, my mother's dreams.

My Aunt may be right. In my mother's dreams, the dead speak. They warn us of unseen dangers and comfort us in our greatest moments of sorrow. Ultimately, they assure us that there is an eternal link from generation to generation.

I nudge my father, "The list?" Who else should I invite? I consider Roberta my police friend and her partner Julie? No, I decide, that is not a good idea. There's really no one else from the station house. After all, it's not my party.

"You're going to invite Vasily and Mikhail? And their families?"

asks my mother. Being gangsters in America is not a disqualifier. These are some of our oldest friends from the neighborhood in Petersburg. If I think about it, Vasily is probably my closest friend here in America.

There were two Russian Americans in high school and a burly guy from college, all from the Brighton Beach neighborhood. But none of them lived in the NYC area any longer. If it was a party for me, I would invite them; one lived in Chicago and the other two were in California. We exchanged Jewish New Year cards and corresponded by e-mail a few times a year. I have never told them about Olga, only Vasily knows of my obsession.

I listened as the others made decisions about old friends, neighbors, and Russian co-workers. In the end, the guest list was easier to create than I had imagined. I was expecting arguments about this person or that but there were no disagreements. It was too easy. I began to worry immediately after we settled on the list. Who did we forget to invite? Who will be insulted by this neglect?

The day arrives. To my surprise, I sleep well and I am refreshed for the many chores that await this day. I have my list of things to be accomplished so I shouldn't forget anything. Uncle Boris and family arrive at eleven o'clock in the morning so I am preparing to leave the house by nine thirty.

Aunt Tatiana quietly slips by my door but I am up and see her. "Did you sleep well?" I ask her. She is spending the night in the guest room so that she can organize everything, especially the caterer's preparation.

"I'll make you an omelet with peppers and cheese. How about tomatoes?" she asks and I enthusiastically respond, shaking my head like an eager puppy waiting for a treat.

My parents are already sitting at the kitchen table, sipping a glass of hot tea. "How many people are coming? Do you have a final count?" my mother asks me.

"We have just about fifty," and I take a list from my pocket.

"Can I see?" My mother's hand moves to snatch my list from my clinched hands.

"No, no," and I pull away my arm. "There has to be some surprises today," and I have this tremendously wide, Cheshire cat grin. I am up to mischief.

My father tenderly strokes my mother's arm and kisses the top of her head. Love is such a powerful force.

Aunt Tatiana and I arranged the important arrivals at separate intervals so my mother doesn't spend the whole day crying. We wanted the tears over by the time the rest of the guests arrived. Uncle Boris and family were first; if the plane was on time and traffic was tame, we should be back in Brighton Beach for lunch. Aunt Maria and the boys were scheduled to arrive from West Hartford with my Uncle Igor and the other cousins by 1 PM. The rest of the guests were told to arrive at 2 PM. Since this was a gathering of many Russian immigrants, 2 PM meant between 3 and 4 PM. Rebbe Rosenberg had been asked to prepare the nuptials at 4 PM as the closing event of the celebration.

I chuckle to myself. This may turn out to be fun.

My mother grabs my forearm and pulls me closer, kissing my forehead. "I know you. You have something planned," and she gives me a gentle zetz on my arm.

I want to blurt out all the plans, but I contain myself. I can't keep the grin off my face, but I finish my delicious breakfast. And if etiquette would permit, I'd lick my plate clean. "Many things to accomplish this morning," I say as I stand.

The caterer arrives just as I leave for the airport.

"I'm going," I yell to the women, as my mother and aunt corner the caterer to discuss how to keep the hot food, hot. I wink at my father since we all know I'm going to pick up my unnamed guests. Wait for my surprise, I'm thinking.

The roads are quiet, the plane is on time, and there are my six relatives from Berlin, standing, waiting for me to pick them up. Everyone is kissing me and hugging me. I have lipstick stains on my shirt collar, but it's wonderful to see them again for such a happy occasion. A courteous and efficient limo driver that I am, the luggage is in the trunk, my uncle buckled up in the front seat next to me, and the others squashed in the back. My young cousins, born in Berlin, sit atop their older siblings, born in Petersburg. I'm a cop so we don't worry about exceeding the maximum limit of passengers in the back seat. My aunt is fanning herself with a German newspaper.

"Hot back there, you want me to put on the air-conditioner?" I ask in German. Seeing my relatives is a perfect opportunity for me to practice my German.

"Are we expected?" my uncle asks although he knows the answer.

I speak to my aunt and uncle. "You know your sister. She'll start bawling as soon as she sees you." I take one hand off the steering wheel and dramatize her wiping away the tears. "She's expecting you, but it's not real until she actually touches you." I reach over and gently grab his shoulder. "She's a tactile person; she likes to touch," and I repeatedly jab his forearm.

"Did you think about what we've been discussing," my uncle communicates directly with me, trying to persuade me that I am needed in Europe. Since a past visit to Berlin, he has sent me e-mails and even letters arguing for the need to re-populate Germany and Europe with Jews, principally those Russian born. We cannot discuss these ideas on the phone while my parents are listening.

"Am I right?" he persists.

His logic is clear and intellectually thought provoking, based on history and today's reality. We should not let the Nazis win by allowing Europe to be 'Judenfrei,' Jew free.

"I'm still listening. I am open to all ideas," I tell him.

"Good boy. I know your mother disapproves, but in her heart, despite all the success and materialism she has earned in America, she is Russian. Nothing can change that. We are all Europeans. Europe needs more Jews."

This is a conversation we must have away from my mother's prying ears. "I'm sure there are employment opportunities for me in Germany or in the Low Countries since I speak German and Russian. Flemish is like German. The Dutch all speak English." My Uncle Vanya, the Cossack soul, is intrigued with the potential adventure. This would certainly produce fireworks from my mother.

My aunt is more comfortable now that the air conditioner is on. She opens her coat and tries to relax. "It's so nice to travel here for this momentous event. Always, I wondered how your mother and father remained together. Truly in love, they are. Prison, hunger strikes, demotions, living in all those cramped apartments, forsaking what each one of them deserved as educated and important members of the old Soviet Union system. It doesn't seem to have dampened their love. Amazing." I see through my rear mirror, my aunt shaking her head in disbelief.

My cousins are sitting in the overcrowded back seat just waiting for us to arrive so they can breathe again.

I turn onto our block and there is my father standing outside the front door, patiently waiting as we pull into the driveway.

He raises his arms over his head and yells out in a big, booming voice. "Look Anna, look who is here."

My cousins tumble out of the back seat. Uncle Boris and my father embrace. "How could we miss this event? I only wish my father was alive," my uncle's voice cracks.

My mother runs out from the backyard. Screaming at the top of her lungs, she tells the world, "Boris, oh, oh, my baby brother." The two hold tightly to each other. The tears begin. She eventually frees my uncle from her tenacious grip so she can kiss my aunt and then kiss the four cousins. For each family member she leaves a souvenir; a few tears on their coats.

Neighbors from all directions observe our visitors. We invite most of them because otherwise how could we continue to stay in the neighborhood.

Aunt Tatiana is too busy with the florist to welcome the Berlin visitors so we walk to the backyard.

Kisses and hugs are in abundance as everyone meets half way under the main tent. Our backyard has been transformed into a gigantic Russian bazaar.

Aunt Tatiana raises her arms towards the sky. "Hashem be praised. Sit and you can all be our food testers." The food severs appear as if by magic and all six pair of hands reach for the beautiful looking appetizers.

I take my father aside. "You haven't shown mama your present?"

"No, of course not. I'm waiting for all our guests to arrive." I know his secret. He has been unusually good about not letting on what he has bought for her. He is not known for keeping secrets.

"Good," I say, as I stuff a frank in a blanket hors d'oeuvre, saturated in dark, deli mustard, into my mouth. The chauffeur is hungry.

It's far more difficult to isolate my mother from her guests and shepherd her away to a quiet spot. But I follow her as she heads towards the house to bring out cold drinks.

"You haven't told papa about the puppy?" I ask

She grabs me under the arm and presses her head to my shoulder. "No, of course not. Natalie is bringing him and with all this excitement I don't want to frighten the poor fellow. I told Natalie to come a little later."

This plan I didn't know about and it worries me. "How much later?"

She is suspicious, "Why?"

"When is she coming?" I don't want her to miss the ceremony.

"Around four," and she stares into my eyes. She points her finger at my nose. "Why? I know you, something's planned?"

"Enjoy this glorious day. The weather is perfect," and I turn away and look for the violinist.

My father is in front of the house worrying about where all the guests will be able to park. I approach stealthily, placing my hand on his shoulder.

He jumps into the air, "Sasha you gave me fright."

"Don't worry," I say confidently. "I made arrangements with neighbors. People will park in driveways along street. That is bribe for inviting them to party." A good Soviet citizen knows the importance of using bribes.

As we peer down the street, my father is counting the driveways and converting the concrete into parking spaces. Uncle Igor's big old Cadillac Coupe de Ville rolls into the old neighborhood. Strangers on the sidewalks stop and stare at the 1950's pink model, glistening in the sunlight. The early arrival gets to park in our driveway.

My father waves to his brother-in-law to move to the top of the class; the steel bumper of the old beauty rests on the fiberglass bumper of my father's practical Toyota sedan.

My uncle moves the front seat forward so the guests can get out. The people in the backseat reluctantly leave the comfort and psychologically reassuring enclosure of the car. Aunt Maria looks as radiant as I remember her.

As an adolescent boy, I had a giant crush on her. She was so glamorous in her furs and thin, statuesque high heels. She could have been a fashion model.

My father and Uncle Igor wrap their arms around each other, and I hug the cousins I know while the unfamiliar relatives uneasily watch.

My father, always a peacemaker, steps forward and stretches out his arms; slowly Aunt Maria moves into his embrace. Their tight grip melts away the years of uncertainties. She bends her head into my father's shoulder and the tears flow. I follow my father's clues, and shake the hand of my tallest cousin while I hug him with my other hand. Then I move on to my other cousin. My father gathers both young men into his arms and the three of them stand together in the driveway, their heads in a huddle.

My mother runs from the backyard. We can hear her coming; she is shouting something but we can't understand exactly what she is saying. The two women, who have not seen each other in 15 years, stop and stare at each other. They stand transfixed in the glimmering autumn sun and then my mother extends her arms. My aunt doesn't hesitate; they embrace, witnessed by friends, relatives and neighbors.

"It was always meant to be that our lives should be entwined.

Alexei comes to me in my dreams, seeks peace, and now I know he can eternally rest," my mother, the seer, speaks. All the others nod in agreement.

"Welcome to my home," my mother, the gracious hostess, says, as she opens her arms in greeting. "Please have something to eat." Among Jews, food is always the ultimate offering and consolation. "Some old friends from Petersburg who now live here sent best Russian vodka," Vasily's family's contribution. Being Russian means that no celebration can begin without vodka so each new visitor is offered a glass of the clear liquid, regardless of their age. The young Berlin-born cousins warily sip the potent drink.

At this moment, the party can end since my mother is reunited with all the people who mean so much to her. "You look wonderful," my mother says in a genuine gesture of reconciliation and appreciation of my aunt's enduring beauty.

Uncle Boris approaches his sister-in-law and nephews. "The years have been kind." He is equally gushing in his sincere testimonial to my aunt's appearance. "You and boys look fantastic. Of course, I would not really recognize them on street. But if I got up close, I see Alexei's eyes. The family resemblance is strong." He kisses her cheeks. "Alexei would want us to be together." My uncle breathes in deeply; we all feel the emotional need to close old wounds and for the family to emerge reborn.

Uncle Boris hugs each of Alexei's sons. "My sister, witch, or some modern Biblical Joseph with her robe of many colors, experiences such vivid dreams that she awakes with her heart pounding and her brow damp with perspiration. She dreams of family united as one. It was said of my father that in his later years that he too had spectacular dreams. He told us once when we were visiting him in his dacha. By this time, he was old man. He had dream and he saw giant bear; he interpreted that to mean Soviet Union. The gigantic animal was attacked by unknown threat, stumbled and fell, but managed to regain his footing and to stand. No one can take Russian out of us. Governments can come and go but Russian soul lives forever." My uncle speaks with the assurance of a man from a family of prophets.

"Food, we all need some hot food and vodka," my father exclaims, and he leads the line of guests back into the backyard. I hear him mumble, "Enough of the supernatural. Your uncle is no better than your mother."

My mother is totally engaged with her relatives and doesn't know the time. The party officially starts at two PM, but no one arrives but my violinist. Then as I watch the hall clock's hands move towards the quarter hour, I hear voices. Slowly, two at a time, like the animals entering Noah's ark, the guests begin to arrive. The smiling guests are loaded with presents that my parents really don't need and will probably donate to a homeless shelter in Coney Island.

My father's boss is an exuberant visitor. Pumping my father's hand, he tells him, "Great, just great. Forty years, Leonid, I can't believe that you are married so long. Who stays married forty years?"

I smile at his boss and he gives me the present. I dutifully take it and place it on a table inside the house. I peer out the living room window to see who else is arriving. I see my Lieutenant and his wife Nancy. They are nearly on time.

They knock on the front door, which I open. She gives me a delicate peck on the cheek. He clutches my hand as we shake. "I had no idea what to get your parents so I made a contribution to a Jewish charity." And she hands me an envelope.

"This is terrific. My parents will truly appreciate your thoughtfulness," I reply, with the utmost respect for his or her decision-making. I walk them into the yard, and try and locate my parents for the necessary introductions.

As we walk along, the Lieutenant laughingly says to me, "Perlov the Protector, Hero of Harbor House, you have a big future in the department. That Interpol case; what a find. You and Sutton will be assigned to a new terrorist unit here in Brooklyn." He stops and faces me. "A promotion is on its way."

I vigorously shake his hand. "Thank you." He doesn't need to know that truth about the tire slashings because the case is moving in a more important direction.

"No thanks necessary. The department needs smart and resourceful people like you. And by the way, speaking of smart people, Roberta passed the sergeant's exam."

My father and the Lieutenant shake hands and talk pleasantries. "You got a smart boy," he tells my smiling father. My father grabs me by the shoulders. "Just like his old man," and we all chuckle.

I watch for Jimmy and his family. I take a slender glass of vodka from one of the hired servers. She winks at me. I can't keep from noticing her sweet looking, innocent face and long legs. As I'm finishing, I feel a sharp slap on my back. I almost spill my drink.

"A Russian party. Forget the beer, it's vodka time," and Jimmy hugs me Russian style while his father looks on and laughs. I shake the men's hands and kiss the women. I need another drink.

The plan is that Marina and her family arrive just before the Rebbe makes an appearance. They are bringing the canopy for the wedding ceremony; my big surprise.

I manage to eat a little food and take another drink from the same server. She has a big smile for me. My impulse is to ask her name but the booze hasn't totally distorted my thinking.

At 3:30 PM, Rebbe Rosenberg arrives. I quickly call Marina on my cell phone at her house, "It's time." I look for my mother's old friend Natalie but I don't see her; hopefully, she'll get here before the ceremony begins.

The Rebbe is alone and stands out in his long beard and dark shabby suit. Physical appearances are not of importance in his world. I walk with him into the crowd.

My mother spots the rabbi and approaches; she is atypically speechless for a few moments. Regaining her composure, she calmly says, "Rebbe, how nice of you to come to our house." Observing the traditional distance of men and women among the ultra orthodox, she doesn't shake his hand or touch him in any way. Their eyes meet.

My father walks towards our honored guest and they shake hands. "Rebbe what privilege."

Rebbe touches my arm and tells my confused parents, "I am here to marry you before Hashem since for forty years you never had the benefit of a religious ceremony."

It was a notion neither of my parents would ever have imagined. It took a minute for them to respond. No one moved; their eyes glanced towards me and back to Rebbe.

My father nodding his head finally speaks, "What a beautiful idea," and his words are genuine, not uttered to please his wife or me. He grabs the rabbi's hands, "Truly righteous act," and his head is still bobbing.

Speech has returned to my mother. "Rebbe who would have thought of such lovely proposal."

He turns his face towards me. "Why your son. He is a righteous man. He protects his people as a police officer and promotes God's message by asking me to perform a marriage ceremony."

My stunned parents stare at me. I feel as if I have two heads. They are deciding is this an act of Uncle Vanya, the Cossack or a pious believer?

"My surprise," I add, and everyone laughs in relief.

The only true believer among my family, Aunt Tatiana, greets our guest with respect. "Rebbe, so wonderful that you are here. I hope you will eat something." She knows of my secret because we had to work the ceremony into what she had planned.

We deliberate in a tight circle deciding on how to proceed. Marina and her father, carrying the huppah, hurry to enlarge the circle.

I give instructions. "Uncles, Boris," and I point to them, "Igor and Viktor," who are standing next to each other talking about cars, "can you hold one of the poles for the huppah?" They obey. I turn and see my cousin Andrei watching the proceedings. "Andrei, would you take one of poles?" He is flattered to be asked. "Yes, of course," and he looks towards his smiling mother.

I have planned the exact spot for the huppah, directing the men to follow. I locate the violinist. "Play something appropriate." He smiles and immediately begins to play Mendelssohn's Wedding March, one of my father's favorites.

I borrow the microphone and speaker from the DJ. He assists me in setting up the equipment.

"Hello everyone." Speaking through the microphone, I see a few eyes look towards my direction.

"Everyone, please," I speak Russian and then English. "Everyone form big half-circle around me. Today, before congregation and God, Rebbe Rosenberg will marry my parents. Please form half-circle around huppah." I point to the four poles carried by my male relatives.

The guests are obedient and we have our big half-circle. The children stand in front of the adults along with the stooped, older people. Here and there guests bring folding chairs for the seniors. Mrs. Chervony is there with her family. Her son Grigori brings her a chair. My mother has emotionally adopted the old woman, making her part of our extended family. She is the last tangible link my mother has to Stalingrad. Mrs. Chervony's present to my parents was a sixty-year-old photograph of my grandfather standing on a tank in the rubble of Stalingrad.

I spy my father. I whisper in his ear, "Give me ring for ceremony." I take the small box and place it in my pocket.

My parents speak Hebrew but are unfamiliar with the words of a marriage service.

"Don't worry," Rebbe says to them, "Just repeat what I say." They nod their heads.

My mother agrees to include some religious rituals in the service. We don't bother with a wedding party marching to the huppah. I will serve as my father's best man. My Aunt Tatiana brings us the ketubah. The Rebbe offers to read it out loud to the guests, but my father says, "It's all in Hebrew and few people will understand it. Let's just show it to guests." Rebbe agrees since it's their wedding party.

I place the microphone in the middle of the circle so that we can hear the words of the rabbi and the responses of the bride and groom. The rabbi unfolds the ketubah and introduces it to the crowd.

"This is the ketubah or marriage contract. Traditionally, it is signed at a reception before the wedding before two witnesses, but since this is an unusual couple we will do things a little differently. Do we have two witnesses to sign?" Lev, my father's chess partner, steps forward and Grigori, Mrs. Chervony's son, raises his hand because only non-blood relatives can serve as witnesses. As the crowd strains their necks to see, my parents sign the document, and so do the witnesses. When we are finished the crowd applauds.

"Instead of reading the ketubah, I invite people to walk over later and look at it."

He continues as a teacher and educator. "Normally, we perform a bedeken ceremony where the groom covers the bride's face with a veil. Do we have a veil?"

My aunt Tatiana rushes forward with a crocheted doily. "Will this do?"

Rebbe takes the decorative material and my father hangs it over my mother's face. It looks more like a pretty rag than a wedding garment but it works today.

"The groom usually wears a kittel, a simple cotton robe that is also worn on Yom Kippur and as a shroud at death. But today a tallit, or prayer shawl, will do." I know that ritual and I am prepared. I hand my father his tallit, which he puts on.

"The bride will circle the groom seven times, as is the custom." My mother, still holding on to her make-do veil, walks around my father.

People in the audience again applaud. Rebbe is startled by the crowd's reaction, but he ignores them.

"The wedding ceremony involves the recitation of seven blessings called the sheva berakhot whose themes include creation of the world and human beings, survival of the Jewish people, the couple's joy, and the raising of a family." Rebbe chants the blessings in Hebrew.

It's time for the ring. I hand the box to my father. The rabbi says to my father, "Take the ring and place it on Anna's index finger." He takes out the ring and does as he is told. "Behold, by this ring you are consecrated to me as my wife according to the laws of

Moses and Israel." Then he repeats it in Hebrew. "Then Anna, of your own free will, you take the ring and place it on your ring finger. And in keeping with Russian tradition, the woman places the ring on her right hand. Please do so." My mother for the first time looks closely at the ring.

"Oh, my God," and the tears begin. It is my father's secret. The ring is a gold copy of their original wedding ring, a paper Cuban cigar wrapper. In their haste when they eloped, all my father's worldly possessions consisted of one Cuban cigar. My father takes out of his pocket a large, old Cuban cigar. "It's the one. I have kept it all these years." And both of them are crying. I help my mother place the ring on her finger. I hand both of them tissues. My uncles are laughing. My Aunt Tatiana is bawling. I can hear her hiccup between the tears.

Most of the crowd is in tears. This is supposed to be a happy affair. The Rebbe is laughing and gently tapping my father on the back. I hand Rebbe the wine cup. The rabbi says the prayer in Hebrew and raises the cup from which my mother and my father drink.

"Does the bride or groom wish to say anything?" asks Rebbe. My parents have not prepared any words to say to each other and they are both overcome with emotion. They can hardly speak.

The ceremony is not over yet, the ritual that everyone knows is still waiting. I show the Rebbe the small glass, which I cover in a cloth napkin. Rebbe places his strong arms around both of my parents. "Now we end the ceremony by having the groom break the glass." I place the covered object on the ground. As on cue, my father regains his composure and smashes the glass with his foot. The popping sound can be heard across the backyard.

Everyone explodes in cries of, "Ah," followed by hand clapping and shouts of "Mazel Tov."

I feel hands slapping me on the back. The pretty server hands me another glass of vodka. I don't remember how many glasses of this Russian spirit I've consumed nor do I remember having eaten anything.

The guests remain in the enchanted circle. My Uncle Boris moves to the center.

He gently touches my mother's hand and intently stares at the ring.

"Oh, Leonid, Leonid, only you could have thought of this," he tells my father.

My mother is still softly crying although she can't possible have any more tears left.

"Toast," my uncle bellows in Russian to the crowd. All eyes focus on his compact, sturdy frame.

"To my sister and her husband. No one would have thought 40 years ago that we would be celebrating this anniversary. My father was shocked and angry."

I'm standing next to my Lieutenant, his wife Nancy, Jimmy and his family, roughly translating my uncle's words into English. Marina is by my side listening.

"She is truly a decendant of our family Uncle Vanya, the Cossack, leaving behind fiancé and career to run off with young, brilliant mathematician from hinterlands that my father graciously allowed to live with us in Moscow." My uncle stops to reflect. "How my father cursed and screamed when he read note my sister left behind. I'm certain Leonid's family was worried."

My uncle raises his glass and we follow. "But skeptics were all wrong and I wish my father was alive to see this day." He holds his glass at least twelve inches above his head.

"To this glorious couple that angry parents, governments, and political ideology could not destroy. To love," and he swallowed the contents of the glass.

The Lieutenant and his wife Nancy repeat, "To love," swallowing the vodka in one mouthful.

Jimmy's father says to me, "I could understand some of that speech. My Russian hasn't left me completely."

It's my turn. All eyes concentrate on my face as I move to the center. It's expected that I should propose a toast.

In Russian, I address my audience. "People ask themselves how did this couple survive together despite all pressures?" I see Marina taking my place as translator. Nancy turns her head towards Marina.

"It's easy to fall in love," I say. "It's understandable how couple could live together for 40 years. But how does couple stay madly in love for 40 years. There is reason for this success. First and foremost, they are best friends and they have always been so, trusting each other, sharing their hopes, ambitions, disappointments and regrets. They have no secrets." I chuckle and remark. "Maybe the presents today were secrets." My audience laughs. Natalie has put the puppy in his new crate away from the crowd.

"My parents are true Russians. They come from long tradition of Russian romantics. In their honor, I'd like to read poem from one of greatest Russian Romantic poets of all times, Pushkin." I take the paper from my pocket.

I can remember our first meeting
When like a miracle you came
Before my eyes a swiftly fleeting
Vision of beauty's purest flame.

Amid the miseries that oppressed me
Amid the world's vain foolish cries
For long your gentle voice caressed me
Your features gleamed before my eyes.

The years went by, wild storms swept past me
Scattering many a youthful dream;
I lost the voice that once caressed me
I lost your features' heavenly gleam.

Shut in my prison's dark damnation
Before me stretched dumb days, dead years,
Deprived of God, of inspiration,
Deprived of love, of life, of tears.

Then from its trance arose in greeting

My soul as once again you came
Before my eyes a swiftly fleeting
Vision of beauty's purest flame."

Among my Russian guests a loud applause in recognition
of a great poet's words of inspiration. The English-speaking in
the crowd just clapped in appreciation for words they didn't
understand but could feel the emotion behind my voice. Hands
appear with glasses of vodka, which I gleefully accept. Every
guest offers me another drink. I stand, just barely, accepting
congratulations while my head is swimming and my balance
fading.

Eventually, I sense that Marina is close to me. I say to her,
"Can I drive you home?"

She laughs and kisses me on the lips. "You are too drunk. I
suggest you go upstairs and sleep it off."

My father approaches with a giant smile. "My boy, my Sasha,"
he is dabbing the edge of his eye, "such beautiful poem. Forty
years, it still feels so new. I remember exactly what we were
wearing when we drove off in your grandfather's car. We never
asked permission." He contentedly sighs. I kiss him on the side of
his head and we embrace.

I am clearly unsteady on my feet. His fatherly advice, "You
should walk to Boardwalk and get some fresh air." The sea was
the ultimate cure for all ailments, especially drunkenness. Since
his Odessa boyhood, my father always associates comfort with
the sea.

Slowly our guests are starting to leave. I follow them to the
driveway, waiting so I could make my way to the beach. Most of
the women kiss me and all the Russian men hug and embrace me.
"Good job," I hear from the many faces that pass me by as they
make their way to the cars parked along the street, in neighbors'
driveways, some on the curb. My exhausted Aunt Tatiana leaves
with her husband, sons and the newfound relatives. The old
Cadillac comfortably holds seven passengers. I wave good-bye to
all the departing guests.

Uncle Boris and family have reservations in a newly renovated hotel near the house. Vasily has some sort of ties to this new establishment and he gives them a price that is almost a present. He drives them to the hotel while his brother Mikhail drives their family home. I wave to them all in my shaky condition.

One foot in front of the other is how I make my way towards the beach. It is a painstaking accomplishment but slowly the smells of the sea grow stronger. On Brighton Beach Avenue instead of going straight towards the Boardwalk, I head under the trestle. Am I entirely conscious of my movements? I don't know. Instinct, or is it desire and lust driving me towards the house. My pace quickens as I head down the street.

There is the house. I open the outside gate and manage to walk up the few stairs without tripping over my own feet. My finger presses against the doorbell. I wait resting my head against the door.

"Oh, it's you," Olga says in surprise, as I stand unannounced and uninvited in her doorway.

"Come in," she replies as I carefully study my feet, trying not to stumble head first onto the living room carpet.

I feel her hand on my back steering me into the room. She helps me take off my thin jacket, throwing it onto a new couch, the tags still attached. I notice how it smells, the way new furniture does.

"What brings you here," she asks as I encircle my arms around her waist and kiss her. I expect to be slapped in the face but instead my wet kiss is met with her moist one.

I breathe in deeply as she wraps her arms around my neck. I realize we are almost the same height. I kiss the nape of her neck and lick the soft skin behind her ear. We face and our lips meet; her mouth opens and I feel her tongue. Her long fingers reach and grip mine as she guides me towards another room. I follow obediently.

The bedroom looks different although I can't tell what's new. My equilibrium is off and I tumble onto the firm mattress. My body bounces up and down as if I was a little kid playing on a trampoline. I sit up and she is next to me.

I am laughing as she expertly weaves her fingers through the buttonholes. My clumsy hands tug and pull, practically ripping off her blouse. She doesn't protest. I continue to kiss her face, aiming for her lips but sometimes missing, instead catching her cheek and nose. I can smell the pungent odor of my vodka breath but she doesn't seem to mind.

Her bra opens in the front but my inept fingers can't seem to uncouple the hooks. She places her warm hands over mine and shows me how it's done. We kiss as the hook opens. I gently push her against the mattress and move her legs until she is lying completely on her back. I am still unsteady but I twist my body so I am above her.

Half-dressed, we laugh and kiss again. She slips off her skirt and helps me remove my belt and pants. Together we peel off her silky panties. This is fun.

My bare legs are muscular and tan, and so are hers. I trace the length of her leg with one finger. She is giggling. But we don't waste too much time admiring our trim, fit bodies.

As I'm kissing her nipples, I feel her pull down my shorts. Her fingers pinch and grab my ass. I'm still drunk but not unable to perform my expected duties.

She helps me position myself. I am a success because she is groaning in my ear as we thrust our bodies together. I expend all my energies pumping my body against hers.

I collapse upon her chest. We continue kissing and she pushes me off of her. We rest on our sides staring at our sweaty, shiny bodies.

Words finally form, "Where are your sisters?" I ask with surprise now that my brain is partially functioning.

She sighs and presses her fingernail slowly down my chest. "Out shopping," she answers, and gingerly kisses my chin. She has small blotches of red where my coarse beard rubbed against her soft skin.

"I didn't plan on this visit," I explain.

She tucks her forehead into the nape of my neck. "I know," she answers.

"It just happened."

Her eyes directly face me. "We knew moment we met that it was our destiny." Her eyes close. "Now that case is finished," and she doesn't finish the sentence.

I start thinking again. The gray cells are passing electrical charges to each other. My investigative nature re-emerges. "I know you weren't there when he died, but you haven't told me whole story."

Slowly her eyes open and she stares at me. She is calm, but I sense a bit worried; the conversation is moving in a direction that she wants to avoid. "Yes I have."

I shake my head. "My dark Russian heart knows something is missing." I crinkle up my eyes and nuzzle my nose into the fleshy part of her cheek. "You can trust me. What really happened?"

She turns away from me.

I take my finger and turn her face to my gaze. "Listen. I am just like Inspector Javert and you are my Jean Valjean from 'Les Miserables.' I will not rest until I know all details. So you better confess." I am laughing as I say these words but my intent is clear.

Her face turns pensive. "I can trust you?" she pleadingly asks.

I nod my head. "I am man of discretion. No one is more trustworthy."

She moves away from my grasp and lies on her back staring at the ceiling. I am a patient man. The moments pass without a sound uttered. Tenderly, I take her hand in my mine.

"What happened?" My tone is not harsh but is one of determination.

She still doesn't look at me. I hear her breath deeply and sigh.

"He didn't take his pills," she finally says. I know that, but I uncomplainingly wait for more details. I let her tell the story at her own pace and in her own words.

Her body moves, her head turns, and our eyes converge. "He was evil man, but I was always grateful to him for giving us place to live."

The silence returns so I progress to a related story. "Are the two women your sisters?" I inquire.

"We could be," she pauses, her voice more self-assured. "We were all from Kiev, young budding gymnasts for Soviet system sent to Moscow together. We are all about same age. Masha is the oldest. We called ourselves sisters when we were still children and adopted names Olga, Masha and Irina, like Chekhov play. Our passports and visas identify us as sisters. Our first teacher in Moscow let us use same surname; she had radical attitude about Soviet system always finding little ways to obstruct and circumvent official rules and regulations." Her voice is no longer meditative but nostalgic.

"We were merely promising and were washed up by time we reached puberty. And we returned to Kiev without purpose. In Soviet system, everyone had to have function. So we were educated in hinterlands, deemed good Soviet citizens, but we were nothing special."

She stops and looks past me towards a poster on the wall. "However, I loved feeling of being on stage in front of audience. I studied acting in Kiev while my sisters followed more academic pursuits. I didn't have body for gymnast but I could be in theater. And when Soviet system collapsed, we all decided we had to leave. Together we would seek our fortunes and new adventures in New World."

This is interesting but not what I want to know. "So you met late Mr. Feinstein and he took you in. At first he wasn't demanding but he changed. Yes?"

Her gaze returns to me. A tiny tear is just visible in the corner of her eye. "Yes, it started so innocently and then I can't explain it but he changed. Irina is right it was pornography." She sniffles. I feel for a tissue box on the nightstand and find one. She gladly accepts my present.

"And then what?"

"Vladimir gets him his Viagra and then we got idea of replacing his heart medicine with placebos. We don't really want to kill him; we couldn't do anything so blatant. But maybe there was another way." She is nodding her head.

"But irony," and she quietly laughs to herself, "is that he actually never took any of his pills except Viagra. We had Vladimir create these fake pills for nothing." Her laughter builds.

"Is that crime?" she implores.

I categorically reply, "Yes."

"Even if nothing happened?" she guiltily asks.

"Did he think you might be poisoning him so that's why he didn't take his pills?" I ask.

"No, he would have said something. Actually, I think Irina was always right about him. Eventually, he wanted to die so he stopped taking his pills. He couldn't outright kill himself so he wouldn't shoot himself; he did it his way, the passive way by abandoning his medicine. That was his way, without confrontation or harsh words. Just don't do it."

"What happened to fake pills?" I inquisitively ask, because I want the full story.

"We flushed them down toilet when we found him dead that afternoon."

"You knew you did something wrong?" I respond in a nonjudgmental way.

"We were afraid but it wasn't till weeks later that we actually found those fake pills tucked away in dust ruffle and realized he hadn't been taking any pills. He killed himself. Right?"

She was a murderess. My Olga did pre-meditate a plan to kill off her husband. Now what should I do? "Um…um," was all I could say.

She edges close to my mouth. "Are you going to arrest me?"

How could I be sleeping with a suspect and then bring her in on charges. "No, I am man of discretion. I promised you I could be trusted." I was caught up in a murder case. I never really imagined that she and the sisters with Vladimir's assistance had perpetrated a crime. I thought they took the passive route, merely letting him die of a heart attack while he lay on the floor groaning for help.

"No," I repeat the word again and again, "No, no," and I dress.

As I leave her bed, we kiss. "Call me," she implores.

My drunken state has left me and I wander the streets deciding what should I do? I could be an accessory after the fact. I pull a quarter from my pocket and place the call.

"Hello, can you meet me at our favorite spot."

"I'll be there in fifteen minutes," comes the reply.

Just like a master timekeeper, he arrives, as the fifteenth minute is about to expire.

"You look terrible," Vasily says, "What's wrong?"

"She killed her husband," and he knows immediately to what I am referring.

"Tell me," and he sympathetically listens to my story.

Then he says. "Do you remember when your cousin was attacked right here on this Boardwalk? Do you recall what your Uncle Viktor did? Did he call police? He went to Mikhail and he told my brother what happened?" He places his hand on my shoulder. Out of his pocket he hands me an apple, which I take. I can't remember when I last had eaten.

"Did your uncle want his innocent daughter to testify in court? And maybe something would happen to evil perpetrator. No, he told Mikhail who this monster was and we took care of it." Vasily hands me a napkin as the sweet juice of the apple coats my hand.

"We went to that guy's family and warned his own father. We said we were watching him and to keep his son in line. What happened? One of the guys spotted him about to approach another innocent girl." I remember this case, although it was spoken about in whispers.

"We put out a warning but he was bad seed and something had to be done to protect neighborhood."

The guy was found washed up on the beach wearing a bathing suit even though it was fall. The police ruled it a drowning. The dead man's family said nothing.

"This is same thing. Feinstein was evil man. And look, he died himself. The sisters and Vladimir, they really had nothing to do with his death. Was crime really committed? Um..um. No," he speaks with authority. "He was bad seed and threat to neighborhood. You can be at peace. They did nothing wrong." He rubs the top of my shoulders.

I sit quietly, thinking, remembering his fat, ugly body lying on the carpet. Olga, my beautiful Olga, what have I done. Can I possible go back on my words? I promised her my trust.

I relax as the breezes turn cooler. I breathe in the salty sea air, contemplating the facts. This need to know what happened has unexpected consequences. I sit staring at the ocean pounding the deserted beach. The winds are picking up and old newspapers fly by us. Vasily is by my side. We do not speak.

The sea air pierces my eyes, causing a tear to form. I wipe away the moistness with the napkin. The truth becomes clear. There is no crime and no need for punishment. It is a case of self-defense. The women feeling threatened by his outrageous demands do what is necessary. The neighborhood is safer with him gone. Yes, it is his own decision not to take his medicine. He is the instrument of his own destruction. Feinstein is responsible.

"Yes, fake pills meant nothing. Death was result of his own hand." I nod my head.

Vasily embraces me in a Russian bear hug. "You see that it was inevitable. Evil man is undone by his own hand." We both shake our heads in agreement. He edges closer to me. "But stay away from that woman. If there is even slightest whispering, no one should associate you with her. Not if you want to stay police officer. Right?"

I know he is right.

"Go home, your parents are worried about you. They think you might have drowned, you have been gone so long."

We hug in traditional Russian style and I head back home to the house. The gulls point the way; they know my father has treats for them and some great leftovers for me. My adoring mother is waiting for me in the kitchen; my doctor girlfriend is waiting for a call. I do make that call and assure her I am just fine.

The sea has cured my drunkenness. Moral ambiguities fade away with hot tea and a dozen franks in a blanket. Make things simple; that is the method for living a life of moral tranquility. A bad man is gone. The neighborhood is freer, the family of the dead man is not asking for facts, and his beautiful widow has suffered enough.

It's funny how the unexpected can change your life. But if I look around me the neighborhood looks the same. I can live with this moral ambiguity because it is clear that there is zilch to be gained by revealing what has happened. The truth seeker now knows what happened. Pinching my skin, I feel the pressure but no regrets or remorse. As a man of discretion, I am sworn to keep my word to a fellow immigrant.

I must stay away from her no matter how strong the impulse is to see her, embrace her, and kiss her because I love being a police officer more than I want her. This is to be my sacrifice. I am from a family that understands sacrifice. Even in this land of life, liberty, and the pursuit of happiness, nothing comes without consequences; there is a heavy price to pay to live in this New Jerusalem.

THE END

CPSIA information can be obtained
at www.ICGtesting.com
Printed in the USA
LVHW050820070719
623350LV00012B/359